JOURNEYS OF T

'You didn't tell him you were having his baby?'

Joanna shook her head. 'I didn't want Oliver to feel obliged to marry me. I still love him, Megan. That's my cross. I want him to be happy. But I can't bear an illegitimate child. The disgrace would kill my parents and certainly ruin me.' She looked up, her eyes pleading. 'You must help me, Megan. No one else can.'

'We could go back to Llanrys. I had to sell grandfather's house in order to pay all his debts, but we could rent a cottage . . .' Megan fell silent, unnerved by the grim appeal in Joanna's eyes.

'I want you to get rid of the baby for me.'

A cold fist closed around Megan's heart. 'Joanna, you don't know what you're asking.'

'Yes, I do. You're as good a doctor as your grandfather ever was. You told me that you were his hands when he shook too much to wield a scalpel, and you were his eyes when he could no longer see the rampant infection in a wound he'd treated. Didn't his patients continue to come to you after your grandfather became senile, because he was the only doctor in that tiny town?'

'While he was alive, Jo. But now he's gone and so has his diploma and his shingle. I'm not qualified, I'm not a doctor and I probably never would be.'

About the author

Katherine Sinclair is the pseudonym of Joan Dial, a bestselling author whose books have thrilled countless numbers of readers. Writing under different pen names her works include historical romances, family sagas, contemporary women's fiction, mystery and suspense. She currently lives in California with her husband.

Journeys of the Heart

Katherine Sinclair

NEW ENGLISH LIBRARY
Hodder and Stoughton

Printed and bound in Great Britain for Hodder and Stoughton Paperbacks, a division of Hodder and Stoughton Ltd, Mill Road, Dunton Green, Sevenoaks, Kent TN13 2YA. (Editorial Office: 47 Bedford Square, London WC1B 3DP) by Clays Ltd, St Ives plc. Photoset by Rowland Phototypesetting Ltd, Bury St Edmunds, Suffolk.

British Library C.I.P.

Sinclair, Katherine
Journeys of the heart.
I. Title
813.54[F]

ISBN 0-450-54040-5

1

How disturbingly similar, Megan Thomas thought, are the sounds and scents of weddings and funerals. The fragrance of flowers hanging in the warm still air of an ancient Norman church, the rustle of taffeta gowns and the crackle of starched shirts. An occasional sigh, a stifled sob, the low murmur of the vicar's voice.

She had not been inside a church since her grandfather's funeral. In the ensuing weeks she had spent many sleepless nights pondering the lies he had told her, but today all her thoughts and sympathy were with her friend Joanna Traherne.

The journey from north Wales to the Cornish coast had exhausted Megan, and she hoped the veil of her bonnet hid her drooping eyelids from her neighbours in the pew on the bride's side of the church.

Opening her eyes as the organ blared forth the wedding march, Megan rose to her feet for the processional. The radiant bride, a glittering ice princess in white satin, swept by on the arm of her dashing groom, but Megan's glance moved swiftly to the frozen-faced maid of honour. She knew Joanna well enough to recognise the depth of the hurt in her resolutely calm expression.

'Are you a friend of the bride or the groom?' a male voice asked at her side.

'The bride . . . well, that is, I went to school with her sister Joanna. I didn't really know Adele too well.'

Although the man's handsome features were tanned almost as dark as those of the swarthy Cornishmen among the guests, he towered over all of them. An imposing presence, Megan decided, but a disturbing one. Brawny shoulders strained the fabric of his fine broadcloth jacket almost to the breaking point, and there was a certain restlessness in his stance, as though secretly he found both the ritual of the wedding and its participants somewhat superficial.

His eyes, which were as dark as his hair, flickered over Megan's mourning gown and black-veiled bonnet. Like her, he had slipped into the church late and been consigned to the very last pew. 'I'm glad Joanna has a friend,' he replied quietly. 'She'll need comforting to get through this.'

Megan had already stepped from the pew to follow the other guests out into the churchyard, but she glanced back at the man in startled recognition that he, like herself, knew that Adele Traherne had just married the man her sister loved.

Swept along with a covey of guests, Megan found herself outside in the mellow June sunshine. How much warmer it was here on the southern coast. The church clung to the side of a steep cliff; far below, the Channel churned against rocky coves where smugglers once brought spirits from France and perhaps still did and where, long ago, wreckers lured ships onto the rocks in order to loot their cargoes.

'Megan!' Joanna's voice called to her and she turned to see her friend coming through the crowd towards her.

They embraced wordlessly. Megan could see the glint of tears in Joanna's hazel eyes. Oh, Adele, Megan thought, why, why? Of all the suitors who clamoured for your hand, why did you have to choose the one man your sister loved?

'Joanna . . .' a deeply timbred male voice interrupted. Megan knew instantly that it belonged to the man who had spoken to her during the processional.

The two young women turned as he approached, and he quickly added, 'Forgive me, I mean Miss Traherne. Although I feel I know you very well, we have not, of course, been formally introduced.'

For the first time Megan noticed his slight accent. It

6

didn't give his speech a foreign sound, but rather flattened the vowels and emphasised some syllables that in England were not ordinarily pronounced.

Joanna looked at him in surprise. 'Surely you can't be . . .'

He gave a small bow, which to Megan appeared more mocking than polite. 'Randolph Mallory, at your service.' He smiled and the resulting changes in his features were pleasing, revealing deeply cleft cheeks and a humorous gleam in his dark eyes that offset heavy dark eyebrows. She noticed, too, that he had a high forehead, but none of these attributes diminished her feeling that, in some indefinable way, this man was dangerous.

'I didn't think you were coming,' Joanna said to him. 'I'm so surprised I hardly know what to say.' She glanced at Megan and said, 'This is Megan Thomas, my dearest friend.'

'We've already met,' Randolph Mallory replied. 'Inside the church.'

Randolph Mallory, Jo's cousin from America. Why hadn't Joanna mentioned that he was invited? Megan wondered. But then, Joanna couldn't have known how intensely interested in America Megan had become since her grandfather's death.

One of the bridesmaids materialised at Joanna's side. 'We're to go to the carriages now. Adele needs you to help with her veil.'

Joanna nodded and murmured to Megan, 'As soon as the reception is under way, we'll talk.' She smiled at Randolph, and Megan noticed a puzzled look lurking behind the smile. 'I can't tell you how happy I am that you came,' she told him.

Megan found herself alone with Mallory. He offered his arm. 'May I escort you to the carriages? I feel you and I are old friends. Joanna mentioned you in several of her letters.'

'Oh?' Megan responded cautiously. 'What did she tell you about me?'

7

'That you're brilliantly clever and something of a maverick –'

'Maverick? I'm not familiar with the word.'

'It's an American expression – one who doesn't run with the herd.

'I understand you were brought up by a physician grandfather who taught you all about medicine,' the American said. 'According to Joanna, you assist him to the extent that you could probably take over his practice.'

'My grandfather passed away recently,' Megan responded.

Randolph Mallory murmured his condolences as he helped her into a waiting carriage and climbed in beside her. They found themselves facing two other wedding guests, an elderly couple who smiled and nodded awkwardly, then fixed their eyes on the stone walls bordering the narrow lane along which the carriage bore them to Traherne Hall.

The house, like the church, clung to a cliff top above a rocky cove into which the indigo sea surged in white-foamed fury. A hard dark line along the horizon indicated the sultry summer day would end in a storm. Megan glanced at the advancing clouds and then at the tables that had been set up on the lawns for the reception. Perhaps the rain would hold off for a while, but already the wind was rising, whipping tendrils of ivy against the age-darkened bricks of the house and rattling the branches of the trees.

Megan moved down the receiving line. When she reached the parents of the bride, Mrs Traherne, who in her maturity was almost as beautiful as Adele, her daughter, peered at Megan without recognition.

'I am Megan Thomas. We met when you visited Joanna at school and again later on, when I spent a weekend here at Traherne Hall . . . It was a long time ago.'

'Of course, how are you, my dear?' said Mr Traherne, who stood beside his second wife. He had Joanna's thoughtful hazel eyes and her rather eager smile, which seemed more vulnerable on Jo's plain features. Joanna's

8

mother had died shortly after her birth, and her father had remarried two years later.

'Megan! Dear child!' Mrs Traherne exclaimed, her tone insincere. 'I didn't recognise you with all that glorious titian hair hidden under your bonnet. But you're in mourning for your grandfather, of course. We were so sorry to hear of your loss. How very unselfish of you to come today, in the midst of your grief.'

Megan was curious to hear their reaction to the arrival of their cousin from America, but before Randolph Mallory reached them Megan found herself standing before the bride, and Adele said rather shrilly, 'Hello, Megan. I don't think you've ever met my husband, Oliver Pentreath? Miss Thomas is an old school friend of Joanna's.' There was a slightly defiant look on Adele's china-doll face.

'I hope you'll both be very happy,' Megan said before moving on.

As she walked across the lawn, the turf felt resilient beneath the thin soles of her slippers. Cornwall was lushly green, the grass luxuriant in a way the craggy hills of north Wales never were.

Accepting a glass of wine from a passing footman, she wandered over to a copse of beech and willows to stand in the shadows in an effort to minimise the effect of her sombre black, which seemed an affront to the festive occasion, although it was ironically appropriate in view of Joanna's loss. The other women in their pastel finery flitted about the gardens like delicate butterflies, and she felt a little like a bat.

'May I join you?' Randolph Mallory appeared so suddenly that she jumped. 'I feel about as comfortable as you appear to be. Are we the only ones who know what's really happening here?'

'Since Adele is now Mrs Oliver Pentreath, perhaps it would behove us to forget any secrets Joanna might have confided? I'm quite sure she would be embarrassed to death if we were to bring up the subject of her past friendship with Oliver.'

9

One black eyebrow twitched mockingly. 'Friendship?'

Wondering how much Joanna had confided in her letters to this man, Megan took a hurried sip of wine, and it went down the wrong way. As she began to choke he smacked her sharply between the shoulder blades. She resisted the urge to smack him back.

'I'll bring you a chair,' he said, and before she could demur he had slipped away and returned with two deck chairs.

Now that she was seated, her good manners dictated that she continue the conversation. 'You came a great distance to attend Adele's wedding.'

'I also had business here in England. I came to buy some Hereford cattle to ship back to the ranch. I feel the era of the longhorn is coming to an end. I had been planning this trip for some time.'

Megan had a fleeting, rather eerie sense of something odd in the tone of his reply, but decided the feeling came from her own fatigue and state of mind. Recent events had taught her to distrust everyone. She hoped this was only temporary, as the feeling was alien to her inborn love of her fellow beings.

'What about you? Will you continue to live in – north Wales, isn't it? – now that your grandfather is dead?'

Fortunately Joanna came looking for them before it was necessary for Megan to answer. 'There you are! Why are you hiding in the trees? Come out at once, both of you. We must laugh and be joyful. This is a happy occasion, remember?' She pulled Megan to her feet, and Megan detected the brittle edge of wine-induced bravado in her friend's voice as she presented them to the other guests.

The rain clouds had not yet reached the coast, but the air was oppressive, almost crackling with the electricity of the approaching storm. The wedding breakfast was served and consumed, the cake cut, champagne toasts offered. Adele and Oliver disappeared into the house and reappeared clad in travelling clothes. A carriage decorated with flowers and streamers was brought around, and they came to the top of the steps leading from the house to be showered with confetti and flower petals.

Giggling, the bridesmaids clustered at the bottom of the steps as Adele waved her bridal bouquet aloft, preparing to toss it to them. She searched the group for her half sister, but Joanna was not among them. One bridesmaid, realising why Adele hesitated, turned and ran back to seize Joanna's hand and pull her forward.

Megan's heart ached for her friend. A dull flush had suffused Joanna's slightly sallow complexion and her lower lip trembled.

The bouquet sailed through the air directly towards Joanna, who made no move to catch it. The flowers fell with a soft sigh to the gravel of the driveway and were scooped up immediately by one of the other bridesmaids. For a split second the half sisters stared at each other; then Adele seized Oliver's arm and they ran lightly down the steps to the waiting carriage.

At almost the same moment the sun disappeared into a billowing black cloud, and the sky was rent by a jagged flash of lightning. Raindrops the size of florins began to fall, and everyone scurried for shelter. In the resulting confusion Joanna grasped Megan's hand with fingers that, even through her lace gloves, felt icy cold. 'We have to talk . . . privately.'

Together they ran up the steps and into the house. Joanna led her down a long hall to a pair of double doors that opened to a solarium running the length of the south side of the house. Here Mr Traherne's orchids were pampered and cared for in their steamy glass-enclosed world. Looking at the exotic loveliness of the blooms, Megan was reminded that this was a rich man's hobby. The Traherne sisters had always known wealth and comfort, but only Joanna had been willing to live as a poor man's wife. Dear Jo, she had not known that handsome Oliver in his threadbare tweeds, a teacher at the village school, was the only heir to a rich uncle in India.

'We won't be disturbed here,' Joanna said. 'I couldn't

11

wait until after everyone left. I had to talk to you right away. Oh, God, Megan, I don't know what to do.'

The tears she had held at bay all day erupted in a flood. Megan slipped her arms around her friend and held her as she sobbed uncontrollably, not attempting to comfort her until her anguish had spent itself. As Joanna's tears began to diminish, Megan led her to a narrow wooden bench used for repotting plants, and moved some clay pots to make room for them to sit down.

They sat side by side, Megan in her black bombazine mourning gown and Joanna in palest peach silk, a colour that suited her not at all and had undoubtedly been selected by Adele. With her dark hair and tawny skin Jo needed strong, clear shades.

For a long time the silence was broken only by the sound of rain beating on the glass roof of the solarium and an occasional strangled sob caught in Joanna's throat. Megan held her friend tightly, wishing she could ease that terrible pain. Poor dear Jo, who had never hurt a living soul, how could they do this to her?

At length Megan took Joanna's cold hands in hers and gripped them tightly. 'It isn't the end of the world, Jo, please believe me. You'll get over Oliver. No one ever died of a broken heart, no matter what the poets tell us.'

Joanna began to cry again, a desperate gasping sound that chilled Megan to the core. 'Oh, Megan, what am I going to do?'

'You're going to go on. Hold your head up and don't let anyone know how you feel. If you act as if you don't care, in time it will be true . . . you won't care.'

Joanna shook her hands free and jumped to her feet. She stood in front of Megan, her eyes drowning. 'I *can't* go on as if nothing is wrong. Oh, God, Megan, haven't you guessed? I'm carrying Oliver's child!'

Megan leaned back weakly, feeling against her back the wooden slats of a shelf that held a row of cymbidiums. The warm earthy odour of bark and humus overpowered the elusive fragrance of the orchids. A moment later the staccato patter of raindrops was lost in a long rumble of thunder. 'Joanna . . . are you sure?'

Joanna dropped to her knees and clutched Megan's hands, burrowing her face into the folds of her skirt like a child hiding from the consequences of her actions. 'Please don't judge me. Oliver and I were secretly engaged for two years. He insisted on saving enough to buy a house before we married, although I would have lived in a hovel with him. We were going to announce our wedding last spring and he persuaded me to . . . that it was all right for us to . . . but then his uncle died and Oliver inherited a huge fortune and Adele began to flirt with him. God forgive me, I could kill her! She knew Oliver and I had an understanding.'

'You didn't tell him you were having his baby?'

Joanna shook her head. 'I didn't want Oliver to feel obliged to marry me. I still love him, Megan. That's my cross. I want him to be happy. But I can't bear an illegitimate child. The disgrace would kill my parents and certainly ruin me.' She looked up, her eyes pleading. 'You must help me, Megan. No one else can.'

'We could go back to Llanrys. I had to sell grandfather's house in order to pay all his debts, but we could rent a cottage . . .' Megan fell silent, unnerved by the grim appeal in Joanna's eyes.

'I want you to get rid of the baby for me.'

A cold fist closed around Megan's heart. 'Joanna, you don't know what you're asking.'

'Yes, I do. You're as good a doctor as your grandfather ever was. You told me that you were his hands when he shook too much to wield a scalpel, and you were his eyes when he could no longer see the rampant infection in a wound he'd treated. Didn't his patients continue to come to you after your grandfather became senile, because he was the only doctor in that tiny town?'

'While he was alive, Jo. But now he's gone and so are his diploma and his shingle. I'm not qualified, I'm not a doctor and I probably never will be.'

13

'Meg, you've told me many times that male doctors have no interest in women's complaints, but I know you studied female anatomy, because I went with you when you bought your books and we told the bookseller they were for your grandfather. And at school you were outraged by the appalling number of women who went to back-street abortionists. I remember you saying that if it weren't against the law, doctors could terminate unwanted pregnancies with a simple operation.'

'Jo, you don't know what you're asking of me! I couldn't . . . Oh, I don't care about the law or getting caught, but I do care about you. I might kill you. It's all very well to study pictures of the female anatomy and know the theory of something, but it's quite another to perform the operation. Please don't ask this of me.'

'I must. There's no one else I trust. I know you could do it. I want you to.'

'I've set bones, lanced boils, and sutured wounds for my grandfather, Jo. His patients were colliers and their families, poorer than church mice. They came to him only in emergencies. By the time he saw them, they were either bleeding or suffocating or in so much pain they couldn't stand it. Their women had midwives deliver their babies, and they put up with their female diseases in stoic silence. My grandfather never even examined a woman, and neither did I.'

'I'm begging you to do this for me, Meg. Please.'

Megan stroked her friend's hair back from her brow, unable to speak or respond. At last she whispered, 'Surely there must be some other way. You could go away and have the child –'

'No! I can't. I won't. Even if I gave up the child, how could I live with a secret like that? If Oliver and Adele were to find out . . . No, it's out of the question. Megan, please, oh, please do this for me. I don't want to go to some old crone with a knitting needle.'

Megan shivered. She knew even better than Joanna how many unfortunate women died of haemorrhages and infections, how many were maimed or left unable to bear another child. It wasn't a fate she wanted for her friend.

'Don't even consider it,' an icy voice interrupted. Randolph Mallory's footsteps had fallen silently on the earthen floor and he appeared from behind a partition festooned with tropical vines. He loomed over the two young women, his face set in tight, angry lines.

2

Megan jumped to her feet and faced Mallory, placing herself protectively between him and Joanna. The rain continued to beat a relentless tattoo on the glass roof of the solarium. 'How dare you sneak in here and spy on us? This is none of your business.'

'I'm making it my business. I won't stand by and let two young women calmly make plans to ruin their lives. Think this thing through . . . Megan, what if Joanna dies by your hand? Can you live the rest of your life with the knowledge that you killed her? And you, Joanna, do you really know what you're asking of your friend? If she's caught, she'll go to prison.'

Megan was so angry, she wanted to slap him, but the look on his face told her he might slap her back. He was a big man, and there was about him a certain lack of gentility, evidenced by an excess of muscle and that outdoorsman's tan, not to mention that hard glaze to his eyes. He had, she was sure, only temporarily stepped out of character for the duration of his visit to the English branch of his family. There was a dangerous quality to this man that suggested he would have his way, no matter what.

Perhaps it was a survival attribute necessary for living in the wild American West. From his stance, he seemed almost ready to restrain them physically.

'Come along, Jo,' she said, taking her friend firmly by the hand. 'We have nothing further to discuss in your cousin's presence.'

For an instant she was afraid he wouldn't move out of their way in the narrow passage between the rows of silent and somehow sinister orchids, but he stepped grudgingly aside. As Joanna went by with her head bowed in shame, he said in a gentler tone, 'You could always go to America to have your child. You might even consider going to New Mexico.'

Joanna merely gave him a stricken look and Megan dragged her out of the solarium as fast as they could move among the brooding orchids.

When they reached the main part of the house, they saw that some of the guests were now departing, anxious to return to their homes before the full fury of the storm erupted. Mr and Mrs Traherne stood at the doors bidding them good-bye, while an elderly butler hurried back and forth bringing coats and wraps. Joanna's step-mother drew her to one side. 'Find Mrs Elliot and ask her to prepare a guest room for Mr Mallory.' She added, in an annoyed tone, 'He might have let us know he was coming.'

'I have to find the housekeeper,' Joanna whispered to Megan. 'Come with me, please. I don't want to be by myself for even a moment. I feel as if I'm choking. As if my head is going to explode.'

As they went downstairs to the servants' quarters Megan asked, 'I take it Randolph Mallory's visit was a complete surprise to you all?'

'Well, I'd written to him about our wedding plans . . . Oliver's and mine. When Oliver jilted me for Adele, I had to tell Randolph that, too, and I did remind him that he'd mentioned buying some Herefords for the ranch and it would be a perfect time for him to come . . . that I needed the comfort of my friends. But I had no idea he'd take me up on the invitation.'

'How did you happen to start writing to him, Joanna?'

'Randolph's mother was my real mother's cousin; she married an American. Randolph wrote to us some time ago to tell us his parents had died. He didn't go into detail, but I assume it was an illness. Father sent a letter of condolence, and . . . I don't know, I just had to write, too. I suppose I was curious about the American West, since we read such frightening accounts of Indian attacks and outlaws there. Anyway, we started to correspond, and his letters were so . . . sensitive, thoughtful, intelligent . . . quite educated. It seemed such a paradox. I'd imagined him to be some sort of cowboy on his father's ranch. I can't tell you how drawn to him I felt – in a friendly way, of course, since I am . . . was in love with Oliver.'

'That big brute of a man . . . sensitive? Thoughtful?' Megan exclaimed, before she could stop herself.

'I must say he isn't at all what I expected. Especially the way he followed us into the solarium and . . . the things he said. He's certainly no gentleman.' Joanna sighed. 'Why can't people be what they seem?'

Why indeed? Megan thought grimly, thinking of her grandfather's lies.

They went into a stone-flagged kitchen where the housekeeper, a wiry little woman whose eyes darted about disconcertingly, was supervising several scullery maids as they washed stacks of dishes.

'Mother says to tell you we have another overnight guest, Mrs Elliot,' Joanna said. 'My second cousin, Randolph Mallory from America.' She paused, then added, 'I'd rather you put him in the east wing.'

Mrs Elliot replied, 'Yes, Miss Joanna. I'll have the bed made up right away.' There was a slight shiftiness to the housekeeper's glance that Megan didn't like. Was her subservient tone a sham that hid her real feelings towards her employers? Megan wondered. Mrs Elliot's deep-set eyes rudely went over Joanna's slender body. 'Are you

17

feeling all right, dear? Been a bit of a strain on you today, hasn't it? Perhaps you'd like a nice cup of tea?'

Megan expected Joanna to reprimand the woman, considering her insolently familiar tone, but Joanna merely replied in a soft voice, 'No, thank you, Mrs Elliot. Come on, Meg, I'll show you your room.

Megan wondered if the woman suspected that Jo was in the family way or if her sly expression just meant the housekeeper knew Adele had stolen Oliver from Joanna. Some people seemed to take perverse pleasure in others' unhappiness.

When they returned to the entry hall a mass exodus was in progress, and the Trahernes were engulfed by departing guests. Joanna said, 'I'd better say some good-byes, too. I shan't be long.' She moved to her father's side, and Megan started towards the drawing room.

The front doors were open, and gusts of damp air wafted in. A young man, his cap in one hand and a yellow envelope in the other, inched around the door jamb and surveyed the crowd uncertainly. As Megan crossed in front of him he said, 'Excuse me, miss. But I've a cablegram here for a Miss Joanna Traherne. Would you be knowing who she is?'

'I'll take it to her,' Megan said. She glanced at the name on the envelope and it was indeed Joanna's; this was not a congratulatory wire for the newlyweds. She slipped it into her reticule and continued into the drawing room, her mind still reeling from the shock of Joanna's predicament.

The room was growing dark. Storm clouds now hung over the house like a grey blanket and the lamps had not been lit. Megan sat on a Queen Anne sofa in front of the fireplace where a vase of summer flowers stood in front of the empty grate. Her weariness had returned and she longed to go to her room to rest, but she felt that Joanna needed her, for it was clear that she was in a delicate emotional state. It wouldn't do for her to think her best friend had turned her back on her, too. Joanna had always been impulsive, and there was no telling what the sight of

Oliver's departure with her sister today might precipitate.

Megan was nodding sleepily when at last Joanna came into the room, her silk bridesmaid's dress whispering as she moved. 'Shall we go up to your room now?'

'Jo, listen . . . I'm too exhausted to think clearly just now. Could we sleep on the problem and decide what to do tomorrow?'

Joanna kneaded her hands for a second, then whirled around and stood facing the marble fireplace, her back to Megan. 'If you won't help me, I'll have to find someone who will. I do mean to do it, Meg.'

'Jo, so much has happened lately in my life, too, that I need a little time to digest what you've told me. We also have to consider the fact that Randolph Mallory knows about you. We don't know what he might do or to whom he might talk.'

Joanna immediately turned around. 'He'll keep my secret. I know he will. His letters are so filled with compassion. The man who wrote to me in such a way must be hiding behind that rather threatening façade.' She sat down beside Megan and stared at the floral display on the hearth. 'I've been so full of my own woes that I haven't asked how you're managing since your grandfather died.'

'Not very well,' Megan murmured. 'I grieve for him, miss him terribly, and treasure the good years we had together, but he left unfinished business, and I don't know how to deal with it.'

'But surely his passing was a merciful release, after these last years of senility?'

Megan drew a deep breath. 'I loved my grandfather dearly, Jo, you know that. He was all I ever had. You remember I told you that my mother died when I was born –'

'And your father left you with your grandfather and you never heard from him again. You never talked about it much, so I knew it was painful to be abandoned by him.'

'I *thought* my father abandoned me, but I was wrong. After Grandfather died, his solicitor gave me a locked box

19

containing the deed to the house and other papers –
including several letters from my father. Letters I had
never seen.'

'Your father had written to you?'

'To my grandfather, while I was still a baby. You see,
my father was also a doctor. His letters were filled with
anguish that he'd been unable to save my mother. After
he left Llanrys he went first to the West Indies and then
became a ship's doctor, sailing between the Indies and
America. He wanted Grandfather to put me on a ship and
send me to a place called Galveston, which is a southern
port in America.'

'America . . .' Joanna repeated thoughtfully, undoubtedly thinking, as Megan had, of the presence here of the
American. 'Your grandfather probably thought a ship's
doctor couldn't care for a baby properly. But he should
have told you about the letters when you were older.'

'My grandfather hated my father,' Megan answered.
'He blamed him for my mother's death, which was quite
irrational, especially for a doctor. God knows enough
women die in childbirth and most doctors won't even
deliver babies –' She broke off, remembering Joanna's
pregnancy. There was no need to remind her that every
woman faced the possibility that childbirth could be a
sentence of death. She quickly added, 'But to conceal my
father's letters from me . . .'

'Meg, your grandfather idolised you. His secrecy is
understandable. He didn't want to lose you. Don't blame
him too much. After all, in all those years your father
could have returned for you.'

'It was clear from the last letters that my grandfather
had written and told my father that I had died as a baby,
soon after he left for the Indies.'

'On, no! How dreadful of him . . . and to think of these
past years when you cared for a senile old man . . . But
perhaps now that you no longer have to care for him you
could go to Galveston and search for your father.'

Megan sighed. 'The letters are twenty years old. I wrote

to the address in Galveston, but there has been no response. I don't even know if my father is still alive. No, I'll probably stay in Llanrys.'

Megan caught Joanna's hands in hers. 'Come to Wales with me, Jo. After the baby is born we'll pass it off as mine and you can come home to Traherne Hall.'

'Dear heaven, then you would be a spinster with an illegitimate child. I couldn't impose that stigma on my dearest friend.'

'I don't have a family to disgrace and I'm not likely to marry. I frighten most men with my ambitions.'

'So you *are* still hoping to be a doctor!'

'Have I ever wanted to do anything else with my life? My grandfather started teaching me medicine when I was six years old. I've had a longer training period than most licensed doctors. But I need a formal education to practice legally. And a way to support myself until I'm qualified.'

'But having a child would be even more of an impediment than being a woman, and God knows that's enough to slam a great many doors in your face.'

'Let me worry about that. Will you come to Wales with me?'

'Will you end my pregnancy for me?'

'I don't dare. I've never attempted to terminate a pregnancy, and I'm not going to practise on my best friend.'

Joanna's lips compressed. She rose. 'I'll take you to your room.'

'Jo . . .' Megan pleaded.

'There's nothing more to be said, Meg.'

They went upstairs silently. Joanna indicated a bedroom on the second floor and said stiffly, 'Dinner is at eight. I'll see you then.'

But Joanna didn't appear at dinner and her stepmother was visibly annoyed by her absence. There were several overnight guests in addition to Megan and Randolph Mallory. Mrs Traherne sent a footman to find Joanna and he returned and stated that she was not in her room, nor had anyone seen her since the wedding reception ended.

21

Randolph Mallory's dark eyes met Megan's across the expanse of white damask tablecloth and she looked away, unwilling to acknowledge the bond of secret knowledge between them.

Mr Traherne said awkwardly, 'It's been a trying day for Joanna. Perhaps she took a quiet walk and lost track of the time.'

'You may begin serving, Hoskins,' Mrs Traherne said to the hovering butler.

As Megan unfolded her napkin she suddenly remembered the cablegram that had come for Joanna. She had completely forgotten it during their earlier conversation in the drawing room.

Dinner progressed tensely, with Mr Traherne asking somewhat distractedly about Mallory's home in America, but obviously feeling embarrassed by Joanna's absence. As soon as she could, Megan excused herself and went back to her room to retrieve the cablegram from her reticule. There was no response when she knocked on Joanna's bedroom door a moment later.

Megan looked down at the yellow envelope and saw that it had not been sealed, the wire had simply been slipped inside it. Was it some urgent message that perhaps should be given to the Trahernes in view of Joanna's absence? On an impulse, she pulled out the cablegram and saw that it had been relayed from a Western Union station in New Mexico, USA: 'Joanna, Impossible to come for the wedding. My thoughts are with you. Be brave. Warmest regards.'

The wire was signed by Randolph Mallory.

3

The gale lashed the Cornish coast with increasing fury, rare for a summer storm. Joanna could hear the wind shrieking across the cove and moaning under the eaves. Around her in the attic, cobweb-shrouded steamer trunks and dust-filmed discarded furniture created grotesque shadows in the deepening dusk.

She fought the waves of pain and nausea sweeping through her and tried to cling to the last shreds of consciousness. She lay on a blanket on the hard wooden floor, a musty-smelling pillow under her head. There was warm stickiness between her legs, and her abdomen was afire.

'You've got to get up,' a distant voice commanded. 'You 'ear me? You can't stop up 'ere no longer. Come on, rouse yourself. You've missed dinner and they're looking for you. I knew I should've said you were ill, but no, you were going to be back on your feet like nothing 'appened. Well, don't blame me . . .'

Hovering mistily above her was a face with a narrow witch's nose and darting eyes that were now filled with fear. Mrs Elliot seized her arm and shook her. 'You've been up 'ere nearly two hours.' In her agitation her carefully cultivated housekeeper's accent had slipped a little, revealing origins quite different from what was indicated on the references she'd presented when she was hired.

'You'll be all right so long as you don't lift nothing nor let a man do it to you again for at least a month.' An unpleasant titter accompanied the advice. 'I've got to get meself back belowstairs now or they'll miss me, too. Now, you get down to your room, do you 'ear?'

Footsteps scurried across the floor. Joanna called, 'No, don't go! Please, wait,' her voice frighteningly weak. She struggled to sit up, retched, and, clutching her stomach, fell back again. The sloping ceiling of the attic rushed towards her, then receded. She felt hot, yet freezing cold, and could not stop shaking. It took all of her strength to whisper, 'Please . . . get Megan. Bring her to me.'

'No! I told you, nobody else must know.'

'She won't betray us . . . Please, I beg you, Mrs Elliot. I feel so ill. Her grandfather was a doctor. She can help me.'

The attic door closed with a soft thud, leaving Joanna alone.

Oh, God, such pain . . . She bit down on her lower lip and tasted blood. The air around her seemed to be filled with the smell of blood. Was it possible that only hours earlier she had bravely marched up here and submitted to the brutal ministrations of Mrs Elliot?

The housekeeper had found Joanna in the throes of morning sickness a fortnight ago and had guessed her condition. When Mrs Elliot slyly suggested that she could take care of the problem for a price, Joanna had at first refused, thinking instead of Megan's medical knowledge. But Megan had let her down, and in her hurt and desperation Joanna hadn't stopped to consider that perhaps it would have been better to wait a few more days, at least until the wedding guests had departed, even though Mrs Elliot said she mustn't delay any longer or it would be too late.

Joanna regretted her impulsive decision to end her pregnancy tonight, but everything had conspired to make her act – not only Megan's refusal to grant her request, but also the knowledge that tonight her beloved Oliver would be consummating his marriage to Adele. It seemed imperative that on his wedding night Joanna should rid herself of the results of his careless lovemaking. A sort of vague punishment for his betrayal.

Then, too, hovering at the back of her mind was yet another disappointment. Randolph . . . Oh, why couldn't he have been her dear sensitive friend in the flesh as well as on the written page? She wished passionately that she had never written begging him to come and get her. At least while he was in America he had thought only that she wanted to escape the humiliation of being jilted by Oliver. But now . . . now he knew the whole sordid truth, and he certainly would not invite a fallen woman to visit his ranch.

What could she have been thinking? That Randolph would come riding on a white horse to pluck her out of her misery? That his very appearance as her champion would make Oliver realise that another man could care about her? How stupidly she'd behaved, over and over again. Her impulsiveness had been her downfall from the very beginning, when she allowed Oliver intimacies that should have been reserved for marriage.

A severe cramp caused her to double over. She buried her face in the pillow and held her breath until the spasm passed. She was soaked with perspiration, her hair clinging in wet strands to her face. Another onslaught of pain assailed her and she slipped away into a void.

She was running down a long tunnel towards a flickering light that never seemed to come closer. Someone was calling her name, imploring her to return. Oliver . . . Oliver, is that you? Oh, my darling, have you come back for me?

Then the flickering light grew brighter and turned into an oil lamp. She felt a cool hand on her forehead. 'Jo . . .'

Megan's voice drifted towards her across a sea of agony. Too weak to respond, Joanna writhed, panting, trying to force herself to protest as she felt the soaked sheet being carefully removed from between her legs where Mrs Elliot had wadded it.

Somewhere in the dimness of the room she heard the sound of tearing cloth, then Megan's voice, low, urgent, but, oh, so comforting. 'I'll try not to hurt you, Jo. You're haemorrhaging and I have to pack your vagina. I'm using my petticoat because I don't have anything else. When I'm finished I'm going for a doctor. I shan't leave you alone for very long, I promise.'

'Can't see a doctor . . .' Joanna gasped in fright and struggled to raise her head, but it flopped back weakly.

'Joanna, you *must* have a doctor. Who did this to you? What instrument did they use?' As she spoke her hands worked efficiently.

'Who . . . told you I was up here?'

'Someone slipped a note under my door. Who did this, Jo?'

'Can't . . . tell. Promised . . .'

'All right, just lie still, don't move. I'm going for −'

She never finished the sentence. The attic door burst open, and there were footsteps and voices and a flurry of confusion. Before a red haze descended like a veil over her pain-racked vision, Joanna saw Megan kneeling beside her, her dressing gown stained with blood. The last sound she heard was her stepmother's anguished scream: 'Oh, dear God! You've killed her.'

4

Joanna hovered in a misty netherworld somewhere between darkness and light. Her limbs were heavy, wooden, and the pain in her abdomen was a writhing serpent. She no longer heard voices and tried to recall something that had been said recently that seemed important . . . but it escaped her.

She remembered Mrs Elliot and felt a shudder ripple

26

through her body. Then she recalled that she'd begged the housekeeper to fetch Megan and that her friend had said she was going for a doctor! Oh, God, no!

Joanna forced her eyes open, and the familiar shapes of her room came into view. She was lying in her own bed. How had she come here? The last she remembered she was in the attic. She had to leave Traherne Hall right away. Mustn't let a doctor find out . . .

It took all of her strength to swing her feet to the floor and stand up on legs that no longer seemed to belong to her. Too weak to dress, she pulled a cape over her blood-soaked nightgown, then began to stuff gowns, petticoats, and undergarments into a valise.

Waves of nausea and dizziness washed over her as she dragged her protesting body to the door. There was no one on the landing, but she could hear the murmur of voices in the hall below. She knew her stepmother and father were anxiously pacing the marble floor, no doubt awaiting the arrival of the doctor who would tell them what ailed their daughter. There was no sign of anyone else.

A hand descended from nowhere, grasping her shoulder in a painful grip. Stifling a cry of fright, Joanna turned to look into the crafty stare of Mrs Elliot. The woman's eyes dropped to the valise in her hand and she nodded, as if in approval. 'Come on, this way, quick now. We've got to 'ide you before they come and lock up both of us. If they can't find you, there's no evidence, is there?'

The woman's muttered words barely registered on Joanna's numbed mind. She felt herself being propelled along the landing to the servants' staircase. For an instant the steps seemed to undulate, and she swayed unsteadily. Mrs Elliot grabbed the valise and dragged her by the hand down the stairs.

The housekeeper seemed desperately anxious to get her out of the house, undoubtedly fearing that she would tell the doctor who had performed the illegal operation. Joanna wanted to assure Mrs Elliot that she would never betray her, but she couldn't seem to catch her breath sufficiently to speak.

Joanna knew it must be very late. The gaslights burned low, illuminating the deserted kitchen; all the other servants would be in bed. Her movements seemed leaden, as in a dream, and she was unable to concentrate on anything but her pain.

When Mrs Elliot flung open the tradesmen's door, a gust of rainwashed air revived Joanna a little. Black clouds obscured the moon, and thunder still rumbled in the distance.

'Wait 'ere,' the housekeeper ordered. 'I'll wake up a stable boy and he can fetch a cart. You'll 'ave to go out the back way, across the fields.'

Joanna sank down on the doorstep, trying to collect her fragmented thoughts. She clutched at Mrs Elliot's skirts. 'Don't tell them.'

' 'Course not. What do you take me for?'

'If you would just tell Mother and Father that I had to go away, that I couldn't bear to stay here and be an object of pity, a jilted woman.'

Mrs Elliot stared at her for a moment, then vanished into the shadows. She returned a little while later with a wide-eyed stable boy who led a gentle mare harnessed to a gardener's cart. The instant the two of them lifted Joanna into the cart, she fainted.

The Trahernes, the village doctor, and Megan were clustered in a sombre group around Joanna's bed. Megan stared at the bloodstained sheet, the damp pillowcase, and the rumpled counterpane. 'She couldn't have gone far. She was too weak.'

'I'm not surprised,' the doctor said acidly. 'What did you use on her? A knitting needle?'

'No! No, I didn't do anything to her . . . except pack her insides. To try to stop the bleeding.'

'And you just happened upon that little bit of medical knowledge, I suppose?' the doctor responded in a voice heavy with sarcasm. 'After all, well-brought-up young ladies are familiar with the dire consequences of botched illegal operations, are they not?'

'My grandfather was a doctor –'

'And you are a criminal abortionist.' The doctor shook a finger under Megan's nose, then turned to Mr Traherne. 'I suggest you send for the constable immediately. This young woman has committed a serious crime.'

'Wait! It wasn't me . . . I don't know who did it, but someone pushed a note under my bedroom door, asking me to go to the attic. That's how I found Joanna.'

'If there is such a note,' Mrs Traherne exclaimed tearfully, 'Megan probably wrote it herself.' She tugged the bell cord beside the bed.

Mr Traherne, his face grey with worry, said slowly, 'Megan, I'm afraid we're going to have to lock you in your room until the constable arrives to talk to you. Pray God that we find Joanna soon and she vindicates you. Doctor, I'd appreciate it if you would spend the night here at Traherne Hall. When we find Joanna we shall need you.'

This couldn't be happening! Megan distractedly pushed her hair out of her eyes. A sleepy-eyed footman appeared, and Mr Traherne ordered him to awaken the other servants and begin a search for Joanna. Then he added, 'As soon as it's light, you are to go to the village and bring the constable.'

Megan clutched Mr Traherne's arm. 'Please believe I did not do this to Joanna. I was trying to help when your wife found us.'

'I caught her bending over your daughter with blood on her hands,' Mrs Traherne cried.

'The penalties for performing illegal operations are severe,' the doctor said. 'Properly so. Joanna will be fortunate indeed if she recovers. If she lives, she is unlikely ever to have another child.'

Mrs Traherne gave a wild cry and collapsed into her husband's arms. Since she had previously shown little love for, or interest in her stepdaughter, Megan wondered if

Mrs Traherne's distress resulted from fear of a scandal rather than concern for Joanna. Mr Traherne, on the other hand, was trembling and beads of perspiration decorated his brow. He looked quite ill, Megan thought.

The doctor reached towards Megan, as though to seize her. 'Come along, I'm going to lock you up. Your mere presence is an affront to decent people.'

'Don't touch me. I am innocent. When you find Joanna, she'll tell you who the guilty one is.'

'If we find her *alive*,' the doctor muttered, giving her a push towards the door.

Megan was still shaking when she was thrust into her bedroom. She heard the door close with a thud and a key turn in the lock.

Where could Jo be? she wondered. She surely couldn't have walked far. Perhaps the haemorrhaging had stopped? Even so, Jo would be terribly weak, certainly in no condition to run away from home . . . unless someone had helped her? But who? Perhaps the person who had performed the abortion . . . who would be afraid of the crime being discovered.

Pressing her fingers to her throbbing head, Megan told herself that Joanna would soon be found and would clear her name. But if she wasn't . . . then Megan would go to prison. If, God forbid, Jo died . . . Megan would face the hangman.

Minutes dragged by interminably. Too exhausted and worried to sleep, Megan listened to every sound. She heard the servants outside combing the grounds, and voices within the hall, occasionally calling Joanna's name.

Just before dawn a key turned, and her bedroom door opened silently. She looked up in surprise to see Randolph Mallory slide quickly into the room and close the door.

'What are you doing here? Did you come to gloat and say "I told you so"? Please leave.'

His dark eyes regarded her with a level stare. 'I've come to offer you a way out.'

'I don't need a way out. I am innocent.'

Megan's heart had begun to pound, but she returned his stare unflinchingly. 'I have nothing further to say to you.'

'You haven't a hope of avoiding prison and you know it. Even if Joanna survives and pleads for you, you've broken the law. If she dies, you will be charged with manslaughter. But there is a way for you to escape. I can get you out of here, if you'll come with me, no questions asked.'

'Go with you? Where?'

'To America.'

For a split second possibilities danced tantalisingly in Megan's mind. Escape from prison, yes, but even more than that, a chance to go to the country where her father might still be living. Oh, how tempted she was! But why did this stranger want to take her to America with him? His expression was unreadable. She asked suspiciously, 'For what purpose?'

A small smile plucked at the corners of his mouth. 'Not for a life of sin, if that's what you're imagining. Oh, you're a beautiful woman, but the world is full of beautiful women. I wouldn't have to resort to trickery if that was all I had in mind.'

'What *do* you have in mind?'

'One thing only – that you come back to the ranch and pose as Joanna Traherne.'

Just as he was posing as Randolph Mallory, Megan thought. The wire from America certainly seemed to indicate he was an impostor. She thought perhaps it would be better to keep that bit of information to herself for the time being. 'You want me to pose as Joanna? But why?'

'Look, we don't have time for long explanations. Suffice to say that I came to take Joanna back to New Mexico. She wrote suggesting that she would not be adverse to visiting the ranch, but that was before she learned of her . . . delicate condition. Anyway, she's disappeared and you're available to take her place. I'm offering you a way out of a difficult situation. But you have to pretend to be Joanna. I'll explain why later. If I'm to get you out, we

31

have to leave before dawn, because that's when they'll bring the law to arrest you.'

'You said New Mexico? I thought you came from the United States.'

'The New Mexico Territory will be part of the United States before long. Statehood is a certainty.'

There was a sudden commotion in the courtyard below. The clatter of horses' hooves, raised voices, a woman's piercing scream. Megan rushed to the window and flung it open. One of the Traherne grooms had ridden in, waving a blood-soaked nightgown. Servants clustered around him as Mr Traherne lifted his wife's limp body into his arms and carried her into the house.

As Megan watched, Mrs Elliot appeared and the groom tossed the bloodstained gown to her. 'I found this at the edge of the cliff. Her slippers are there, too. She must have flung herself over, poor lass. 'Spect her body will wash in with the next tide.'

Megan gripped the windowsill and closed her eyes in mute horror. She felt Randolph's hand close over her shoulder. 'They'll haul you off to prison for certain now. We've only got minutes,' he said urgently.

She drew a deep breath. 'All right. I'll go with you.'

5

Joanna came to her senses briefly, but the bouncing of the cart caused another onslaught of pain and she drifted out of consciousness again.

The stable boy stopped the horse and leaned back to shake her. 'Miss? Miss, please wake up and tell me where to take you. The 'ousekeeper she said to take you to the station, but you can't get on a train if you can't stand on your feet.'

The clouds overhead parted to reveal the stars, then vanished behind a canopy of branches. She could hear the roar of the incoming tide far below and knew she was near Dutchman's Point, a finger of land protruding into the Channel not far from Traherne Hall. The lane forked here, one branch turning inland and leading into town and the railway station, the other disappearing into dense woods that sprawled at the edge of an unstable cliff above a treacherous snarl of rocks in a tiny cove two hundred feet below.

The stable boy's white face came into focus again, wavering before her like a ghostly moon. 'Miss . . . please miss. I'm sorry. I'm thinking you're dying and they'll blame me. I'm going to leave you 'ere and fetch Mrs Elliot. She'll tell us what to do.'

Joanna felt the boy's arms around her, and she was half lifted, half dragged from the cart. She tried to protest, to beg him not to leave her, but everything rushed away again in a welter of weakness and pain.

The void into which she pitched seemed to last only seconds, but when she came to her senses again she could feel sunlight on her face and hear birds chirping somewhere near. She was lying on something soft and sweet-smelling, like a potpourri of fragrant grasses and dried herbs.

Opening her eyes, she saw that she was lying just inside the entrance to a cave. Before her was a panorama of sky and sea and beneath her a homemade mattress protected her body from the rocky ground. She was covered by a blanket and there was a pillow of dried grasses under her head.

Turning her head, she looked into a pair of brilliant blue eyes set in a craggy, clean-shaven face that at first glance seemed to have been assembled in haste and handled before it was set. The nose had been broken and was now

33

slightly misplaced, but the eyes, though wary, expressed kindliness and did not belong with the fierce expression on the ravaged face. One of his ears was misshapen and protruded through a shaggy mop of dark hair. His cambric shirt, although clean, was tattered.

If Joanna could have summoned the strength she would have screamed. As it was, she could only regard the man in silent terror. So the stories of the hermit of Dutchman's Point were true.

As her eyes flickered open the man said, 'My name is Magnus. I interrupted an old woman trying to bury you in the woods. When she saw me coming she picked up a bundle and ran. After I brought you here I heard a commotion on the cliff top and somebody shouting that he'd found a bloodstained nightgown and slippers. I wondered why the old hag hadn't shoved you over the cliff instead of burying you – didn't make sense that she wanted it to *look* like you drowned when she could just as easily have thrown you into the sea. God knows you looked like you were already dead anyway. But then when I realised what had happened to you . . .'

Joanna closed her eyes again in shame. Mrs Elliot hadn't wanted her body found because she didn't want anyone to know of the botched abortion and possibly trace it to her. The housekeeper had been unaware that Joanna's secret had already been revealed to her parents. If Magnus hadn't come upon Mrs Elliot in the act of putting her into a grave it was unlikely anyone would have unearthed a body in the woods. Nor would it have been unusual if her body had not washed up with the tide, since there were so many rocks and underwater caves that bodies did not always return to shore.

'Miss . . . ?' A rough hand touched her cheek gently and her eyes flew open. She tried to move her lips to speak, but words wouldn't come. Gradually she became aware of several facts that her first terrified glance had missed. The man bending over her was young, still in his twenties, and he had been handsome before he acquired the broken nose

34

and misshapen ear. There was tensile strength in his lean, muscled body and the sinews of his arms knotted like ropes as he reached for a tin cup that sat on a ledge above her head. His big hand cradled Joanna's head gently but firmly as he raised it to press the cup to her lips.

When she clamped her mouth shut he ordered roughly, 'Drink. It isn't poison. If I'd wanted you dead, I could have left you where you were.'

The liquid tasted a little like chamomile tea and was very refreshing. She lay back after draining the cup and murmured, 'Thank you. If I could just rest for a while . . . Then perhaps you could help me get to the railway station? I must get away.'

'You're too weak to move. You've a fever and you're bleeding bad. I'll do what I can for you. Dunno much about female troubles, but I can bring your fever down.'

Joanna felt too numb to protest. Was there no end to the depth of her humiliation?

Magnus stood up, crouching beneath the low ceiling of the cave. He was tall and muscular, with broad shoulders and powerful chest muscles. His upper arms bulged beneath his shirtsleeves, and his skin was darkly tanned. He spoke like a Cornishman, but his speech carried a hint of travels to distant places and, though uneducated, suggested native intelligence.

When the rumours about the Dutchman's Point hermit began, there'd been talk in the village of forming a search party to look for a possible escaped convict who had somehow managed the impossible and crossed Dartmoor. But no escapes had been reported from the grim prison that was surrounded by treacherous moors. Most of those who attempted to cross Dartmoor had perished. Besides, none of the local men wanted to go after a desperate man hiding on that sinister peninsula, where one false step could send a man into a bottomless crevasse or over the unstable cliff to the rocks below. Eventually it was decided that if the hermit didn't steal anything from the village or bother anyone, he would be left alone.

'I'm going to the stream to get some fresh water,' he said, 'You'll feel better after you're bathed.'

Joanna closed her eyes in numb resignation. This had to be a nightmare.

Weighed down with grief over the death of her dearest friend, Megan followed Randolph Mallory's orders unquestioningly, with only her instinct for self-preservation keeping her going. She reminded herself that she had not killed Jo, and yet the nagging thought persisted that perhaps if she had ended her friend's pregnancy Joanna would still be alive. Her body would probably wash up with the next tide and Megan would be charged with murder.

Randolph had evidently been confident that Megan would run away with him. He had concealed a ladder in the ivy outside her window and, as soon as the courtyard cleared, he instructed her to climb down and wait for him in the copse of trees near the side gate, which was used mainly by grooms and gardeners going to and from the stables and kitchen garden.

It was now getting light rapidly, but only minutes after Megan reached the copse she heard the thud of hooves and Randolph appeared, riding a big chestnut stallion and leading a smaller black mare. Megan's travelling bag was fastened to the mare's saddle.

'Can you ride?' Randolph asked, jumping lightly to the ground. Although he was a big man, he moved not exactly with grace but with a certain precision that suggested perfect control over every muscle.

'A little,' Megan said. She had to pull up her skirt, since he had not bothered to find a sidesaddle.

He lifted her easily onto the mare's back and said, 'Follow me and don't stop for anything. If anyone sees us, we're just a couple of wedding guests out for a morning ride.'

With their travel bags lashed to their saddles? Megan

36

thought. Not likely. Still, Randolph had evidently scouted a route across the Traherne farmland and as they cantered towards the rising sun she decided this man knew exactly where he was going and what he was doing.

They reached the village an hour later and went to the blacksmith's shop. Megan waited on the street with their bags as Randolph led the horses inside. He appeared a moment later, took her arm, and began to walk.

'We've missed the morning train to London, but there's one to Bristol in half an hour. With luck we can get a ship there. If not, we'll take a train north to Liverpool.'

'What about the horses?'

'I told the blacksmith they belong to the Trahernes. He'll have them shod and returned to the hall. I doubt the stable master will mention this to the Trahernes, since several guests took horses to help search for Joanna. I said my good-byes last night, and they believe I'm on my way to London on business, so they won't connect your disappearance with my departure.'

Megan waited until they were safely aboard the train before looking him straight in the eye and saying quietly, 'Now you'd better tell me exactly who you are and why you are pretending to be Randolph Mallory.'

As his dark eyes flickered over her face, he seemed to be wondering how much she knew. 'How did you find out?'

'A cablegram came from Randolph last night, saying he couldn't come to the wedding.'

'I overlooked that possibility. Why didn't the Trahernes say anything about it?'

'No one saw the cablegram but me. It was delivered just as the bride and groom were leaving. It was addressed to Joanna and I meant to give it to her, but . . . You haven't answered my question. Who are you and what are you up to?'

'My name is McQuinn. Randolph Mallory is my friend, just as Joanna Traherne is yours. I manage the Diamond T, which is near the Mallory ranch. The absentee owner is an Englishman. I visited him in London just before I came to Cornwall.'

'But why the masquerade? If you've nothing to hide, why didn't you tell the Trahernes who you really are?'

'I believed Joanna would go to New Mexico if she thought her cousin Randolph was travelling with her, but I doubted she'd go such a distance with a complete stranger.'

'But what about the real Randolph Mallory? Where does he fit into this puzzle? He couldn't have been aware of what you intended to do, or he wouldn't have sent that wire.'

'Sufficient to say he would have welcomed Joanna with open arms, once she was there.'

'But Joanna is dead. You want me to impersonate her. Why?'

His expression closed, shutting her out. 'I've told you all I intend to. You and I made a bargain and I've kept my part of it. Besides, you're hardly in a position to make any demands.'

'Mr McQuinn –'

'My friends call me Quinn.'

'I doubt you and I will ever be friends. Do you have a first name?'

'Sure. Ramblin' Jack.'

'I don't believe you.'

'Suit yourself.'

Megan leaned back against the antimacassar on her seat, wondering if perhaps facing a judge in England might be less dangerous than going to the American wilderness with a total stranger. After all, she was innocent of hurting Jo . . .

Memories of Joanna drifted into Megan's mind and at once a great sadness gripped her. First she had lost her grandfather, now Jo. The two people who had meant most in the world to her. The magnitude of the tragedy diminished everything else. She almost hoped that she was journeying into danger. Perhaps it would distract her tormented mind from the grief that racked her every thought.

6

Joanna was too ill to be more than vaguely aware of the man who cared for her during the following days. At times she seemed to leave her body and hover somewhere above the cave in the rocky cliff where the hermit named Magnus fought to save the life of a woman who was a complete stranger to him. She seemed to be merely an observer to the fact that in bathing her fever-racked body he was also seeing her nakedness. Her clothing had mysteriously vanished, so he dressed her in one of his own cambric shirts.

He spoke gruffly, yet showed great patience, coaxing her to drink, to eat. Once, as he lit a fire over which to cook the fish he had caught, she came to her senses long enough to protest that someone might see the flames and be alerted to their presence.

Magnus regarded her quizzically. 'You fear someone might come after you, then? That old crone who tried to bury you alive in the woods?'

'I thought perhaps *you* might be in hiding.'

'Not to worry. from the sea a fire would be one more speck of light on the land, and it can't be seen at all from any other direction. We're well hidden by the woods and this cave can only be reached by means of tunnels through the cliff, which no one else knows about. When you're feeling strong enough to get up, don't blunder out the mouth of the cave. There's a sheer drop to the rocks below.'

Joanna silently considered the fact that she was completely at this man's mercy. She was dependent upon him for her every need and could not even find her way out of the cave without his help. She asked quietly, 'Why are you doing this for me?'

'I know what it is to be without a friend in the world.'

'I don't know how I shall ever be able to repay you. I'm so grateful.'

He promptly disappeared into the darkness at the back of the cave. Joanna glanced about his living quarters. He had carried driftwood up from the beach and, from it, had fashioned rough cupboards to hold his food and pots and pans. One portion of a ship's hull atop a pair of boulders formed his table. Next to it stood a bench. A lantern was perched on a rock ledge next to a cluster of seashells that he had evidently collected and displayed for their beauty.

A tear sprang to Joanna's eye. This was his home and he clearly endeavoured to make it comfortable and cosy, yet every item in it seemed to call attention to his loneliness. There was only one plate and one cup, which he shared with her. One chair, one narrow bed, which he had given up for her.

When Magnus disappeared for long periods he usually returned with a fish or a lobster. Apparently he made other forays for supplies, since he had flour and tea. Joanna didn't ask questions, though; she had quickly learned that curiosity was likely to make him disappear, and she felt lonely and frightened when he left her by herself in the cave.

'You're a lady,' Magnus said suddenly one evening. 'You're no scullery maid seduced by the master. What happened? Did your father throw you out because your lover refused to marry you?'

Any lingering hope that he was unaware of the true nature of her malady vanished. She answered, 'I ran away.'

'Because the man refused to marry you?'

'Why do you question me so? It's none of your business. Have I asked you why you were in prison?'

She caught her breath, appalled at having said such a thing. But why else would a man choose to hide himself from the world? If he wasn't an escaped convict, Joanna knew he had committed some crime and was hiding from the law.

He rose abruptly and went to the fire. She heard the spatter of grease as he dropped two fish into the pan. A little while later he came back and helped her sit up. Wordlessly he handed her the tin plate with one crisply fried herring, and she began to eat with a real appetite for the first time since she had left home.

Magnus took the pan and the remaining fish and disappeared into the shadowy tunnel at the rear of the cave.

When she had finished eating, she placed the plate on the ground beside her and looked at it curiously. If Magnus was an escaped convict, then where had he found the cooking utensils, plates, blankets, and so on? He surely hadn't brought them from prison with him. The mattress upon which she lay had been made by stuffing dried grasses inside a sack that appeared to be made of canvas. A sail, perhaps? Did he also have a boat? Someone must have aided him in his escape. She wondered who it was.

She allowed her hands to stray to her stomach, which was now concave. Although she felt a deep sense of loss that she would not bear Oliver's child, that emotion was overlaid with relief, which produced such feelings of guilt that she forced herself to think of the future.

Where could she go now and what could she do? A wave of panic washed over her and she called, 'Magnus! Magnus, are you there?'

He came back instantly, as though he had been waiting for her summons. 'What is it? Do you hurt? Are you bleeding again?'

'No . . . no, I'm all right. Just . . . lonely. A little frightened. I remember you said Mrs Elliot put my nightgown and slippers at the edge of the cliff. Do you know what happened to the cape I wore?'

'She had wrapped it around you like a shroud. I burned it after I brought you here, because it was bloodied and covered with the dirt and forest humus from the grave she put you in.'

By now she would have been presumed to have drowned, Joanna thought, and she shed a tear for her father's grief but wondered sadly if Adele and her mother would not be relieved to be rid of her. If they thought she was dead, then her disgrace was gone with her. They were all better off. Oh, but the agony of never seeing any of them again was too much to bear.

'So you found me naked and near death,' Joanna whispered. A lesser human being would have left her to her fate, she thought. How would she ever repay this man? She had nothing in the world to give him.

'Or perhaps at the beginning of a new life?' Magnus suggested. 'Bringing with you nothing from the old.'

'How wise you are,' Joanna murmured, feeling suddenly sleepy and secure. They didn't speak again, but his shadowy presence comforted her.

When she awakened at dawn he was sitting beside her, but he wore his fishing clothes so she knew he must have left during the night. Although she'd grown accustomed to his battered features it was still a jolt in the clear dawn light to wake up and find him watching her.

'Have you a place to go?' he asked.

She swallowed a dry lump in her throat. 'Don't worry about me. I have plenty of places to go.'

His eyes drifted to her bare feet. 'You can't go far barefoot and dressed in a man's shirt.'

This morning he seemed to be accompanied by a warm, yeasty odour . . . surely it couldn't be? But it was! Reaching behind him he produced a crusty loaf of freshly baked bread and handed it to her.

Famished, she took two delicious bites before mumbling, 'Where on earth . . . ?'

His big hand went behind him again and this time returned with a cotton dress of the kind worn by farmers' wives. A moment later there was a shawl and a pair of shoes, one of which was missing some of its buttons. 'You'll have to do without underwear, and the shoes will be too big.'

'You stole these things!' she burst out, spraying crumbs.

A pulse beat in his temple and his lips clamped together. 'Damn you, I'm no thief.'

'Magnus, I'm so sorry. Please forgive me. It's just that these clothes are . . . used.'

'Of course they are. They're from a pawnshop. I traded fish for the bread and the clothes. Get dressed. It's time for you to go. I'll get the boat ready.'

After he left, Joanna donned the dress and shoes. Both were too large. She carefully folded Magnus's shirt and laid it on a rock.

A cold fear gripped her. He was sending her away, but where on earth could she go? If she had the price of a train ticket she could go to north Wales to Megan, but she had no money.

When Magnus returned, he surveyed her for a moment. 'Funny how breeding always shows. Even in those clothes you look like a lady.'

Unsure how to respond, she ran her hands through her tangled hair, which hung about to her shoulders. She wished she had pins so that she could put it up. Magnus's idea of what a lady looked like was very different from her own. 'Where are you taking me?'

'Back to your own kind, if we're lucky.'

'But you don't know who I am or where I came from, so how can you know my kind?'

Shrugging, he said again, 'You're a highborn lady.'

'Could I stay with you for a little longer? Perhaps I could do something to earn my food.'

He threw back his head and laughed. It was the first time she'd heard him laugh and she would have appreciated the full-bodied sound had his amusement not been directed

43

at her. Besides, it conjured up a ludicrous picture of her cleaning fish and coaxing driftwood to burn. She'd never lifted a finger to do anything for herself in her entire life. Why, she didn't even know how to put up her own hair, as she'd always had a maid.

She said defensively, 'I'm not completely useless. Besides, I was joking. I don't really want to stay here with you. It . . . it isn't proper.' Oh, goodness, had she really said that?

He gave her a pitying glance and jerked his head towards the back of the cave. 'Come on, then, give me your hand and stay close.'

He led her into the darkness, and they crouched as they moved through a dank tunnel that gradually became so small they had to get down on their hands and knees. She had to bite her lip to keep from crying out as they squeezed through a narrow aperture into another chamber of the huge cave. Here the darkness was filled with the sound of rushing water.

'It's low tide,' Magnus shouted over the hollow roar of the sea. 'We're on a ledge. Slip off your shoes. The water is only knee deep.'

Joanna did as she was told and felt his hands touch hers as he took her shoes from her. 'Now hold on to my back and I'll lead.'

She tried to hold up her skirts as they stepped into icy water, but was so afraid of being separated from him that she soon gave up and clung to him for dear life.

Underfoot the sand shifted and felt slimy while the receding tide tugged at her skirts until she was sure she would be dragged off her feet.

At last there was a glimmer of light ahead, and soon she and Magnus emerged from the cave onto a pebble beach. A small boat was pulled into the shelter of a cluster of rocks.

Magnus began to drag the boat towards the water and glanced at her over his shoulder. 'Unless you can climb the sheer face of the cliff, you'd best get in.'

Without hesitation, Joanna did so, and he pushed the boat into the water and jumped in.

She watched as his large, capable hands rigged the sail. 'Have you always been a fisherman?'

'No.'

'Oh. I just thought . . . your hands . . .'

'A bruiser's fists. I was a pugilist. A boxer. Did you think I was born with a face like this?'

The wind caught the sail and the boat skimmed effortlessly over the smooth sea. Feeling spent from the effort of crawling through the caves, Joanna leaned against the rough wood of the bow and wondered again why he had chosen to live as a hermit. He had to be an escaped convict; there was no other explanation.

She didn't ask where he was taking her because all at once she wasn't sure she wanted to be parted from him. But she felt that this apprehension was merely a reaction to her weakened physical state, as she considered the possibilities.

He would probably drop her at one of the tiny fishing villages along the coast. She didn't dare think what she would do after that.

'Have you any wifely skills?' he asked abruptly.

Joanna's mouth opened in a startled O.

'Oh, don't panic. I'm not about to ask you to marry me. I'm thinking if you're domesticated you could get a job as a housekeeper.'

'I . . .'

His glance was slightly contemptuous. 'Foolish question. You've been waited on hand and foot since the day you were born.'

'I do have an education,' Joanna said defensively. 'Perhaps I could find a position as a governess.'

'Nobody's going to trust you with their children unless you've got references.'

He muttered something under his breath and set about changing the position of the sail to take a different tack. She wasn't sure how much time had passed as she dozed,

45

lulled by the warmth of the sun and the rocking of the boat.

When she opened her eyes, he had again turned towards the shore and her eyes widened in fright as she saw they were headed towards what appeared to be an impenetrable barrier of rocks. The Cornish coast was riddled with tiny coves and inlets, and many of them had lured sailors onto unseen reefs or swirled small craft into rocks less formidable than the ones she could see.

Catching sight of her face, Magnus smiled grimly. 'If you're a religious woman, now might be the time to say a prayer or two.'

She closed her eyes as Magnus manoeuvred the craft through a perilously narrow opening in the wall of rock. Moments later they were in a deserted cove. She was still shaking as the side of the boat scraped the edge of a rocky cliff into which were hewn rough steps. Magnus helped her out, and she could see the incoming tide was already splashing over the lower steps. He tied the boat to a jagged extrusion of rock and offered his hand to help her up the slippery steps. She took it gratefully and didn't look down at the swirling water as they climbed upward.

The steps led to a fish cellar containing a row of wooden barrels and some fishing nets. An oil lantern burned low, illuminating a narrow staircase that took them from the cellar to a stone-floored kitchen.

Before Joanna could catch her breath or begin to worry about whose cottage they had broken into, Magnus said, 'Wait here,' and disappeared through a door.

The fisherman's cottage was sturdily built to withstand the coastal gales. Although she could hear the low rumble of voices through the stout timbered walls, she could not distinguish what was said.

She looked around. The kitchen was clean and neat, and smelled sweetly of the bunches of dried sage and thyme hanging from the beamed ceiling. Gleaming pots and pans decorated one wall and a bright copper coal scuttle stood inside a brass fender surrounding the fireplace. The sink board and stove were scrupulously clean. Her wandering gaze went finally to the far end of the room where a scrubbed wooden table and chairs stood.

In the centre of the roughly carved table was a delicate crystal vase, which held, to her surprise, a waxy white orchid – hardly the type of flower one expected to find in a humble fisherman's cottage. For an instant she thought of the greenhouses at Traherne Hall and her father's collection of orchids, and a wave of homesickness washed over her.

Minutes later Magnus returned with a woman whose appearance caused Joanna's eyes to widen. She was regally tall, with exotic features – high cheekbones, flaring nostrils, and slanting amber eyes that flickered over Joanna with undisguised interest.

Although the sun was now high in the sky, the woman still wore night attire of such a revealing nature that Joanna felt herself blush. An almost transparent kimono was loosely knotted about her tiny waist. Her high swelling breasts and dark nipples were clearly visible beneath the translucent silk. Straight black hair hung past the woman's waist, and she wore slippers trimmed with marabou feathers.

This was no fisherman's wife; in fact this was a creature beyond imagining. Although her complexion was the colour of creamy coffee, her features appeared to be less African than a blend of Asian and European. But surely in no culture on earth did a respectable woman flaunt herself before others so shamelessly. Joanna wondered if this could possibly be one of the ladies of the evening she and Megan used to giggle and wonder about. But where could such a woman have acquired a rare white orchid? Joanna's father knew of only a couple of other growers. Like him, they were aristocrats, hardly likely to be acquainted with this woman.

Magnus cleared his throat and fixed his eyes on Joanna, perhaps as embarrassed as she by the woman's dishabille. 'This is my friend Delta. She's going to help you. You can

47

trust her. She's got friends who will inquire about a position for you, and you can stay here until she finds one. And if you change your mind and want to go home, she'll see you get there.'

He started for the door and Joanna asked faintly, 'You're not leaving?'

Turning, he looked at her with hard cobalt eyes, and unaccountably she shivered. Such coldness in those eyes now, all trace of kindliness gone. 'Take my advice, lady, and go home. Throw yourself on the mercy of your family. The world's a hard place for a woman alone.'

'I've never even told you my name –' she began.

'There was no need.'

He opened the door, and in the instant before he disappeared back into the fish cellar she called, 'Thank you –'

Delta opened the kitchen door behind her and called, 'Lizzie!' A moment later a plump, sullen-faced young girl wearing an apron appeared.

'The lady needs breakfast. Make us a pot of tea, too.' Delta pulled out a chair and sat down at the table opposite Joanna, scrutinising her from head to toe. 'What's your name?'

'Joanna –' The name Traherne was fairly well known throughout Cornwall, so she did not finish the statement.

Delta said, 'Joanna's good enough. We will invent a new surname for you later, yes? Magnus says you're educated but useless. This is true?'

'I've never actually worked for a living,' Joanna replied defensively.

'Well, I expect we'll find a position for you somewhere. There's a place for everybody somewhere, yes?' There was a melodic lilt to her voice and the merest hint of an unfamiliar accent, and when she spoke she gestured extravagantly with her beautiful hands. She had long, tapered fingers and perfect oval nails. Occasionally she would pause, extend her arms as if in flight, and then, hands fluttering, she would shrug and stretch her slim body with artless grace. Joanna was sure that she and Magnus had aroused Delta from her bed, despite the lateness of the hour.

Lizzie reappeared with a plate of cold ham and thickly sliced bread. She placed a butter dish and a pitcher of milk before Joanna, put the teapot beside Delta, and went back into the kitchen.

'Magnus isn't much of a talker,' Delta said, pouring herself half a cup of tea. 'How did you two meet?'

Lizzie returned with a bottle of rum and filled Delta's teacup with it.

'He . . . helped me,' Joanna said. 'Rescued me, I suppose you could say.'

Amber eyes regarded her quizzically, but the woman made no comment. She drank the tea and rum mixture in a single long swallow.

'Are you a good friend of his?' Joanna asked.

Delta's full lips curved into a provocative smile. 'You might call us friends.'

'Have you known him long?'

'It's been a few years since he was introduced to my brother by the Marquess of Queensberry.'

Joanna looked at her blankly, unable to believe a member of the titled aristocracy was acquainted with either Magnus or this woman and her brother.

Delta enjoyed her confusion for a moment and then explained, 'Magnus and my brother fought each other in the ring. They were both boxers.'

'Oh, I see.' To be polite Joanna nibbled a piece of ham, although she was too intrigued with her hostess to be really interested in food. 'Magnus is a fugitive, isn't he? Was he in Dartmoor prison?'

The amber eyes narrowed. 'You're not accusing me of harbouring an escaped convict, now, are you?'

'You can trust me. Please . . . I'm aware he spent time in prison. Just tell me what he did.'

Delta leaned forward, eyes alert, watching her reaction. 'He killed a man.'

Joanna gasped, but Delta went on unconcernedly,

satisfied that she had again shocked her unexpected guest. 'In the ring, mind you, in a fair match. Magnus was challenged by a young fellow who was boxing champion of his college. Turned out his head was made of glass. His father brought charges. He was rich, and Magnus was poor. They trumped up assault charges, and Magnus was convicted and sent to Dartmoor.'

'How ghastly!'

'He took a chance, coming here. The dead fellow's brother has an estate not far away.'

'Oh, dear heaven! I hope he isn't caught on my account,' Joanna exclaimed. 'Why on earth would he come here?'

'Because he knows he can trust me to keep my mouth shut, just as you've got to keep yours shut. Don't tell a living soul he's been here. If you do and he's caught, I'll probably kill you. You understand?'

Joanna shivered at the fierce gleam in Delta's eyes and didn't doubt she would carry out her threat. This woman cared about Magnus a great deal. To attempt to change the subject Joanna asked, 'Does your brother live here with you?'

'No.' Delta stood up abruptly. 'I live here alone except for Lizzie. But I have a regular visitor. A gentleman friend. You'll have to stay out of sight when he comes.'

Joanna awakened with a start, unsure where she was. After weeks of living in the cave with Magnus, she was surprised to find herself lying on a feather bed surrounded by the shadowy outlines of furniture. To her right she could make out window shutters painted with silver lines of moonlight. A cool breeze, salt-laden and smelling of all the mysteries of the sea, found its way through the shutters, along with the rhythmic slap of water against the rock below.

The room was cold and she recalled leaving the windows wide open before closing the shutters, so she swung her feet to the floor and crossed to the window. She was about to close it when she saw the dark outline of a boat in the narrow channel through which Magnus had sailed into the cove. She had been amazed that he could find that tiny opening in broad daylight. This boatman surely must be mad to risk it at night, even in the moonlight.

Curious, she watched the boat glide towards the steps leading to Delta's fish cellar. A man jumped out and quickly tied up the boat. As he straightened up, she saw he was tall and lean and he moved like a young man. But then, as though instinctively sensing that someone was watching him, he raised his head and looked up.

Joanna quickly stepped back out of sight, but not before the moonlight had flooded the man's hawklike features so she could see that he was no longer young. He looked at least forty, and perhaps the moonlight dealt harshly with his features, but in that cold light his expression seemed arrogant and cruel.

Unable to help herself, Joanna peered around the edge of the shutter again, and at that moment Delta appeared on the steps below. In two quick bounds the man reached her and swept her roughly into his arms.

Before Joanna could look away, he captured Delta's lips in a passionate kiss while his hands tore off the filmy kimono she had worn all day. She stood naked on the steps, proud as a Greek statue, as the sea spray dampened her flesh. He caressed her breast briefly, then bent and took it into his mouth.

Delta seized his head in her hands and buried her face in his hair, cradling his face to her bosom with a tenderness that seemed inconsistent with her usual icy demeanour.

Joanna wrenched her eyes away and, heart thumping, sank down onto her bed. She wondered if they would make love right there on the sea-washed steps or if the man would sweep Delta up into his arms and carry her to her bedroom.

Recalling Oliver's fumbling seduction, accomplished in darkness and haste, Joanna felt a pang of envy. She could not conceive of casting all discretion to the winds and giving herself up to such unbridled passion. Delta must indeed be one of those creatures she and Megan had speculated about – not, perhaps, a lady of the evening, but at the very least a kept woman. Joanna had always imagined that kept women lived in luxury, but this humble fisherman's cottage gave the lie to that assumption.

Perhaps this man had brought Delta the orchid? If so, then he and his family would surely be known to Joanna, whose father knew all the orchid fanciers in Cornwall. She had not recognised him, but she had caught only a brief glimpse of his face. Whoever he was, it was imperative that he not learn of her presence in the cottage, in case this information was relayed to her parents.

A woman's laugh drifted up and through the open window, low and sultry like the murmur of the sea kissing a sun-drenched shore.

Joanna covered her ears with her hands and tried to shut out the sound. She felt lonely, bereft, and vaguely uneasy, as though the arrival of Delta's lover in some obscure way was a portent of her own future.

7

Megan and Quinn sailed for New York aboard one of the new White Star liners that now plied the Atlantic. On the second day out of port they ran into a summer storm that gave most of the passengers *mal de mer*. Megan, too, felt queasy and would have retired to her cabin had not Quinn ordered her to put on a coat and accompany him to the upper deck.

'You'll feel better if you can see the horizon,' he insisted and, despite her protests, dragged her up on deck.

'Keep close to me if you want to stay aboard the ship,' he warned. 'The deck's as slippery as grease.'

She had to cling to him as they crossed the slanting deck. At the rail he kept his arm around her as the ship heaved and pitched beneath them, but the sharp, briny tang of the wind did revive her. Following his instructions, she fixed her gaze on the distant horizon and felt some of her nausea disappear.

After a moment she became uncomfortably aware of Quinn's body pressed to hers and tried to inch away from him. So far they had circled each other like wary tigers meeting on neutral ground, neither prepared to give an inch, and Megan didn't care for this sudden switch to the roles of protector and protected.

Feeling her pull away from him, Quinn removed his arm immediately and she lurched along the rail, frantically trying to keep her balance. Her bonnet flew away in the wind and she watched it land on the surface of the water below as her hair whirled free of its pins.

She felt a certain perverse satisfaction in seeing the expensive bonnet wash away. Before sailing from Liverpool Quinn had insisted upon providing her with a complete new wardrobe. He'd pointed out that Randolph would not believe she was Joanna if she appeared in her drab mourning gowns. Megan had quietly fumed, uneasily certain not only that he took pleasure in abruptly ending her mourning period but also that he sensed her own dislike for the drab black garments, which gave little comfort to her or anyone else, especially her dead grandfather.

As the wind invaded her skirts and they ballooned around her, she grasped the slippery rail with one hand while holding down her dress with the other.

His expression saying 'I told you so' more clearly than words, Quinn extended his arm towards her. 'You'll find it easier if I take the force of the wind for you. Or you can go below again and heave up what's left of your breakfast.'

'I'll go below before I'll allow you to put your arms

53

around me,' Megan retorted stubbornly, although she would have preferred to remain on deck. She grasped the damp rail and planted her feet apart, gulping the reviving air into her lungs.

'Suit yourself. But if you slip and break a limb, the rest of the journey is going to be damned uncomfortable for you. The voyage is the easy part of the trip. After we reach New York, there'll be days on a train and then some rough country to cross, probably on horseback, since the stage doesn't go near the Mallory ranch.'

'You didn't doubt that Joanna would be able to make the journey. Why worry about me?'

'Perhaps because you'll be less likely to ask for help. There's a certain damn-you-I'll-do-it-myself attitude about you.'

He turned his head away from her, and his next words were lost in the shriek of the wind and hollow roar of the sea.

'What did you say?'

'Nothing I'd better repeat.'

'Now that we're safely at sea, I'd like to ask a question,' she said. 'Has it occurred to you that the Trahernes will surely write to Randolph Mallory and tell him of Joanna's death? What happens then?'

'A letter will take several months to reach him, even assuming they write immediately, which is unlikely. We'll have arrived and accomplished our purpose long before then.'

'I suppose it's futile to ask what that purpose is.'

'You assume correctly.'

'There is one thing you'd better keep in mind. If I find that you have some nefarious scheme planned to defraud Joanna's family, I will consider our agreement terminated, even if it means I have to stand trial for killing Jo.'

He gave her one of his penetrating glances but said offhandedly, 'You didn't kill her. She leapt from the cliff top. But then, the law deals harshly with abortionists, too. As for the rest, your masquerade has nothing to do with money. In fact, Randolph Mallory is just as wealthy as the Trahernes. Maybe more so.'

The ship lurched and Megan slid into his waiting arms. She glared up at him. 'At least tell me about him. What's he like?'

'He's a gentleman. Courtly, well mannered, educated, refined . . . the last man on earth you'd expect to find living on the wild frontier.'

'The exact opposite of you, then? Since you are rude, ill mannered, ill bred, arrogant, overbearing –'

'Oh, come on,' he said, 'tell me what you really think of me.'

Pulling free of his arms, Megan made her way cautiously along the rail. 'I think I'll go back to my cabin. I feel better now.'

'Since you found out Randolph is a gentleman?' he murmured, moving quickly to open the door to the companionway. 'I bet you do feel better.'

The storm had passed by the following day, and that evening the passengers cautiously took their places in the dining salon. Megan had been assigned a seat at a table for six and found herself with an English family travelling to America for the wedding of one of the two pretty daughters who accompanied them.

'Don't approve one bit,' the bewhiskered father said sternly, although it was clear he was totally under the control of his three giggling females. 'Should be marrying one of the fine young Englishmen who asked for her hand. But, no, she was bowled over by this rather brash young man from Virginia who was on what he called his grand tour.' He broke off, his ginger moustache twitching in indignation.

His wife gave him a reproachful glance. 'Darling, for all you know, Miss Traherne might also be going to marry an American.'

Her younger daughter sighed dreamily, 'Like that simply devastating man you were talking to on deck yesterday?

He had to be an American. They not only speak and dress differently but move differently as well. Had you noticed? Especially that one. One is very much aware he is a male.'

Her mother gasped. 'A well-brought-up young lady does not notice how any man moves, and certainly doesn't comment on it.'

The bride-to-be leaned towards Megan confidentially and inquired, 'Is he a riverboat gambler? My fiancé gave me a book about America and I saw a picture of a gambler. Your friend has that rather bold look . . . oops!' She broke off as Quinn came into the dining room and made directly for their table.

Introductions were offered, relief that the seas had subsided was expressed, and Megan spent the remainder of the meal watching the two English girls flirt with Quinn, who treated the entire family to a barrage of charm that stunned her. At the wedding she had been too concerned about Joanna to notice that Quinn was thoroughly at ease with people, capable of intelligent, witty conversation, and far more skilled in the gentle art of flirtation than she would have suspected. She found herself lapsing into silence, hard put not to frown disapprovingly at the two young women who hung on his every word.

'Ah, yes,' he remarked, gazing at the bride-to-be, 'I believe warnings should definitely be given about the danger in placing eligible young American males and English females, or vice versa, in close proximity with one another. I'm not sure what happens, but it seems to be a volatile combination. A thunderbolt always strikes.'

'Or perhaps lightning?' Megan suggested, finding her tongue at last. 'And someone is burned.'

Quinn's eyes met hers, locked, and held. 'Oh, I'm quite sure lightning wouldn't dare strike you.'

Before Megan could respond, he turned to the unengaged sister and smiled. 'I understand that the orchestra will play after dinner. With your father's permission I'd like to ask for a waltz.'

Later, as she watched the two of them dance – the

56

girl held firmly in Quinn's arms as he whirled her with surefooted ease over the swaying deck – Megan felt her resentment deepen. Not that she wanted to dance – indeed she would have refused if he had asked her to, since she was still in mourning despite her pretty pale green satin gown. But it seemed an affront to her for him to dance with a perfect stranger while she was left to sit and watch.

She watched for a few minutes, aware all at once of what the girl had meant when she spoke of the way Quinn moved. He seemed to be accustomed to unstable ground under his feet. He had learned to tread carefully. But with every step he took, she became more aware of his physical presence. Those straining shoulders, the long legs . . . dear heaven, where were her thoughts taking her? A pox on that flighty young thing for suggesting that he was an impressive physical presence, even if it was true.

Megan quickly left the salon and returned to her cabin.

One by one the days slipped away, marked by an uneasy truce between Megan and Quinn. She excused herself each evening after dinner and spent her time alone in her cabin. She imagined Quinn dancing with the English girls, and probably with every other woman on board, and decided she wouldn't give him the satisfaction of being a witness to his popularity.

On the last night before landfall the captain gave a gala party, but again Megan slipped out of the dining room immediately after dinner. Reluctant to go to her cabin and shut out the sound of music and laughter, she made her way to the bow of the ship and stood at the rail, searching the darkness for the first glimpse of land.

'We won't make landfall until dawn.' Quinn stood at her side. He had approached so silently that she jumped.

'What are you doing here? Did you run out of dance partners?'

'Are you volunteering?'

'Certainly not.'

'Perhaps dancing is against your religion?'

His usual bantering tone was missing, and she sensed an

underlying seriousness to the question that puzzled her. She wanted to reply that she loved to dance and hadn't had the opportunity to do so for so long that it was agony to hear the music and not have a chance to whirl around the floor. Instead she said, 'It isn't against my religion. I'm in mourning. Had you forgotten?'

'Ah, yes, mourning . . . It's your way of punishing yourself because you're alive and someone else is dead?'

'Not at all. It's a way to show love and respect . . . Oh, I don't wish to discuss it with you. How could you know what Jo and my grandfather meant to me?'

'Your grandfather's practice was in a coal-mining town, I believe. Since you assisted him, you must have seen some sights most young women are spared.'

A quick vision flitted through her mind, a memory of colliers with crushed limbs and worse, from the almost daily accidents down in the pit, along with gruesome recollections of the results of terrible fires and cave-ins. Yes, she'd seen more human suffering than most women. 'Are you insinuating that I should be grateful my grandfather is dead so I no longer have to assist him?'

'No, nothing like that –'

'If you'll excuse me, I believe I'll retire. We're arriving at dawn, and I shall want to be on deck to see your famous New York Harbour.'

She thought she heard him sigh as she walked away, but perhaps it was only the rising wind.

The train pulled away from the east bank of the Rio Grande and rumbled into the Jornada del Muerto, a stretch of arid desert extending for ninety miles down the centre of New Mexico.

Megan sat in a window chair, opposite Quinn, who, she noticed, had begun to study her intently as they drew nearer their destination. His questions had also grown more frequent and more personal. Why hadn't she married? Most women her age were already mothers, weren't they? What had become of her parents? Why had she spent her life with her grandfather and why hadn't he made better provision for her after his death? Megan's usual response was that none of this concerned him.

She tensed now, expecting another embarrassing question, as he looked at her in that disconcertingly direct way he had. But instead he remarked, 'This railroad line is brand new. Built by eastern speculators who don't know a damned thing about the West. The fools overlooked the danger of spring flooding from the Rio Grande, and they ignored the fact that cloudbursts will send walls of water thundering into those dry arroyos. The rails will be under water, and bridges will wash out. More than one train has plummeted to disaster off a washed-out bridge.'

Megan leaned forward in alarm, her gaze sweeping the pale vista of sand to the distant mountains.

Quinn added, 'This time of year we'll be safe enough.'

'But surely you should warn someone what might happen during the spring floods?'

He raised an eyebrow. 'You think they'll rip up track and reroute it? It's cheaper to leave a few locomotives and cars lying on their sides in the mud.'

She leaned back against the seat, feeling her tension return. The closer they got to the Mallory ranch, the more she regretted having agreed to impersonate Joanna. She was sorry, too, that Quinn believed she had performed an illegal operation on her friend, thereby causing her death. But then, she wondered, why should she care what he thought of her? She had begun to admit to herself that she found him extremely attractive in a purely physical sense, but since she disliked him in every other way, this seemed paradoxical, to say the least.

'Joanna was your closest friend,' Quinn remarked a few minutes later. 'You had no secrets from each other . . . but I wonder if she read any of Randolph's letters to you.'

'We hadn't seen much of each other during the past few years, since we left school. I was taking care of my grandfather and couldn't leave him to visit Cornwall. Nor did I want Jo to visit me because . . . well, Granddad was rather difficult. I didn't even know she was corresponding with Randolph.'

'Hmm . . . that might present a problem, then, since I have no idea what he wrote her – only what she wrote him. He didn't show me her letters, of course – his integrity wouldn't allow that – but when I saw which way the wind was blowing, I decided to take a look for myself.'

'You read her letters?' Megan asked, outraged. 'Is there no limit to your . . . your prying, meddling, underhanded sneaking –'

Quinn held up a hand to stop her. 'It was necessary. I had to know if there was any chance of her coming to New Mexico. You see, I knew he was in love with her . . . or rather, with her letters.'

'Are you sure he's never seen a picture of Jo? If he has, he'll know that I'm not –'

'No. She never sent a picture. Randolph fell in love with the woman who revealed herself in a more important way – by sharing her thoughts and feelings.'

Baffled, Megan stared at him. Quinn certainly didn't fit the role of matchmaker, and in any case, why would Randolph need one? He could simply have travelled to Cornwall to meet Jo or invited her – suitably chaperoned, of course – to visit him. If only he had . . . perhaps he could have spared her Oliver's betrayal.

The full impact of what Quinn had told her suddenly struck her. 'Dear heaven! You surely don't intend to present me, pretending to be Joanna, as a prospective bride for your friend?'

His eyes acquired a shuttered look that caused her hackles to rise. That expression meant he would hold back far more than he'd divulge. He merely shrugged. 'Nature, as they say, will take its course. But with your looks, if you could tame that shrewish attitude you affect sometimes . . . If you could act like Joanna – sweet, gentle, ladylike –'

'Are you saying I'm not a lady?'

'I'm saying that around me you've behaved in a some-what outspoken manner. Anyway, if you could act like

Joanna, I daresay you could very easily become Mrs Randolph Mallory . . . and, I might add, as such you'd be safe from the long arm of British law, since Megan Thomas would no longer exist.'

Megan leaned back, all the breath leaving her body. This was preposterous, unthinkable. Quinn was surely mad to consider such a plan. Above all, *why* had he gone to such lengths to bring Joanna and Randolph together? And why, with Joanna dead, had Quinn felt compelled to find a substitute for her?

Obviously the two men were friends and confidants, as she and Jo had been. Megan considered what true friendship meant. There was nothing she and Jo wouldn't have done for each other. Well, there was one thing – Jo's last request. Megan felt tears well up in her eyes and turned her head quickly so he wouldn't see them.

'It's all right to weep for your friend,' Quinn said in a tone more gentle than she'd yet heard from him.

She brushed her hand across her eyes and allowed herself a moment to grieve for Joanna. At school they had been drawn to each other because both had pursued their education with far more enthusiasm than the other girls at the boarding school, but whereas Joanna loved books, music, and art, Megan was more inclined towards science and mathematics. They were regarded as odd by the other young ladies, who were preparing to spend the rest of their lives doing nothing more demanding than planning dinner parties for the idle rich.

Megan thought, We were arrogant, aloof, certain that we were superior intellectually. We didn't need anyone else, because we had each other. It was a perfect friendship. Oh, Jo, how I shall miss you! Even during periods when we didn't see each other, it was a comfort to know you were always there . . . but now . . .

She forced herself to think about their different personalities. It was true that Joanna was soft-spoken, ladylike, gentle, whereas Megan was outspoken, direct, inclined to be impatient with affectations. She didn't hesitate to fly into a rage if the situation warranted it, while Jo would do anything to avoid unpleasantness or any kind of a scene. Their education had been similar, but their family backgrounds were worlds apart. Still, Megan had known and understood Jo well enough to impersonate her. But if this meddling man believed she would do so in the hope of catching a rich husband, he was sadly mistaken.

Again the question nagged her. Jo had said that Randolph's letters revealed him to be a wealthy man who was courteous and gentlemanly. Surely such a man could pick and choose among young ladies eager to share his life? Unless . . . he was physically so repulsive that he frightened them away? Of course! Why hadn't she considered that possibility before? It made sense . . . no photographs had been exchanged. She recalled, too, Quinn asking about the sights she had seen in her grandfather's surgery. Dear God, was that the reason? Was Randolph hideously deformed or monstrously ugly in some way?

Megan drew a deep breath, considering whether to ask Quinn point blank if this was the case. Would he reply honestly? Probably not. Besides, what difference would it make? She was thousands of miles from home with no means of support. No matter what kind of monster Randolph turned out to be, she would have to accept his hospitality, at least for a while.

The train slowed down and began to climb out of the desert and ascend a slow curving grade. Quinn leaned forward and stared into the empty space of the Jornada. Megan saw what had captured his attention. A distant cloud of dust whirled and eddied, then separated into a fairly large group of horsemen.

'I don't like the look of this –' he began.

The remark was never completed as the train window suddenly shattered. Quinn pulled Megan to the floor. In the instant before she fell she heard the crack of another gunshot.

Women and children screamed. Bullets smashed into

windows. For a few seconds there was utter confusion and all Megan could be sure of was that the train was attempting to pick up speed, grinding over the track and swaying wildly as it attempted to outrun the attackers.

8

'Justin Bodrath at your service, dear lady,' an educated voice drawled.

Joanna was waiting in Delta's kitchen with her back to the door. At the sound of the strange voice she spun around and looked into a pair of pale grey eyes that regarded her lazily. He was in his late thirties, immaculately dressed, and leaned on a silver-knobbed ebony cane, as though too weary to stand erect. He was slightly built and his face was haggard with dark circles under his eyes and an unhealthy sallowness to his complexion. A drooping moustache added to his melancholy appearance.

'Miss Joanna Smith, I presume? Please! Do not lower your eyes. I understand your dismay at my appearance, but never fear – it is not a nurse that I require. In fact, I find most members of the medical profession tiresome. My dissipated look is mostly due to chronic insomnia, I do assure you. Now, I understand from Delta that you're educated and willing to work.'

A gentleman, Joanna thought, and obviously well-to-do. How odd that he would even consider hiring someone only on the recommendation of a woman like Delta. The best Joanna had hoped for was that some local shopkeeper or seamstress would hire her.

'Y-yes,' she stammered. 'I am seeking a position.'

'Good. I need an amanuensis. Are you ready to leave?'

'You have no questions to ask?'

'None. Do you?'

Joanna shook her head.

'Let's be off, then,' Justin Bodrath said. 'I have a carriage waiting.'

Having cast caution to the winds thus far, Joanna could see no point in worrying now about what the future held in store for her, but still she hesitated. 'I would like to thank Delta for her hospitality . . . but she's still asleep.'

'You can return to thank her later if you feel you must, but I shall leave a token of our gratitude in a more tangible form, which she will expect.' There was a faint hint of scorn in his voice as he withdrew a wallet from inside his jacket and deposited a pound note on the table.

Joanna bit her lip. 'I do hope she won't be insulted.'

'My dear Miss Smith, you obviously don't know Delta very well. She insists upon payment for all of her . . . services.'

There was no mistaking the innuendo, and Joanna felt a twinge of indignation but made no comment. She decided she would indeed return to thank Delta for all she'd done, and she would bring a little gift, if possible.

He held open the door for her, and they went out onto the cobbled street.

The village sprawled untidily around a mine, probably the tin mine that Delta had mentioned. Two sleek horses harnessed to a gleaming carriage attended by a strapping young coachman awaited them. Joanna noticed that the horses and coachman looked a great deal healthier than Justin Bodrath.

The hour-long journey to Justin Bodrath's home was accomplished in silence except when he pulled a large white handkerchief from his pocket, covered his mouth, and coughed. Noting his pallor and sunken eyes Joanna wondered if he was consumptive.

They travelled inland away from the sea and came at last to a lush valley dissected by a peacefully flowing river.

Trees and shrubbery were profuse in this part of Cornwall, and green meadows gave way to pampered lawns as they approached their destination. The softness and beauty of the countryside and the glory of the estate grounds had not prepared Joanna for the starkness of the house, and she felt a sudden chill as they approached it.

After passing a gate house with battlements, they followed a gravel drive to a bleak granite structure devoid of ornamentation and showing only narrow windows. At one corner of the house, adding to its fortresslike appearance, a crenellated turret rose in medieval splendour.

Justin murmured, 'When the house was built back in the fourteen hundreds, my ancestors were involved in a blood feud. There are slightly larger windows that look into an inner courtyard. It's rather bleak-looking because Cornish granite is extremely hard and difficult to carve.' He gave her a sidelong glance. 'I'm assuming that, with a name like Smith, you are not Cornish.'

He paused to cough again. This time the paroxysm lasted longer than the others and was more severe. By the time it ended, the carriage had stopped before a great arched entryway with a pair of studded oak doors that opened instantly. Two uniformed footmen hurried down the stone steps to the gravel drive and opened the carriage doors.

'Welcome to my nameless home.'

'Nameless?' Joanna was acutely aware of her cotton frock and shabby shawl as the footman handed her down from the carriage.

'It's referred to as Bodrath House by the locals, but it was once called something else entirely. Heaven knows what, since my family didn't want the name perpetuated.'

As they walked towards the entry, he continued, 'The blood feud I mentioned . . . I regret to say the family who built the house were all wiped out by my ancestors who were their enemies and who then moved in. The Bodraths were evidently fierce warriors in those days. One would hardly credit that I was their sole remaining descendent, would one?' He turned and looked at her. 'But I expect

Delta told you that I am the last of the star-crossed Bodraths?'

Before Joanna could respond that Delta had told her nothing, since for the last two days Joanna had remained hidden in her room while Delta's lover visited her, Justin began to cough again. It seemed the closer he came to the house the more severe the attacks.

A stony-faced butler awaited them at the front door, and Joanna felt his disapproval long before she crossed the threshold.

Dark panelling and the narrow windows, which admitted little light, created an oppressive gloom within the entry hall. Justin said, 'This is Paxton. He'll show you to your room. I'm fatigued from the journey and must rest. We shall talk later.'

Joanna found herself alone with the butler as Justin disappeared through one of the ground-floor doors. The butler said, 'This way, miss,' his tone frosty.

She was taken to the servants' wing and shown a small barefloored room furnished only with a bed, a chair, and a wardrobe.

'The footmen inform me you have no luggage,' Paxton remarked. 'Since we have no female servants here, I cannot provide you with a change of clothing. No doubt Mr Justin will have instructions for you in this regard. Remain here until you are sent for.'

Wondering how a house of this size could possibly be run solely by men, Joanna walked to the narrow window and looked out across the most beautiful garden she had ever seen. She saw a profusion of summer flowers and well-tended shrubbery surrounding a fish pond, which was fed by a waterfall running over smooth rocks. Beyond, she caught a glimpse of the valley through the gently moving branches of a copse of beech and willow. The grimness of the house seemed an affront to such beauty.

She sat down on a hard narrow bed and wondered exactly what an amanuensis was required to do, at the same time speculating on the extremely unusual lack of female servants at Bodrath House. But the thought that superimposed itself over every other was that she missed Magnus more than she would have ever believed possible.

Joanna awakened with a start, unsure where she was and why her heart was thumping madly. In the instant before she struggled to sit up, she recalled stretching out on the bed in the barren little room that was her new home at Bodrath House.

The sky outside her window was now dark, and she remembered that she had waited in vain for hours for Justin Bodrath to summon her. Still disorientated and only half awake, Joanna called, 'Come in.'

The bedroom door opened and Paxton appeared, carrying several garments. 'Mr Justin will be going to the dining room shortly. It's time for you to dress for dinner. I've brought toilet articles and some clothes down from the attic for you.'

Paxton placed the clothes on the bed. Although scarcely worn, they were long out of fashion and smelled strongly of camphor. The butler straightened up and looked at her. His manner was not at all the calming one of the butlers she had been accustomed to. He reminded her of the captain of a ship whose crew needed a firm hand. Indeed, there was a definite military bearing to his rigidly erect posture.

'I'll return for you in half an hour,' he said in a tone that brooked no argument.

The moment the bedroom door closed behind him she ran to the washstand and poured water from the pitcher into the bowl. After a cursory splash she picked up a hairbrush and dragged it through her tangled locks. The dresses Paxton had brought her were all too wide and too short, and the matronly styles suggested they had once belonged to Justin's mother. She selected a fragile charcoal silk with a lacy jabot.

Precisely thirty minutes later Paxton again knocked on her door. Joanna followed him out onto the landing and down the staircase. He marched with military precision, shoulders back, head high. She felt a little like a soldier being escorted through a barracks. Looking around her, she decided that was exactly what Bodrath House was like. Spartan, severe, drab, with not a touch of softness or luxury. There were no carpets, curtains, or ornaments of any kind. Just vast barren rooms and bleak halls furnished with the absolute minimum of unadorned furniture.

They passed a dining room where three footmen were setting the table. All were strapping young men. Paxton led her into an adjacent drawing room where Justin huddled in a chair, looking frail and wan and swathed in a heavy plaid blanket, despite the warmth radiated by a blazing fire in the hearth. Joanna noted with surprise that the mantelpiece clock indicated it was eleven in the evening, long past the usual dinner hour.

'Ah, there you are, Miss Smith.' There was a touch of impatience in Justin's tone. 'Forgive me if I don't rise, but I'm feeling a little poorly just now. Paxton, you may serve the wine.'

Paxton asked, 'One glass, I presume, sir?'

'Of course. We must keep Miss Smith's head clear for the night's work.'

Joanna stood awkwardly beside the fireplace, wondering if she should assume the subservient demeanour of a servant. Was an amanuensis a servant, or would she be considered more in the governess class? Never having encountered a female amanuensis, although she understood they were becoming more common, Joanna wasn't sure.

Justin didn't speak again until Paxton handed him a glass of wine. He sipped it and said, 'I do hope you're not too tired to begin work immediately. I realise it couldn't have been too restful for you at Delta's cottage, with all the comings and goings.'

Joanna shifted her weight to her other foot, her sixth sense warning her to be careful how she answered questions about Delta. 'Comings and goings?'

'Her gentlemen visitors. I understand they're legion.'

68

'She had only one visitor,' Joanna responded defensively and immediately realised this was the information he was seeking.

His sunken eyes came instantly to life. 'A big bruiser with a battered face, broken nose? Probably came into the cove through the suicide gap.'

Magnus, Joanna thought, tensing. Dear heaven, did Justin suspect that he was at large? She shook her head, her mouth dry. 'No, her visitor had rather pointed, hawklike features. He was an older man and certainly couldn't be described as a big bruiser.'

'Ah, the viscount. Delta's latest lover, an old fool who will surely kill himself trying to act like a young fool over her. No, I don't mean him. It was he who told me he'd seen another boat approaching the cove one night, but it veered off upon sighting his boat. The man at the tiller, he was sure, was a murderer who had escaped from Dartmoor, the Lord knows how. No one else ever has and lived to tell the tale. I expect he managed to survive crossing the moors because he was a local man. I never believed, as everyone else did, that he perished crossing the moors. They should have hanged the bastard immediately after his trial, but the judge gave him a life sentence instead.'

'I saw no such man,' Joanna said firmly, surprised at how easily the lie sprang to her lips. 'Why would he go to Delta?'

'He was a friend of her brother.'

'Then, if the convict did indeed survive the trek across the moors, perhaps he went to Delta's brother.'

'I hardly think so. Delta's brother was killed in a fall from the cliff just before Magnus went to trial.'

Joanna digested this silently.

'Tell me, Miss Smith, what was the name of the mutual acquaintance who introduced you to Delta?'

She cleared her throat. 'When we met, you said you had no questions to ask me.'

'I did indeed. Very well, you shall remain my lady of mystery.'

'Mr Bodrath, I'm anxious to hear the nature of my work.'

'We are going to write my family history. You see, Joanna, since my line will end with my death, I have decided that if I can't leave a son behind as testimony to the fact that the Bodraths once walked the earth, then I should at least leave a written record of the somewhat gaudy splash we Bodraths made while we lived.'

Justin began to cough and covered his mouth.

When he recovered, he said, 'Now, I should explain that male servants are a family tradition. You will recall I told you that the Bodraths were warriors. My grandfather spent most of his life serving his country in the outposts of our empire. He was a military man and was never comfortable around women. Alas for my grandmother, who spent most of her life alone in this house. She died before he retired and came home, at which time he brought his army batman and several former noncoms to serve him. The male servant tradition was continued by my father: he also was a career army officer. My brothers and I were brought up by tutors and valets and never knew the tender touch of a woman.'

'Your mother . . . ?'

'Died when my younger brother was born, a year after my birth. My older brother, Neville, followed family tradition and went into the army. I, regrettably, was never strong enough.'

Joanna said, 'You mentioned a younger brother . . .'

All the life went out of Justin's eyes again. He slumped in his chair. 'How I miss him,' he said softly, a world of sadness in his tone. 'Harry was the light that lit all of our lives. When it was snuffed out, we fell apart, we Bodraths. Neville was so distraught that he recklessly led a charge against a Zulu uprising and was killed . . . not cleanly in battle, but slowly at the hands of his captors, and before the news of his death even reached us, my father succumbed to heart failure. My own ill health began then. It was as if

70

none of us wanted to go on without Harry. I truly believe that both Neville and my father wished their own deaths upon themselves. They would have lived had Harry not been murdered.'

'Murdered! Oh, how ghastly!'

An angry flame flared in the sunken eyes again. 'So now you will understand why I have vowed to use all my resources to track down the convict Magnus . . . but this time he won't go back to Dartmoor, I promise you. This time his miserable life will be ended just as he ended Harry's young life.'

9

Where had Quinn carried those guns? He now had three pistols, one of which he quickly passed to a fellow passenger aboard the beleaguered train as it thundered through New Mexico.

Quinn had produced the guns with the alacrity of a magician, and now the two men were smashing the windows and firing at the horsemen who rode alongside the tracks. Quinn seemed as much at ease with left-handed shooting as with right. As his pistols spat fire, Megan heard the other man say, 'Nice shootin', mister.'

She was unsure exactly what was happening, because every time she raised her head Quinn shoved her down again. But when the train began slowing on the long uphill grade, it seemed certain the bandits would catch up soon and leap aboard. What would happen then? She felt cold fear form in the pit of her stomach.

Over her head she heard someone say, 'They're

outrunning us. They'll catch up with the engine soon and get the driver.'

With a screech of brakes the train ground to an abrupt halt, flinging passengers in every direction. In the resulting confusion Megan scrambled to her knees and took one terrified glance through the window. Half a dozen men, kerchiefs tied over the lower part of their faces, were approaching.

She clutched Quinn's arm. 'Throw away the guns – quickly, before they shoot you. You can't fight so many.'

He glanced down at her, as if remembering she was there. He shoved both guns into his belt and offered his hand to help her to her feet.

The bandits were now swarming aboard the train. Men put their arms around their sobbing wives, and children hid their faces in their mothers' skirts. The robbers swaggered through the cars demanding money and valuables; as they entered the car ahead of the one Megan and Quinn were in, he suddenly grabbed her wrist and yanked her through the door to the connecting platform between their car and the one behind it.

'What are you doing?' she gasped.

'I'll jump off the train first and catch you.'

'But you've left all your valuables behind.'

At that instant they heard a gunshot inside the car. 'That's why,' Quinn said grimly. He leapt from the train, turned, and held out his arms.

Megan unhesitatingly jumped into them.

'Get down on the ground and crawl under the train,' he instructed. He gave her a slight push and she crawled beneath the car. He followed. From their position behind the wheels they could see the horses, hooves kicking up dust several cars down the track as they pawed the ground nervously awaiting the return of the robbers.

'They left only one man with the horses,' Quinn whispered. 'And he's not looking this way.' He rolled over onto his back, pulled a pistol from his belt, and reloaded it. 'You see those boulders alongside the track on the other side of the train? When I tell you, run for them.'

'They'll see me,' Megan protested, her heart pounding.

'The train will be between you and the man with the horses. The others are busy inside.' He rolled to his stomach and pointed his gun at the lone horseman. 'If he looks in your direction he's a dead man. Go! Now.'

Megan hesitated only a second, and then more shots and a yell from inside the car sent her dashing towards the rocks. She flung herself to the ground behind the boulders and lay panting, afraid to look back to see what was happening.

Seconds later Quinn hurtled over her head and crashed down beside her.

'What –' Megan began, but he clamped his hand over her mouth.

'Keep quiet and keep your head down,' he whispered in her ear. 'I'm going to circle around behind the train and get aboard the caboose. They disarmed all the passengers, so they won't expect a rear attack.'

Megan turned cold. 'No! You can't – you'll be killed.'

But he was already on his way.

She was unsure how long she lay in the broiling sun, holding her breath. Raucous laughter and the muted sobbing of women came from the direction of the train. She hadn't had time to grab her bonnet, and the midday heat radiating from the rocks caused waves of dizziness and blurring of her vision. The barren vistas of the Jornada seemed to undulate under the shimmering heat. Mirages formed and dissipated, floating grey phantoms that suggested cool lakes and beckoning ponds of cool water. Megan blinked, momentarily unsure if she was awake or dreaming.

Then all at once the air was filled with gunfire, shouts, the thunder of hooves as the horses bolted. Megan covered her ears to shut out the din, terrified that Quinn was dead and that at any second her hiding place – and her connection to him – would be discovered.

Minutes passed before she heard Quinn's voice over her head. 'You can open your eyes now. You're safe.'

Her eyes flew open. He was silhouetted against the sun and she blinked up at him and blurted out, 'You're still alive.'

'You sound disappointed. Come on, the engineer's getting up steam.'

He helped her to her feet and then turned on his heel and strode back to the train. Before Megan reached the nearest door she heard Quinn issuing orders. 'Put the bodies in the baggage car. We'll tie up the two gunmen who are still alive. We can take turns keeping an eye on them.'

By the time she reached the train, he was waiting to offer his hand. She looked up at him. 'You . . . killed four men?'

He pulled her up and stared at her. 'Funny thing about a lot of people. They won't act unless someone leads them. No, I didn't kill four men. When I came blasting in through the rear, a couple of the other passengers found their courage and jumped two of the bandits. Now maybe you'd care to make yourself useful.'

That still left two men he must have killed, Megan thought. 'What do you want me to do?'

'You've been bragging about how much you know about medicine. Now's your chance to show us. Three passengers in the next car were shot. See what you can do for them. We'll be at Rincon in an hour, if you can keep them alive until then . . .'

Megan was already running down the aisle in her haste to reach the wounded passengers.

One was an older man, heavy and florid-faced. He was unconscious and his ruddy complexion was already turning blue. She saw at once that he had not been shot. He had probably suffered a heart attack and there was little she could do for him. She directed his weeping wife to make him comfortable and to mop his brow with a cool cloth. It would give her something to do.

Megan turned her attention to the other two men. One was clutching his arm and cursing, the other had a blood-spurting shoulder wound. The train blew steam and began to inch forward. She pulled up her skirt and began to tear strips of fabric from her petticoats.

'Someone cut away his shirt,' Megan said. 'We've got to stop the bleeding. You men, stop gawking and check the other cars. Perhaps there's a doctor aboard.'

By the time word came back that there was no doctor, Megan had slowed the bleeding with a pressure compress hastily fashioned from her petticoat. She turned to the other man, who was still cursing, and gently peeled away his shirtsleeve.

'The bullet didn't go in very deep,' she told him. 'I can get it out if you'll let me. The sooner the lead is out, the sooner the wound will begin to heal.'

'Lady, I'd be grateful.' He grinned, although his eyes registered pain. 'Sorry about the cussing. That danged thievin' hombre just shot me for no damn good reason.'

'Does someone have a box of matches? I'll need some more cloth, too. One of you ladies is going to have to donate part of your petticoat.'

One of the men produced a box of matches and another handed her his knife. 'Where did a pretty little thing like you ever learn to treat gunshot wounds? Same place you learned to talk with that cute accent?'

'I treated a couple of injured poachers once,' Megan said cautiously, recalling that she was supposed to be Joanna Traherne, from Cornwall, not Wales, who had no knowledge of medicine. She would have to be careful when she arrived at the Mallory ranch not to display any skills Joanna could not possibly have. She added, by way of explanation, 'They'd been shot by the gamekeeper on my father's estate.'

'Where you headed, missy?'

'I'm going to visit the Mallory ranch. I believe it's south of Silver City.'

'Is your pa one of them absentee owners?' He turned to another passenger and said, 'That part of the territory is carved up into some mighty big spreads, and some of 'em are owned by Englishmen.'

Megan ignored the question as she held a match flame to the tip of the knife and then went to work removing the slug.

Quinn appeared just as she finished bandaging the wound. Her patient was now flipping the bullet in the air with his good hand and looking cocky. Megan's eyes met Quinn's briefly and she thought she saw respect in his gaze, or perhaps it was merely a reflection of what was in her eyes. He had, after all, saved the day.

The buckboard bounced over a rutted path towards the Mallory ranch, and despite her fatigue, Megan looked around her with growing interest. The New Mexico Territory was certainly beautiful now that they had left the bleak desert behind.

A herd of well-fed longhorn cattle, unlike any she had seen in England, grazed along a meandering river lined by cottonwoods and willows. The valley swept upward to the slopes of the hills, where lighter greens met the darker hues of the pines.

'We'll be there before sundown,' Quinn remarked, urging the horses forward at a fast trot.

'Are we expected today?'

'I sent Randolph a wire from Albuquerque. He knows we'll be in sometime tonight.'

She looked from the deepening shadows of the valley to the clouds spilling like golden waterfalls down the pale turquoise canopy of the sky. Fluffy pink cloud-figures rose from the southern horizon over a lavender and smoky grey background while brush strokes of scarlet and green and yellow feathered away to the west. 'I've never seen anything more awe-inspiring,' she said softly.

Quinn glanced down at her. 'Neither have I.' He let his eyes linger on her face for a moment.

76

Abruptly he reined the horses to a halt.

'What is it?' Megan asked. 'Is something wrong?'

'No . . . yes. I'm not sure this is such a good idea after all.'

'Isn't it a bit late for doubts? Randolph is expecting us.'

'He's expecting *Joanna*.'

'Don't worry. I'll keep my end of the bargain. I'll *be* Joanna. Soft-spoken, ladylike. I've been rehearsing the part since we sailed from England. You mightn't have noticed, but I haven't uttered one single word in Welsh.'

'You mean you normally speak Welsh?'

'In Wales we do – to one another. We all speak English, too, but we often let a bit of our own language slip in. Some things can be expressed only in Welsh.'

'And some things,' he said quietly, 'can't be expressed in words at all.'

Puzzled by his tone, she turned to look at him. In the red light of the setting sun his expression seemed less mocking, more open. For an instant she felt close to him in some way she was unable to define. She even swayed towards him, her face upturned, half expecting him to kiss her, if only in a gesture of friendship. It would have been improper, of course, but he was not a man who observed the rules of propriety . . . and they'd had an eventful journey together.

Then he added, 'You're a remarkable young woman. Brave as well as beautiful. I didn't believe you at first, about your part in Joanna's misfortune, but now I'm sure you were only trying to help her.'

'How many times must I tell you that it was not I who did that dreadful thing to Joanna? If I had, I wouldn't have mangled her like that.'

He was silent for a moment, staring at her through the deepening shadows. 'I believe you,' he said. 'I didn't, until now. Listen – you don't have to go through with this charade. I can turn around right now and take you back to Silver City. This is a big country, Megan. You can go anywhere you choose, do anything you want. I'll give you a stake and you can pay me back when you're on your feet.'

'I don't understand. Why the sudden change of heart?'

'When I first met you, I decided you were just a little too beautiful and far too intelligent for your own good, with an attitude that makes a man wonder if his britches are buttoned. I guess you aren't aware of it, but most young women are more deferential towards men. Your attitude makes a man want to cut you down to size.'

Megan was outraged. 'That is the most conceited, demeaning, idiotic observation I've heard you make, and God knows you've made some absolutely ridiculous, stupid, patronising —'

He seized her face in his hands and kissed her full on the mouth. Taken completely by surprise, Megan didn't react for a moment. She was aware of the warmth of his lips, of their insistent pressure and pulsing rhythm, of the tiny eddy of his breath blending with her own. More than anything, she was aware of the rush of feeling through her own body, a breathless, heady sense of discovery, as if he had allowed her to tap into feelings she had never explored.

Her first instinct was to respond, to soften her lips and welcome his. But the echo of what he'd just said hammered at the back of her mind. She jerked back, put her hands on his chest, and pushed him away. She sensed rather than saw his faint smile, as it was now almost completely dark.

'At least you didn't slap my face.'

'I wouldn't dignify the liberty you took by responding to it in any way.'

'Then let me analyse the situation for you. We could suppose that I didn't want to be on the receiving end of another barrage of derogatory adjectives. You have a real knack for using them, by the way. Or we could be honest and admit that we were enchanted by the sunset and the presence of an attractive member of the opposite sex.'

'Speak for yourself.'

He laughed softly. 'I suppose you deny that only seconds earlier you were looking at me in a most inviting manner . . . practically asking to be kissed. A gentleman always obliges a lady in that regard – not that I'm a gentleman, of course. But I'm well aware that hell hath no fury like a woman scorned.'

Megan tried to contain her fury. 'If I were a man, I'd take that whip from you and beat you senseless for that remark.'

'If you were a man, we wouldn't be in this situation.' He picked up the reins.

They rode in silence for a few minutes until the road ahead forked. Megan asked in a tight voice, 'Are we going on to the ranch?'

'If that's what you want.'

'Perhaps we could tell Randolph the truth. The whole story about Joanna.'

Once again he reined the horses to a halt. This time he turned and grabbed her arm in a painful grip. 'That isn't one of our options. If you go on, then by God you pretend to be Joanna, do you understand? Swear to me that you'll never tell him, no matter what. If you commit yourself to this, then it's all or nothing.'

Shaken by the intensity of his command, Megan nodded.

Abruptly he released her, and the next moment the buckboard lurched forward. He didn't speak again, and Megan watched him covertly. Anger was written in every line of his body and in the breakneck pace he now forced on the horses.

As they drew nearer to the Mallory ranch the way was lighted by lanterns hung from trees and fences. Megan could make out the shadowed outline of a long rambling building built on a sheltered ridge, overlooking bunk-houses, workshops, and an orderly array of corrals filled with horses and livestock. They passed an orchard and a grove of cottonwoods. Shade trees had been planted in a parklike setting all around the grounds.

The rambling building proved to be the ranch house, which was set behind a series of archways in the Spanish style. Megan and Quinn passed through a wrought-iron gate and into a small patio illuminated by oil lanterns. They approached the front doors, which were flanked by huge clay pots trailing blossoms that were unfamiliar to Megan.

Quinn pushed open the front door just as a smiling olive-skinned woman came hurrying across the tiled floor. 'Señor Quinn, *Bienvenido! Cómo está usted?*'

'I'm well, Consuela. This is Señorita Traherne.' He turned to Megan. 'Consuela is Randolph's housekeeper and a real treasure. Watch how you treat her. This isn't England and good help is hard to find.'

'I'm not in the habit of abusing servants,' Megan replied shortly. He managed to arouse her indignation with every word. She wondered if he did it deliberately.

'She speaks a little English, so watch what you say.'

Still smiling broadly, Consuela gestured for them to follow her. The rooms flowed one to the other through more archways, and Megan saw that the walls were tremendously thick – several feet, she guessed. Despite the heat of the day, evening had brought a chill to the air, and within those insulating walls the house was quite cold. The rooms they passed through were furnished with massive Spanish Colonial pieces carved from dark mahogany.

They entered a room filled with flickering firelight. A huge log blazed in an open fireplace, the light dancing on a dining table set for the evening meal. Megan was surprised to see covered dishes made of silver and delicate bone china on a white linen cloth. But her gaze went directly to the man seated at the head of the table. As they walked towards him she was vaguely aware of the greetings passing between Randolph and Quinn, but the words floated, undigested, over her head, as she stared at the most handsome man she had ever seen.

Randolph Mallory had golden hair that formed a bright halo in the firelight. His carved cheekbones drew attention to gentle blue eyes that were fixed upon her with equal astonishment.

'Welcome to my home, Joanna. I can't tell you how glad I am that you came or how surprised I was to hear you were here in New Mexico. But – I feel I know you well enough to say this – I'm astounded that in your letters you described yourself as plain. Why on earth would someone as lovely as you refuse to send a photograph?'

'Your cousin is excessively modest, Randolph,' Quinn said, and Megan bridled at his sarcasm, although it seemed lost on Randolph.

They had reached the head of the dining table and Megan, whose gaze had been fixed on Randolph's face, now realised that he had not risen at her approach. She saw also that he was not seated in one of the elaborately carved high-backed dining chairs. Why . . . he was sitting in a wheeled bath chair of the sort used by invalids.

He had extended his hands towards her, and she took them, wrenching her eyes from the wheelchair to his face. He was regarding her with a wary, apologetic expression. 'Now you know my little secret, Joanna. I'm a prisoner of this damned chair. I should have told you in my letters, I know, but . . . how can I explain? In our correspondence I could be a whole man again. I didn't have to risk being the object of your pity or having you regard me as different from other men. You see, Joanna, the accident that killed my parents left me unable to walk. My legs were crushed, and I'm paralysed.'

10

Although Joanna was shaking, she spoke to Delta calmly. 'Why would you send me to work for Justin Bodrath, knowing that he is Magnus's sworn enemy? What were you thinking of? You didn't even warn me . . . Why, I could have given away the fact that Magnus is the hermit of Dutchman's Point!'

Delta twisted her sinuous body and tossed her silken mane of black hair. She regarded Joanna over her shoulder, then continued nonchalantly to trim the stem of an orchid. Lizzie, her sullen face alight with the anticipation of an argument, remained at Joanna's side, having shown her into Delta's parlour.

'But you didn't give him away, did you?' Delta said. 'So why are you angry with me? You have a good position with the wealthiest man in this part of Cornwall. How many such positions did you think would be available to you? Such gratitude!'

'I don't mean to sound ungrateful.' Joanna sank into the nearest chair, truly contrite. 'It's just that it was horrible, hearing Justin Bodrath call Magnus a murderer. And I live in fear that I'll mention his name without thinking about it.'

'Go and attend to your work, Lizzie,' Delta snapped to the gaping maid. She turned to face Joanna, her amber eyes speculative. 'You sound like a woman who cares enough about a man to fear for his life, but perhaps what you feel for Magnus is only the fascination of a lady for a brute.'

Joanna felt herself flush. 'Magnus isn't a brute! He's the kindest, gentlest man I've ever known. I owe him a great debt of gratitude. He saved my life. Naturally I care what happens to him.'

She felt uncomfortable and wished she had not come. The past week had taken its toll on her weakened health, and she experienced a wave of faintness. Justin Bodrath insisted upon working only after dark. Joanna sat up with him every night poring over old journals and letters, then went to bed exhausted at dawn. Justin slept most of the day, but Joanna, unaccustomed to such hours, tossed and turned and dozed fitfully.

'But you *are* fascinated by Magnus. Admit it,' Delta persisted. She leaned forward, her eyes glittering with amusement. 'Do you wonder what it would be like to be taken into those great muscular arms? To feel those huge hands on your body? Oh, his poor face is the worse for wear, of course; yet it has a certain animal appeal, yes?'

'Please, you are embarrassing me.' Joanna rose to her feet, gripping the back of the chair in order to steady herself. 'I must go now; Mr Bodrath's coachman is waiting for me. I rode to the village with Paxton when he came in to buy provisions.'

Delta gave a small snort. 'Tell me, my lady, in the household you came from, did the butler ever go out for provisions?'

It hadn't occurred to Joanna, but it was true of wealthy households that most of what was needed was either grown on the estate or delivered by local tradesmen. In the rare event some item was urgently needed, one of the junior servants would be sent on the errand, certainly not the butler.

Delta went on, 'Paxton drove you through the village in an open carriage to find out if anyone knew you. He's no doubt questioning everybody now, trying to find out who you really are. Tell me, are you free to roam about Bodrath House?'

Joanna had very little freedom, she realised. She stayed

83

in her small room until she was summoned to dinner shortly before midnight each evening. On those occasions when she had attempted to leave her room, a footman had materialised outside her door and asked what he might bring for her. It was clear she was expected to stay out of the way when not actually working with Justin. The night's work was done in Justin's study. 'I stay in my room most of the time,' she answered.

'Listen to me, Joanna Smith. You say you owe Magnus a debt. I'm going to tell you how to repay it. Somewhere in Bodrath House, among that regiment of men commanded by Paxton, is someone, or something, that will tell us how Harry Bodrath really died.'

'But I understood he died in a boxing bout with Magnus.'

'Magnus knocked him unconscious, but Harry was still alive when he took him home. Besides, Magnus was forced to fight against his will. My brother Joss knew all that happened that night and would have testified for Magnus. But somebody killed Joss before the trial. I want to know who. I want vengeance against that man. I swore it on my brother's grave. I want Magnus's name cleared, too, because I love him. You'd better know that before you set your own cap for him. You may enchant him with your refined ladylike ways, but you'll be no match for me in the end. I know how to enslave a man in ways you couldn't even imagine.'

Joanna's mind was reeling. 'But if you love Magnus, how can you give yourself to that man who visits you?'

Delta laughed, a harsh, brittle sound. 'You show no surprise about anything else I tell you. The only thing that shocks you is that I love Magnus. Surely you must have guessed. Who do you think helped him escape from prison? Why do you suppose he knew he could trust me to help you?'

'I'm shocked – horrified – by what you've told me. I had no idea you believed your brother was killed. I'd assumed it was an accident when Justin said he fell from a cliff top to his death.'

Delta gave a small gasp. 'There! You see! Justin had him thrown from the cliff. How else would he have known how Joss died? When my brother's body washed ashore, the men in the village thought he'd been dashed against the rocks after wrecking his boat in an attempt to get through the suicide gap during a storm. But I knew better.'

The heavy brass knocker fell against the front door, an impatient rapping that signalled Paxton's return.

'You'd better go,' Delta whispered. 'He won't come in here. Keep your eyes and ears open. You must try to find out what happened after they took Harry home that night.'

Wondering if she was returning to the home of a murderer, Joanna felt her hand shake as she reached for the door.

Magnus's great fist smashed down on Delta's wood table, sending splinters flying and toppling the delicate vase holding the orchid. 'Damn you to hell, Delta! What were you thinking of? You've put the lass in danger. Christ in heaven, I can't believe you'd send your worst enemy to Bodrath House, let alone a frail little thing like Joanna who never did you any harm.'

'I sent her there for you – for Joss. To clear your name and bring my brother's murderer to justice.'

'And just how did you imagine Joanna could do that?'

'By keeping her eyes and ears open. Someone in that house – Paxton or one of those soldier-footmen of his – saw something that night or heard something later. Joanna owes you her life; this is a way for her to repay you.'

'I don't want her to repay me. I just want her to be safe –' He broke off, flushing.

Delta's eyes narrowed to catlike slits. 'I knew it! You're in love with her! You've fallen in love with that whey-faced little slut.' She spun around, grabbed the vase, and raised it over her head to hurl at him.

He was upon her before she realised he had moved. His hand seized her wrist and the vase crashed to the stone-flagged floor. 'Don't ever call her that again, do you hear?'

'She got rid of a baby. You told me so yourself – when you came here to ask me how to keep her from bleeding to death. But now all of a sudden she's a pure little virgin again. How did she manage that, Magnus? That's a trick I'd like to learn.'

'Bad girls don't get themselves in trouble, Delta. Only the good girls get caught. You of all people should know that.'

She spat in his face and he released her. For an instant they glared at each other, and then she fluttered her long silky eyelashes. 'I only wanted to have someone at Bodrath House who could help us,' she said wheedlingly. 'They won't dare harm her. She's a Traherne; her father is one of the wealthiest men in Cornwall.'

Magnus seemed to slump inside himself, as though he were hearing what he'd suspected but didn't want to accept. 'How do you know that?'

She twirled the orchid in her fingers. 'I'm a witch.'

Realisation dawned in his eyes. 'Your fancy man . . . of course. He found out for you. And after you swore to me you'd tell no one about her, ask no questions.'

'Have I ever broken my word to you? I didn't ask. He mentioned that he'd won first place for his prize orchid in the flower show because his arch rival hadn't entered one due to the accidental death of his older daughter, Joanna Traherne. Magnus, Joanna's family thinks she's dead. Does she know that?'

'I think she suspects it. If I hadn't frightened that old woman off, she would have made sure Joanna was dead before she flung the dirt and branches over her. I wouldn't be surprised if the Trahernes paid the old woman to get rid of Joanna . . . Wouldn't be the first time the upper classes have tried to bury their mistakes.'

'What if they find out she's still alive, then? Her father has a seat in the House of Commons. He wouldn't want a scandal to get out involving his daughter.'

'The Trahernes are not going to find out, are they?'
There was an edge of flint to his voice.

Delta glided towards him, wrapped her arms around
him, and nestled her head against his chest. 'You can trust
me, Magnus. You know that.'

He raised his hand to pat her shoulder approvingly, but
she turned her face upward and kissed his mouth. At the
same time her fingers were busy with the buttons of his
trousers.

'Delta . . .' he said hoarsely, but she had reached her
goal with practised ease, and she caressed him, murmured
enticingly against his mouth, her body pressed to his,
moving languidly.

She laughed softly as he became aroused. Her tongue
slipped between his teeth, darting playfully. She caught
one of his hands and brought it to the warm flesh of her
breast, and he felt her taut nipple thrust against his palm.

'Don't . . . do this to me,' he said raggedly.

With a quick shrug of her shoulders she sent her silk
kimono slithering to the floor. Her body was perfection, a
soft glowing gold, like a priceless statue.

He fought long-suppressed urges with the desperation
of a drowning man, but she was relentless. He could not
stop her hands, her lips, or resist the promise of her eyes.
Scarcely aware of what he was doing, he allowed her to
draw him towards the hearthside rug and push him down
on his knees.

She sank down before him, her breath sweetly hot
against his mouth. Then, pulling away, she began to writhe
like a serpent, swaying back and forth, her long black hair
falling first to one side and then to the other. for a moment
he was mesmerised, blind with desire even while he loathed
himself for giving in to her.

Then he gave a strangled cry and jumped to his feet.
'No, by God, Delta, it's not right. I want you, yes, but I
don't love you, and you . . . you don't love any man, you
just possess them. I'll not be one of your playthings.'

Her eyes were glazed, trancelike, and for a moment

she continued her swaying, lost in her own sensual spell, unaware her prey had escaped. She reached forward, apparently expecting to touch him, but grasped empty air. She jumped then, as though awakening, and searched the room with eyes suddenly dagger-bright.

'You want me because I'm the only man who can resist you, Delta,' he said heavily. 'For the love of God, have mercy. Your brother was my best friend, and I want to be your friend, too. Don't do this anymore.'

'It's her, isn't it?' The way in which she spat out the words reminded him of the hiss of a striking snake. 'It's that damned Joanna. Do you think she'd care if you made love to me? Ha! You're so far beneath her she doesn't even know you have feelings like other men. You fool, Magnus. You were just another servant to do her bidding. The upper classes think the rest of us are put on the earth to serve them. Haven't you learned that by now?'

He moved towards the cellar door, walking stiffly, his shoulders braced as though he bore a heavy burden.

Her eyelids drooping, neck and shoulders aching with fatigue, Joanna examined the faded sepia photograph Justin Bodrath had placed on the desk before her. It was a formal picture of Justin's father and his three sons.

Oil portraits of all of the Bodraths hung in the gallery, but Harry Bodrath had not lived to his twenty-first birthday, when his portrait would have been commissioned.

Justin reached up and turned the gas mantel higher. Somewhere out in the night an owl gave a mournful cry. 'Here we are in all our decadent glory. The Bodraths as they were before Harry died. God, we were a good-looking family, weren't we?'

Joanna blinked, forcing her tired eyes to focus, first on the older man who stared sternly from the centre of the picture. The family resemblance to Justin was unmistakable, though his father had been a robust, military man while Justin was currently plagued with ill health. Neville, the firstborn son, was also the spirit and image of their father, but Joanna's gaze moved swiftly away from him as she found the face of the murdered Harry Bodrath.

'Harry was so beautiful, wasn't he?' Justin sighed. 'A Greek god, perfect in body and face. He was the youngest, and perhaps we all spoiled him. That's a rather petulant pout he's wearing, and the picture doesn't do him justice at all . . .'

Justin droned on, rhapsodising about the dead and deified Harry, as Joanna stared at Harry Bodrath's handsome face and wondered what would have happened to everyone, including herself, had he not challenged Magnus to a boxing match.

11

Megan slept late the morning after her arrival at the Mallory ranch, but when she appeared in the dining room she found that Randolph had waited to have breakfast with her.

His smile of greeting lit up his face. 'Good morning, Joanna, how charming you look. Please, come and sit as close as you can so I can feast my eyes on you.' He rang a small silver bell, and Consuela bustled in carrying a covered dish.

Megan thought of Joanna as she returned Randolph's greeting and took the chair he indicated. How would she ever be able to maintain this masquerade? she wondered.

'I suppose Quinn has already had breakfast,' she remarked as Consuela served an omelette with tomato sauce.

'He left late last night to return to the Diamond T

– that's the ranch he manages for an English absentee owner.'

Megan felt a twinge of disappointment. Oddly, she had dreamed about Quinn last night. She told herself sternly that the dream was merely the result of his unexpected kiss.

Randolph said, 'I hope you like the huevos rancheros. The salsa is somewhat spicy. I should have asked Consuela to serve foods that you're accustomed to, but . . . well, to be honest I didn't think of it until now. I've been so excited about meeting you at last. Joanna, you'll never know how much your coming here means to me. I can't wait to show you around the ranch. As soon as we've eaten I'll take you on the grand tour.'

Megan hadn't realised that she'd cast an involuntary glance in the direction of his bath chair until he added, 'I can handle a buckboard. One doesn't need legs to hold on to the reins. I am paralysed from the waist down, but my arms are quite strong.'

A bite of the spicy eggs temporarily took Megan's breath away, which she decided later was perhaps fortunate, as she might otherwise have asked for more details about his paralysis, in terms a layperson would not have used. It occurred to her then that she would have to take care not to reveal her medical knowledge. Above all, she would have to bite back any spontaneous Welsh exclamations.

After breakfast, at Randolph's suggestion, Megan changed into sturdier shoes and put on a hat. When she went outside she found he was already seated in the buckboard. Two ranch hands were waiting, holding the reins of their horses. One man stepped forward to help Megan up beside Randolph, and as the buckboard began to move, the two ranch hands mounted their horses and followed.

'I don't want to frighten you, Joanna,' Randolph said, 'but I'd prefer you don't go anywhere by yourself. There are still a few bands of renegade Indians roaming the territory, and we get more than our fair share of thieves and rustlers. Even though we're only touring the ranch this morning, it's necessary to have a couple of men accompany us, as my land stretches for miles and law and order, as you know it in England, hasn't quite reached the West yet.'

Quinn had evidently not mentioned the attempted robbery of the train, and Megan decided she wouldn't either.

The countryside was so lovely that it was difficult to imagine it being spoiled by lawlessness. Megan found herself exclaiming at each new delight. After a while she asked, 'How far are we from the ranch Quinn manages?'

'The two ranches are adjacent to each other; their common border is marked by a river. Quinn visits me whenever he can get away. I hope you two will be good friends. He can be . . .'

'Difficult?'

Randolph smiled. 'To say the least. I sensed a little hostility between the two of you last night. That surprised me because I thought you'd be exactly the kind of woman who would bowl him over.'

Joanna was that kind of woman, quiet, reserved, deferential, Megan thought. Almost instantly she wondered if she could learn to be the kind of woman who could bowl over a man like Quinn. She had battled these ambivalent feelings towards him from the start and found them disturbing. Even more disconcerting was the fact that Quinn was constantly on her mind.

'But to my complete amazement he was able to persuade you to come,' Randolph continued, 'and for that I shall be everlastingly grateful to him.'

'Oh, look!' Megan cried as the buckboard rounded a bend in the trail. 'Cowboys!'

A trio of riders skilfully drove several stray calves back in the direction of the main herd of cattle, and Randolph stopped the buckboard so that she could watch.

'I can no longer ride a horse,' Randolph said. 'But as soon as I can bear to let you out of my sight, I'll have Chuck, my foreman, help you choose a mount for yourself.'

Megan recalled with a jolt that Joanna was an experienced horsewoman, accustomed to riding sidesaddle and wearing ladylike broadcloth riding habits. Her own riding experience consisted solely of that awkward and uncomfortable journey from Traherne Hall to the railway station with Quinn. Although he'd threatened that the final leg of their journey would also be on horseback, he'd relented and bought a buckboard to transport her and her baggage to the ranch. She'd have to find an excuse to decline Randolph's offer of a mount.

After a while Randolph again urged the horses forward at a trot, and a pleasant couple of hours later they came to a riverbank lined with cottonwoods and live oaks. To Megan's delight, Randolph lifted a blanket from behind the seat, revealing a picnic basket. 'I thought perhaps we could have lunch here.'

The two ranch hands who had followed helped him out of the buckboard, then took the horses downriver to drink. Megan unpacked tortillas and cheese and cold roast beef and spread the food on a checkered cloth on the ground.

Randolph was propped against a tree, his legs stretched out in front of him, covered with a blanket, despite the warmth of the day. Megan wondered if he kept his legs hidden because the flesh and muscle had begun to atrophy. She longed to tell him that her grandfather used to encourage the families of crippled colliers to move their paralysed limbs and massage the flesh to try to keep them from withering, for, as he put it, one never knew when the medical profession might find a way to restore the lost control.

The sun climbed higher in the sky and the day was hot, but the river murmured over the rocks, and overhead the leaves of the cottonwoods whispered. Sated by the food, Megan found herself relaxing so completely that she lay back in the sweet-smelling grass and, arms stretched over her head, sighed contentedly.

Randolph spoke softly, 'It's so good to find you're not

brooding over recent events. After your last despairing letter I feared . . . Well, never mind my fears. But tell me, what did Quinn say to you to persuade you to come? That rascal never even hinted he planned to visit you in Cornwall, let alone ask you to come back with him.'

Megan felt her jaw tighten, but she forced a smile. 'I was a little upset at the wedding. He convinced me that I needed to get away from . . . everyone.'

'Would it help to talk about Oliver?'

Megan looked away quickly, but Randolph continued, 'When I received your letter telling me he was going to marry your sister, I felt a mixture of rage and relief. Rage that he'd hurt you and relief that you were not lost to me.'

'Lost to *you*?'

He flushed slightly. 'I feared if you married, our correspondence might end. Anticipating your wonderful letters made my life worthwhile again. We shared so much of ourselves, our thoughts, feelings, secret dreams.'

He reached out and touched the back of her hand lightly. 'I used to think that if ever we met, and you weren't shocked to find me in that damned chair, that we'd talk easily, in the same way we wrote to each other. But' – he withdrew his hand from hers and shook his head slightly – 'frankly, I'm baffled. You're . . .'

Not what I expected, Megan finished silently for him. Aloud, she said quickly, breathlessly, 'Randolph, this is all so new and strange to me – the country, the ranch . . . meeting you. I need a little time to get used to . . . speaking to you instead of writing.'

'Of course. How thoughtless of me. Let's not even attempt to discuss personal matters for a while. Ah, but we can discuss the books we've read recently. You wrote that you were engrossed in a novel by Hardy, so I sent to New York for it.'

Megan groaned inwardly. Joanna loved to read novels and poetry. She understood music, art, drama. How on earth could Megan, whose own reading was confined to newspapers, medical articles, and scientific journals, possibly participate in an intelligent discussion of the books he and Joanna enjoyed?

Randolph was waiting with an eager expression on his handsome features and, feeling wretched for lying to him, Megan sat up and clapped her hand to her forehead. 'Randolph, I seem to have developed a terrible headache. I think perhaps it's because I am unaccustomed to the heat.'

At once he was concerned, contrite that he had overtaxed her. He whistled and the two ranch hands came immediately to help them back onto the buckboard.

Megan, who was in perfect health and never suffered from headaches or any other minor aches or pains, was treated to a great deal of solicitous attention by both Randolph and, when they returned to the ranch house, Consuela. Megan found herself lying in a cool, darkened room with a cold cloth over her eyes, feeling like the fraud she was, convinced that retribution was bound to descend upon her for her deception.

Inevitably, after a moment she began to think about Quinn again, wondering what he was doing and when she would see him again.

That evening and all during the next few days she managed to steer the conversation away from dangerous subjects by the simple tactic of asking questions about New Mexico, about the ranch, and about Randolph's life before and after the accident that had killed his parents and paralysed him, although he never talked about the accident itself.

It was quickly evident that, although he had once taken an active part in running the ranch, his heart had never truly been in it. Apparently he had always preferred gentler pursuits and, left to his own devices, probably would have spent his days reading, playing the piano, and submitting poems and sketches to small literary magazines.

Megan reflected upon the twist of fate that had given him so much of what he desired from life while taking away his parents and the use of his legs. Why did it so often happen, she wondered, that one seemed required to trade so dearly for one's desires?

One evening at dinner she could not help commenting on how different he and Quinn were and asking how they had met.

Randolph raised one golden eyebrow in surprise. 'But I told you about him in a letter.'

Megan wanted to slap herself. 'Yes, of course, but I've forgotten how you met. I suppose it didn't interest me until he came to England and I realised how different the two of you are.'

'We met across a poker table. Quinn won everything I carried on me as well as a silver-trimmed saddle I recklessly wagered. I was sixteen at the time and devastated – didn't know how I would face my father. The following day Quinn rode over here and returned the saddle with a stern warning about the evils of gambling. At the time he was working as a drover, pushing cattle herds north, and I was fascinated by the fact that he was educated, worldly, not at all like the ignorant cowpokes we usually encounter. He told us he'd recently been mustered out of the army – the cavalry, I believe – but we never did learn much about his life before he came to New Mexico. Anyway, a year or so later he was back in the territory again, and he came to see me. He got into the habit of dropping by whenever he was in the area. He even saved my hide once when I was accosted by outlaws between here and Silver City. After that, my father recommended him for the job of running the Diamond T.'

Randolph sighed deeply. 'That wasn't very long before the accident.'

Placing her knife and fork neatly across the centre of her plate, Megan patted her lips with her napkin and smiled. 'Yes, I remember now. You did mention your meeting in a letter.'

He was watching her curiously. 'While we're discussing our letters, you never did answer the question I asked when you first arrived: Why did you describe yourself as plain? Why, in fact, did you refuse to exchange photographs? Oh, I know what you wrote when I asked you to send me a picture – that it would be fun not to see exactly what we looked like; that way we could imagine each other to be anything we chose. Then when I begged you to give me a hint, you wrote that you had plain features and' – he paused as the ticking of the grandfather clock in one corner of the dining room seemed to grow louder and Megan's fingers tightened on her napkin – 'and brown hair. Joanna, your hair is gloriously red.'

Megan let out her breath carefully, wondering if she should claim that she used henna, but before she could speak the lie, he continued, 'I thought you would bring up the subject yourself, and confess . . .'

So he knew she was an impostor! What would happen now? She picked up her wine glass and took a sip. 'I was going to, Randolph, honestly. It's just that these past few days –' She was about to say that the days had been so wonderful she didn't want them to end, but he leaned forward, his eyes twinkling, amused.

'There's no need. I realised almost immediately what you'd done. In one of your very first letters you mentioned your school friend, Megan Thomas, and how much you admired her because, as you put it, she was utterly fearless. You also said that she had auburn hair and green eyes. Like a fool, I replied that I didn't care for red hair, as it usually went with a quick temper. I then asked you to tell me what you looked like. Joanna, dear Joanna . . . it never occurred to me that you'd probably encountered that stupid myth about red-haired people before and were sounding out the waters, as it were, to find out how I felt – that, in fact, you had described *yourself* to me. Then when I wrote that I didn't care for red hair, you decided that since there was little likelihood we would ever meet, you would simply substitute your own brilliant looks for those of your plain little friend.'

During this recital Megan's mouth had dropped open.

Too surprised by his explanation to speak, she studied him warily.

He laughed, delighted. 'Oh, Joanna, you lovely thing! Can you imagine my absolute delight to find that the dear, sweet, sensitive woman who penned those letters to me is not a plain little dove after all, but a vibrantly beautiful young woman! To find those qualities of understanding and compassion and such appreciation for the finer things of life in one who looks like you . . . Oh, Lord, listen to me. I'm doing it again. Generalising. But you must admit that most beautiful women tend to be a trifle self-centred and spoiled.'

Megan was too stunned to speak for a moment. finally she said warily, 'I feel awful about having misled you.'

'But I misled you to a far greater degree. I never told you of my paralysis. Don't you see, it didn't really matter to either of us what we looked like on the outside, because we'd discovered the essence of each other, the really important parts of our hearts and souls, through our letters.'

Consuela came into the dining room carrying a bowl of fruit, and Megan was glad of the pause to collect her wits. She had been on the verge of confessing her deception. But now she remembered her promise to Quinn that she wouldn't divulge her identity, and she also recalled that she was accused of having murdered Joanna. Heaven only knew what Randolph, feeling about Joanna as he did, would do if she confessed this to him.

When Consuela departed, Randolph refilled their wine glasses. 'Let's drink a toast to no more secrets between us.'

As the days passed, Megan found that Randolph was a charming and considerate host. He frequently made wry remarks about his bath chair – 'that damned chair,' as he called it – but he was so completely without self-pity that Megan found herself drawn to him in a way she had not expected.

They quickly established an easy camaraderie that, on

her part, included strong feelings of protectiveness, as if Randolph were a favourite brother who had been wounded and she the sister who would take care that nothing ever hurt him again.

It was soon clear why Randolph and Joanna's correspondence had meant so much to each of them, since they were indeed kindred spirits. If only Jo hadn't died, if they really could have met . . . Perhaps if Jo had borne Oliver's child, she and the baby and Randolph could have become a family, since Randolph probably could not become a father himself. Still, Megan decided, that was not meant to be.

Randolph was so hungry for someone to talk to that he didn't notice that Megan usually answered his questions with another question, thus avoiding discussions of novels and poetry with which she was unfamiliar.

Megan might have begun to relax and enjoy her new life, which was a far cry from taking care of her bedridden and senile grandfather, had it not been for one nagging fact: As the days passed, she found herself thinking about Quinn constantly, missing his presence, his banter, even his high-handedness. She wondered if Randolph would suspect how she felt if she suggested inviting Quinn over for dinner, and was about to risk it when Randolph himself suggested it.

'You know,' he said quite suddenly one day, 'I've just realised that Quinn hasn't been to visit us since he brought you here. I must send a rider over to the Diamond T to ask him to come. He's probably staying away to give us time alone. I feel guilty that I haven't missed him. He's been a good friend and companion, but I've never been able to discuss Russian novelists with him, or the French Impressionists, or Byron.'

'What *did* you talk about with him?'

'Oh, his travels – he's been everywhere. The various jobs he's had – he's done just about everything. Before . . . the accident he was like an older brother to me. Took me under his wing and taught me how to shoot, to travel the territory safely, to camp under the stars without losing my scalp to an Indian or my hide to a grizzly. He took me to Silver City to some of the less notorious clubs. I suppose I was a bit of a mama's boy before I met Quinn. I was an only child, my mother was overprotective, and my father was always busy. Anyway, Quinn would come riding into the territory and hang about for a time. Then off he'd go again.'

Megan waited to hear that Quinn would be coming to visit, but Randolph had evidently forgotten to send a rider to the Diamond T, as several days passed and he made no mention of it. He had not asked how long she intended to stay and she certainly was not going to bring up the subject, but he had begun to talk of events in the future she might enjoy, a play to be performed at the theatre in Silver City, a famous singer who was to appear in another nearby town.

Late one evening as she rose to say good night, Randolph reached out and caught her wrist. 'Joanna, would you . . . could you give me a good-night kiss?'

She bent and brushed his lips lightly with her own, closing her eyes as she did so and imagining it was Quinn's mouth she kissed. At the same time she wondered what the real Joanna would have felt at that moment.

12

Joanna climbed the staircase to her room, aching with weariness after a long night's work. Oh, how she wished Justin Bodrath could work as normal people did, in the daytime. She feared she would never become accustomed to nocturnal toil.

Entering her room, she was about to close the draperies to shut out the dawn light when she noticed a large seashell lying on the window ledge outside. After opening the window, she picked up the shell. Tucked inside it was a scrap of paper upon which was written, 'Come to Delta's cottage. I'll wait in the fish cellar for one hour after dawn each day for three days.'

It was unsigned, but it had to be from Magnus. She was surprised because she hadn't thought he could read and write.

Although exhausted from the night's labour, she splashed cold water on her face, donned a riding habit that had belonged to Justin's mother, and slipped down the stairs. She was uncomfortable wearing a dead woman's clothes and felt vaguely spectrelike in the ancient silks and bombazines, but the broadcloth habit was still in style.

At the bottom of the staircase she paused, listening, but the house was silent, the menservants not yet moving about. She walked out through the main door and made her way to the stables. Justin had given her permission to ride any of his horses, most of which were gentle mares used for pulling his carriage, but so far she had been too exhausted and too weak from her illness to take him up on the offer.

A sleepy stable boy aroused a groom, who found a sidesaddle and strapped it onto one of the mares for her. Minutes later she and her mount were galloping towards the sea.

As she expected, Delta was still in bed at this early hour. Lizzie answered Joanna's knock on the door and silently conducted her to the door leading to the fish cellar.

Magnus was standing at the foot of the stone stairs. He pulled his woollen cap from his head as she approached. 'Thank you for coming, Miss Traherne.'

She caught her breath. 'So you know who I am. How did you find out?'

Pulling out one of the empty fish barrels, he carefully wiped off the top so that she might sit on it. He hovered over her for a moment, as though wanting to do more for her, then crouched in front of her, his craggy face earnest and concerned. There was deeply felt sympathy in his eyes. 'I've some bad news for you, and I wish there was a gentle way to break it to you.'

'Has something happened to a member of my family?'

'Your father . . .'

Her mouth was dry. 'Oh, no . . .'

'It was very sudden. Heart failure. Delta only just found out, but he passed away shortly after I found you in the woods.'

Joanna buried her face in her hands. She felt that she had killed him, just as surely as if she'd put a knife into his heart.

'I'm so very sorry,' Magnus went on. 'They think you're dead, too. In the village they say you accidentally fell from the cliff and drowned. Do you want me to take you home now, to be with your mother?'

She looked up at him. 'My mother died a long time ago. I'm not sure my stepmother would welcome me back.' Her voice broke. 'It was . . . my disgrace that caused my father's death. You know what a pariah a woman in my circumstance is.'

He bit his lip, his face expressing his wish to deny what she said, but he was too honest for that. At last he said, 'Ah, damn it, society may condemn the woman, but you must put the blame where it belongs, Joanna, squarely on the shoulders of the man who deceived you. Don't blame yourself. He's the one who broke his promise. If he hadn't, none of this would have happened. You must know how many first babies come a bit too early in a marriage. Put it behind you now, lass. You'll find someone else to love.'

'How very kind you are, Magnus, but I know how plain I am. I'm resigned to spending my life as a spinster.'

'Plain? You?' He sounded genuinely amazed. 'Why, you're plain like the sky is plain where it meets the sea. Oh, you're not flashy pretty like some women, but there's

101

such warmth in your eyes, such gentleness in your sweet face –' He broke off, flushing a dull red.

Joanna stared at the damp floor in an agony of shyness.

Magnus bit his lip. 'I'm sorry. I had no right . . .' He paced the damp floor for a moment and then turned to her again. 'I don't know what Delta was thinking about, sending you to work for Justin Bodrath. You can't go back there. If you won't go home, is there not someone else you can turn to?'

Megan, she thought immediately. An elusive worry about Megan nagged at Joanna, but she was unable to think of a reason for it. She recalled Adele's wedding and Megan's refusal to perform an illegal operation, but she remembered nothing between the moment when Mrs Elliot brought on the miscarriage and the instant when she awoke to find Magnus bent over her in the cave. She replied, 'I have a dear friend. Her name is Megan Thomas, and she used to live in a little town called Llanrys in north Wales, but I don't know where she might be now.'

'And when did you see her last?'

'At my sister's wedding. But I'm afraid I was so full of my own misery that I never learned where she intended to go after that. She'd recently lost her grandfather, and I'm not sure that she went back to north Wales.'

'I'll try to find your friend for you,' he said, 'but please don't go back to Bodrath House. Delta will find somewhere else for you.'

'No, love,' a silky voice at the top of the stairs said. 'Delta will not. Miss Traherne will return to Bodrath House and find out who killed my brother and Harry Bodrath, because if she doesn't, Delta will tell the Trahernes what Joanna did – *everything* Joanna did.'

'Delta . . .' Magnus's voice was a low growl as he started towards the stone stairs, but Joanna rose swiftly and caught his arm.

'It's all right. I intended to go back to Bodrath House. I will do what I can to clear your name, Magnus. I owe you that for saving my life.'

'You owe me nothing, and I won't have her threatening you,' he declared angrily. 'I see now why she was eager to bring you here – to try to blackmail you. Delta, if you go near Joanna's family, I swear to God I'll –'

'What?' Delta asked huskily. 'Beat me? Why, darling, I would enjoy that.'

Blushing, Joanna fled.

After Joanna returned the mare to the stables, she hurried to Bodrath House and, not wishing to ring the front door-bell, slipped in through the tradesmen's entrance.

Several young menservants were at work in the kitchen, baking bread, polishing silverware, scrubbing pots and pans. Although they glanced at her, no one spoke. She nodded a brief greeting and then walked quickly along the corridor that connected the servants' wing of the house with the main hall.

She had reached the foot of the staircase when a door opened behind her and a steely voice spoke. 'While you are in the master's employ, miss, you will not leave the premises without permission.'

Turning to face Paxton, Joanna felt herself tremble. She made a conscious effort to remind herself that he was merely the butler, despite his field marshal's demeanour. 'Mr Bodrath did not restrict my movements, Paxton. In fact, he gave me permission to go riding.'

'Within the boundaries of the estate only, miss. If you wish to go outside the estate, then one of the staff will accompany you. Don't be deceived by the tranquillity of the valley, most of which is owned by Mr Bodrath. We're not far from the edge of Dartmoor, and we never know when an escaped convict might come our way. The unwary can find themselves in dire peril.'

'Thank you for your concern, Paxton,' Joanna said. 'Now I must get some rest.' She fled up the staircase, feeling his disapproving gaze follow her, the echo of what sounded frighteningly like a threat ringing in her ears.

* * *

Magnus beached his boat and made his way up through the cliffs to his cave, still in a state of great anxiety about Joanna. After she left, he had argued with Delta, but she adamantly refused to retract her blackmail threat, and Magnus feared where Delta's jealousy of Joanna might lead.

He stood at the end of the promontory known as Dutchman's Point, watching the restless channel churn about the rocks below, thinking how the arrival of a frail young woman had changed his life.

After the horror of his imprisonment and his harrowing escape across the moor inches ahead of searchers and bloodhounds, he had been content merely to be free after he reached the sanctuary of the caves. The days had passed pleasantly; he had spent them fishing, hunting, even paying an occasional visit to Delta's cottage so that he was not entirely without human companionship. He had looked upon her as his friend, as her brother had been.

Joss had told Magnus that Delta was once the mistress of a French plantation manager on their native island of Martinique. When her lover was discharged for thievery, he took Delta and Joss to Normandy and then brought them here to Cornwall. The Frenchman smuggled wines and spirits from his own country through the suicide gap to the fish cellar below the cottage where Delta now lived. Delta had promptly turned him in to the customs and excise men, taken the profits from his last sale for herself, and bought the cottage. The unfortunate Frenchman now languished in prison, and Delta had found a titled Cornishman, an avid sailor and orchid fancier, who provided for her.

Magnus had never encouraged Delta's attentions and, since she was flirtatious with all men, didn't realise that her pursuit of him was serious. He truly believed she had helped him escape from prison because of his friendship with Joss; had he known the truth, he would not have taken Joanna to her.

The thought that Joanna was at this very minute in

Bodrath House made Magnus's skin crawl. Memories of the boxing match with Harry Bodrath – and the reason for the fight – pounded in Magnus's mind like a hammer against an anvil. He didn't know for certain who had killed Harry, but he surely knew the reason. What if Joanna should uncover that dark secret? Wouldn't her life be in danger, too?

He had no choice. Despite her wishes, he couldn't leave her to the sinister mercies of Justin Bodrath. Magnus went back into his cave, having reached a decision.

Late that afternoon he left his boat in a deserted cove and made his way into the village near Traherne Hall. He stopped the first man he met on the lane and asked if he knew where the former schoolmaster Oliver Pentreath, recently married to Adele Traherne, now lived.

The man looked at him curiously. 'Why, he moved up to Traherne Hall with his bride, after Mr Traherne died.'

Thanking the man, he asked for directions.

It was almost dusk when he reached the hall and stood before the wrought-iron gates, in awe of the splendour of Joanna's home. Magnus had known from the start that she was a lady, but he had not imagined that she came from a family as wealthy as this. The gap between their stations in life became a chasm as he surveyed the great house.

He had fought his feelings of tenderness towards Joanna to no avail. After she left the cave, he had experienced a loneliness greater than any he'd ever known, and seeing her again this morning had caused such a rush of feeling that he knew now he was deeply, irrevocably in love with her.

The knowledge brought no joy, only pain, because as he opened the gate and began to walk towards the house, he knew it was a hopeless, impossible love.

13

Megan surveyed herself in her dresser mirror and decided that she looked altogether too excited, girlish, and eager. It wouldn't do to let Quinn know how much she had looked forward to seeing him again. He was coming for dinner tonight at his own request, having sent a note saying he would like to see her and Randolph as he had something important to tell them.

Although she didn't dare speculate about what that something important might be, it was difficult to extinguish the hope that she had been on his mind as much as he'd been on hers. And if so, perhaps . . .

She had never much concerned herself with her looks – Joanna had often gently chided her for her somewhat careless appearance – and in fact she was often as untidy and ink-stained as she had been as a student. During the ocean voyage to America, however, Megan had wielded brush and comb more vigorously and, of course, Quinn had provided her with the kind of wardrobe she never would have purchased for herself, even if she had been able to afford it.

Torn between wanting to look her best and fearing that too much primping would make her feelings for Quinn obvious, she gathered up her hair and snatched it back from her face, pinning it into a fat bun at the back of her head. Several wavy wisps promptly escaped, but she forced them back. That was better; she looked sterner now. But the dress was still too pretty, a vivid jade silk that made her eyes look like enormous emeralds.

Since she had not yet summoned Consuela to help her button the dress, Megan peeled it from her shoulders and went back to the armoire to choose another. The gold taffeta was too bold, she decided. The pale grey shantung would be demure were it not for its décolletage. She certainly didn't want to show off her breasts. A day gown? No, that would be too casual. She finally settled on the grey shantung, but slipped a lace shawl about her shoulders and pinned it over the low-cut bodice.

Her heart beating a little too rapidly, she went down the long, cool corridor towards the dining room, thinking again how very well suited to a man in a bath chair this Spanish-style bungalow was, with its wide halls and arched entrances.

Randolph's wheelchair was pulled into position in front of the roaring fire. The thick adobe walls of the house kept out the day's heat and it was often necessary to have a fire in the evening.

Quinn stood with his back to the fire, a glass in one hand, as he gestured with the other. He was resplendent in a well-cut suit she hadn't seen before, a ruffled shirt, and a bow tie. Randolph was laughing at something Quinn had said.

Quinn's eyes met hers over the top of Randolph's golden head. In that second, as their eyes locked, she felt her heart thump madly and her knees grow weak. Never, ever before had a man had this effect on her. He looked foreign, a little menacing, overpoweringly male. Until Quinn appeared in her life Megan had never given much thought to her own femininity, except to bewail the fact that it kept her out of most medical schools, but now she was aware of every single nerve and vein in her body.

Randolph swivelled around and saw her. 'Ah, Joanna! How lovely you look.'

'In spite of the matronly hairstyle,' Quinn added, grinning as if he knew of her inner turmoil.

'Now, Quinn,' Randolph admonished, 'don't go riling my dearest penfriend and most treasured houseguest.'

'Your *only* penfriend and houseguest,' Megan said, smiling as she approached.

'Besides, with hair the colour of a brand-new copper penny, there isn't much you can do to make it unattractive,' Randolph added. He reached out to her in his customary greeting after they had been apart, if only for minutes, and she slipped her hand into his.

The gesture did not go unnoticed by Quinn.

Randolph looked up at her with an expression of such joy that Megan felt humbled and more than a little uneasy. If Quinn had come to tell her he loved her, she knew she would leave with him. How would Randolph react? Surely it would be better to go now, before he had grown too accustomed to having her here.

Somewhere nearby Quinn murmured something about a glass of wine, or would she prefer whisky?

She withdrew her hand from Randolph's and sat in the fireside chair closest to him. 'Wine, thank you.'

As he walked over to the liquor cabinet, Quinn said, 'When I first met the Mallorys, I was surprised that they lived in this genuine hacienda surrounded by Mexican and Indian furniture and artifacts. Their bunkhouses were filled with some of the toughest hombres this side of the Pecos, and yet the family observed many European customs. Wine drinking and dressing for dinner, for instance. Randolph's father was something of a roughneck, but he married a cultured woman.'

Randolph glanced at Quinn curiously. 'My mother and Joanna's mother were cousins. She's well aware of my parentage, Quinn.'

Quinn covered the slip smoothly. 'I was about to say that it's almost like old times, having another cultured Englishwoman here.'

Randolph said, 'Over the years you've done a lot for me, Quinn, but nothing to equal the wondrous gift of bringing Joanna here.'

Quinn's eyes flickered over Megan's face and he raised his glass. 'Here's to friendship.'

Yes, Megan thought, relieved, of course! She and Quinn could still be friends with Randolph.

'Quinn was just telling me about a family of skunks that took up residence at the Diamond T during his absence in England,' Randolph said to Megan.

'I had to buy new clothes for tonight,' Quinn said. 'The smelly critters had sprayed everything in the house. Before I routed 'em, they even got the clothes I had with me on the trip.'

'Skunks?' Megan asked.

'I forgot,' Quinn said. 'You don't have them in England.' He described the animals briefly, then added, 'By the way, Randolph, there's a grizzly in the area. I saw his tracks yesterday, and he got one of the Diamond T cows. Better warn your hands.'

They settled down to dinner and Megan resolved to sit quietly and let the men dominate the conversation, as Joanna would have done. Quinn spoke of road agents on the loose and fears in town that a war party of Apache might have broken out of the reservation and headed their way. Then, almost in the same breath, he spoke of an opera company coming to perform in Silver City and how an expensive orchestra imported from San Francisco was playing at one of the saloons.

The exhilarating mixture of stalking danger and imminent culture that came together on this raw frontier fascinated Megan. Despite her resolve, she found herself asking questions and offering opinions. She wanted to know when New Mexico might become a state, and who paid for expensive orchestras and opera companies. What about schools, hospitals? Newspapers? Politics?

'Why, Joanna,' Randolph said, his expression one of amazement. 'I had no idea you were interested in such things. I got the impression from your letters that you were happier to remain inside the walls of your father's estate and leave the rest of the world to its own follies.'

Quinn's dark eyes flashed her a warning glance. 'I'm sure it's the novelty of her first venture out of England.'

Megan murmured, 'I don't know what's come over me. I was always painfully shy, and as you say, I much preferred solitude to social contact.' The accurate description of Joanna sprang easily to Megan's lips and she added lightly, 'Perhaps your wonderful New Mexico air has affected me.'

Quinn rose. 'I've eaten far too much. Why don't we go for a walk? It's a fine clear night but cold. We'll need coats and a blanket for Randolph –'

'No,' Randolph said at once. 'I'd rather not go outside. The night air seems to give me phantom pains in my legs. You two go.'

They both protested, but he insisted. 'Go, or you'll make me feel guilty. I'll sit by the fire and finish the last chapter of Robert Louis Stevenson's new book.'

'Randolph –' Megan began.

'Please, Joanna. You've been cooped up with me and hauled around in the buckboard . . . Why, you haven't even been riding since you arrived. There's no need to pretend your limbs are useless just because mine are. Go for a moonlight stroll with Quinn. I want you two to be the best of friends.'

Quinn gave a how-can-we-argue gesture, and Megan, her pulse racing at the prospect of being alone with him, nodded. They didn't speak until they had walked some distance from the house. Then Quinn said, 'Do you think he suspects that you're not Joanna?'

'No, but I feel terrible for deceiving him. He's the sweetest, kindest man I've ever known. I considered breaking my word to you and telling him the truth – but I couldn't do it. He would be heartbroken to learn Jo is dead. We have to find a gentle way to –'

'He's besotted by you. But you know that. Joanna's letters were only the foundation. An equal part of his love belongs only to you. To the way you look, move, laugh. You're a very animated young woman, exciting to be with.'

'I'm surprised to hear compliments from you.' Her heart-beat had speeded up again. He was expressing his own feelings for her, she was sure.

They had reached a grove of cottonwoods along a shallow stream that flowed swiftly over smooth rocks. Quinn stopped suddenly, caught her by the shoulders, and turned her to face him.

'He's going to ask you to marry him. He told me so tonight. He believes you've accepted his paralysis and that he has a chance of winning your affection. He's living in a fool's paradise, convinced that the romantic, idealised love expressed in your correspondence will be enough to sustain a marriage.'

She could hear Quinn's torment now; it was in his voice, in his self-accusing tone. He regretted the masquerade, wanted her for himself. Perversely she felt the need to rub salt into his wound. 'But wasn't this your plan from the very start? To bring Joanna here to be Randolph's wife? Tell me, why. *Why*?'

His hands fell from her shoulders. 'Because I feel a certain responsibility for him, because I care what happens to him, and because he was turning into a recluse. Aside from Consuela and his foreman, he talked to no one but me. He never left the ranch; some days he never left his room. He'd already entombed himself. He was sinking deeper and deeper into depression. He loved a woman he'd never met, but he was afraid to meet her. I thought he might kill himself when Joanna wrote that she was going to marry Oliver. Fortunately the next mail brought the invitation to Oliver's marriage to her sister and the news that Joanna had been jilted.'

Megan was silent for a moment. Then she asked quietly, 'Are you saying that you think now you made a mistake? That you shouldn't have brought me here and that it would be wrong for me to marry him?'

'I'm telling you that if you accept his proposal, you'd better recognise from the start what kind of a marriage you'll have. Because if you commit yourself to it, there'll be no turning back. Any hopes and dreams Megan Thomas may have had will have to be forgotten.'

'I wanted to be a doctor,' Megan said, 'But I couldn't

111

go to medical school because I had to take care of my grandfather. I hoped once I arrived in America I might be able to go to Galveston and find my father . . . but the chances that he's still alive are very slim, and even if he is, how could I find him? This country is so vast, it's beyond imagining. I hoped some day to return to England and prove that I didn't kill my best friend. Yet that, too, seems impossible. My hopes and dreams are unattainable. It's time for me to accept that and go on with my life.'

'You'll marry Randolph?'

She looked up at him. One side of his face was lit by a beam of moonlight that penetrated the canopy of cotton-wood leaves. A bold face, unafraid, ready to take on anything life presented. He stood erect, broad-shouldered, strong. He would never withdraw from the world, he would always rush at life headlong and savour every moment of it, good and bad. How exciting it would be to journey through life with such a man! At his side perhaps her own dreams could still come true.

His arms were curved slightly at his sides and she had a sudden urge to feel them around her, to be pulled close to him, and to have him kiss her again as he had the night they arrived, just before he suggested they call off the masquerade. Oh, why hadn't she agreed then, while there was still time to spare Randolph's feelings? In retrospect it seemed likely that only her curiosity about Randolph Mallory had driven her on, because hadn't she, even then, felt this magnetic physical attraction for Quinn?

'I can't marry Randolph,' she answered, her voice low, husky with the passion she felt. Suddenly all of nature conspired against her – the moonlit evening, the sweetly pungent scent of sagebrush, the murmur of the stream, but most of all the nearness of this man, who had been on her mind waking and sleeping. Caution forgotten, she stood on tiptoe and flung her arms around his neck. 'I don't know how or why it happened, but . . . I love you '

Her fingers tangled in the smooth thick hair at the back

of his neck, and she pulled his face down so that their mouths could meet.

For an instant the kiss was a hungry, breathless blending of warm lips, hot breath, a pent-up need that throbbed through every nerve in her body. His hands slipped under her coat, and she felt his strong fingers encircle her waist, burning through the thin material of her gown to the flesh beneath, which in turn seemed to pulse with new energy. She felt as though she were on the brink of some incredible discovery, the unlocking of some inner core of her being to which only Quinn held the key.

Then, abruptly, his mouth grew slack and he pushed her away from him. She swayed on her feet, bewildered.

When he spoke, his voice was strained, despite its harsh edge. 'You don't know what you're doing . . . or saying. You've spent your whole life in a little Welsh village, insulated from the world by an old man who taught you all about healing broken bodies and nothing about human nature. You're only weeks out of that cocoon. For all your cocky courage, you're still an ingenue. What do you know of the world, or of men?'

'You said I was beautiful,' Megan whispered, hating the desperation she heard creeping into her voice. 'You said I was exciting to be with . . .'

'And so you are. And, yes, I want you. A part of me wants to push you down in the grass right now and take you. There was a time when I would have, with never a moment's regret. But I won't do that to Randolph. For me you'd be a moment's pleasure; for him you represent the rest of his life.'

Megan felt as though he had slapped her. Somewhere in the pit of her stomach a seed of realisation began to sprout. She had committed woman's ultimate folly. Oh, God, she had thrown herself at a man who didn't care for her! How could she have been so foolish as to speak first? It was not the female prerogative to declare love; it never had been. Women were the chosen, never the choosers.

'You shouldn't have said those things to me. You

shouldn't have kissed me,' she whispered, thankful for the concealing darkness that hid her flaming cheeks.

'I said only what Randolph would have told you if he could have gathered his courage.'

'What gives you the right to be his voice?'

'Whatever little I can do for Randolph will never be enough to repay my debt to him. Good God, hasn't he told you?'

'Told me what?'

'It's my fault his parents are dead. It's my fault he can't walk.'

Megan gasped. 'What do you mean . . . your fault?'

'Exactly what I say. Come on, we're going back. I haven't given Randolph my own news yet.'

Grasping her arm, he propelled her, not gently, back along the pathway to the house.

'Aren't you going to tell me what happened? Why you feel you were responsible?'

'No. If Randolph wants you to know, he'll tell you.'

They reached the house and went inside. Megan blinked in the sudden glow of lamp and firelight. Randolph said something; she was unsure what. Her emotions seemed to roar in her ears.

Then Quinn said, 'I can see you two have established a real fine friendship here and I'm glad, because I'm going away.'

'Away? From the Diamond T?' Randolph asked. 'I thought you were happy there.'

'It was all right, for a while. But I never intended to settle down. I've been here longer than any other place. No, I'm through ranching. When I was in England I told the owner I wanted to quit, and he asked me to find a replacement. I found that man yesterday, and so I'll be hitting the trail tomorrow.'

14

'You're very quiet this evening,' Randolph said the next night at dinner.

Megan's scarcely touched dinner had congealed in a pool of scarlet salsa on her plate. The last rays of the setting sun painted vermilion stripes across the atrium adjacent to the dining room, adding to the red haze that blurred her vision.

At the sound of Randolph's voice, she started, abruptly recalled from her silent reverie.

'If you're concerned that your arrival here caused Quinn to leave,' he continued, 'consider that he must have made plans before he left for England. He did say he'd told the owner of the Diamond T of his intentions.'

'What makes you think I would be concerned about Quinn?'

'Your sensitivity, Joanna. You're worried that you may have come between two friends. I sensed the friction between you and Quinn the moment you arrived. I even wondered if it had its origins in . . . well, if he'd somehow tricked you into coming here. But of course, he'd never do such a thing, and I realised that, like the true friend he is, he's been hanging around here even though he wanted to move on long ago. He feels he can go with a clear conscience now because I have you for company.'

Megan's feelings were less about Quinn than about her own stupid declaration of love to him. If only she could take it back! How would she ever be able to face him again?

Randolph reached across the table, turned his hand palm upward. 'Give me your hand, Joanna.'

Megan placed her hand in his, but did not feel comforted as his fingers closed around hers. He used his arms and hands a great deal, gesturing, touching, as though to compensate for the lack of movement and feeling in his legs. She looked at him, wondering if the extent of her misery shone from her eyes.

'It's time we discussed the future,' Randolph said. 'Our future.'

Megan waited, detached – seeing, hearing, but curiously uninvolved, as though he really were addressing her dead friend Joanna, using her as a medium.

'We've carefully avoided talking about Oliver or Adele, or your parents,' he said. 'I thought perhaps you'd want to send a wire to your family that you'd arrived safely. Since you haven't mentioned them, I wonder if the whole Oliver business caused an estrangement between you and your parents and sister.'

'I . . . sent them a cable from New York –' Megan began. 'No, that isn't true. Randolph, I can't lie to you.'

His fingers tightened on hers. 'Please, Joanna, don't say anything else until you hear what I have to say. What happened back in Cornwall is over. When you wrote to me of your despair, when you begged me to come and take you away, I swear I would have, if I could have. But I couldn't bring myself to tell you the real reason I couldn't come. I had no idea that Quinn would go to Cornwall or I would have asked him to tell you everything that I was too cowardly to put into a letter. But, good friend that he is, he sought you out anyway.'

'Randolph, I –'

'Please hear me out. I knew, when you came back with him, that you had come to America to start a new life. Joanna, you must have guessed from my letters that I grew to care for you . . . no, more than that, to love you with all my heart. I loved you before I ever met you. I fell in love with the woman who penned all those wonderful

116

letters to me. Then when you walked into my house, you took my breath away with your beauty. I would never ask for anything else from life if you'd stay with me, share my home, my life . . . Joanna, will you marry me?'

She had anticipated this moment. She knew that Randolph was not seeing the real Megan Thomas. This soft-spoken, subservient creature was an invention. He was seeing Joanna's soul in her body, but how long could she hide the real Megan . . . the woman who appalled so many men? Opinionated, bossy, ambitious, everything men hated in a woman? The woman who had sent Quinn running?

But as she looked into Randolph's devoted eyes, all of her rehearsed refusals seemed inadequate and she faltered.

'Joanna, don't answer for a moment. Although I expect no disclosures from you, in fact do not want to hear any, there are some things I must tell you. I know I can't be a husband to you in the real sense of the word, but I can offer you companionship, a devoted heart, and financial security. In addition to the ranch, my parents left me a copper mine, and my grandparents left me shares in several eastern companies, one of which is a railroad. If you will be my wife, there is nothing in the world that you can't have, including complete freedom to go anywhere you choose. I shan't expect you to stay here at the ranch with me all the time. Just knowing you'll be coming home to me will be enough.'

Megan felt tears well up and she blinked. How easy it would be to say 'Yes, I'll marry you.' And who would be hurt if she did? Certainly not poor dead Joanna, or Quinn, who would probably never return for fear she might throw herself at him again. Still she hesitated, worried about the foundation of deception on which such a marriage would be built.

She drew a deep breath. 'Randolph, you asked me earlier if I was worried that I might have caused Quinn to leave. There is something about your friendship that

117

concerns me. He told me it was his fault that your parents are dead and you are in that chair. Is that true?'

A veil of remembered pain descended over his eyes, creating indigo shadows. Megan looked at his handsome face and recalled something Joanna had said once, about mortals who were so perfect in mind and body that the gods became envious and punished them.

'Joanna, don't ask me to go into detail about what happened. It was an accident that Quinn never meant to happen. You don't need to know any more than that. Quinn will be back to see us one of these days, and I don't want to tell you anything to cause you to dislike him any more than you do already.'

'I don't dislike Quinn. It's he who doesn't like me.'

'I'm sure that whatever happened between you was only a misunderstanding. But, Joanna, please, I don't want to know what you think about him. Tell me how you feel about me, about the prospect of being my wife.'

'Randolph, I . . . I'm afraid I don't love you.'

He studied her hand, curled in his. 'It doesn't matter. I love you enough for both of us. The greater gift is mine. It's far more enjoyable to love than to be loved, you know. If you care for me at all – and I know you do from your letters –'

'I'm not . . .' Oh, God, she had almost blurted out that she was not Joanna. She couldn't do that to him, not now, not after Quinn had deserted him; he couldn't lose Joanna, too. 'I'm not the same person who wrote those letters,' she finished lamely. 'I changed . . . after Oliver married Adele. But I do like you very much, and I've been happy here with you. If that's enough for you . . .'

His smile of joy flooded his face. 'Oh, it is, it is. There's a preacher in Manzanita Flats who'll come out here to perform the ceremony. You don't mind if it's a quiet affair?'

In a daze Megan listened to the plans for her wedding, which was to take place within the month.

*   *   *

118

In the Blue Goose saloon in Silver City Quinn regarded his hand, queens over jacks, and doubled his bet. Although it was still hours until sundown, gamblers sat behind stacks of silver and bags of nugget ore. Most of them had guns strapped to their sides.

The orchestra from San Francisco played in the background as money seemed to float in the air, changing hands, wafting back and forth. He'd almost forgotten how eager miners and cowpokes sometimes were to part with their money.

Lallie Kendall, perkiest of the Blue Goose girls, a strawberry blonde with innocent china-doll blue eyes and a fashionable hourglass figure, moved in beside him and rested her hand on his shoulder. She knew better than to talk while the game was in progress, but she was obviously bursting to impart some news or gossip – or perhaps she wanted to hear about Quinn's trip to England. As he waited for the other bets to be placed, Quinn concentrated on his cards, knowing where his mind would take him if he allowed it to wander. Back to a red-haired Welsh woman with fire in her eyes and a complete lack of feminine wiles, a woman he found both supremely appealing and utterly exasperating.

His full house prevailed, and, tiring of poker, he picked up his winnings. Lallie followed him to the bar, one plump arm tucked into the crook of his elbow. 'Took your sweet old time comin' to see us, Quinn. I heard you been back from Europe more'n a week now. What was it like? And what's all this I've been hearing about you leaving the Diamond T? Listen, have I got news for you – I'm getting my own place.'

The bartender placed two glasses of whisky in front of them and Quinn drained his. 'Your own place, Lallie? Where?'

'Manzanita Flats. I got me – what d'you call it? – some backers. They're building my very own place for me. Gonna have chandeliers and everything.'

'Manzanita Flats? You think you'll get much business there? It's kinda off the beaten track, isn't it?'

'Not anymore. Railroad's coming in. Ain't you heard? The Diamond T and the Mallory ranch will be able to put their cattle right on the train. No more driving the herds north. Heck, Quinn, why are you pullin' up stakes now, just when we're getting civilised around here?'

She laid her hand on his arm and looked up at him with a little-girl smile. 'You wanna go upstairs?'

Before he could reply, a man burst into the saloon calling for volunteers to form a posse. 'It's the Chiricahua Kid,' he yelled. 'The army's chasing him in the south, but he just killed a family not more than three miles from town.'

An uproar broke out as men hastily gathered up their winnings and rushed out into the street. Quinn remained at the bar. 'Who the hell is the Chiricahua Kid?'

'They don't know for sure he's a Chiricahua,' the bartender said. 'That's just a name the army hung onto some redskin renegade. Nobody knows where he come from. But all the signs he leaves say Apache.'

Quinn thought about Randolph and Megan out at the Mallory ranch. But there were plenty of hands to protect them and he had warned them he'd heard there were renegade Indians running loose.

'You going with the posse, Quinn?' Lallie asked.

'No. They've got too many men as it is. Any redskin worth his salt will hear 'em coming miles off.'

He was glad to leave the Blue Goose. He disliked being indoors gambling and drinking in a cloud of tobacco smoke while the sun was still shining. But concentrating on the cards was profitable, and it distracted him from attempting to answer unanswerable questions, the first and most compelling of which was why he had lied to Megan about his feelings for her. He told himself that his friend loved and needed her and that he had a debt of honour to settle with Randolph, but he knew that was not sufficient reason to deny his own feelings.

Perhaps, Quinn thought as he climbed into the saddle and rode down the street, Megan herself was the reason he had been unwilling to accept the love she offered. From almost the first instant he met her she had professed two burning ambitions: to find her long-missing father and to become a doctor. Even when she despaired of ever achieving either goal, he sensed in her an unquenchable thirst that would never be slaked. He had to ask himself if he could accept the possibility of her love for him being only a temporary state, a way of filling a void in her life. And if that was the case, what would happen if she found her father and he could somehow get her into medical school? Quinn had no wish to be discarded, even for a few years, in favour of a career. Randolph, on the other hand, would be content to wait patiently at home for Megan. He might even enjoy her absence, since he could write long letters every day, the way he used to do with Joanna. He had seemed to enjoy the correspondence more than the companionship of having Megan live with him.

Several times Quinn had been on the point of riding out to see Megan, wanting to talk about her ambitions, about the possibility that she might want to return to England. He wanted to say 'I love you, but I need all of you, all the time,' but his pride wouldn't allow that kind of confession.

Waiting in Silver City for Doc Sedgewick to arrive didn't help Quinn. The town was too damn close to her. But Quinn had never failed to respond to a call for help from a friend, and once again Sedge, an old friend from Quinn's army days, was in trouble. The irony of Sedge having what Megan desired so desperately – a medical diploma – was not lost on Quinn. Not that Sedge's license to practice did him any good. Nobody in the territory would trust him to treat them.

Feeling a desperate need to be alone, Megan slipped out of the house as the sun climbed high in the sky and a lazy midday heat settled upon the countryside. Most of the hands were eating, and Randolph was closeted in his office with Chuck, discussing ranch business.

She felt uncomfortable whenever the lanky foreman with skin like old leather appeared. His faded grey eyes

121

rarely met hers and apart from an occasional 'Yes, ma'am' or 'No, ma'am,' he seemed oblivious to her presence, as though if he ignored her she might go away.

Most of the previous night she had lain awake, assailed by doubts about the wisdom of her decision to marry Randolph, cringing inwardly each time she remembered declaring her feelings to Quinn.

Walking briskly down the path beaten into the meadow surrounding the corrals, she headed towards the dense growth of cottonwoods lining the river, wanting to be out of sight of the house as quickly as possible.

It was cool in the shade of the trees, and the sound of running water brought a sense of peace. She continued to walk, not worrying about getting lost, since she knew she could merely follow the river back to the house.

At home in north Wales she had often walked for miles. She enjoyed being alone with nature again, feeling the earth beneath her feet and smelling the fresh scent of leaves and grasses in her nostrils. She had time to be alone with her thoughts, or not to think at all if she chose, merely to savour the sun-warmed solitude.

But all at once the riverbank became too densely overgrown and rock-strewn for walking, and she was forced to detour away from the water.

In a surprisingly short period of time she could no longer hear the sound of running water and, attempting to retrace her steps, found herself plunging ever deeper into a maze of ferns and saplings until she came to a barrier of rocks.

She was in a narrow glen, a dense canopy of interwoven branches overhead and a carpet of humus under her feet. The cathedral-like silence was broken only by the buzzing of insects and the chattering of birds.

'Oh, Megan,' she said aloud, exasperated at herself. She couldn't be lost. All she had to do was go back to the point near the river where she had detoured inland, then follow the water back to the house. But where was the river?

The countryside here was so different from Wales. There she would simply have walked until she came to a lane, or she could have climbed a hill to get her bearings. She'd never be far from a village or a farm or some recognisable land-mark. But in this wild country there were no lanes, and it was miles to the next ranch, while the sparse settlements were hours or even days away by horse or buckboard. A vast emptiness claimed the western part of América; the land did not yet belong to the few settlers who had braved incredible hardships in order to build homes here.

She was about to go back to the gap in the bushes through which she had entered the glen when she heard the sound of snapping branches. Someone was moving down the same trail she had taken.

At first she felt relief, thinking that someone had come looking for her. But then she realised it was too soon for her to have been missed – and whatever was coming down the trail was making too much noise to be a man.

A fetid animal odour drifted in on a stirring of air, and something large crashed through the undergrowth towards her.

She realised, panicking, that behind her was a sheer wall of rock she couldn't possibly climb.

Then, no more than ten feet away, a bear emerged from the brush and, seeing her, uttered a heart-stopping snarl and rose up on its hind legs.

15

Joanna's fingers had cramped around the pen, and she laid it on the desk in order to rub her hands together. The closely written page of the Bodrath journal danced in front of her eyes.

The study had grown cold as dawn approached, and her desk sat in a window alcove some distance from the fireplace. Justin, bundled in woollen cardigans and shawls, sat near the dying embers of the fire. Without turning his head to look at her, he asked, 'Have you finished?'

She'd noticed before that his hearing was extremely sensitive. No doubt he'd heard the pen touching the wooden desk. 'Not yet. I have writer's cramp.'

'The typewriting machine I ordered should arrive tomorrow.'

'I do hope I shall be able to learn how to use it.'

'Of course you will. As it is, the work is progressing far too slowly.'

'But we only started the actual writing a few days . . . nights ago.'

'Yes, yes, but I think perhaps we're going about the whole thing the wrong way. Instead of beginning when the Bodraths acquired the estate, I believe it would be more interesting to tell the saga backwards, as it were.'

'Backwards?'

'Start with the present. With myself, the last of the Bodraths, and how I came to be in this situation.'

As usual, he was holding a metal box on his lap. He tapped the box with one finger, as if it contained the answer to a riddle.

Each evening when they entered the study, Justin unlocked one of the wooden cabinets that lined the walls and produced bundles of letters, diaries, and musty documents. He handed them to Joanna, who sorted through the material and extracted the information needed for the Bodrath journal. He always took that small metal box out of the cabinet, but he did not give it to her. Once she saw him go to a brass plaque on the wall and open it to reveal several keys hanging from hooks inside. He used one of the keys to unlock the metal box, but he did not open it.

He continued. 'Yes, that's the way to go about it. Might as well exorcise all the demons first, though it will be

124

painful to have to write of Harry –' He broke off, coughing.

After a moment he was silent. Joanna picked up her pen and resumed writing. The work helped direct her thoughts away from the tragedy of her father's sudden death. It worried her that instead of grieving she found herself unable to believe that her father truly was dead, although she knew Delta and Magnus had no reason to lie. She wondered if the fact that her father had always been a rather distant and unapproachable figure had something to do with her present lack of emotion regarding his death.

'Perhaps when you've finished the Bodrath journal,' Justin said minutes later, 'you might write the story of the mysterious Joanna Smith.'

'It would make dull reading, I'm afraid,' Joanna said carefully, something in his voice warning her to beware.

'Dear child. I know that you have secrets to keep hidden. That is what made you perfect for the task of recording the Bodrath secrets. Your own past precludes your prematurely revealing ours. The Bodrath journal, you see, will never be read by anyone but you during my lifetime, which will, of course, shortly be coming to an end.'

'Please don't say that, Mr Bodrath.'

'But it's true. Oh, the physicians say that if I were to move to a warmer climate – Italy, perhaps – I might live an extra few months. But I should hate to die anywhere but here. I merely mention this fact in order to remind you not to discuss the journal with anyone except me – especially when we begin to write about Harry –'

He began to cough again. The paroxysm intensified, and he clapped his handkerchief to his lips.

Joanna hastily rose and poured him a glass of water, but when she offered it he shook his head and pointed to the bell cord, indicating that she was to summon Paxton. The burly butler would carry his frail master up to his bed, and no more work would be done tonight, since Justin insisted that she write the journal only when he was present. When the night's work ended the study was locked. Justin kept the keys fastened to his watch chain.

As usual, a simple meal had been laid out for her in the breakfast room, and as she sipped cocoa and nibbled toast, she felt both relief and anticipation. Relief that Paxton had apparently not told his master of her departure from the estate the previous day, and anticipation that when she began to write about Harry Bodrath she might learn something that would prove he was still alive after the boxing match with Magnus.

She had finished breakfast and was on her way to her room when Paxton met her in the hall. 'The typewriting machine has arrived. The salesman is here to explain its use to you. I put him in the library.'

A beaming rotund man waited in the library beside a formidable-looking machine. 'This is the latest model, with the newest arrangement of keys,' he explained. 'As you'll see, the back is hinged so you can swing the carriage up to see what you've written. You return it by depressing this foot pedal on the floor.'

Joanna gazed at rows of keys, one for each lower-case letter and one for each capital, in addition to separate keys for several other characters, and found to her surprise that she was less intimidated by the machine than excited at the prospect of learning to use it. It seemed to be a harbinger of the future, her own as well as that of all the businesses and professions that would be affected by it.

'A fad, I'm sure,' Paxton said disdainfully. She jumped, not realising he had followed her to the library. 'And a noisy one, to be sure. It's a good thing the house is solidly built, or the clattering would probably keep us all awake at night.'

The salesman rolled a sheet of paper into the machine. 'Perhaps you'd like to try it, miss?'

Joanna cautiously struck several keys.

'I didn't think the master would go this far,' Paxton said. 'I believed by now he would have tired of the idea of writing a journal and sent you packing.'

Joanna watched, fascinated, as the salesman raised the carriage and showed her she had typed the word Harry.

Paxton read it, too, and frowned. 'You do realise how ill Mr Justin is? Are you aware that terminally ill people often indulge in wild flights of fantasy?'

'Is that so?' Joanna murmured.

'Quite so. I shouldn't pay too much heed to anything he tells you.'

Joanna looked up at him. 'I am an amanuensis. It isn't my place to make judgements about my employer's state of mind.'

He flushed and she realised he had taken her remark as a chastisement. She was amazed by her own temerity when she did not make haste to apologise to him. One of Megan's exasperated remarks echoed again in her mind: 'Oh, Jo, must you let every man you meet wipe his feet on the back of your neck?' Megan would be proud of the way she was learning to stand up for herself. She couldn't wait to find out where Meg was so that she could write to her.

Magnus presented himself at the tradesmen's entrance to Traherne Hall. The footman who answered the bell hesitated for a moment, then evidently decided that Magnus was too formidable to argue with, and invited him to wait in the kitchen.

Twisting his cloth cap in his hand, Magnus tried to ignore the stares and giggles of the scullery maids and the ferocious scowl of the cook. Although he had asked to speak with Mr Oliver Pentreath, he expected the footman would probably fetch the butler instead.

Magnus had never questioned Joanna about the old woman who had tried to bury her alive in the woods. He had assumed that the hag was a villager who performed illegal operations. Every village had a woman who took care of such problems with potions or scalding hot baths or by tightly binding the pregnant woman's abdomen or by pounding her with heavy objects. And if none of those tactics worked, the woman would insert a variety of instruments into the womb. Death by bungled abortion was not an uncommon occurrence.

The kitchen door opened and the footman returned. Magnus caught his breath as he looked at the woman who accompanied the footman. It was the same old witch who had pulled branches and bracken over Joanna and left her for dead.

She surveyed Magnus with narrowed eyes and pursed lips. 'I am Mrs Elliot, the housekeeper here. State your name and business, please.'

'My name doesn't matter. I have a message for Mr Oliver Pentreath, and I'm to give it to nobody but him.'

She held out a mottled hand. 'I'll see he gets it.'

'It's not written down. I'm to tell him something.'

A sound like the hiss of escaping steam came from her thin lips. 'And what makes you think Mr Pentreath will deign to see the likes of you?'

Magnus racked his brain for something of sufficient urgency to cause Pentreath to see him. He would have to be careful not to give away to this woman that it concerned Joanna. 'Tell him . . . it's a matter of life and death.'

'Whose life and death?'

'A . . . lad who used to be one of his pupils . . . Please, Mrs Elliot.'

She sniffed. 'The family will be coming down for dinner soon. I may or may not mention it. What's the boy's name?'

'He won't remember it, probably,' Magnus answered hoarsely. 'Joe . . . Joseph, a frail lad, he is.' Would Oliver Pentreath connect the name Jo with Joanna? Probably not, since he believed Joanna was dead.

Magnus spent two hours in a corner of the kitchen, sweat beading on his forehead, wondering every time the door opened if it would bring Pentreath or the police.

When he thought he could no longer stand the tension, the door opened and a man in evening clothes entered the kitchen. He was slightly built, with smooth dark hair and soulful eyes. He had a vaguely scholarly air, and Magnus

128

thought perhaps women might be drawn to his rather mournful countenance, which suggested that of a tormented poet.

So this was the man to whom Joanna had given all of herself, her love and trust. Magnus resisted an urge to pick up Oliver Pentreath and hurl him across the stone-flagged kitchen.

Rising to his feet, Magnus said, 'If you're Oliver Pentreath, we'd better talk in private.'

Oliver hesitated, nervously eyeing the tall and muscular body of Magnus, his battered features and worn clothing, then without a word turned and walked back through the inner door. Magnus followed him into a small office that probably was used by either the butler or the housekeeper. Oliver closed the door. 'Well?'

'Joanna Traherne isn't dead. I know where she is. She needs someone to take care of her. I thought, since her father has passed away, I should come to you.'

Oliver drew in his breath sharply. 'You're sure it's she?'

'Oh, yes.'

'I wondered why we never found her body. Where is she? Is she . . . all right?'

'She didn't have your child, if that's what you're asking, but she damn near died when she lost it.'

Oliver turned ashen. He sank down on the nearest chair, hand clapped to his forehead. 'Oh, God! I didn't know . . .'

Magnus cursed himself for speaking without thinking and at the same time almost, but not quite, felt pity for the man. Evidently Joanna had not told him of her pregnancy. Perhaps Oliver Pentreath was guilty only of being fickle, not callous.

'Look, I can't hang about here,' Magnus said. 'Joanna – she calls herself Joanna Smith – has taken a position with Justin Bodrath. I daresay you've heard the name.'

Oliver looked up sharply, as though seeing Magnus for the first time. 'I have indeed. His brother was murdered . . .' His voice trailed away and Magnus wondered if he was now connecting the broken nose and cauliflower ear with his former profession and recalling that Harry Bodrath supposedly died in a boxing match. If so . . .

'Joanna was very ill,' Magnus explained. 'When she recovered she was afraid to come home, because her parents knew she was with child. They found out about it on the day of your wedding to her sister. Lucky for you they didn't know who the father was. Then when we heard her father had died suddenly . . . well, she blames herself for that, I think.'

'And so does her stepmother,' Oliver murmured. 'It wouldn't be a good idea for Joanna to come here for a while.'

'She wouldn't anyway. But there's something else you'd better know. The woman who got rid of the child for her also tried to bury Joanna alive in the woods. That woman is the housekeeper here, Mrs Elliot. I expect she was trying to bury the evidence of her crime.'

Oliver had turned a sickly green. He cleared his throat, tugged at his collar, but did not comment.

Magnus shifted his weight, anxious to leave. 'Joanna hopes to get in touch with her friend Megan Thomas. Do you know her address?'

'No, I don't. She was here for our wedding but left rather abruptly afterwards. Is she . . . is Joanna really all right now?' he asked again.

Magnus nodded, considering what to do next. 'You can go and see her at Bodrath House,' Magnus said. 'And perhaps before you go you could make some inquiries about the whereabouts of Megan Thomas.'

'How did you come to know Miss Traherne, pray tell?'

'That doesn't matter now.'

Oliver's dark eyes had lost their mournful look and acquired a cunning stare. 'Ah, but it does. Obviously you're concerned about her, and you must have helped her in some way. For that, my good man, you shall be

130

rewarded . . . No, I absolutely insist! Stay here. You'll be quite safe. I'll be back in a moment.'

Before Magnus could argue, Oliver was on his feet and through the door with the alacrity of a weasel. Only when Magnus heard the key turn in the lock did the words 'You'll be quite safe' acquire meaning.

He put his shoulder to the solid door, but by the time he battered it down, two grooms waited outside, each pointing a shotgun squarely at his chest.

Awakening to the sound of knocking on her bedroom door, Joanna glanced at the sunlight filtering in through the window shutters and then at her clock. Ten in the morning? Surely Justin could not be summoning her at this hour?

She slipped out of bed, donned a dressing gown, and went to the door. A footman waited on the landing. 'A gentleman here to see you, miss. Says he's your brother-in-law.'

Joanna blinked. Surely, it couldn't be . . .

'He's in the library. Mr Paxton said to fetch you down.'

'Thank you. I'll go to him immediately.'

Her fingers shook as she hastily dressed. Brother-in-law. Sister's husband. *Oliver.* She made her way to the library.

Her first thought, upon seeing Oliver again, was how very small and insignificant he looked. She'd remembered him as taller, sturdier, and much, much more handsome.

He stood in the centre of the room, his hat in his hand, and although he had cast aside his battered tweeds in favour of a tailored suit and a fine linen shirt, she was momentarily taken aback at her complete lack of emotion at the sight of him. He might have been a stranger, rather than a man she had once loved to distraction.

'So it really is you,' he said, quietly.

'Is it true that my father passed away?'

'Yes, I'm sorry. It was very sudden. He didn't suffer.'

She closed her eyes briefly. Then, composing herself, said, 'I was told that Adele and Mother believed that I'm dead, too.'

He glanced away. 'They told all their friends that your death was an accident. That you'd foolishly gone walking alone along the cliff top and fallen into the cove. Since I was informed you are here under an assumed name, I presume you have no intention of returning from the dead. Let me assure you that no one else at Traherne Hall knows your whereabouts.'

'How did you find me?'

'Joanna, how could you have done this terrible thing to your family? We mourned you. We even had a memorial service for you. Do you realise that Adele and I cut short our honeymoon when we heard the false report of your death?'

'How very inconvenient for you,' Joanna murmured.

The sarcasm, unusual for her, was lost on him. He paced back and forth in front of the fireplace for a few seconds, then turned to face her again. 'Can you imagine the terrible guilt I felt? Your stepmother told me she believed you had . . . deliberately jumped from the cliff because I jilted you.'

Oh, dear, you poor thing, Joanna thought, compressing her lips to keep from speaking the thought aloud. She felt rising anger, uncharacteristic for her, at his attitude. Oddly, it occurred to her that she was reacting more like Megan than her own former meekly accepting self.

Listening to Oliver ramble on about what people would think if she suddenly reappeared as if resurrected from the dead, Joanna was thankful that only her parents and Megan knew that she had been carrying Oliver's child when she disappeared. But then he said, 'You should have told me you were in the family way, Joanna. I had a right to know.'

She walked over to the nearest chair and sat down. 'Who told you that? How did you find me?'

'A rather frightening-looking individual came to Traherne Hall. He had the battered face of a pugilist and when he told me you were working for Justin Bodrath I remembered instantly where I had seen my visitor before.

His photograph appeared in the newspaper after he was convicted of beating Harry Bodrath to death. I recalled too that he had escaped from Dartmoor, but was presumed to have perished on the moor. This was some years ago, but I knew I wasn't mistaken. It was the same man.'

Fear clutched Joanna. 'Oh, what a risk he took –'

'*He* took? What about me? I found myself confronting an escaped felon. How on earth did you meet such a man?'

'He saved my life. He's the hermit of Dutchman's Point. He'd been living there peacefully for some time, not bothering anyone. Where is he now?'

Oliver shrugged, his eyes not meeting hers. 'Hiding, I daresay. Joanna . . . I've missed you.'

'Missed me?' she repeated blankly.

He crossed the room and took her hands in his. 'At first I was dazzled by Adele, by her beauty, her gaiety. But . . . oh, God, forgive me for saying it, but there's nothing else to her . . . nothing below the surface. I can't talk to her. She's not interested in anything except clothes and parties. And she's as cold as ice. I've missed your warmth, your passion –'

Shocked, Joanna wrenched her hands free of his grasp. 'Oliver, this is quite improper.'

'Ever since the convict came and told me you were alive, I've been wondering what we could do, searching for a solution,' he went on, a feverish gleam in his eyes. 'I can't do anything about my marriage, of course, since it's a fait accompli. Adele and I have moved into Traherne Hall, and already I feel uncomfortable in it. I'm not sure my uncle did me a favour, leaving me a fortune. At heart I'm still a country schoolmaster, more at home in a cottage. The prospect of the society whirl into which Adele will plunge me as soon as our mourning period is over terrifies me. Even now we have guests and musical evenings constantly. How I long for peace and quiet, for your sweet arms, Joanna –'

'Isn't it a little late for regrets, Oliver?'

'No, no. It's never too late. Don't you see, we've been

given a second chance for happiness? Oh, I'll continue to play the dutiful husband to Adele, but there's no need for you and me to be apart. I'll find a nice little house somewhere and visit you often. You can't return to Traherne Hall, of course, and we'll have to be very discreet. It would be better not to let your stepmother and Adele know you're still alive. They blame you for your father's death, you know.'

'You're suggesting I become your *mistress*?' Joanna asked incredulously.

He ran his hands through his hair in a distracted manner. 'I want you to be my dear love, as you were in the past. My dearest, my feelings towards you are as strong as ever. Don't you understand? I was bewitched by Adele, but the spell is broken. It's you I want.'

'You'd better leave,' Joanna said, her voice shaking with anger.

'I know I hurt you, and I do beg your forgiveness. But please, Joanna, don't let foolish pride keep us apart. You can't possibly stay here, working in an all-male household that has a most sinister reputation.'

'I have nothing further to say to you, Oliver,' Joanna said. 'I'll send a footman to show you out.'

She turned to leave and he called after her, 'You're overcome with emotion. You thought our love affair was over. You need time. Send a message when you're ready to talk to me.'

Joanna had Oliver escorted out, then spent most of the rest of the morning pacing restlessly in her room, exhausted but in too much turmoil to sleep. Although she was angry that Magnus had gone to Oliver, she realised that he had done so out of concern for her and at tremendous risk to himself. She was touched by that.

At last, just before noon, she lay on the bed and drifted off to sleep.

She was awakened by someone shaking her arm and slapping her face, not gently. Opening her eyes she looked up into Delta's livid face.

'Delta! How did you get past the servants?'

Her lovely olive-skinned face was contorted with fear and anger. 'It's all your fault. You did this. Get up, get out of that bed. I'm going to kill you.'

Struggling to come to her senses, Joanna found herself dragged from the bed. 'Did what? What happened?'

'Don't pretend you don't know that Magnus went to your family, to the Trahernes.'

'Please, you're hurting my arm.'

'I'm going to pluck your eyes out of their sockets and your tongue out of your head. I'm going to do to you what they'll do to Magnus.'

Fear clutched Joanna. 'Magnus has been caught?'

'Didn't your fancy man tell you? They locked Magnus up at Traherne Hall and sent to Dartmoor for warders to take him back. They'll surely hang him this time.'

16

In blind terror Megan turned to run back into the glen. Her foot caught on a root and she sprawled on her back among the decaying leaves.

The bear reared over her, so close she could see red pinpoints of light in its eyes and saliva oozing from its jaws. The rank smell of the animal was overpowering.

Her fingers closed around a rock on the ground beside her. She picked it up and hurled it at the bear's head, screaming, 'Go away! Leave me alone!'

The rock caught the bear a glancing blow on the side of his head and he gave a low growl and started towards her again.

She closed her eyes to shut out the horrid vision of approaching death.

There was a whirring sound, then a grunt, followed by a crash. Opening her eyes she saw the bear on the ground, still twitching, a feather-tipped arrow protruding from its neck and a second one from its back.

At the same instant the bushes parted and the archer who had saved her life appeared. He and Megan regarded each other silently.

Megan looked at the first Indian she had ever seen. She was too startled to be afraid or to consider that perhaps she had been spared one kind of death only to face another.

Her first thought in that moment was to marvel at how clean the man's buckskin shirt and leggings were, at how well groomed his shoulder-length black hair was. His eyes were as black as obsidian, and strongly carved cheekbones were balanced by a high forehead, which was bound by a dark red bandanna. He moved noiselessly in high-topped moccasins and, when he was close enough, bent over the bear's carcass and pulled out his arrows.

Megan lay where she had fallen, staring at him in fascination as he carefully cleaned the arrowheads and replaced the arrows in a quiver slung over his shoulder. When he was finished he turned to look at her.

'Do . . . do you understand English?' she asked, her voice a croak. 'Thank you. Thank you for saving my life.'

He continued to stare unblinkingly.

She cleared her throat, wondering how to communicate with him, wondering what his intentions were, wondering if perhaps this was nothing more than a vivid dream. She said again, 'Thank you. I am grateful to you.'

Clasping her hands together, she held them over her heart, then extended her arms towards him, hands open, palms upward, hoping to convey her gratitude.

The Indian reached out, caught one of her hands, and pulled her to her feet. She gasped with surprise, but forced a smile to her lips.

Releasing her hand, he stared for a moment, then

beckoned to her, turned, and moved silently along the narrow path through the undergrowth.

Feeling less threatened by him now, she followed, giving the bear's carcass as wide a berth as the path allowed. Perhaps the Indian was an army scout or some other 'tame' Indian. She felt no fear of him, indeed was sure that nothing ever again could terrify her as much as the bear had.

A short time later she found herself back on the river-bank, at the exact spot where she had lost her way.

The Indian pointed in the direction of the ranch house, then turned to leave.

'Wait – please. May I know your name? Mine is Meg . . . I mean. Joanna. I live at the Mallory ranch.'

The black eyes met hers briefly. 'A-chi-tie.'

Seconds later he was gone. Only the stirring of the branches of a sapling he'd brushed against testified to the fact that he'd been there at all.

Megan hurried back along the riverbank to the house, thankful to be back within the stout adobe walls. Randolph looked up from the book he was reading as she burst, breathless, through the archway leading to the dining room. The table, set for lunch, and Randolph's casual smile of greeting, stopped her headlong rush.

Her walk, her encounter with the bear, and the appear-ance of the Indian – was his name A-chi-tie or did that mean good-bye? – had all taken place in the space of an hour or so, and she realised she had not been missed. She decided it would be foolish to relate what had happened, since doing so would surely result in a ranch hand dogging her footsteps everywhere she went. In the future she would have to remember how closely the wilderness pressed in upon the ranch and be more careful where she walked.

'I bet I know what you've been doing,' Randolph said, wheeling himself towards the dining table. 'You curled up somewhere with a book and forgot about lunch. No, don't look guilty, I understand perfectly. We've been so busy getting to know each other that we haven't had time to read. We must remedy that. I suggest we set aside a period each day when we can indulge ourselves, either together or separately.'

As usual, Megan listened and nodded in agreement. After taking her place at the table, she picked up her water goblet and drank thirstily. Consuela appeared, the yeasty odour of fresh baked rolls preceding her, and behind her was the ranch foreman, Chuck.

Chuck's lanky height and sun-etched features, the complete lack of spare flesh on his body, reminded Megan of rawhide. He could have been any age from thirty to fifty. On the rare occasions when he spoke to her, he usually talked in monosyllables. She was quite sure he had taken a dislike to her on sight, and she wondered what she had done to cause this, but his feelings were evident in his scowling glances and the way he vanished whenever she appeared.

Today, however, he was obviously bursting to speak in her presence. 'Pardon me for barging in, Mr Mallory. But we just got word that the Chiricahua Kid and his gang killed a family between here and Silver City. He may be headed this way. Maybe we should post some extra guards on the stock tonight?'

Randolph turned at once to reassure Megan. 'He wouldn't be likely to attack a ranch of this size – we've too many men – but he might try to take some horses.'

There was a crafty gleam in Chuck's faded eyes as they met Megan's, and she realised that he wanted to frighten her. Before she could comment, he added, 'Mr Mallory is right, ma'am. The farm the Kid attacked was isolated, just a man and his wife and two young 'uns. I hear he –'

'Spare us the details, Chuck,' Randolph interrupted. 'Post extra guards and tell the hands to work in pairs.'

Megan waited until Chuck and Consuela departed before asking, 'Who is the Chiricahua Kid?'

Randolph frowned. 'A redskin renegade. Nobody knows for sure, but it's believed he may be a Chiricahua Apache who didn't go to the Florida reservation with

Geronimo. The Apache are perhaps the most fierce and bloodthirsty of all the tribes. They were the last of the hostiles to fight the settlers, and a few of them are still roaming the territory. They're nomads and it's believed they hide out in the Mexican mountains and occasionally come foraging through Arizona and New Mexico. No need to worry, Joanna, but stay close to the house.'

For a split second Megan considered the possibility that the Chiricahua Kid and A-chi-tie were one and the same, but she decided immediately that it was impossible. Surely the man who had saved her life could not have murdered a woman and her children?

'Too bad Quinn picked this particular time to leave,' Randolph remarked.

'Would you feel safer if he were here?'

His hurt look was quickly masked, but she could have bitten off her tongue at the unthinkingly callous remark. He said, 'With a gun in my hand, Joanna, I am just as capable of defending us as any other man, if it comes down to that. I meant that Quinn is one of the few men who understands the Apache. Quinn was with the Fourth Cavalry when they rounded up Geronimo and his Chiricahuas and shipped them off to Florida. He always said that they were done in by their own people – Apache scouts with the army. Didn't he tell you he was in charge of the scouts?'

'No,' Megan said. 'He told me very little about himself. He talked mostly about you.'

Randolph's expression softened, but there was an ironic twist to his mouth as he commented, 'Selling me to you, no doubt.'

'No,' Megan said quickly. 'His friendship with you is important to him, and it has nothing to do with me.'

As the days passed the fear that the Chiricahua Kid might strike again diminished. One of the Mallory cowboys reported finding the coyote-ravaged carcass of a bear near the river. The bear had been skinned, but no one had seen any hunters on Mallory land.

Two weeks went by, and Randolph asked Megan if she would like to go into Silver City to buy a trousseau.

'Oh, yes, I'd love to go into town,' she said at once. She didn't really need any more clothes, but the prospect of being in a real town with people was irresistible. Apart from Randolph, she saw no one here on the ranch except Consuela, whose English was limited, and the laconic Chuck. On the rare occasions when she addressed the hands, they usually displayed an agony of shyness, regarding her as if she were an alien creature from an unknown land. To make things worse, her conversations with Randolph were becoming increasingly strained, and she often caught him watching her in bewilderment.

'When can we go to Silver City?' she asked.

He looked away. 'I . . . I don't care to go into town, Joanna. Chuck will take you.'

She felt a guilty twinge of relief. A day in town and a respite from affecting Joanna's dulcet tone and bookish manner would be welcome indeed. Her spirits lifted for the first time since Quinn's departure.

'As soon as you've selected the material for your wedding dress and asked the dressmaker when she can have it ready, we'll be able to set the date,' Randolph said, and her spirits sank again.

The following day she climbed aboard the buckboard and, with Chuck at the reins, set off for Silver City. While Chuck went to the bank, picked up the mail, and made some purchases for the ranch, she would go to the dry goods store and buy dress lengths, then visit a dressmaker.

As the buckboard rolled through the lush valley, she glanced sideways at Chuck. 'Have you been with Mr Mallory a long time?'

'Came out west with his father.'

'Ah, so you were here when –'

'He met Mrs Mallory in New York. He had business there and she was visiting. She should've gone back to England. Reckon she thought the territory would have cities like New York. She weren't never happy here. Too

140

lonely for a woman, 'specially one like her. Too refined – "genteel," I guess the word is.'

Megan was curious about the accident, not about Randolph's English mother, but she listened quietly, since Chuck seemed inclined to talk for once.

'She sent for fancy china and such from England, made old man Mallory dress up before he went to the table.' Chuck gave a short laugh. 'Recall one time – before Consuela came – we had this old hombre for a cook and Mrs Mallory got a shipment of goods from Europe – cans of fancy salmon. She threw this big dinner party. Guests from all over the territory. Well, the table was set with her fancy china and all, and she tells the cook he forgot to bring out the salmon. So he goes into the kitchen, couldn't find his can opener, so takes the top off the can with an ax, and brings the can, jagged edges and all, and puts it on her fancy-set table.'

Chuck laughed, relishing the memory, and Megan smiled.

'Still, she stuck it out. I'll give her that,' Chuck went on. 'Though she sure tried to turn Randolph into a sissy. Her and the old man were always at each other's throats over the boy. Then Quinn showed up.' Chuck broke off, scowling, and fell silent.

When he didn't speak again for what seemed like several miles, Megan said, 'I take it you weren't fond of Quinn.'

He glanced at her and for one awful moment Megan wondered if he suspected that she missed Quinn more than a prospective bride should have. But he said, 'I like folks to wear their true colours.'

'I'm not sure I know what you mean.'

'Well, here comes a drifter, a gambler, says he's a drover, done some cowpokin', served in the army.'

'This wasn't true?'

'Sure it was true. Only no drifter ever talked like him or had fancy manners like him. Why, he even picked up one of Mrs Mallory's porcelain vases and told her exactly how old it was and where it come from. Now, Quinn told

141

us plenty about soldiering in the territory and pushing herds north, but he didn't tell one single thing about where he was *before* he showed up here.'

Megan felt herself bridle. 'Many people are reluctant to talk about their past, especially those who migrate here. Why do you find it unusual in Quinn?'

''Cause she thought he was a gentleman and he let her.'

She? Mrs Mallory? 'But you don't think he's a gentleman?'

'Sure didn't act like one with her, did he?'

'You mean . . . Quinn and Mrs Mallory –' Megan was shocked speechless.

'Now, I'm not blaming her. Old man Mallory was a diamond in the rough, didn't know nothing about books and china and such, and Quinn, why, he not only takes the boy under his wing, but he sweet-talks the mother, too. I ain't saying Quinn had it in his mind to . . . you know . . . with her. She was a handsome woman, but a lot older than him. Still, he led her on and that's no lie.'

'And the accident . . . ?'

'We'd been rounding up strays along the Gila River, been gone for a couple of days, come back to find a note from her. She'd gone to the Diamond T, to Quinn. The old man was tired, but he saddled up again and so did Randolph, and off they rode. She'd taken the fancy carriage he had made for her in Silver City. I dunno what happened when they got to the Diamond T. Seems they carried her out to the carriage. The old man was holding her, and Randolph was driving the team . . . bringing her home. Only they lost a wheel and crashed into a gulch. Randolph was thrown clear, but they were trapped inside.'

Megan was aware of the shaking of the buckboard, the sound of the horses' hooves striking the ground, and the warmth of the sun on her back, but she felt cold, numb, and unsure if her sadness was due to sympathy for the Mallorys or her shattered illusions about Quinn.

'So now you know what happens when a man marries the wrong woman,' Chuck said, his voice so deathly quiet that Megan had to strain to hear him over the creaking of the buckboard.

'And maybe, missy, you'd best do some pondering about your own wedding plans.'

17

Joanna glanced at the clock in her bedroom. It was almost eight, still three hours before Justin would appear to begin the night's work.

By now her letter should have been delivered by Delta's messenger to Traherne Hall, with instructions to give it to no one but Oliver. She prayed it would reach him before the arrival of warders from Dartmoor to take Magnus into custody. She dared not contemplate what his fate might be if he was returned to that dreaded place, since escape would be added to his previous conviction.

She had written, 'My dear Oliver, if you will see to it that your prisoner is set free immediately, I will agree to the arrangement you proposed to me this morning. As ever, J.'

Her hands felt icy cold as she reached for the doorknob, and she hesitated before stepping out on the landing. If she was ever going to get into that locked box in the study, it had to be tonight.

Taking a deep breath, she left the sanctuary of her room and made her way along the upper gallery towards the east wing of the house, where Justin's bedroom and private sitting room were situated. The portraits of the warrior Bodraths silently observed her progress along the dimly lit hall.

A pair of oil lamps in wall sconces flanking one door suggested that this might be Justin's room. She stood outside, listening. No sound penetrated the heavy oak door.

Heart hammering, she slowly turned the knob and pushed the door open. The moon had risen, sending fingers of pale silver light through the narrow shutterless windows.

A curtained four-poster bed stood in the centre of the room, and the sound of laboured breathing testified to the fact that Justin was asleep behind those curtains.

Joanna looked around. Like the rest of the house, the room was spartan, furnished with only the necessities – the bed, a carved mahogany wardrobe, a chest of drawers. A door on the opposite wall undoubtedly led to a dressing room that contained the washstand.

Holding her breath, she crossed the room swiftly to the chest of drawers. Justin's gold watch chain, to which the keys to the study were attached, was not on the valet tray. She slid out the top drawer. There were no keys in it, or in any of the other drawers.

She tiptoed into the dressing room. A marble-topped washstand holding a porcelain pitcher and bowl stood against one wall. A shelf above the bowl held toilet articles, but the watch chain was not there, either. Perhaps Justin actually wore it to bed, or draped it over a bedpost. She would have to risk opening the bed curtains to look.

As she was about to leave the dressing room someone knocked on the outer bedroom door and Paxton's voice spoke softly, 'Mr Justin, sir . . .'

Joanna drew back against the dressing room wall, her fist against her teeth to keep them from chattering with fear. It was too early for the butler to awaken Justin. What was he doing here now?

Footsteps crossed the bare wood floor, then stopped. She could almost see Paxton's gaunt hand opening the bed curtains. She heard his voice again, 'I'm sorry to waken you, Mr Justin, but –'

A groan and a muffled curse. Then an explosive burst

144

of coughing. Joanna froze, fearing Paxton would come into the dressing room to get a drink of water for his master. But then Justin said, 'What is it, man? Lord, I'd only just closed my eyes.'

'The young woman is not in her room. The boy who was supposed to be watching her door dozed off and she's gone. I've sent him to the stable to see if any of the horses are missing. She may have gone back to that mulatto whore's cottage. If so, you should not allow her to come back. No good can come of her being here. I've told you this before.'

'And I've told you, Paxton, that I need an amanuensis. I can't die in peace unless I finish the journal.'

'I could assist with the journal.'

'No, my dear fellow, you couldn't. It requires far more education than you possess, not to mention writing skills that are quite beyond you. It's possible Joanna is upset about her brother-in-law's visit and has left us anyway, but let's not jump to that conclusion yet. Tell me, did you learn who the brother-in-law was?'

'Not yet. He used the Smith alias. How many others do you think the mulatto will send to spy on you? Mr Justin, why do you tempt fate so?'

'It's the only excitement left to me nowadays, Paxton. Surely we're capable of outwitting such people? And if not . . . if someone does in fact learn too much, then we are also capable of dealing with that situation, are we not? Go away now and let me rest. If Joanna returns, all well and good. If not, then you, my faithful servant, may learn to typewrite this night.'

Paxton's footsteps crossed the room; the landing door opened and closed. Justin coughed again, and the bed creaked.

Joanna remained glued to the dressing room wall, her mind racing. The conversation she'd overheard had possessed a curious undertone, not at all typical of the exchange between master and servant. There had also been the implied threat, that they were 'capable of dealing with

145

that situation' – if someone learned too much. Were Justin and his butler conspirators? Perhaps in the murder of Delta's brother, Joss?

Don't think about it now, she cautioned herself silently, or you'll probably faint.

She waited until the sound of Justin's laboured breathing told her he was again asleep, then slipped out of the dressing room and approached the bed.

For a second she stared at the heavy velvet curtain, fearing that if she pulled it back she would disturb him. His breathing was erratic, with long pauses followed by gasping, choking sounds.

Her fingers closed around the edge of the curtain and she inched it back.

She saw the watch chain immediately, a dull gold gleam against the darkness of the mahogany bedpost just above Justin's head.

As she reached for it, he stirred, turning his head. She snatched her hand away. Her heart was now thumping so loud that the sound seemed to fill the room.

Holding her breath, she reached for the chain again. Her fingers closed around the heavy gold watch and she slowly eased it upward, a fraction of an inch at a time, taking care not to let the keys rattle against one another.

As the watch chain cleared the top of the bedpost, a bony hand closed around her wrist. Justin opened his eyes and regarded her with a malicious smile.

18

Megan felt her senses quicken as Chuck handed her down from the buckboard and she was surrounded by the bustle of Silver City.

So many people on the street, so many coaches and wagons and carts. People coming, going, the sound of music and laughter drifting out of doors left open to catch the afternoon breeze. Why, there were more trees and flowers here in town than she had seen throughout the countryside all the way from the Mallory ranch, a journey that had taken most of the day. Chuck had not even stopped to eat the picnic lunch Consuela had packed, claiming it was too dangerous because of outlaws and renegade Indians. Megan wondered what he would say if she told him about A-chi-tie.

They checked into a small hotel, then walked around the block to a street of stores.

'This here is the best dry goods store in town,' Chuck said, indicating the establishment in front of her. 'There's a dressmaker lives over the store. They should be open another hour or so. If you have to wait to see the dress-maker you could have a sarsaparilla in the drugstore next door. They got 'em one of them new soda fountains. You can walk to the hotel from here, so I won't come back for you.'

'I shan't need you again until we're ready to leave,' Megan said. 'I know you have ranch business to take care of, so just leave a message at the hotel desk to let me know what time you wish to go.'

Chuck gave her a long hard stare that was no doubt meant to convey to her again his disapproval of her decision to marry Randolph.

Her initial outrage that the foreman had tried to warn her away had, during the last leg of their journey to Silver City, given way to understanding. Chuck had evidently witnessed the unhappiness of Randolph's mother and feared that history was about to repeat itself, that another upper-class Englishwoman would create havoc for herself and those around her on this wild frontier. Perhaps if the real Joanna Traherne were marrying Randolph that would be true. But as the granddaughter of a poor country doctor, Megan had never been accustomed to luxury.

She went into the store and, waiting for the proprietor to finish with a customer, she fingered bolts of satin and taffeta and calico and gingham. Although Randolph wanted a quiet wedding, he would probably expect her to wear a white bridal gown. Since they were not going away on a honeymoon, she didn't need any travelling clothes.

Randolph had suggested that, since she had 'forgotten' to bring a riding habit, perhaps she would like to have one made, but the idea of riding sidesaddle over this rough terrain was daunting. Joanna perhaps could have managed, but Megan had already decided she was perfectly happy riding in the buckboard. Perhaps she would simply forget to have a riding habit made.

She selected ivory satin for her wedding gown and ecru lace for a veil, along with the simplest pattern she could find. 'I understand you have a dressmaker on the premises,' she said.

'Yes, ma'am, Sophie Grace's got somebody with her right now, but Lallie should be about done; she's been up there for hours. Reckon they're just gossiping. You go right on up – stairs over there on your left.'

Megan went up a narrow wooden staircase to the mezzanine overlooking the store. There was only one door, but when she knocked there was no answer. She waited.

148

The proprietor called up to her, 'Go on in, ma'am. Door's never locked.'

Megan opened the door and stepped into a maze of worktables littered with dress patterns, scissors, and scraps of material. Gowns in various stages of completion were pinned to several dressmaker's dummies, and, near the window, the latest Singer treadle sewing machine stood in all its shining glory.

For a moment she was unaware of the curtain that divided the room, this side obviously being the work area. 'Hello?' she called uncertainly. 'I'm looking for the dressmaker.'

A woman's face, taut with worry, appeared around the curtain. 'Didn't he tell you I had somebody up here?'

'Yes. I'm sorry. I didn't mean to intrude. But the gentleman downstairs said it was all right to come up, that you were probably finished with your previous client. You are Miss Grace?'

The woman came around the curtain. She was about thirty with strong Slavic features that would have been striking had it not been for those tight lines of worry. 'Name's Sophie Grace. You couldn't pronounce my last name. What can I do for you, Miss . . . ?'

'Traherne. Joanna Traherne. I need a wedding gown.'

'Ah, you're getting married.' Her face relaxed into a hesitant smile that vanished as someone behind the curtain groaned.

Megan was about to apologise and withdraw when from behind the curtain there was a sharp little cry of fear and pain. The next moment a hand clutched the curtain and a pale blond young woman staggered into view. She wore a bright fuchsia dress that reached to midcalf and was hiked up at one side to reveal a black lace petticoat that drew the eye to black mesh stockings. Megan's eyes went at once to the bright red stream that trickled down one leg.

'Sophie Grace, for God's sake do something,' the young woman gasped. 'I'm bleeding to death.'

Without hesitation, Megan hurried to the young

149

woman's side and slipped her arm around her. 'Come on, lie down.' She glanced at the dressmaker, whose eyes had widened and who now wore a look of fear. 'Do you have a bed? Help me get her to it.'

Behind the curtain stood a bed, a potbellied stove, a table, and several chairs. They helped the young woman lie down on a bloodstained sheet and Megan said, 'Let's get her clothes off.'

'I just let her rest here,' Sophie Grace said. 'She came in for a fitting this morning and took sick. I swear to God, we didn't do anything to bring this on.'

'Get me some warm water and clean cloths. I saw some white muslin out there on your worktable.'

Megan pulled off her gloves and then unhooked the fuchsia dress. When the dress and petticoats were off, she covered the woman's upper body with a blanket and smoothed her red-blonde hair back from her forehead. 'What's your name?'

'Lallie . . . Lallie Kendall.'

'How far along were you, Lallie?'

China-blue eyes, round as a doll's, regarded her warily.

'I need to know, Lallie. Because how far along you are will tell me what must be done. I can help you if you tell me the truth. I know a little about medicine.'

'I missed my time about eight weeks ago.'

'You need to have the inside of your womb scraped, Lallie. We must go to a doctor.'

'No!' Lallie struggled to sit up, and Megan had to restrain her. 'No, for God's sake, don't bring the doctor.'

'You won't get into trouble for having a spontaneous miscarriage, Lallie . . . You're sure you didn't do anything to bring this on?'

'Please don't fetch the doctor. One of the other girls went to him and . . . oh, God, she's got this terrible problem with her insides. Her pee keeps draining into her female passage.' Lallie thrashed about, clutching Megan's arms. Tears streamed down her cheeks, leaving glistening rivulets through a heavy layer of face powder.

Sophie Grace returned with a basin of water and a roll of muslin. She looked at Megan expectantly.

Megan's eyes met Lallie's, and she recognised the hope and terror in her gaze; she'd seen that look before, in Joanna's eyes. For an instant her friend's face was superimposed over that of the dance hall girl. Megan wavered, remembering. If she walked away and Lallie did not get medical help . . .

'Oh, God, no, not again,' Megan said aloud. She turned to Sophie Grace. 'I don't have the instruments I need, and we've no ether. Perhaps I could improvise with a kitchen knife. Lallie, I'll be as gentle as I can. Do you think you can lie still? It's very important, and there will be some pain.'

Lallie's hands grasped hers feverishly. 'Yes, yes. Anything. Please, help me.'

Megan turned to Sophie Grace. 'Can you find me a clean apron? Put on some water to boil. You can use the water in the bowl to wash her. Oh, yes . . . and lock that door.'

As Megan gently rolled down Lallie's net stockings, she considered the fact that although a licensed physician had carelessly punched a hole in Lallie's friend's vagina, this girl unhesitatingly allowed a complete stranger to perform a curettage on her. Because I'm a woman, Megan thought. We're all sisters, and our bodies are less mysterious to us than they are to men. We need more women doctors, so we can minister to one another. Why do they make it so difficult for a woman to get into medical school?

The dry goods store had closed by the time Megan was ready to leave, and as Sophie Grace unlocked the door for her she asked, 'You sure you don't want me to walk back to the hotel with you?'

'No, it's not far. You stay with Lallie. Let her sleep as long as she can. I'll come back in the morning to look at her, but don't hesitate to come for me if she gets feverish or begins to bleed again.'

'Reckon we should measure you for your wedding dress tomorrow, too?' Sophie Grace asked with a grin.

Megan gave her a tired smile and nodded. She'd completely forgotten the original reason for her visit to the dressmaker.

The street was still filled with people, and several curious looks were directed at her as she walked by. When a pair of cowboys staggered towards her and one of them mumbled, 'Howdy there, Red, you lookin' for me?' she realised why she was the object of the stares. Here, as in most places, 'nice' women did not venture out alone at night. She quickened her pace.

Music drifted from a storefront saloon. It was unlike any music she had ever heard before – a raucous cacophony that somehow formed a melody that was joyous, uplifting, yet curiously sad, all at the same time. She paused, intrigued by the sound, and at that moment the swinging doors yawned open as someone left the saloon.

For an instant the brightly lit interior formed a tableau – mirrors behind the long curving bar, small tables packed with gamblers and drinkers, the musicians . . . Why, the musicians were black men. She had only seen one other black in her life – the conductor aboard the train that she and Quinn had taken. But in the split second before the doors swung closed again, one other face leaped out of the crowd.

He sat facing the door, his cards folded inside one hand, a gaudily clad dance hostess standing beside him, her arm around his shoulder, as he flipped coins into the centre of the table. Quinn. Casually playing cards in Silver City when she imagined him journeying far away, perhaps agonising over what might have been between them had he not owed a debt of honour to Randolph. His continued presence in the territory seemed an affront to Megan, the final insult.

She walked on quickly, angrier at Quinn than she'd ever been before.

Quinn tossed his cards onto the table and said, 'Deal me out.' He stood up and walked over to the bar.

If Sedge didn't show up soon, he was going to be too late. Quinn was tired of killing time in endless poker games waiting for him.

Quinn had learned early in life that he had an exceptional memory that made him an excellent card player. Since he invariably won, however, there was no longer any challenge in poker, and he didn't particularly enjoy the game. Still, when he needed a stake, he often sought out a poker game with men who were eager to be parted from their silver. And he was sure that money, or the lack of it, was Sedgewick's current problem.

Quinn had met Sedge when both men were serving with the Fourth Cavalry during the final days of the bloody wars with the Apache. Both were misfits, educated men thrown into the company of rough-and-ready professional soldiers. Sedge, the company doctor, had fled west from Boston following a scandal with a very young female patient. He insisted he had been in love with the girl and wanted to marry her, but her father had threatened lawsuits and an end to his medical practice.

As an army doctor Sedge had soon learned to drown his sorrows in drink, for which he unfortunately had a limited capacity. It had been Quinn's observation that a proclivity for strong liquor seemed to be one of the hazards of the profession. After a series of incidents requiring disciplinary action, Sedge had disappeared at a time when he was most needed. A patrol had been ambushed and had returned with five badly wounded men, three of whom had died before Sedge was found. He had been delivering a breech-birth baby for a Chiricahua squaw. That incident had been the last straw for the commanding officer of the fort, who had promptly booted Sedge out of the cavalry. Only Quinn knew that the woman was Sedge's lover and the child was his son. Women, it seemed, were Sedge's second weakness.

Quinn himself had left his family in the East partly in rebellion against a father who expected him to take over the family printing business and partly to escape the smothering attentions of a doting mother and older sisters.

153

Like many young men he was drawn to the western frontier by the promise of adventure and unlimited opportunity. His stagecoach had come upon the remains of a wagon train and, horrified by the mutilated corpses left by Geronimo's Chiricahua Apache, Quinn had promptly enlisted in the Fourth Cavalry.

Four years later, wiser in the ways of the Indian after leading Apache scouts, he had learned to respect and understand the Apache, to feel guilty about their treatment at the hands of soldiers and settlers. Torn between loyalty to his own people and pity for the nomadic Apache who had been driven from their desert hunting grounds and settled in a stinking Florida swamp, he returned to civilian life, restless, rootless, to search for the ideals he seemed to have lost somewhere among the sun-washed plains and stark gorges and chasms of the Southwest.

It was after midnight when Sedge at last arrived at the saloon. Quinn was surprised to see no evidence of a recent binge. Sedge had sandy hair that he rarely combed and the emaciated features of a martyr.

Quinn said, 'Let's get out of here. I want you away from the smell of whisky so I can savour the experience of having a conversation with you while you're sober.'

'It's Migina, Quinn,' Sedge said. 'This time I know for sure what happened to her. I know where she is.'

They went outside to the now-deserted street. A full moon was rising over the dark bulk of the mountains to the south. Quinn said, 'Oh, God, Sedge, are you still pining for her? How many more wild-goose chases will you go on? Or worse, send me on? She's dead. Accept it. She and the boy have been dead for years.'

Migina, whose name meant Moon Returning, and for whom Sedge had been kicked out of the army, had vanished with her infant son after a raid by Mexican troops on the Sierra Madre *rancheria* where she had fled after one of Sedge's drunken binges. He had followed fruitless trails ever since, searching for her.

'All the braves in the *rancheria* were killed, but the

154

women and children were taken to San Carlos and distributed among the Mexican troops' families as slaves,' Sedge said. 'She's still alive, still there.'

'Who told you this?'

'A Mexican I met out along the Rio Grande. He remembered her, Quinn. He described that little scar she had on her forehead and said her boy had light hair, like mine.'

'The Mexican said all this *after* you gave him several bottles of your magic elixir, I presume?'

'Quinn, I don't dare go south of the border; I'm wanted in Mexico for horse stealing. It's a trumped-up charge, but I'd never make it back alive, even if I were in any kind of shape, which I'm not. My kidneys are rotten and my liver is worse. My team's as bad off as me. Half the time me and the horses are in so much misery we can barely make a couple of miles a day.'

'So you want me to go to San Carlos and find out if Migina and the boy are there. Did it occur to you that after all this time she might be some Mexican's squaw? In which case the locals might not take kindly to a gringo taking her out of the country.'

'Quinn, please . . . for old times' sake.' There was genuine pleading in his voice. Not that it was necessary. They both knew that Quinn would go.

19

Megan felt as if she were being borne on a swiftly moving tide towards an uncertain future, powerless to prevent unthinkable events from taking place. Until the very last moment she was sure some stroke of fate would prevent her marriage to Randolph, but her wedding day dawned and she found herself standing beside his wheelchair murmuring the vows that would bind them together for the rest of their lives.

Consuela and Chuck witnessed the simple ceremony, and Megan felt the foreman's hostility even more strongly than Randolph's nervous joy.

Consuela, giggling and flushed, served them a festive dinner, and to hide her uneasiness, Megan drank far too much wine. Afterward she sat on the hearth rug beside Randolph's chair, and he put his arm around her, his fingers playing with her hair, and read to her from a well-worn volume of poetry.

His voice, low and resonant – what a wonderful voice he had, she thought – murmured Shelley's words: '"O wild West Wind, thou breath of Autumn's being,/Thou, from whose unseen presence the leaves dead/Are driven, like ghosts from an enchanter fleeing,/Yellow, and black, and pale, and hectic red . . ."'

The warmth of the fire, the soothing touch of his fingers in her hair, the mellow taste of wine, and, not least, the soothing sound of his voice, all conspired to make her fall fast asleep.

Awakening with a pounding headache in her own bed the following morning, Megan forced herself to wash and dress and go down to breakfast. Unable to meet Randolph's eyes, she said, 'I'm so embarrassed about last night . . .'

Randolph smiled and said, 'My very dear Mrs Mallory, you were exhausted. Please don't apologise. Come and give me a kiss.'

She kissed his cheek. 'How did I . . . Who . . . ?'

'Chuck carried you to your bed.'

Megan made a silent vow never, ever, to take too much wine again.

It was quickly evident that Randolph expected to make no changes in their living arrangements. She did not share his bedroom, and Consuela continued to run the house.

156

There was little for Megan to do, and since Chuck had picked up a large shipment of books on their trip to Silver City, Randolph seemed content to spend most of his time reading and expected her to do the same. He did suggest, however, that since there had been no further reports of the activities of the Chiricahua Kid it would be all right for her to go riding, as long as she stayed on Mallory land, within sight of the hands.

On the afternoon of her third day as Mrs Randolph Mallory, she and her new husband sat at opposite sides of the living room, books on their laps. Randolph was obviously lost in the novel he was reading, and Megan envied him the ability to live the lives of the people in the book, while she idly turned pages and tried to stifle a yawn.

She rose, stretching her arms over her head to relieve cramped muscles, and walked to the window overlooking the entrance to the house. Seconds later she blinked and wondered if she was hallucinating.

Coming towards the house was the most elegant carriage she had ever seen. It was adorned with lacquered pictures, brass lamps, and a fringed top of green and gold. The surrey was pulled by a sleek pair of horses, and as it drew to a halt, she saw that it was driven by an Oriental of gargantuan size. He jumped to the ground as lightly as a dancer and handed down his passenger, a pretty, plump young woman dressed from head to toe in brilliant jade green. She looked vaguely familiar.

Megan said, 'We have visitors,' and ran to open the front door before the green-clad woman reached it. The huge Oriental waited with the carriage.

At close range Megan recognised her visitor as Lallie Kendall, whom she had last seen languishing on the dressmaker's bed.

'Howdy, Miz Mallory, I sure hope you don't mind me dropping in,' Lallie said anxiously.

'I'm delighted to see you, Lallie,' Megan said sincerely. 'Please come in. How are you?'

157

'Real good, thanks to you.' Lallie squeezed Megan's hands, her big blue eyes registering so much gratitude that it was not necessary for her to put her feelings into words.

'Who is it, dear?' Randolph's voice came from the archway leading to the living room.

'Lallie, this is my husband. Randolph, may I present Miss Lallie Kendall?'

Randolph's face was in shadow, and a long minute elapsed before he responded to Lallie's cheery 'Pleased to meet you.'

'Yes, well . . . I'll see you when you've finished with Miss Kendall, Joanna.' He turned his wheelchair abruptly and went back into the living room.

Megan felt the snub as much as if it had been a slap. A small sound of dismay escaped from her lips, but Lallie said quickly, 'It's all right. I shouldn'ta come. I knew better. But I had to see you, Miz Mallory.'

'I must apologise for my husband's rudeness,' Megan began.

Lallie clutched her hand and spoke in an urgent whisper, 'We need you real bad. I got me a place in Manzanita Flats; it ain't far from here. Could you come and look at one of my girls? There ain't no doctor in town, and I doubt I'd be able to get one to travel down from Silver City. I hoped you'd come back with us, but I don't want to get you in trouble with your husband.'

'Of course I'll go with you,' Megan said. 'If you'll just wait until I have a word with my husband.'

'I'll wait out in the surrey,' Lallie said hastily.

Randolph didn't lower his book when Megan entered the room. She said, 'That was inexcusably rude of you.'

He closed the book carefully and regarded her with an expression she'd never seen on his face before. 'I can't believe you'd bring a creature of that sort into my house. Don't you know what she is? Joanna, I know you've led a sheltered life, but even you can't be so naive as not to recognise . . . Where on earth did you meet such a woman?'

The angry comments she'd been about to make were checked when he addressed her as Joanna. 'In Silver City,' Megan answered quietly. 'At the dressmaker's. Randolph, I shan't invite her to come back, since her presence obviously distresses you, but I can't be rude now she's here. I'm going for a ride in her new carriage.

She left the room quickly before he could respond, or, worse, before she lost her temper and screamed at him as Megan would have done. Running to her room, she went immediately to the closet and, reaching for the key she had hidden in the pocket of one of her coats, unlocked the steamer trunk she had brought with her. At the bottom of the trunk, concealed under a shawl and winter skirts, was her grandfather's medical bag.

As she left the house, Chuck emerged from the bunkhouse, no doubt to get a closer look at the surrey. She held the black bag close to her side, hoping he wouldn't recognise it for what it was. She imagined rather than saw the amazement on his face when she was helped aboard the carriage by the Oriental driver.

'This here's Mr Chang,' Lallie said. Mr Chang bowed politely, and seconds later they were rolling down the path tamped into the red earth, startled ranch hands popping up to view the carriage as they passed by.

Megan ran her fingers over the green leather upholstery of the carriage and sighed at the sheer sensory pleasure of touch.

Lallie laughed. 'Some rig, huh? Wait till you see the Jade Palace.'

'The Jade Palace?'

'My place in Manzanita Flats. Green's my favourite colour, so we decided to do the place in green, and one of the gents what's backing me named it the Jade Palace.'

Megan glanced towards Mr Chang's broad back and whispered, 'Does he understand English?'

Lallie nodded. Megan decided to save her inquiries about the sick girl until they arrived at the Jade Palace.

It was even more ostentatious than the carriage, despite

the fact that Manzanita Flats boasted only a single street consisting of a general store, a saloon, a blacksmith, and an abandoned stage station, surrounded by a straggle of small farms. However, the carriage passed gangs of workers laying railway tracks, and the stick skeletons of new buildings rising in the steel wake of the approaching railroad promised rapid growth of the town.

Entering a circular green-carpeted foyer dominated by a chandelier of such gigantic proportions that Megan thought of the midnight sun reflecting off polar glaciers, they were met by a trio of nervously fluttering young women, all clad in elegant, if gaudy, ball gowns.

'Where's the doc?' one demanded.

'Hurry, for chrissake, she's nearly dead,' another added. The third girl looked at the black bag in Megan's hand. 'Well, lookee here! I ain't never seen a lady doc before.'

'You're not seeing one now, either,' Megan responded as she was borne along in the centre of the group past a handsomely carved bar towards a magnificent curving staircase. Except for a white-haired gentleman drinking at the bar, the Jade Palace appeared deserted.

Turning to Lallie she asked, 'Is it female trouble again?'

'Could be, I reckon. She's got terrible pain in her belly. Came on real sudden.' They reached a landing, and Lallie led the way to the last door, which opened onto another, narrower staircase beyond. 'Our private rooms are up here,' Lallie said, then, more sharply, 'You girls get back downstairs. Miz Mallory don't need no audience.' She closed the door firmly in their faces, cutting off a barrage of protests.

At the top of the second staircase there were four rooms, and Lallie directed her into the last one. A black woman with a profile as arresting as the head on an ancient Egyptian tomb sat beside the bed holding the hand of a lovely dark-haired girl who was writhing in agony.

Lallie said, 'You can go now, Beata. We'll take care of her.' The black woman rose and, nodding to Megan, left the room.

Megan laid her hand on the girl's brow and felt a raging fever. 'Where do you hurt?'

'Stomach . . . awful pain.'

'In one side?'

'No. All over. I got me a pain in my back, too.'

'She can't keep any food or water down. Vomits it all right back up,' Lallie volunteered.

'When did the fever start? Has she had chills with it?'

'Yeah, how'd you know?'

Megan pulled back the sheet and began to gently press the girl's abdomen, eliciting groans.

After a moment she straightened up and motioned for Lallie to step outside. On the landing Megan whispered, 'She may have an abscess. I watched my grandfather operate on one once, but the patient died. I've read about the operations done by a man named Henry Hancock in London, and a doctor in Boston named Reginald Fitz did a study of this disease. He calls it appendicitis. Lallie, I'm afraid it's usually fatal.'

'Sweet Jesus, no! She's only seventeen. We can't just let her die.'

'We have to find a qualified doctor who is willing to attempt an operation.'

Lallie wrung her hands. 'The closest is in Silver City. I tried to get him to come, before I came for you. But folks in Silver City think we're overrun with redskins and outlaws all the time out here, and the doc refused to make the trip. Could we take her to him?'

'I don't think she could tolerate the journey. Is there no one else?'

'Doc Sedgewick, but he don't count. He was an army doc at the fort, got kicked out for drunkenness. He travels about the territory in a wagon now, mostly pulling teeth and selling tonic water.' Lallie gestured helplessly. 'Miz Mallory, you gotta realise, not many doctors will set foot in a house of sin.'

Megan had not until this point considered the true nature

161

of the business conducted at the Jade Palace. She decided it was the least of her worries. 'He'll have to do. Where can we find him?' Megan was already halfway down the stairs.

Lallie caught up with her at the foot of the curved staircase that descended into the foyer. 'Wait a minute. I got an idea. I know somebody who might persuade Doc Sedgewick to come. They were in the army together, and it just so happens my friend is in the dining room right now.'

'Dining room?' Megan asked, surprised.

'Why, sure. This is a high-class establishment.'

'Let's go and talk to him.'

'Come to think of it, he's a friend of yours, too,' Lallie said as they crossed the foyer and entered a luxuriously appointed room filled with the aroma of good food. The sound of soft music came from a grand piano on a dais. Waiters in white jackets carried silver trays to small tables at which were seated well-dressed men. Some of the men had pretty young women with them, but many were alone.

Lallie made a beeline for one of the tables, and Megan followed, a drum beginning to beat in her head as she saw who was seated there, watching their progress with amused astonishment.

Megan listened as Lallie conveyed in a series of swift whispers their need to find Doc Sedgewick and persuade him to come to the Jade Palace.

When she finished, Quinn rose to his feet, his eyes on Megan. 'You'd better come with me. You'll be able to explain the urgency better than I will.'

'Good idea,' Lallie agreed. 'You'll be safe with Quinn.'

'Will I?' Megan asked icily.

Quinn gave a small bow. 'My dear Mrs Mallory, is there time to offer my congratulations upon your recent marriage?'

Did a shadow momentarily flicker in the depths of his eyes, or had she imagined it?

162

'One congratulates the groom, not the bride,' Megan responded.

'You want Mr Chang to take you?' Lallie asked.

'We'll travel faster on horseback. Could you get a mount for Mrs Mallory?'

'Sure. I'll see you both out front.' Lallie sped away.

Quinn gestured for Megan to precede him to the door. 'You didn't waste any time tying the knot.'

She glanced up at him. 'Randolph would have sent you an invitation to the wedding, but you didn't deign to let him know where you were.'

He shrugged. 'I wasn't sure where I was. Can't you help the girl yourself without calling in a doctor?'

'No.'

'Come on, then, but I'm warning you, Sedgewick hasn't practised medicine as you know it for years.'

20

Adele Pentreath pushed her husband away. 'Oliver, don't. You'll ruin my hair.'

He sighed and released her, his frustration mounting.

She sat down at her dressing table and patted her smooth golden coiffure. 'I don't understand why I can't at least have a look at him. I've never seen an escaped convict.'

'You've never seen a rampaging bull elephant, either,' Oliver said mildly, 'and I'd as soon have you encounter one as that beast I've got locked up in the cellar. The man battered his way through a very solid door and took a shotgun away from one of the servants before we subdued him.'

Adele shivered in shocked delight. 'What did you do?'

The second footman had used the stock of the shotgun on Magnus's head, knocking him unconscious, but Oliver shrugged as though he had single-handedly overpowered a man twice his size, implying that the details would be too distressing for his wife's delicate sensibilities. Magnus had been carried down to the cellar, securely tied with harness straps, and locked in a storage room.

'I'm not sure I shall be able to sleep tonight, knowing that awful man is on the premises, locked up or not,' Adele said.

'You could sleep in my bed,' Oliver suggested hopefully.

'Darling, only lower-class husbands and wives share sleeping quarters.'

He regarded his wife's exquisite features, reflected in her dressing table mirror, and contemplated how frequently she reminded him of his humble origins. Sometimes he thought that the woman who was now Mrs Oliver Pentreath and the dazzlingly pretty, pliant young woman he'd courted – or had she courted him? – were two different people. Oliver became bewildered whenever he asked himself why he had married the wrong sister. Joanna had never made him feel lowly or inadequate; she had understood him, cherished him. Adele, on the other hand, regarded him much in the manner of one confronted by a slobbering hound who has crawled back to lick the foot that kicked him.

'How awful that he witnessed Joanna's suicide,' Adele said.

'But worse that he came here to blackmail us,' Oliver responded. The Trahernes had circulated the story that Joanna had foolishly gone walking alone on the treacherous cliffs near Dutchman's Point and had fallen to her death. Oliver had seen no reason to let the family, especially Adele, know that Joanna was still alive. For one thing, Joanna herself had chosen to remain out of sight, and for another, he found it oddly exciting that, when Joanna accepted his offer of future living arrangements, he would in fact be making love to a ghost.

164

'You don't think . . . that the convict killed her, do you?' Adele asked suddenly.

'No, no, I don't,' Oliver replied quickly. It wouldn't do for her to get off on that tangent. 'Besides, the man will surely hang when they add the escape charge to his earlier conviction. Remember, we don't want your mother to know that this criminal ever laid eyes on Joanna. It would upset her too much, and besides, there's no point in telling her. We must keep the Traherne name from being associated in any way with an escaped convict.'

Distractedly, he reached out and caressed the creamy perfection of Adele's bare shoulder. She tensed and brushed away his hand.

Sighing, Oliver said, 'I suppose I'd better dress for dinner.'

'Mmmm . . .' Adele was now so engrossed in the selection of a perfume from the array of cut-crystal bottles assembled on her dressing table that she seemed unaware of his departure.

In his adjoining room, Oliver saw that his valet had laid out his evening clothes, and he frowned at the stiffly starched shirt. How much simpler, yet infinitely more fulfilling, life had been when he was a country schoolmaster.

A knock on his door heralded the arrival of his valet. He wondered how servants knew the precise moment at which their services were required as he called, 'Come in.'

'Ready to dress for dinner, sir?' the valet inquired. 'The butler asked me to bring this letter to you.'

Oliver recognised Joanna's handwriting instantly. His heart leapt. He tore open the envelope and read her note. To the waiting valet he said, 'I'll dress later. Come back in half an hour.'

When he was alone, Oliver reread the note. So Joanna wanted the convict released. The man had helped her and she felt compassion for him, however misguided. Joanna was so soft-hearted, she really needed to be protected from herself. Obviously an escaped prisoner could not be turned

165

loose on society, but it appeared that if Joanna was to be restored to him, she would have to be made to believe that the convict was free.

Oliver allowed himself a moment to remember the precious hours he'd spent with Joanna in quiet conversation, and the wonder of their physical union. How warm and pliant she had been, a gossamer cocoon, a warm vessel into which he could pour himself with abandon. He felt himself grow inside his britches, remembering. Unlike Adele, Joanna did not dress provocatively. In fact her gowns were quite matronly and all-enveloping, and it had been a wonderful shock to find an exquisite body under the layers of heavy petticoats and constricting whalebone.

With a tremor of anticipation, Oliver thought rapidly that he could rent a cottage, perhaps in some secluded cove farther along the coast, and first thing in the morning he would journey to Bodrath House and pick up Joanna. Why, by this time tomorrow she could be lying in his arms . . .

Magnus dragged the leather strap binding his wrists back and forth across the jagged edge of a broken brick protruding from the wall of the cellar. He'd been sawing for hours, but it seemed the brick would probably crumble before the leather snapped.

Since the local constable had not come for him – no doubt because Oliver did not want anyone to know that Joanna had been saved by a convict – Magnus guessed that word of his capture had probably been sent to Dartmoor. If so, there was little likelihood that guards would come for him before tomorrow.

He tensed as he heard the sound of footsteps on the cellar stairs somewhere beyond the locked storage room door. Seconds later the door opened and a ribbon of yellow light spilled across the stone floor. A grey shadow scurried back into its hole.

There was a stifled cry of dismay. 'Ugh! I hate rats.'

Magnus blinked, startled. A woman's voice had spoken.

He strained to see the face beyond the raised lantern and caught a glimpse of golden hair.

'Stand up, please,' the voice commanded. 'I want to see how big you are.'

He struggled to his feet, hampered by the bonds on his ankles as well as the fact that his hands were bound behind him. There was an awed gasp, then a moment's silence.

'Good gracious. No wonder you frightened the wits out of the servants. Oliver, too, I think, although he wouldn't admit it. They'll probably hang you, you know.'

The oil lantern was placed on the floor near him and she came closer, a young woman clad in a black evening gown that set off the ivory perfection of her features. She peered at him as though he were some caged beast. 'Can you speak, or are you mute?'

'I can speak. I'll do tricks for you, too, if you untie me.'

She giggled nervously. Now that his eyes had become accustomed to the light, he saw that she was exquisitely pretty, although her beauty was marred by a downward turn to her mouth that suggested discontent. He decided she must be Adele, Joanna's sister, wife of Oliver.

'If you'd fetch me a drink of water I'd be grateful, Mrs Pentreath.'

'Oh!' She stepped backward. 'How did you know who I am?'

'You're not old enough to be Mrs Traherne, and you're not dressed like a scullery maid. 'Course you could be a footman with a liking for women's clothes.'

'You're quite a wit, aren't you?'

'A thirsty wit, milady.'

She picked up the lantern and disappeared through the door. Magnus thought she'd left for good, but a moment later she returned with a bottle of wine. 'There isn't any water down here. Will this do? It's a rather good sherry.'

'Can you open it?'

This problem had evidently not occurred to her. He said, 'Put the cork up to my mouth. I'll do it.'

She hesitated, then stepped closer and held up the bottle.

167

He said, 'Hold tight, now,' then gripped the cork in his teeth and pulled. It came free and wine splashed on both of them. Adele giggled again and held the bottle to his lips as he drank. When he finished she backed away, watching him.

He slid down to the floor again, his hands finding the broken brick behind him in order to resume sawing at the leather strap binding his wrists. 'You haven't asked about your sister.'

'I don't want to hear the grisly details. I wear this dreary black mourning gown for my father, not for Joanna. How can I grieve for a sister who was so selfish?'

'*Selfish*?'

'Suicide is a supremely selfish act. Mother says so. It punishes those left behind.'

'Your husband didn't tell you?' Magnus felt a chill of horror. 'Joanna didn't commit suicide. She's alive and well.'

Adele's mouth dropped open. 'Where is she? Why did she let us think she was dead?'

'She was very ill,' he said cautiously. He knew he would have to be careful not to give away too much. 'By the time she recovered enough –'

'It wasn't my fault that Oliver preferred me,' Adele said. 'Joanna was always jealous of me, you know.' A petulant note crept into her voice. 'She did this whole rotten thing just to punish us, didn't she? Does she know she killed Father with her wickedness? I suppose now she'll come back and embarrass the rest of us to death.'

'Look, Mrs Pentreath, Joanna doesn't want to come home. She wants to go to her friend, Megan Thomas. I came to ask your husband to help me find her. Do you know where Miss Thomas is?'

'No, I don't. She used to live in north Wales.'

'Will you go to Joanna and help her? She's working for Justin Bodrath. If they take me back to Dartmoor, she'll be all alone and I fear for her.'

Adele retreated to the door. 'Mother is going to be

furious.' She turned and fled, leaving the door wide open.

At that moment, the leather binding Magnus's wrists gave way.

Joanna's fingers moved over the keyboard of the typewriter, slowly finding the letters she sought. If she concentrated on the keys, looking only from the machine to her notes, she was less aware of her surroundings.

At first, after Justin had ordered Paxton to lock her in the Cromwell retreat, the confining walls and low ceiling of the tiny chamber had terrified her. It was like being sealed into a tomb. There was barely enough space for one chair and the table that supported the typewriting machine. She had to lower her head when she stood up, and there was no room to move around the table.

The chamber had been constructed during the time of Cromwell and Charles I as a place in which Loyalists could hide when the Roundheads came searching for them. Windowless, cold, and damp, the walls clammy, it smelled like a grave.

Beside the typewriter sat the metal box Justin had kept locked in the study. He had flung it on the table just before he locked her in. 'There . . . that's what you were curious about it, is it not? Feast your eyes on the contents. It no longer matters to me, because my brother's murderer has been caught.'

'Magnus!' Joanna had cried.

Justin's eyes had gleamed. 'So you do know him. Don't bother to deny it. Magnus has been caught. He's presently locked up at Traherne Hall. Ah, I see that name also means something to you.'

He had coughed, then added, 'By the way, the Trahernes recently suffered a tragedy. Their elder daughter died. So you see, dear, there's no one on earth who knows or cares that you're locked in here. When the Bodrath journal is complete, I might even let you out. But since you've demonstrated that you can't be trusted, for now here you stay.'

Joanna stopped typing and rubbed her hands together to ease the stiffness of her fingers. She raised the lid of the metal box again and looked at the contents. Lying on top was Harry Bodrath's death certificate.

The injuries described were consistent with blows received in a boxing match, and the certificate also stated that the doctor had observed that violent vomiting and convulsions had occurred shortly before death.

So he had died by Magnus's hand after all, although not until hours after the boxing bout. Joanna was still trying to cope with that realisation as she agonised over what would become of Magnus now and why he had gone to Traherne Hall. But of course she had asked him to try to learn Megan's whereabouts! No doubt that was the reason he had taken such a risk. Reaching for the trapdoor leading out of the chamber, she rattled it again, but it remained locked.

Justin surely had slipped over the edge of reason. How could he do this to her?

She had not yet looked at the other papers in the box. They appeared to be more old letters, and she had waded through a mountain of those already. But now she wondered what set these particular letters apart from the others so that Justin had kept them locked away. Picking up a yellowing sheet of paper she unfolded it and read: 'Unless the rest of the money is forthcoming, your father will be informed of your brother's perversion.'

The words danced dizzily in front of her. Obviously this was a blackmail threat. But to whom? To Justin, about Harry? Or to Harry, about Justin? There was also that third brother . . . Neville.

The trapdoor opened suddenly, clattering back against the stone floor of the chamber. Paxton's head appeared. "You may come out now. The master is asleep.' He offered his hand to help her, but she ignored it.

Once she was standing upright again she glared at him. 'You are both going to be prosecuted for this. You are holding me against my will.'

170

Paxton's cold eyes glittered and she thought, amazed, that he looked as if he might be about to cry! He said slowly, 'Mr Justin is dying. The doctors are with him now. You'll be free to leave shortly. Mr Justin wanted to be sure the murderer of Mr Harry was safely in custody before he let you go. He was afraid you'd go home and release the man before he could be taken back to Dartmoor. As soon as we hear from Traherne Hall I'll let you know. In the meantime you may rest in your room.' He gestured for her to precede him up the stairs.

Joanna hesitated. 'I'm very sorry about Mr Bodrath, Paxton. I'm sure his rather irrational behaviour is due to his illness. Will you tell him I bear him no ill will?'

'I regret he no longer is aware of others.'

As they walked up the great staircase Joanna asked, 'What will become of the Bodrath journal now? We've done so much work on it.'

Paxton's lips compressed into a tight line. 'It was only a distraction for him in his final days. There is no one left to care or even be curious about the Bodraths. I shall burn it.'

As she entered her room and heard the key click in the door behind her, it flashed through Joanna's mind that there was one reward for her hours of labour: she had learned how to typewrite, a skill that might be useful when she again sought a paying position.

But her main concern now was how to escape from the house and make her way to Traherne Hall. She prayed she could reach Magnus before he was sent back to Dartmoor.

21

Megan surveyed the painted wagon and bedraggled horses with dismay. It looked more like a tinker's cart than a conveyance suitable for a travelling doctor. The sign lettered in peeling gold on the side of the wagon read 'Dr Sedgewick's Elixir, guaranteed to cure rheumatism, gout, insomnia, ague, baldness, and general debility.'

Quinn had already dismounted, but she remained in her saddle, and she realised she was frowning when he glanced up at her and said, 'Don't sit in judgement until you know him. He's a damn fine doctor when he's sober.'

He walked around to the rear of the wagon and called, 'Hey Sedge, you in there?' He climbed inside.

They'd had a hard ride, and Megan was breathless. At first she had balked when Quinn suggested the journey would be easier on her if she donned a pair of his britches and rode astride the horse. 'Many women out here do. Our terrain isn't exactly suitable for sidesaddles and you, Mrs Mallory, are not much of a horsewoman. Besides, nobody but me will see you.'

She supposed she should be glad they'd found the doctor so quickly and that she'd been spared having to make conversation with Quinn en route.

Quinn's head appeared at the front of the wagon. 'He's in here, asleep. I'll tie our horses to the back of the cart, and we'll haul him over to the Jade Palace.'

She slid to the ground and Quinn took the horses around to the back of the wagon. Returning, he offered his hand to help her up into the passenger seat. She took it, but avoided looking into his eyes.

Glancing into the back of the wagon she could make out the shape of a man, sprawled amid a clutter of cooking utensils, blankets, boxes. 'Don't you think we should wake him?'

Quinn picked up the reins and urged the horses forward. 'No. He'll probably refuse to come if we do.'

'Where are we?'

'This is Diamond T land. He was probably looking for me.'

'I heard you were friends in the army and that he was thrown out for drunkenness. Is that also why you left the army?'

'I've always been able to hold my liquor.'

'That isn't an answer.'

'What was the question?'

'Oh, never mind.' Megan held on to her seat with both hands as the wagon lurched over the bumpy trail. 'Don't you realise this is a waste of time? That man in the back is sleeping off a drunken binge.'

'We'll fill him full of coffee.'

'He'll be incapable of performing an operation.'

'Becky needs surgery?'

His use of the girl's name momentarily distracted Megan. Evidently he was well acquainted with the ladies of the Jade Palace and their services. Realising that, she was surprised at the twinge of pain she felt. 'Yes, I think so. But few doctors know how to perform this operation; it's very new.'

'Did your grandfather do it?'

'Yes. Once. The patient died.'

'Do you know how to do it?'

'My grandfather made an incision near the umbilicus –' She broke off. 'I can't do it.'

'What if Sedgewick can't do it either? Will Becky die?'

'That's in God's hands.'

'No, I don't think so. It's in yours.' They rode on in

silence for a few minutes. Then Quinn asked, 'What does Randolph think about your hanging around with Lallie Kendall and the Jade Palace girls?'

Megan realised with a start that she had completely forgotten about her husband. She decided to worry later on about what she'd tell him. For now, Becky had to be her first concern. 'He wasn't too happy when I left with Lallie.'

'How did you meet her, anyway?'

'We met in the dressmaker's in Silver City,' Megan answered shortly.

'And you invited her to the Mallory ranch? For Pete's sake, haven't you any sense?'

'No, I didn't invite her. She came to ask me to help Becky.'

He gave her a suspicious sidelong glance. 'How did she know you could help?'

'Damn you, stop questioning me!' Megan shouted. 'You have no right. You walked out of my life and out of Randolph's life. You are not our keeper.'

'Wh-what — Where'n hell . . . ?' A raspy voice came from the depths of the wagon, and a second later a haggard face topped with a wild thatch of sandy hair thrust itself between them. It was an arresting face, with high cheekbones, melancholy eyes, and full lips, too sensitive to give credibility to his contrived sneer.

'How are you, Sedge?' Quinn said. 'Say hello to Mrs Randolph Mallory.'

The doctor turned bloodshot eyes in Megan's direction. 'A redhead, huh? I didn't figure Joanna for red hair. How 'bout you, Quinn? Say, where we going, anyway?'

'Dr Sedgewick,' Megan said carefully, 'I am the daughter and granddaughter of physicians.'

'Bully for you,' he mumbled as he climbed unsteadily onto the wooden seat between her and Quinn. Despite a fresh breeze, he brought with him a strong smell of whisky.

'I merely tell you that to let you know I have lived my whole life with a practising doctor and . . . in fact, assisted him many times in his surgery.' She paused. 'Are you familiar with the work of the Berlin surgeon Rudolph Kronlein?'

Megan could hardly believe the change that came over the unkempt doctor at the mention of the German surgeon. It was as if a magician had waved a wand and transformed Sedgewick from a drunken derelict into an alert, intelligent being. 'Kronlein? You betcha! He's doing the same work as one of our American physicians. You heard of Reginald Heber Fitz? He described the pathology and symptoms of what he called appendicitis.'

It didn't seem possible that a man who had spent the last several years hawking elixirs and pulling teeth on the western frontier would be aware of the latest medical advances; still, hoping against hope, Megan asked, 'You've studied their methods?'

'I've *read* about 'em; I still get all the medical journals. There's been a bunch of case reports and articles the last few years. I guess every surgeon worth his salt is operating on the appendix these days.' The wistfulness in his voice suggested that, like many men whose professional lives had been destroyed by inebriation, he regretted having allowed that to happen.

The wagon had reached the outskirts of Manzanita Flats, and Sedgewick looked around curiously. Megan said quickly, 'I served as surgical nurse at many of my grand-father's operations, Dr Sedgewick. I would be honoured to help you. You're the only man for a thousand miles who can save Becky's life . . .'

Somehow she kept up a constant stream of chatter as Quinn took one of the doctor's arms and she the other and they propelled him, wide-eyed, into the Jade Palace.

Just before they reached Becky's room, Quinn gripped his friend's arm and said quietly, 'Help her, Sedge, and I swear to God I'll find out for sure what happened to Migina and the boy. She's not in San Carlos, but I'll find out, somehow, where she is now.'

* * *

175

Megan walked slowly down the staircase, oblivious of the well-dressed ranchers now crowding the Jade Palace bar, the pretty young women who moved among them, and the couples who passed her on their way up to the private rooms. Her mind raced, filled with images, questions, theories. She was bone-weary, elated, alive in a way she had not felt for some time.

Halfway down the stairs she became aware of Quinn. He stood with one elbow resting on a newel post, watching her. Her first impulse was to race down the remaining stairs and fling herself into his arms. Then reason prevailed as her memory returned. Quinn had rejected her, and she was Randolph's wife. She felt as if she were collapsing in on herself.

He ran up the stairs, took her hand, and pulled her arm through his. 'Are you all right?'

'Yes, yes. Just a little tired.'

'What about Becky?'

She smiled. 'I think she's going to be all right. We can't be sure, but if she doesn't develop peritonitis, she should recover completely. The abscess was between the cecum and the abdominal wall and didn't appear to have spread into the peritoneal cavity –' She broke off, then added hastily, 'Dr Sedgewick did an excellent job. I was impressed with his skill.'

He stared at her.

'What is it?'

For a moment he didn't answer. Then he shrugged and said, 'That smile of yours . . . be careful how you use it.'

'Not even you are going to make me angry now, Quinn, so don't tease.' She was bursting with the need to share her excitement. 'I'd almost forgotten the feeling – the challenge, the sheer battle of wit and will against disease. It was just like the days before Grandfather became senile. Why on earth would a surgeon with Dr Sedgewick's skill throw away his training, his knowledge . . . himself?'

'One of the things you're going to find out, living in the

territory, is that a lot of people are like you. They came here to make a fresh start. It's better not to pry into anybody's past.'

Especially yours, Megan thought, as they reached the ground floor.

He asked, 'Would you like a drink before I take you home?'

She clapped a hand to her mouth. 'Oh, lord! Randolph!'

Quinn's mouth twisted into a cynical smile. 'Lallie sent Mr Chang out to the Mallory ranch with a message that you were taking care of a sick girl.'

'But Joanna couldn't . . . wouldn't –'

'Look, there's no point in worrying about it now. Come on.' He took her arm and led her to a door on the far side of the foyer.

They went into a room furnished with a handsome black lacquered desk and several matching cabinets. Megan let out a sigh of relief.

He looked at her with amusement. 'What's wrong? Did you think I was going to take you into one of the pleasure suites?' He pulled out a chair. 'This is Mr Chang's office.' He opened one of the cabinets. 'Brandy, whisky, or wine?'

'Plain soda water, if there is some. I want to keep a clear head, to remember all that happened this evening.' She looked around. 'Mr Chang's office? I thought he was Lallie's coachman.'

'And bouncer and office manager and representative of the real owner of the Jade Palace, here to keep an eye on his interests.'

'The real owner?'

'A railroad baron. Mr Chang came out here with a gang laying track, but from what Lallie says he's a business genius, not to mention being formidable enough in size to scare off any troublemakers. He poses as a bouncer and drives her around in her fancy surrey because her customers wouldn't take kindly to a Chinese running the place.'

177

Quinn brought her a glass of soda water and she sipped it, acutely aware that he stood only inches away. She didn't look up at him.

He said quietly, 'I saw how Sedge's hands were shaking, even after we filled him up with coffee. You did the operation, didn't you?'

She drew a deep breath. 'Quinn, there is an extremely powerful group of doctors in your country, the American Medical Association. They would surely see to it that any unlicensed practitioner of medicine was severely punished. They would also indict any licensed physician who was a party to such a procedure. To answer your question . . . Dr Sedgewick performed the operation.'

'So be it.'

Raising her glass she added, 'As soon as I've finished this, I must go. There's no need for you to take me; I'm sure Lallie and Mr Chang will see me safely home.'

'Isn't it a little late to start worrying about being alone with me? We travelled six thousand miles together. Will another five or six miles compromise you?'

She rose to her feet and looked him straight in the eye. 'When I travelled six thousand miles with you I was not only a single woman but also a fugitive. I am now Mrs Randolph Mallory, and I've already embarrassed my husband once today. I won't have you return with me in tow, like some wandering steer you've roped.'

He grinned. 'A heifer would be a better simile.'

Ignoring him, she went on, 'The last time we were alone I made certain foolish admissions to you. I was infatuated with you. Looking back, I believe it had something to do with your recklessly brave handling of the attack on the train. I'd never known a man like you before, and I suppose I was fascinated by you. You must remember, I spent my life with a man who endeavoured to save lives, while you . . ."

Megan wasn't sure what happened next. Her voice trailed away. Quinn took the glass from her hand and put it on the desk. They stared at each other. Then she was in his arms and his mouth was on hers and the blood pounded

178

in her ears as for a moment she yielded all of her senses to his control, to the desire she felt, that despite her best intentions, threatened to flare to flash point.

Weakly she raised her hands, but she could neither push him away nor stop him from speaking the words that once she would have given anything to hear.

'Megan, after I left you, I made it all the way to Santa Fe. I spent days and nights playing poker, drinking, trying to forget. But I couldn't get you out of my mind. I woke up one morning with a hangover like I haven't had since I got out of the army, and I rode day and night to make it back here. I reached Silver City the day the announcement of the wedding appeared in the paper. You and Randolph were married the day before I got back.'

All the blood drained from her face. 'Why do you tell me this now? Are you trying to restore my lost dignity, is that it?'

'No, no. Don't you understand what I'm telling you? I love you. Oh, Megan, *how* I love you.'

'No!' Her reply was almost a scream. 'Don't say it. I can't stand it. *It's too late.*'

'Megan, this isn't the time and it certainly isn't the place. But when I saw you coming down those stairs tonight I knew what a fool I'd been. My feelings for you had been growing all the way across the Atlantic. You'll never know how many times I walked the deck of that damn ship, wondering how the hell I was going to turn you over to Randolph.'

'But you *did* take me to him. I think I know why now. You had an affair with his mother, and when he and his father tried to take her away from you there was a terrible accident that resulted in Randolph being crippled and both parents killed. Encouraging me to marry Randolph was an attempt to assuage your guilt.'

His hands fell away from her. 'Randolph didn't tell you that.'

'No. It was Chuck.'

'I don't give a damn what Chuck thinks, but I do care

179

what you believe. There was no affair. Randolph's mother was a beautiful, unhappy woman who misunderstood my sympathy for her.'

'Oh?'

'I come from a very old Philadelphia family, Megan. Mrs Mallory could have been my own mother, or my older sister, thrust down on a raw frontier, trying to bring some sort of order – culture, even – to the household of a man who had no time for it. I felt sorry for her, and for Randolph. I guess I spent more time with them than I should have. Maybe I should have read the warning signals, but I didn't. Nothing prepared me for the day Mrs Mallory arrived at the Diamond T with a suitcase. If her husband and son hadn't come for her, I'd have taken her back home myself. I swear to God.'

'Then why did you feel guilty enough to go to England to try to get Joanna to come to Randolph?'

'I told you. I went to England to meet with the owner of the Diamond T and to buy Herefords. It's true I felt sorry for Randolph and, when I met her, just as sorry for Joanna. I saw how miserable she was that her sister had stolen her beau, and I pictured her and Randolph together – two lonely people who needed each other.'

'That doesn't explain why you asked me to come instead.'

'You were in a jam. It seemed tragic to let a woman like you hang for murder. I wanted to provide a new identity for you and a companion for Randolph. Hell, I'm not sure any more what happened after that. Except that you're here, married to Randolph, and I love you and you love me, so where do we go from here?'

'Nowhere,' Megan said. She turned her back to him, images tumbling over one another in her mind. The nights she'd cried herself to sleep, the hours she'd agonised over her foolish declaration of love, the fact that for a little while this evening she had been engaged in a desperate battle to save a girl's life and during that time no one else, not even Quinn, had mattered. Superimposed over everything else was the sadly reproachful face of Randolph.

When she turned to face Quinn again she was composed. 'You didn't allow me to finish what I started to say earlier. I was trying to tell you that what I felt for you was the fascination of opposites – infatuation, temporary, curable. I got over it very quickly after you left. I'm sorry, Quinn, but you're wrong. I don't love you; I never did.'

For an instant, when he drew a sharp breath, she almost wavered, but forced herself to go on, 'You will get over it, too. We're totally dissimilar creatures, from different ends of the world. We met and became curious about each other – so curious that we mistook our feelings for love. But curiosity isn't love, is it? Don't be embarrassed because you made exactly the same mistake that I did.'

She walked to the door, turned, and looked back at him. 'If you're going to be in the neighbourhood for a while, I wish you'd call on Randolph. He's missed you. Good night, Quinn. Thank you for finding Dr Sedgewick for us.'

It was after midnight when Mr Chang delivered her safely to the door of the ranch house. A lantern had been left lit, and the door was unlocked. She walked into the house and saw at once that Randolph, seated in his wheelchair, was waiting for her under the archway leading to the living room.

'Randolph . . . you shouldn't have waited up for me.'

'Will you have a glass of wine with me before you go to bed?'

She hesitated. 'I'm very tired.'

'Please, Megan. We must talk.'

She stopped dead in her tracks. *Megan*. The name resonated in her head, like the echo of a gigantic bell. Slowly she walked past him into the living room. The fire was still banked high, casting a red glow on adobe walls and a golden gleam on polished mahogany.

Turning to face him, she asked, 'How long have you known?'

'From the beginning, I think.'

'What made you suspect?'

A ghost of a smile hovered about his mouth. 'For one thing, you're simply too beautiful to be Joanna. No woman who looks like you would describe herself in her letters as plain. But there was more than that. Several times I mentioned something we'd discussed in our correspondence and you didn't respond. It's evident, too, that you aren't fond of reading novels or poetry. Nor are you an art fancier. You didn't even comment on the paintings I've collected. But I suppose what really gave the game away was Joanna's letters. You see, she wrote to me at length about her dear friend, Megan Thomas, the doctor's granddaughter who wanted to be a doctor herself.'

'But you didn't say anything –'

'No. I wanted you to stay, on your terms. On any terms. Do you remember when the subject of your lovely red hair came up? I made up an explanation for it. I was the one who rationalised every discrepancy in your story. Nor did I ever question Quinn about you.'

'But . . .'

He rolled his chair towards her and, when he was close enough, held out his hands. She sank into the fireside chair and put her hands into his, squeezed his fingers briefly, and then let go. 'How could you want me to stay after I lied to you? I don't understand –'

'Then let me tell you about loneliness. About waking in the night and staring into the darkness and thinking that the dawn will never break and even if it does it will bring another empty day. About wanting so desperately to have someone to talk to, to share my thoughts with. Someone who would stay with me even though she was not being paid to be here . . . Someone I could touch . . . Can you know what it's like never to feel the touch of a human hand? The night we were married you sat at my feet and I stroked your hair, explored the contours of your lovely face, kissed the nape of your neck . . . I was in ecstasy.

182

Megan, my legs are paralysed, but my mind isn't, and in my mind I wanted you more desperately than any whole man ever yearned for a woman. I thought perhaps, in time, we could even consummate our marriage. When you'd had time to get used to the idea. Oh, not in the way most married people do, but . . .'

Megan leaned back, suddenly finding it difficult to breathe.

His handsome face was drawn into tight lines. 'Megan, I don't know how it would have been if Joanna had come. All I know is that you walked into my life and instantly it was worth living, brighter in every way. Instead of waking up and staring into the darkness, I woke up and thought of all we would do that day, of things I wanted to tell you. You brought to me happiness such as I'd never known. Just watching you is such a pleasure . . . listening to your laughter, the dear nearsighted way you have of scrutinising anything that interests you. Your curiosity, your quick grasp of what would be new and baffling to most young women. You're so animated, so vivacious, you seem to cast a golden aura over everything and everyone you come near.'

Letting out her breath slowly, Megan said, 'You haven't asked why I posed as Joanna. Aren't you curious about the circumstances of my coming here?'

'As there have been no letters from Joanna since you came, I assume she was privy to the deception, although it seems out of character for her.'

'Randolph, I'm sorry . . . There's no gentle way to break this to you. Joanna is dead.'

He was silent. In the fireplace a log burned through and fell in a shower of sparks. The clock on the mantelpiece ticked away several minutes. At length he said, 'I can't seem to grasp the fact that she's gone. I'll probably go on looking for a letter from her for the rest of my life. How did it happen? A sudden illness?'

'An accident.' There was no need for him to know all the details, but he was waiting expectantly, so she added,

'A fall from the cliff. She probably struck her head on the rocks in the cove below and drowned. I'm sure it was mercifully quick.'

Randolph's expression was stricken. 'Oh, God . . . she didn't commit suicide over Oliver?'

'No, no, I'm sure it was an accident.'

'Quinn knew, of course? Was it his idea that you pretend to be Joanna?'

'Yes. But don't be angry with him. You see, I was in trouble . . . accused of a crime I hadn't committed, but the circumstantial evidence against me was overwhelming. He suggested I pose as Joanna in order to escape and, well . . . one thing led to another.'

'I can hardly be angry with him. Besides, he's gone.'

'Actually, he's back. I saw him tonight in Manzanita Flats.'

'Then no doubt he'll call on us.' Randolph leaned forward, looking past her into the dying embers of the fire. 'So you came under duress, not because you wanted to.'

'That's not entirely true. When my grandfather died, I learned that my father came to this country long ago – to a place called Galveston. He may still be alive. I thought perhaps if I could find him he might be able to help me get into medical school. Something my grandfather was reluctant to do in England, because he needed me at home.'

She sighed. 'But I spoke at length with one of your doctors tonight and it seems the male bastion of medicine is as sacrosanct here as it is in England. It's almost impossible for a woman to get into medical school.'

Randolph seemed to shrink into his wheelchair as she spoke and, realising her thoughtlessness, she slid from her chair to the hearth rug in front of him. Taking his hands in hers, she drew them to her lips and kissed his fingertips. 'Randolph, you are the dearest, most considerate, kindest man I've ever known. I don't expect you to forgive my deception, and I'll understand if you want a quiet

184

annulment of our marriage. But I do want you to know that I've come to care a great deal about you and I'd give anything if I could undo the hurt I've caused you.'

He looked into her eyes, searching for answers he evidently did not find. 'Tell me, Megan, if you could have anything in the world you wanted, would you choose to stay here with me?'

She hesitated, feeling as if she were on the edge of something unexpected and a step in the wrong direction might cause irretrievable loss. But the weeks of lying and weaving a web of deceit had taken their toll and she silently vowed never again to be less than honest with him. 'All my life, since I was five years old, all I ever wanted was to become a doctor.'

'Thank you for answering truthfully. Now I think the first thing to do is to send off your application to a couple of medical schools. At the same time we'll try to locate your father. What's his name?'

'Dr Davydd Morgan Robard. My own real full name was Megan Thomas-Robard, but no one ever used it because I always lived with my grandfather and he was Dr Thomas. But how can we possibly find my father after all this time?'

'There is an excellent detective agency called the Pinkertons. If your father is still alive they'll find him.'

'Randolph . . . I don't know what to say. Do you realise that if by some remote chance I'm accepted into medical school – women are often shut out, but if a miracle occurs and they take me – I'll be there for years, and after that will come internship and residency . . .''

He reached out to push a strand of hair back behind her ear. 'Perhaps I could persuade you to spend your vacations here with me. Maybe, when you have a moment to spare, you'll write.'

A tear trickled down Megan's cheek. 'Oh, Randolph, don't be so damned nice. I can't bear it.'

'I'm not being nice, I'm being selfish. I'm searching for a way to make you a part of my life. If I know you'll be coming back to me, then I'll have a reason to live.'

Megan flung her arms around his neck and kissed his lips.

22

Joanna waited until dusk had fallen and then bundled a change of clothing and her toilet articles inside her shawl. Since she had not yet been paid for her services, she reasoned that the few borrowed garments and toilet articles she took had been honestly earned.

She climbed out of her window and stood on a narrow parapet some thirty feet above the courtyard.

The cobblestones below beckoned ominously, and she clutched the window frame, wondering how she was going to descend to the ground without falling and killing herself, or at least breaking her limbs.

There were no trees close by, nothing but precarious footholds in the granite blocks of the wall. One slip and she would plummet to the courtyard below with nothing to break her fall. There was no point in even trying to climb down.

Reluctantly she swung her legs back over the windowsill and stood again in her locked room. She went to the door and pounded on it. 'I know someone is out there. Please, I must speak with you. Open the door, I beg you.'

Seizing the doorknob, she rattled it and screamed that she would jump out of the window unless the door was opened.

She heard the key in the lock. Quickly, she picked up a heavy brass vase that stood on the mantelpiece and ducked behind the door. As the young footman stepped into the room she brought the vase down on the back of his head with all her might.

He gave a startled grunt, then crumpled to the floor. Joanna stood over him, still holding the vase, aghast at what she'd done. For a moment she considered bringing a cold cloth for the footman's head and perhaps holding her smelling salts under his nostrils. Then all at once voices and footsteps approached along the vaulted corridor that led to Justin's bedchamber.

Quickly she drew back into the room and closed the door. Would they notice that the footman was no longer outside her door? Paxton posted sentries as if he were still in the army. But as the voices drew nearer she strained to hear through a crack in the door and realised that Paxton was not out there, only the physicians who had been called to examine Justin.

A strange voice, low and sonorous, said, 'I suggest we wait until the butler summons us to come back, and he surely will before this day ends. Otherwise one of us will have to return to write the death certificate, and personally I've no desire to remain in this mausoleum any longer than necessary.'

The footsteps moved on by. The doctors had evidently been sent from the sickroom. Paxton genuinely cared for Justin and no doubt he wanted to be alone with his master in his final moments, which meant that Joanna need not fear either of them apprehending her. On the floor the unconscious footman began to stir. Snatching up her bundle of belongings, she ran from the room.

Downstairs, the main hall was deserted. The doctors had probably gone into the drawing room to wait. She decided to go through the servants' wing in order to leave the house as near to the stables as possible.

On her way she noticed that the ladder leading to the Cromwell retreat was still hanging down and the trapdoor was open. In his haste to return to his dying master, Paxton had evidently forgotten to lock it. She paused, then on impulse went up the ladder into the room.

Quickly she gathered up the completed pages of the Bodrath journal, then tipped the contents of the metal box into her shawl. Paxton had said he intended to burn them, but perhaps these papers contained evidence that would exonerate Magnus.

She saw no one as she slipped out through the tradesmen's door and crossed the courtyard towards the stable. Would the grooms allow her to take a horse? Perhaps if she commanded them imperiously enough.

A huge shadow loomed in front of her and she cried out in fright as muscular hands seized her shoulders.

Then the moon slid out from behind a cloud. 'Joanna, it's all right. It's me.'

Joanna flung herself into Magnus's arms, feeling safe, protected, at last. She felt him tremble, but he held her close and murmured that no harm would come to her now.

At last he gently peeled her away from him and took the knotted shawl from her hand. 'Come on, we'll have to walk as fast as we can to Delta's cottage, and we have to get there before dawn. The authorities know I'm alive and free, so there'll be searchers and bloodhounds looking for me. They're bound to go to Delta and find my boat in the cove.'

Taking her hand, he led her away from the house. They didn't speak again until they were safely off the Bodrath estate.

'I was so afraid for you,' Joanna said. 'Justin said you were locked up at Traherne Hall.'

'Don't worry about it now. Save your strength; we've a long walk ahead of us.'

'I should have known Oliver would not let you go, no matter what I promised –' She bit her tongue in dismay.

'Damn him,' Magnus growled. Then, more gently, 'You should not have troubled yourself over me, Joanna. I'm not worth it.'

'You are worthy of my deep and lasting devotion, Magnus. I shall never forget what you did for me.'

'There is nothing I wouldn't do for you. I'm your most humble servant.'

'We must go far away, Magnus,' she said. 'Please take me away with you. There's nothing for either of us here.'

'You can't stay with me. They'll hunt me down now for sure. Before, they thought maybe I'd died on the moor, but now . . . there's nowhere for me to run.'

'We'll leave the country, then,' she declared recklessly. 'I have a friend in America who will help us, I'm sure.' Yes, she thought, even though Randolph had turned out to be so different from his letters, and even though he knew of her shame, still that gentle man she had written to must be lurking somewhere behind that fearsome façade.

Magnus stopped walking abruptly and turned to face her. In the moonlight his craggy features seemed carved out of impenetrable rock. 'No matter where we go, your world can never be mine, Joanna, nor mine yours. We can't ever be more to each other than we are now.'

Joanna wanted to plead with him not to reject her. She longed to tell him that she couldn't stand to have another man abandon her. But instead she whispered, 'How did you ever become such a snob?'

'Don't make fun of me, Joanna.'

'I'm sorry. I didn't mean to hurt your feelings. But you must stop building this insurmountable barrier between us.'

'It wasn't me who put it there. It was there all along and always will be.'

Joanna turned and stumbled away from him, tears blinding her. She had done it again, she realised miserably. She had offered her heart to a man who didn't want it. Until that very moment she hadn't even known that she loved Magnus.

He came after her and caught her in his arms, sending her bundle of belongings to the ground. For an instant he held her and they stared at each other, acutely aware of the silvery light of a new moon, the rustling of leaves in the breeze, and the sweet scent of late summer in the meadow beside the lane. Most of all, each was aware of the closeness of a cherished being.

Then his face blurred as it came closer, and she raised her mouth to receive his kiss. He was tentative at first; then he claimed her lips in a sweet blending of warm breath and yielding flesh that was so filled with promise that Joanna felt as if she were soaring towards some distant star.

Magnus groaned and thrust her roughly away from him. 'Ah, God Almighty, what am I doing? This is madness. My station is so far below yours that I've no right even to touch your hand. Forgive me, Joanna.'

'Why do you ask forgiveness when I welcomed your lips, your caress? How can it be wrong to be close to one who cares for you, for whom you care . . . ? You do care for me, don't you, Magnus?'

'Yes, I care for you.' His voice was ragged with emotion. 'I care too much to saddle you with a hunted felon, an escaped convict . . . Come, I'll take you wherever you want to go, and as soon as you're safe with your own kind, we'll say good-bye.'

'Is there nothing I can say to you to keep us together?'

'Ah, Joanna, don't you see? It's wanting what we can't have that does us in. We think that if something, or somebody, is out of reach, then to possess it would make us happy. But it wouldn't. Chances are, it would make us more miserable than we were before. 'Specially when it comes to the wrong matching up of men and women. Because most of what we think that person is is nothing more than what we've made them in our own minds.'

'If you think I've bestowed shining armour on you in my mind, you're wrong, Magnus. All the manly attributes I see in you have been shown to me in your every action.'

The moon slipped behind a cloud briefly, and Magnus glanced up at the sky. 'Come on, we must get to my boat and away from here before they raise a hue and cry for me at Traherne Hall.'

As if in response to the thought, at that moment the sound of horses' hooves broke the silence. Someone was riding hard and fast down the lane from Bodrath House.

The footman would have reported her missing by now. Joanna remembered Justin's secret box and partially written journal, tied into her shawl with her gown and underwear. Surely those few papers weren't important enough to cause Paxton to send someone after her?

Magnus grabbed her hand and yanked her towards the hedgerow. 'I'll go first. You follow.'

The branches of the hawthorn snapped under the onslaught of Magnus's big hands and brawny shoulders. but the thorns still tore at Joanna as she fought her way through the hedge after him. They broke into a run, Joanna following blindly, her breath grinding in her chest.

The sound of horses' hooves faded, and clouds began to race across the pale crescent moon. They plunged on through the darkness. At last Magnus stopped to allow her to catch her breath and she looked around at the shadowed countryside, aware now of the change in their surroundings. Gone were the trees and meadows and hedgerows; the earth undulated in bleak hillocks strewn with rocks and bits of scrub. A few gnarled bushes fought for survival here and there, and there was something sinister about hollows filled with pitch-black shadow.

Anxious to be gone from this dismal place, Joanna stumbled forward, ahead of Magnus. A second later he caught her around the waist, lifted her into the air, and put her down behind him.

'We're on the moor now, Joanna. You must stay behind me. Another step and you'd have been in a bog. Quicksand, lass. It's been the death of many a convict who tried to escape.'

23

Megan stood at the window watching the path that wound up the rise towards the house. A rider was approaching at a furious pace, sending plumes of dust flying behind him. Several cowboys ran from the bunkhouse, and he shouted something as he rode pell-mell for the house.

Calling to Randolph that they had a visitor, she hurried to open the front door.

Quinn vaulted from his horse and ran towards her. Beyond the arched façade of the house she could see Mallory ranch hands taking up positions behind makeshift barricades. Sandbags had appeared as if by magic, and rifles were quickly passed to the crouching men. Quinn pushed her back into the house.

'A cavalry troop from Fort Apache is chasing the Chiricahua Kid and his renegades this way. The army should be here before dusk, but we might have to hold them off until then.'

'What can I do to help?' Megan asked calmly.

'Round up all the ammunition you can find and get ready to reload rifles. Better get Consuela to help you.'

As she raced to find Consuela, Megan recalled the robbery of the train that had brought them to New Mexico and silently thanked the fates that Quinn had happened to be nearby to help them face this new peril. She'd overheard enough hastily terminated conversations between the ranch hands about the atrocities committed by the Chiricahua Kid to know that his band of murderous thieves was now large enough to put all of them in real danger.

Consuela began to cry and crossed herself the instant Megan mentioned the Chiricahua Kid.

Leaving her cowering in the pantry, Megan went in search of Randolph.

His wheelchair was near the front door and she heard Quinn's voice, low and urgent: 'They killed a party of travellers only two miles out of Manzanita Flats. A scout is on his way to Fort Bayard and with any luck the army will intercept the bastards if they head that way, but it looks as if we're in for –'

Both men turned and saw her approach. Randolph, who was loading a rifle, said quickly, 'Don't worry. The Indians may not even come this way.'

Several things occurred to her simultaneously. She hadn't seen Quinn since their last emotional exchange when he'd confessed that he loved her; he didn't know that Randolph was aware of her true identity; and Quinn had no idea that she'd applied for admission to several medical schools in the East.

'Randolph's right,' Quinn said. 'The Kid prefers to attack small spreads. He's not likely to take on a dozen men.' The look he exchanged with Randolph suggested that neither of them believed this. Quinn turned and left the house through the front door.

Randolph finished loading his rifle and positioned his bath chair in front of the window beside the front door, which afforded a clear view of the only approaches to the house. There could be no attack from behind, because the house was nestled back against a sheer wall of granite.

Megan moved to his side. 'Randolph, please station one of the other men here. In your chair you're too exposed.' Seeing the hurt that flickered in his eyes, she quickly added, 'You can't manoeuvre the chair and fire a gun at the same time.'

'You'd be surprised what I can do if I have to. Megan, there are some boxes of shells in the storeroom next to the kitchen. Will you bring them? Get the other rifles from the gun case, too, and the shotgun.'

She quickly collected several boxes of shells, the shotgun, and two more rifles, then placed them near his chair. 'Quinn said I should reload the guns, but I don't know how,' she confessed. 'I've hated firearms since the first time I helped my grandfather treat a gunshot wound.'

'I'll show you how. I want you to keep a pistol with you at all times. I'll show you how to use it and if . . . the renegades break through –'

It wasn't necessary for him to finish. The bodies of two Mexican women had been found several weeks after the Kid and his men had abducted them. What had been done to the two women during the time they were forced to ride with the outlaws was something Megan didn't want to imagine.

Silently she watched as Randolph showed her how to load the rifles and the pistol. Finally he loaded the shotgun. 'You don't have to aim with this,' he explained. 'You can point it in the general direction of any intruder and it's guaranteed to stop them.'

Megan sat on a high-backed wooden chair in the hall. An uneasy silence seemed to have settled over the entire ranch. There was no sound within the house, and outside even the corrals were quiet, as if the horses, like the humans, sensed approaching danger.

Randolph regarded her with a wry smile. 'Up till now the Kid's been like a ghost. Pops up here and there, then disappears into thin air, leaving bodies and burned farms and wrecked stagecoaches in his wake. But with the troops from Arizona and a patrol from Fort Bayard, they're bound to catch him this time. You're probably going to witness the last Indian attack in the territory.'

Megan gave a small smile. 'When we tell of it in the future, we'll probably exaggerate outrageously.'

He smiled back, his eyes warm with love and admiration. 'Nothing daunts you, does it?'

'Oh, yes.'

'Well, you certainly don't show it.'

'My grandfather taught me that fear is the most

194

communicable of all the diseases. I learned to be frightened without showing it. You say the Chiricahua Kid is like a ghost. Does anyone know anything about him?'

'Not who he is or where he came from.'

'He must be filled with hatred, if all the stories of his atrocities are true.'

They were silent for a moment. Then Randolph said, 'The cavalry from Fort Apache will probably need feeding when they get here. We'd better warn Consuela.'

'She's in the pantry, praying for deliverance, I think. I'll tell her later.'

'I wonder if any of Quinn's old buddies will be with the troop. He was with the Fourth Cavalry.'

'In Arizona?'

'Yes. He left the army after Geronimo and his braves were shipped off to Florida. Quinn felt the Chiricahua Apache had been betrayed.'

'In what way?'

'They were told that in order to make a peace treaty they'd have to be counted, so the braves went willingly to the fort. The army promptly disarmed them and announced that they were prisoners of war. They were marched to Bowie Station. Quinn was there. He said the band played "Auld Lang Syne" as the Apache were packed like cattle into boxcars and shipped off to Florida. They've been dying like flies in a swamp there ever since. They were desert dwellers, nomads. Quinn's disillusionment with the military had begun before that, but –'

A burst of gunfire and a bloodcurdling yell from outside interrupted him. 'Get away from the window,' Randolph instructed. 'Take the shells into the living room. When I need you to reload, I'll slide a gun across the floor to you.'

Heart hammering, Megan grabbed the boxes of shells and drew back away from the window. 'I'll stay here. Surely nothing will penetrate twelve inches of adobe?'

A barrage of explosions outside muffled his reply. Randolph used his rifle butt to smash the window and fired at the unseen raiders. When he'd emptied the rifle he tossed it to Megan, who crouched on the floor and reloaded.

She could hear bullets whining through the air and muffled thuds as several of them buried themselves in the adobe walls. Surely one or more bullets would eventually find Randolph where he calmly sat in his wheelchair? A cold pool of fear for him formed in the pit of her stomach, but he had ignored her earlier protest, and she learned that he never retreated from a position he had taken.

Minutes later Quinn dragged a bleeding cowboy into the house, laid him at Megan's feet, then raced back outside to the accompaniment of rapid rifle fire from Randolph. Megan placed a cushion under the wounded man's head and then ran to her room to get her grandfather's medical bag.

Smoke from the rifle fire hung in a purple haze over the hall and the din outside sounded as if an army were attacking. Megan tore the wounded man's shirt away from a spreading pool of blood. Consuela crept from her hiding place and took over the reloading of Randolph's rifles.

A short time later two more ranch hands were in need of Megan's care. She worked quickly, sure of her tasks now, concentrating on staunching the bleeding. The removal of bullets would have to wait until later.

The sun sank lower, and dusk began to settle, with no sign of the cavalry from Fort Apache or a patrol from Fort Bayard. A glance through the window over Randolph's shoulder revealed that several of the Mallory cowboys were slumped over the barricades, obviously beyond her help.

A flickering orange light flew through the air, and she saw to her horror it was a flaming arrow. Seconds later the bunkhouse roof was ablaze.

Quinn and Chuck backed into the house through the front door, firing as they came. They slammed the door shut and dropped the bolt. Quinn's face was smoke-grimed, and for an instant Megan was back in Llanrys with her grandfather, waiting at the pithead as the coal miners brought up their dead and mangled comrades from the dark depths of the earth following a cave-in or a fire or some other catastrophe. Quinn wore the same expression of urgency and purpose.

The gunfire stopped and the ensuing silence resonated about the house, more frightening than the noise. Randolph said, 'Good God . . . surely they haven't killed all the other hands? How many men does the Kid have?'

'Three or four of our hands deserted us before he got here,' Chuck responded. 'Murphy may still be alive, but we can't get to him.'

'The scout probably didn't make it to Bayard,' Quinn said, 'and I guess the cavalry went to the Diamond T. No doubt they're all enjoying a good meal while their Apache scouts track the Kid here . . . which means the scouts will have to go back for them. Still, it can't be much longer now. We can hold out.'

As if to give the lie to his statement, a flaming arrow flew through the window, narrowly missing Randolph. It imbedded itself in the velvet cushion of a sanctuary bench and sent flames shooting up the wall. Quinn seized a rug and beat them out.

When he had stamped out the last spark he said, 'It's almost dark. I'll ride to the Diamond T and make sure the troop doesn't get lost. If they're already lost, I'll get help.'

'No!' Megan cried, more fearful for his safety than for her own. The three men turned to look at her. She added lamely, 'You can't possibly get out; they've obviously surrounded the house.'

For an instant Quinn's eyes locked with hers, as if daring her to admit that she cared whether he lived or died; then he said, 'I'll make it, but in the unlikely event I don't . . .' He put a pistol into her hand.

She looked down at it uncomprehendingly.

Randolph said quietly, 'If they break in, don't let them take you alive, Megan.'

Quinn looked from one to the other. '*Megan?*'

'We'll save the explanations until you get back,' Randolph said.

'But they're trying to burn down the house,' Megan cried, sure that if Quinn left she would never see him again.

'The roof's tile and the walls are adobe,' Chuck said in a tone more suited to addressing a backward child. 'This is the only window that opens to the outside. We'll deal with any fire that comes this way.'

Megan saw now the wisdom of the Spanish hacienda style of architecture, with all rooms opening onto an interior courtyard.

'I'm going out the back way,' Quinn said, looking at Megan. 'Come with me and watch to see if I make it up the ridge behind the house.'

Megan followed him along the corridor and through the kitchen to the back door. 'It's too dark to see whether you make it up the ridge.'

'I know. I needed a kiss for luck.'

He pulled her into a close embrace, and his mouth found hers, claiming her lips with a hungry ardour that Megan responded to instantly. For a moment she allowed the rush of passion to drive away fear, even reason, and then sanity returned. Gasping for breath, she twisted her face away from his.

'Stop it! Are you mad?'

'He called you Megan. Doesn't that change everything?'

'It changes nothing. I'm still his wife.'

'There's more to being a wife than having a slip of paper say it's so.'

She pulled free of his grasp and ran. Halfway back along the corridor a burst of gunfire shattered the silence and she skidded to a stop, a scream trapped in her throat. He was dead; they had shot him as he left the house . . . or was he only wounded? Blindly she turned and stumbled back, oblivious of everything but an overwhelming fear that she had lost Quinn forever.

Wrenching open the back door, she was about to rush out into the darkness when rough hands grabbed her and pulled her back.

'Where the hell do you think you're going?' Chuck demanded, slamming the door shut.

'Quinn's out there!'

Chuck looked down at her with contempt. 'He's long gone.'

'But the shooting –'

'That was your husband persuading a couple of hombres to get away from the front door.'

He looked at her for a long moment and then turned his back and walked away. That look on his face lingered in her mind as she followed him back along the corridor. Was it possible that Chuck had been close enough to overhear her conversation with Quinn? Worse, could he have observed their kiss?

Something rattled overhead. Chuck stopped and looked up. 'Damn. They're on the roof prying off the tiles. If they set the rafters afire . . . Go warn your husband. Tell him I'm going out to try to pick 'em off.' He disappeared in the direction of the living room, which opened to the inner courtyard. Moments later shots again rang out.

Megan flew back to Randolph's side. He had closed the shutters over the window and now sat facing the door. Consuela huddled against the wall, motionless, her eyes glazed.

Randolph looked at Megan. 'Where's Chuck?'

Before she could finish telling him, something formidably strong battered against the shutters, which gave way. Randolph fired three shots in rapid succession. At the same instant, the wooden rafters over their heads began to splinter under the assault of hatchets. Megan snatched up the shotgun, pointed it towards the ceiling, and pulled the trigger.

There was an earsplitting explosion, the shotgun bucked violently, and she found herself flat on her back, choking on smoke. A body fell from above and crashed down beside her on the tile.

A distant sound filtered through her dazed senses. 'Randolph . . . do I hear . . . music?'

'That, my dear,' he answered hoarsely, 'is a cavalry bugle . . . and it's blowing a charge.'

She sat up and wrapped her arms around his legs, burying her face in his lap. 'I'm surely going to wake up in a minute . . .'

Outside there was the thunder of horses, gunfire, yells, and shouted commands, then finally a voice calling, 'Hullo, the house! Anybody in there? I'm Cap'n Hutchison, Fourth Cavalry.'

Megan uncoiled her stiff limbs, rose, and went to raise the bolt on the front door, carefully stepping over the body of the man she'd brought down from the roof. She avoided looking at him.

The blue-uniformed officer who stood outside touched his cap and said something, but Megan didn't hear what it was. She blinked into focus a group of soldiers who dragged a buckskinclad prisoner towards the house.

'Ma'am,' Captain Hutchison continued, 'we've got him. That's the murdering redskin that's terrorised the entire territory. You can tell your children you saw the Chiricahua Kid captured.'

Megan stared in disbelief at the captured man. It was A-chi-tie, who had saved her from the bear.

24

Joanna felt sure her strength would give out long before they crossed the corner of Dartmoor that led towards the coast. As they covered only a small part of that inhospitable terrain to evade pursuers, she marvelled that Magnus had managed to escape from the grim prison that loomed over the heart of the moor.

When at last they reached the doubtful sanctuary of Delta's cottage, Joanna was so exhausted she nearly collapsed. But as she rested in a chair while Magnus told Delta all that had transpired, her reason warned her that neither of them would be safe as long as they remained in Cornwall.

Seated at Delta's kitchen table, Magnus finally fell silent. Delta looked from one to the other, her eyes narrowed.

Recognising the furious disappointment on the other woman's face, Joanna said breathlessly, 'So you see, there is no one left to avenge yourself against. Justin Bodrath is dead. He was consumptive, and I'm sure he died a horrible, choking death, gasping for breath. Surely death is punishment enough for whatever part he played in your brother's murder?'

'What about Magnus? Is he to be hunted down and hanged? You were supposed to find out how Harry Bodrath died.'

'The death certificate indicated he died as a result of the boxing match –'

'I don't want to hear about certificates!' Delta cried. 'What can a bit of paper tell us? Only that a man is dead, not why he died or by whose hand.'

'The certificate described injuries, symptoms . . . I'm not a doctor, but they sounded like the injuries a man would receive in a fight.' She wondered even as she spoke if perhaps one day Megan might look at that certificate and tell her more. She was glad she'd had the foresight to bring the Bodrath documents with her.

Magnus said, 'What does it matter now, anyway? All the Bodraths are gone. And I'll be gone, too, as soon as the wind comes up and I can set sail.'

Delta moved restlessly around the kitchen, her body as sinuous as a cat's. 'I'll start packing. There's nothing to keep me here now that Justin Bodrath's gone. I'm going with you.'

'Delta, you can't come with me. If – God forbid – we're caught, you'll be guilty of aiding a fugitive. I must go alone. I'll sail across the Channel and –'

'And what? You don't speak French. How will you survive in France?'

'Magnus,' Joanna put in, 'why not go to America? I could give you a letter of introduction to my cousin there. I'm sure he would help you get started again.'

His eyes softened with love as he looked at her. 'But where will you go? I didn't find out where your friend Megan is. Maybe you should think about going to your cousin in America yourself.'

Delta said, 'Magnus, I'd like to go to America.'

Joanna put in, 'The newspapers are full of appeals for immigrants. They want settlers for the western part of the country, which is where my cousin lives.'

Delta picked up the orchid that decorated her table and twirled it in her fingers. 'I have a little money put away. Enough to get you and me to America, Magnus.'

'If anybody goes to America, it should be Joanna.'

'I don't have enough money for three passages.' Delta's voice was almost a hiss.

Magnus took Joanna's hands in his, ignoring Delta's venomous stare. 'I must know you're safe somewhere.'

'I can't go back to my family, Magnus. I just can't. If I'd been able to collect my salary from Mr Bodrath, I would have travelled to my cousin in the New Mexico Territory, also. As it is, I shall find a position. Don't worry about me.'

'We're wasting time!' Delta said sharply. 'They'll have you back in Dartmoor if we don't leave now. Magnus, for God's sake . . . we can all go.' She fumbled with a loose brick beside the fireplace, then reached into a hidden compartment and produced a tin box. 'Damn it, we'll have to travel steerage if all three of us go.'

'Delta, I'll pay you back as soon as I can. I promise,' Joanna said.

Magnus's expression as he gazed at the two women was

that of a male helpless to deal with female determination. 'The sun's coming up. There's not much space in the boat for belongings. Don't pack too much. What will you do about Lizzie?'

Delta shrugged indifferently. 'She can find another job or she can stay here and earn a living the same way I had to.' She glanced down at Joanna's bundle of belongings. 'I'll find a bag for you.'

'Please hurry,' Joanna replied.

Paxton looked at the body of his late master, draped in white satin and lying in his coffin. In a few minutes he would be sealed away in the family crypt forever. Paxton bent to kiss the waxen cheek and whisper his last good-bye.

'I swear to serve you in death as I did in life. No scandal will ever touch your name. I promised to find Harry's murderer, and I shall keep that vow, even if it takes the rest of my life and all of the wealth and property you left to me.'

Straightening up, he walked from the room. He marched slowly from room to room, checking to be sure his orders had been carried out. The furniture had been draped with dust sheets; the dishes were packed away.

It had been careless of him to leave the Cromwell retreat open, allowing the Traherne girl to steal the secret box and the Bodrath journal, and he was furious that the groom he'd sent after her had not been able to catch up with a single frail little female on foot. But no matter. She would return to her family, and he could retrieve Justin's possessions, or, if she was truly foolish, she might stay with the convict. Paxton rather hoped for the latter. It would serve her right.

His footsteps echoed through the hall as he moved from room to room. A deep stillness had fallen on the house, as if the very walls knew that the era of the Bodraths had ended.

Paxton left his inspection of the portrait gallery until last. The senior footman waited, white sheets folded across his arm, to cover the paintings after Paxton had looked at them one last time.

'Give the covers to me; I'll do it myself,' Paxton said.

'The man you were expecting has arrived,' the footman said. 'I left him outside. Shall I bring him into the house?'

'Have him wait in the hall by the front door.'

The footman nodded and departed, leaving Paxton alone with the long line of Bodrath portraits. The painted faces seemed to stare at him expectantly. He went first to the old warrior he had served through several bloody campaigns and, ramrod straight, saluted him.

'You saved my life. Brought me to the only home I've ever known. You charged me with the care and upbringing of your sons, and I made them my own. I think perhaps I was more a father to Neville and Harry and Justin than you were.'

Paxton covered the portrait with the dust cloth. His former commanding officer's eyes seemed to watch him until the last second, and the message in that burning stare was clear: *You're a good soldier, Paxton. I know I can count on you to do your duty*.

Moving quickly down the ranks, he covered the other portraits, then went slowly downstairs to the hall, his fingers trailing along the banister.

A man of gargantuan size stood awkwardly at attention by the front door. He was young, no more than nineteen or twenty, his boyish face contrasting oddly with his Goliath's body. Paxton noted with satisfaction the unblemished features, the huge fists, but, more important to his purpose, the crafty stare in the small eyes as they darted greedily about the great hall of the Bodraths.

Paxton walked around the man, examining him from every angle.

'They said you might give me work,' the young man said, apparently unable to endure the silence.

'I expect you're wondering why you were merely dishonourably discharged from the army, instead of being court-martialled.' When there was no immediate reply,

Paxton snapped, 'Answer me at once when I speak to you, Hollis.'

'Yes, sir. Yes, I did wonder who got me out.'

'It was I. You see, I heard that, before you were brought up on charges, you were a promising boxer. Knocked out every opponent without being touched yourself. But then there was that unfortunate charge of assault and battery and . . . but you know the rest.'

'Yes, sir.'

'Very well, Hollis, I think we understand each other. I bought you, you see. I now own you, body and soul. Without me, you will drift into a life of crime and end up at the end of a rope.'

Hollis cleared his throat. 'What do you want me to do for you, sir?'

'Eventually, when we catch up with him,' Paxton said, no flicker of emotion showing on his face, 'you are going to beat a man to death with your bare fists.'

25

The bunkhouse fire had burned itself out, and Consuela was in the kitchen preparing food for the soldiers, who were pitching tents on the open range. A detail had been ordered to remove bodies and round up the horses that had been released from their corral by the raiders.

Captain Hutchison was well pleased with his men. A dozen renegades were dead, their leader was in custody, and the stragglers who had escaped would be tracked down by the cavalry's Apache scouts at first light.

Megan finished bandaging the shoulder of the lone

surviving cowboy as Chuck watched her suspiciously. She looked at Randolph, who slumped wearily in his wheelchair.

'I don't care what the soldiers say,' she declared angrily. 'That man *can't* be the Chiricahua Kid.'

'Then what was he doing skulking about on our land?' Chuck growled.

'He lived here peacefully, without you even knowing about him, for weeks before the attack. He lived alone, I'm certain. He was never part of that murderous gang.'

'You shoulda told us you'd seen a redskin on ranch land,' Chuck said, and muttered something under his breath about greenhorn foreigners with not enough sense to come in out of the rain.

Ignoring him, Megan appealed to Randolph again, 'Would a man capable of murdering and torturing men, women, and children have saved me from that bear?'

Randolph pressed his palm to his forehead. 'I'm still trying to grasp that you wandered off and encountered both a bear and an Indian and never said a word about it. Didn't it occur to you that Chuck or one of the men should have investigated?'

'Investigated? Tracked him down and tied him up like an animal, you mean, just as the soldiers have done.'

'Megan, you're new here. You don't understand what it was like in the territory a very short time ago. Settlers were constantly battling the Apache, who are the most bloodthirsty of all the tribes.'

Megan was silent, lost in thought. Then suddenly she exclaimed, 'Oh, dear God! I was so concerned about A-chi-tie that I completely forgot about Quinn! Quick, we must send soldiers to find him.'

Chuck's deep-set eyes regarded her knowingly and she looked away quickly, sure now that he suspected how she felt about Quinn.

Randolph said, 'Captain Hutchison told me that Quinn is at the Diamond T. I'm sorry, I should have told you before, but you were busy taking care of the wounded.

What a blessing your medical knowledge has proved to be . . .' His voice trailed away, and it was clear from his expression that something troubled him deeply.

'What it is?' Megan asked. 'Is something wrong? It's Quinn, isn't it? Was he wounded, hurt? Is that why he didn't come back with the cavalry?'

'He broke his leg, Megan,' Randolph said. 'His horse threw him just before he reached the Diamond T, and he crawled the last few yards. The cook at the Diamond T set the bone for him. He'll be fine, but he couldn't ride back here.'

'There's something you're not telling me,' Megan insisted. She glanced at Chuck, who muttered something about finding a place to sleep, then helped the wounded cowboy to his feet.

'Tomorrow you could ride over to the Diamond T with the cavalry and see that Quinn's leg is set properly,' Randolph said when they were alone. 'One of their hands can bring you back.'

'Randolph, for the love of heaven, tell me what it is that makes you look at me as if I were about to disappear in a puff of smoke . . . Oh!' she broke off, her excitement rising. 'That's it, isn't it? Chuck picked up the mail just before we were attacked. There was a letter from a medical school –'

'Megan,' Randolph interrupted swiftly, 'there were three letters. Forgive me, I opened them so I could prepare you for the worst if necessary. I'm sorry. All three medical schools rejected your application for the same reason.'

She slumped into a chair, hope fading. 'Because I'm a woman.'

'No.' Randolph wheeled his chair closer to her and took her hands in his. 'Not because you're a woman. Because . . . you're too old. They wouldn't take a twenty-five-year-old man, either. They say it simply takes too many years to train a physician. They can't give space in medical school to anyone whose useful life as a doctor would be limited . . .'

Megan wasn't listening. She rose as if sleepwalking and left the room.

A campfire was burning low in the field where the soldiers had pitched their tents. Except for the shrill cacophony of the crickets' night song, silence had fallen on the Mallory ranch.

Megan crept past the charred shell of the bunkhouse, glanced back over her shoulder, and, detecting no one following, hurried towards the smokehouse.

The sentry posted outside stiffened, rifle at the ready, as she came into view. He lowered his gun. 'Ma'am, it don't pay to creep up on a man like that. You're liable to get yourself shot.'

Megan held up a cloth-wrapped plate. 'I brought some food.'

'Thank you kindly, ma'am, but I had supper.'

'This is for the prisoner. Stand aside, please.'

The sentry's mouth opened in astonishment. 'Ma'am, I can't let you go in there. Look, that murdering scum don't deserve to be fed, but if it'll make you happy, give me the plate and I'll take it to him.'

Megan took a step back. 'And will you feed him also? As I recall, his wrists were bound behind his back with rawhide thongs when he was put into the smokehouse. No, my good man, you are on my property and you will not dictate to me. I'm going inside to feed him. You can remain out here as you were ordered.'

She thought he might actually shoot her as she reached for the latch of the smokehouse door, but he said, 'Hold on there. I'll light the lantern for you.'

He stood respectfully aside, gun pointed at A-chi-tie, who lay on his side, bound hand and foot, on the dirt floor. The smell of greasy smoke was overpowering, and Megan bit back a cry of alarm as a scorpion scurried over the toe of her shoe, startled by the sudden light.

The lantern's yellow glow fell on the Indian's face. His jaw was badly bruised, and there was an oozing bump on his forehead. He looked at her, recognition in his eyes,

208

and tried to scramble to his feet. The sentry pushed him back down.

'Ya-tah-hey,' the Indian said, looking at Megan.

Megan turned questioningly to the soldier.

'Well, I'll be . . . I reckon whoever hung the moniker "Chiricahua Kid" on him had never met him.'

'Why do you say that?'

'He just greeted you in Navajo. He ain't no 'Pache.'

'I knew it!' Megan exclaimed. 'I knew he couldn't be the one.'

'Oh, hold up there, ma'am. He's the Kid all right. We caught him not fifteen feet from the house.'

He was probably coming to help us, Megan thought. She looked around. 'Will you pull him up into a sitting position? Perhaps near the door . . . the smoky smell in here is horrible.'

The sentry obligingly leaned his rifle against the wall and grasped A-chi-tie's shoulders. When the Indian was up on his knees, the soldier felt the cold muzzle of his own gun prod the side of his head.

He turned and stared up the length of the barrel at Megan. 'I'm sorry,' she said quietly, 'but you have the wrong man. Cut his bonds.'

For a second she thought he would refuse, but then he shrugged. 'You turn him loose, he won't get far. He's got a busted ankle.'

He took a knife from his belt and slid the blade under the Indian's bonds. The rawhide took what seemed an age to give way.

Megan prodded the soldier with the rifle again. 'Now lie down on the floor with your hands behind your head.'

A-chi-tie pulled himself upright by clutching the door and as he hopped out of the smokehouse Megan saw that the sentry had been right; the Indian obviously couldn't bear to put any weight on his right ankle. He turned to look at her and said something in his own language, then began to hop away. She kept the rifle pointed at the sentry.

A-chi-tie disappeared into the shadows.

The sentry twisted his head to look up at her. 'Now what?'

'Now we wait to give him a chance to get away.'

Megan sat on her bed watching in stony silence as her clothes were carefully packed by a tearful Consuela.

Randolph said, 'Chuck will take you to Deming and put you aboard a train. He'll send a wire to the Pinkerton agent in Galveston who has been searching for your father. The agent's name is Denby. He'll meet the train and take you to a hotel.'

'I'd rather stay here and face the consequences,' Megan answered. 'I feel as if I'm running away.'

'I don't think you understand the seriousness of what you did. Interfering with the army, setting free a murderer. Apart from any possible charges Captain Hutchison might bring against you, when the word gets out that you turned the Chiricahua Kid loose –'

'He *isn't* the Chiricahua Kid,' Megan said for the hundredth time.

'It doesn't matter. If he isn't the Kid, then the real renegade is still free and he'll kill and plunder the territory again. You know we aren't completely without law and order here. The man you call A-chi-tie would have been safer in custody. He'd have been given a fair trial, and if the real Chiricahua Kid had struck again, that would have proved they had the wrong man.'

'I've heard of your lynching parties, Randolph. I saw how A-chi-tie had already been beaten. He wouldn't have lived long enough to stand trial. Besides, holding a post-mortem on what I did serves no purpose. I just can't leave you to face the wrath of the entire territory alone. Please allow me to stay long enough to explain –'

'It will all blow over as soon as the real Chiricahua Kid is captured. In the meantime it's better that you aren't here. I'll let you know when it's safe to come back.'

Chuck knocked on the open bedroom door. 'We've got

210

to go if we're to make it to Deming in time to catch that train.' He picked up her bags.

Consuela hugged her and murmured, *'Vaya con Dios*,' then dissolved into tears and ran from the room.

Randolph watched Megan sadly. 'I shall miss you.'

Megan stood up. 'I don't know why. I've caused you nothing but trouble since I arrived. How different it might have been for you if I really had been Joanna . . .'

The train thundered across the sand-swept vistas of the south-western deserts, and Megan marvelled at the vast emptiness of the country. So few towns, so few farms. She was glad to see that there were several uniformed soldiers aboard the train, which she hoped would prevent another attack by outlaws. On her last train journey she had been accompanied by Quinn. As she settled back into her seat, she at last allowed herself to think about him.

Her departure from the ranch had been so abrupt there hadn't been time to ride over to the Diamond T to say good-bye, and she couldn't help wondering what Quinn's reaction to her banishment would be.

After a few minutes of what she decided was pointless speculation, she concentrated on what lay ahead instead of what was irrevocably lost. Had the Pinkertons found her father? Was he still alive, and if so, was he a practising physician?

Galveston proved to be a town built on an island off the coast of Texas in the Gulf of Mexico. Megan was met at the station by the Pinkerton man, Denby, and taken to what he assured her was the finest hotel in Galveston.

Denby was a bespectacled, studious-looking young man with sandy hair and a nervous habit of tugging at his shirt collar as if it felt too tight. He informed her immediately that he had not been working on her case but that as soon as she was settled in he would return to the office and see what the latest report revealed.

She unpacked, had lunch sent up to her room, then stood on the balcony hoping to catch a whisper of a breeze coming across the water. The air was oppressively still and humid. On the street below she saw that the houses were built well above the ground, with many steps leading to their doors; some structures appeared to be built on stilts.

How slowly the minutes dragged by when one had nothing to do, and how she hated idleness. If her father was alive and practising, she hoped she could persuade him to let her work with him, at least until she returned to New Mexico . . . if she returned. That was another question that hovered uncertainly in her mind.

Down on the street she saw Denby crossing towards the hotel, and she went back inside to await his arrival, silent prayers fluttering like caged birds . . . Please let my father be alive. Let him be practising. Above all, let him like me.

Denby, who was carrying an important-looking portfolio, sat stiffly in a chair, alternately tugging at his collar and shuffling papers.

When she was ready to scream with tension, he finally announced, 'Your father spent several years as a ship's doctor, mainly aboard merchantmen plying the Caribbean, calling at Galveston occasionally. Then on one trip he met a lady here and they were married. He settled here with her and went into medical practice, mainly treating rich hypochondriacs. His wife came from one of Galveston's oldest and wealthiest families, and her connections pretty much determined his patients.'

He paused, tugging at his collar, and Megan asked quickly, 'Is he dead?'

'No, no, he's alive, but . . . well, something happened, three or four years ago, that caused him to give up his practice and . . . well, he became a recluse, a complete hermit. He has a fine big beachfront house, but he has walled it in, except for a small opening to the sea. Even that has steel wire barriers out past the tide line, so no one can walk in from the beach.'

'And doesn't anyone have any idea what happened to cause this withdrawal?'

'Well, we think the main problem was that . . .' He

paused. 'It was rumoured that your father had reverted to his old habits.'

'What old habits?'

Tugging at his collar, Denby muttered, 'Drinking too much. He'd been kicked off several ships for being drunk, but he apparently overcame the problem during the first years of his marriage. I'm sorry, Mrs Mallory. You've come a long way on a fruitless trip. Your father will not see you. My firm sent him a letter informing him of your imminent arrival, and we received in return a curt note stating that you must be an impostor, as he had no daughter.'

'He believes I died in infancy,' Megan said. 'But I have proof of my identity – my birth certificate, even some letters in his own handwriting. Please give me his address so that I can inform him of this.'

Denby's eyes gleamed behind his glasses. 'You're not giving up? Good. Sure, I'll give you the address. I'll take you out there myself.'

26

For days Joanna lay on a narrow shelf in steerage as the immigrant ship pitched and heaved its way across an ocean already churning with autumn squalls. During the journey, she endured misery such as she had never imagined. The days and nights at sea were filled with the wailing of infants, muffled curses, moans of seasick voyagers. In the close quarters the stench of vomit and urine and unwashed bodies sickened her. The rolling of the ship tossed passengers about unmercifully, and many were injured.

Delta disappeared from the steerage quarters the second day out of Southampton and didn't return. Magnus was closeted away somewhere with the other single men and not allowed to enter the women's section, so Joanna had no contact with either of them. The seas were so heavy that the passengers were not allowed on deck. Seasick and lonely, Joanna wondered if she would live to see America.

It was with vast relief that she heard the excited shout that reverberated about the ship proclaiming that land was in sight. She went up on deck to see New York Harbor materialise in a thin early-morning mist, and cheered with the others when at last the ship nudged the dock; unaware that the ordeal of Ellis Island lay ahead.

She saw Magnus briefly as she and the other passengers were herded into what reminded her of a cattle shed. He waved encouragingly, although his face was creased with concern. She was poked and prodded by a doctor and then questioned by a man whose Irish brogue was so thick she could understand very little of what he asked. She had an uneasy feeling he considered her mentally deficient when she looked at him blankly in response to a query. Nodding and smiling seemed to help, and he wrote slowly and labouriously on an official-looking document. All she was sure of was that he had her name, which she gave as Joanna Smith. Continuing to use the alias seemed an appropriate penance for the shame she had brought to the name Traherne.

The immigration official established that she had no relatives in New York and no job to go to, and seemed not to hear her stammered explanation that she hoped to travel to a friend in the New Mexico Territory, as he was already stamping his ledger. He waved her along.

It was like being in prison, she decided, as days passed and still she was not released. No, this was worse than prison, she realised, for she had no idea when she would leave the island; at least a prisoner knew the length of his sentence. What had become of Magnus? And where was Delta, whom she had not seen since they boarded the ship?

Prospective employers came to see the newly arrived immigrants, but they wanted women who could use sewing machines or were skilled in other tasks that were beyond Joanna's ken. Then, miraculously, one day she was taken to the gates leading to freedom and reunited with Magnus.

She hugged him and babbled over and over how glad she was to see him. He told her sheepishly that he'd had to say she was his common-law wife and promise to support her.

'I don't care if you told them I'm your trained monkey,' she replied. 'Let's get away from this dreadful place as fast as we can. Where is Delta? I didn't see her for the whole voyage.'

Avoiding her eye, Magnus replied, 'She took up with one of the ship's officers on the crossing. Said she couldn't stand being in steerage. He whisked her off Ellis Island in no time, too. I didn't see her for a bit. Then she came knocking on my door.'

Joanna's joy at being reunited with Magnus dwindled at the prospect of sharing living quarters with the beautiful Delta. 'She's . . . with you now?'

'We've a room in what they call a tenement. It's not the kind of place you're used to living in, but I thought it would be better than Ellis Island.'

'I'll only need a place until I can send a wire to Randolph,' Joanna replied. 'We'll manage until then.'

The tenement proved to be a nightmare that was, if anything, worse than Ellis Island. Joanna's heart sank as she followed Magnus up the interminable flights of grimy stairs, passing scarred walls and battered doors that did little to contain cooking smells and the abrasive sound of squabbling.

Magnus paused outside a door on the sixth floor, his expression tense. 'Joanna . . . Delta's been feeling poorly. I got work as a labourer and I've had to leave her alone a lot. She wouldn't let me fetch a doctor, but now that you're here, p'raps you can get her to tell you what ails her.'

He opened the door, and Joanna tried to disguise her

dismay as the shabby room came into view. Delta, looking painfully thin and lethargic, lay on a bed in one corner of the room. She regarded Joanna balefully.

Joanna picked her way carefully through the clutter to the bed. 'I'm so sorry you're not well. Now, don't worry about anything. We won't leave for the New Mexico Territory until you're well enough to travel.'

Magnus said, 'I can still get a half-day's work in if I leave now. Will you be all right, Joanna?'

'Yes, thank you. But would you stop on the way and send a telegram? Send it to Randolph Mallory, Mallory Ranch, near Manzanita Flats, New Mexico Territory. Just say I'm in New York and ask if I may visit the ranch.' She paused, 'No – ask him to wire train fare for three and say I'll repay him.'

'You don't need train fare for three,' Magnus said at once. 'He's your cousin, not ours. I'll work until I can pay my own way and Delta's.'

'But Magnus, I owe Delta for my passage here,' Joanna protested.

'Let me take care of that. You just see to yourself. This is no place for you. The sooner you go to your cousin the better. I'll change the wire for you. I don't want charity from anybody.'

Surprisingly, Delta said nothing and Magnus left before Joanna could argue.

Delta looked up at her expectantly, as though she hoped Joanna would miraculously transform the depressing room and window view of the grey city into the spotless cottage she had left behind on the ruggedly beautiful Cornish coast.

She's here because of Magnus, Joanna thought. She really does love him, even though she can't be faithful to him. Well, I love him, too, and I'm sure he loves me, so the choice will be up to him. Perhaps in the United States, which claimed to be a classless society, he would no longer feel a class barrier between them.

Placing her bundle of belongings on the floor, Joanna

216

touched Delta's smooth brow. 'You don't seem to have a fever. How long have you been ill? Perhaps you ate something that disagreed with you.'

'I should think you'd know what ails me,' Delta said, her amber eyes flashing triumphantly. 'I've got the morning sickness. I'm with child.' She paused, then added, 'But I'm not going to do what you did. Oh, no. I'm going to have this baby and I'm going to marry the father.'

Joanna felt a coldness begin somewhere deep inside her. 'Magnus told me you were . . . engaged to an officer aboard the ship.'

Delta snorted indelicately. 'That was over the minute he got me off Ellis Island. Men are such fools. They believe everything you tell them. Surely you know whose baby this is. Magnus and I have been living together just as we did before he went to Dartmoor.'

'You and Magnus . . .' Joanna said faintly. 'He's . . . the father of your child?'

'I told you he was my man.' Delta stretched her arms over her head and yawned. 'The sooner you're on your way to wherever you're going, the better. You can't share a room with a married couple.'

Joanna blindly turned away and made a pretence of tidying the room, feeling as though her heart had shattered into a dozen pieces and all of them had lodged in her throat. Somehow she knew she would have to put on a brave face until Randolph replied to her wire.

But his reply, when it came, was baffling: 'Unsure why you are in New York. Assume your father's there. Too soon for you to come back to ranch. Please write and explain.'

On her first foray out into the teeming streets of the city Joanna found herself pinned against a shop window, terrified of the bustling pedestrians who surged along the sidewalks in a human wave. There were more people than she had ever seen congregated in one place, and there were so many horse-drawn wagons and new horseless

217

carriages, filling the air with noise and smoke, that she was afraid to cross the street.

Magnus had given her directions to the Western Union office. To get there she had to ride a streetcar, but she wasn't sure she could even walk to the corner where she was to catch it without being trampled in the crush of humanity.

The city was deafening, filled with the raucous shouts of vendors, grinding wheels, the clatter of horses' hooves, the strangely exciting harmony of voices conversing in many different languages.

A tiny ginger-coloured kitten suddenly darted out of the shop doorway behind her, somehow avoided the hurrying feet on the sidewalk, and pounced upon a piece of paper blowing along the gutter. A second later an eddy of wind lifted the paper out into the street and the kitten chased after it.

Joanna didn't stop to think. When she saw horses and wagon wheels bearing down on the helpless little creature, she plunged into the street and snatched up the kitten seconds before the driver of an ice wagon yanked on the reins to force his team to swerve away from her.

Clutching the kitten to her breast, Joanna stumbled back to the sidewalk. The iceman berated her soundly for her foolhardiness, pointing out with his colourful epithets that she had risked her own skin and his, to say nothing of the lives of animals that were far more valuable than a cat – his horses. Several passersby also chided her for almost causing a serious accident.

She crept back to the shop, her cheeks flaming. A harassed-looking man wearing a blood-spattered apron came running out of the door leaving a trail of sawdust in his wake. He took her arm and led her into what she now saw was a butcher shop.

'Oh, thank you, miss, for saving the kitten. My daughter would've been brokenhearted if it had been run over. It's hard to keep pets when you live over a shop on a street as busy as this. Here, sit down and catch your breath.'

He pulled a chair out from behind the counter and she sat down. The kitten had wrapped itself around Joanna's neck and was purring loudly. The butcher carefully removed the tiny animal from her shoulder. 'You just rest a minute while I take Tiger upstairs to my little girl.'

Joanna looked around. Sides of beef and pork hung from steel hooks behind the counter, and a glass case was filled with cut meat, sausages, organ meats, and soup bones. The shop was scrupulously clean, but the gamey smell of raw meat didn't help the fluttering in her stomach. She had lost so much weight during the voyage due to seasickness that her shrunken stomach rebelled under far less provocation.

The butcher returned, carrying a glass of water. 'I saw you standing out there. Were you waiting for somebody?'

She accepted the water gratefully and took a sip. 'No . . . I was just a little overwhelmed by all the people.'

'My name's Jacob. Just moved into the neighbourhood, did you?'

'Yes, the day before yesterday.' A day and a half of cleaning the room and catering to Delta's constant demands, with no opportunity to speak privately with Magnus, who returned from his work late at night, grimy, tired, and looking more defeated each day.

He would hang a blanket across the room and sleep on a lumpy couch while Joanna had no choice but to share the double bed with Delta, who whispered that she was taking Magnus's place and should hurry off to New Mexico. Joanna lay awake each night for hours, listening to the sounds of the city, wondering how the pampered Miss Traherne could possibly have been reduced to such circumstances.

She smiled apologetically at Jacob the butcher. 'My name is Joanna Smith. I suppose I must seem foolish to you.'

'More like a fish out of water. A very refined sounding fish, I might add. Are you looking for work?'

She glanced nervously at his chopping block and meat

cleavers, and a broad smile spread over his face as he evidently read her mind. 'I don't think you'd be strong enough to heft sides of beef, Miss Smith. But one of my customers used to work uptown for a nice family. She's had to give up her job to come home and take care of her sick mother. I could put in a good word for you, if you're interested.'

'A . . . servant's job?' Joanna asked hesitantly.

'Parlour maid to a very well off family,' he answered with a touch of triumph in his tone, as if he were delivering unexpectedly welcome news. 'Nice uniform to wear and a day off every other week. You look like you could handle it, and you speak the language. Plenty of young women would kill for that position, I can tell you.'

'I would live with the family?'

'Well, yes, of course you would.'

'Oh, Jacob,' Joanna breathed, 'I can't tell you how glad I am that I took shelter against your shop-window!'

Jacob had insisted upon giving her some of his best stewing beef to show his gratitude for the rescue of his daughter's kitten, and that evening Magnus returned to find a pot of stew bubbling on the oil stove in the corner of the room.

Since Joanna had no idea how to light the stove or how to prepare the stew, she had been forced to ask for instructions from Delta, who lay in bed, fanning herself with an ostrich feather and complaining about how ill she felt. Joanna had saved her news for Magnus's arrival.

'. . . And the parlour maid who had to give up the job lived just around the corner, so Jacob sent his wife to speak to her. And he has one of those new telephones, so he called Mr and Mrs George Abercromby – and tomorrow I am to go for an interview,' Joanna concluded breathlessly.

Magnus laid down his fork. 'But what about your cousin in New Mexico? I thought you wanted to go to him. Did you send another wire?'

'No . . . no, I didn't. Oh, I know you said I should, that

perhaps my first telegram had become garbled en route. I think it was his reply that was mixed up, but still, the meaning was quite clear. He doesn't want me to visit him.' She glanced towards the bed, wishing they could speak in private. Delta picked at the food on her plate, watching them from beneath half-closed eyelids. Her magnificent breasts had grown even more plump during her pregnancy and were scarcely concealed under a wisp of silk night-gown.

'Magnus, I didn't tell you this before,' Joanna continued in a low voice. 'I met Randolph Mallory at my sister's wedding. He . . . he knew of the trouble I was in.'

'And you think that's the reason he doesn't want you to visit him. I see.' Magnus digested this silently for a moment. 'But a maid's job . . . Joanna, this won't be like working for Justin Bodrath.'

'We had parlour maids at Traherne Hall, so I do have a vague idea of their duties,' Joanna said, staring longingly at his callused hands resting on the edge of the table and wishing she could slip her own cold hands into his.

'Well, you haven't got the job yet,' Magnus said. 'I'll take you uptown tomorrow for the interview. I don't want you wandering into any more butcher shops.'

'But don't you have to go to work?'

'I lost my job today. The work is finished.'

A groan came from the bed.

Magnus stood up. 'Don't worry. With luck I'll be picking up some money tonight. Joanna, I hope you don't mind if I don't eat your stew till later. I don't usually eat before a fight.'

Joanna caught her breath. 'A fight? You mean a boxing match?'

'Well . . . it's a bare-knuckle prizefight.'

Delta sat up in bed. 'I want to come and watch.'

'You'll stay where you are,' Magnus said. 'You're too ill.'

Joanna clutched his arm. 'Oh, please don't fight! It's such a brutal sport. You might be hurt. There must be some other way to earn a living.'

He looked down at her, his eyes fierce and tender and alight with an emotion that was deeper than despair. 'Will you walk down to the street with me? I want to talk to you.'

'Magnus!' Delta whined. 'I don't want to be left alone.'

'We won't be a minute. You'll be all right.'

'You don't need to take her outside. I've already told her . . .' Delta began, but Magnus, ignoring her, took Joanna's hand and led her from the room.

27

With the help of Denby, the Pinkerton agent, Megan found a beachfront cottage, open in front to a long stretch of sand and protected on three sides by a densely planted screen of brightly coloured oleanders. Denby assured her that the cottage was not far from the sprawling seaside home of Dr and Mrs Robard, with its high walls and private beach to keep intruders at bay.

Megan strolled along the beach, hoping to catch a glimpse of her father, perhaps bathing in the sea since the Gulf waters were still warm despite the arrival of autumn.

Since she had always used only her grandfather's name, hearing her father referred to as Dr Robard underscored the fact that he was truly a stranger to her. She sent him a note, apologising for her abrupt appearance and begging him to see her so that she could explain, but it came back unopened, marked 'return to sender.'

Her vigil revealed that only tradesmen called at the Robard house. She waylaid a butcher's boy one morning and asked if she might deliver the parcel of meat he was carrying.

The boy looked at her in amazement.

'I'll give you fifty cents,' Megan offered. American money was still an enigma to her, but this sounded like a princely sum.

A greedy hand grabbed the coin instantly. He gave her the meat, then grinned. 'Won't do you no good to knock on no doors. They never answer. Just put the meat in the icebox by the back door.' He jumped on his bicycle and rode off.

So even the tradesmen did not gain entry. Megan pushed open a solid wood gate and stepped into a jungle of overgrown oleanders through which a narrow path wound its way to the side of the house.

The house itself stood behind a formidable army of unfamiliar trees, which shaded the house so densely she thought it must surely be like a catacomb inside. As the butcher boy had indicated, a large wooden icebox stood outside the door.

There was no bell, and so Megan knocked on the door, gently at first, then louder. There was no response. She pounded and called, 'Dr Robard! I must speak with you.' Still no answer.

After bruising her knuckles on the door for several minutes she put the meat into the icebox and followed the path as it meandered around the house. All of the windows were shuttered, presenting blank eyes to the world. There was one other door, apparently the main entrance, but no one responded when she beat a tattoo with a tarnished brass lion's-head knocker.

She fished in her purse for a notepad and pencil and wrote: 'Dr Robard, I'm staying at the old Merrifield cottage just down the beach. I have something that belongs to you and which I'd like to return.' She signed the note with her birth name, Megan Thomas-Robard, and pushed it under the door. After all, she did have some of her father's old letters.

On her way back along the overgrown path she paused as she heard a faint cry. It came from within the house and sounded like the cry of a child – the angry, frustrated cry that a very young child might give when its wishes are thwarted. Although Megan waited for a few minutes, it was not repeated.

Puzzled, she walked back to her cottage. Denby had not mentioned that the Robards had a child. Was it possible she had a young half brother or sister? The possibility made her even more eager to gain entry to the house.

Several days passed and there was no word from her father. Denby had evidently cabled Randolph of her safe arrival, for a wire came: 'Miss you desperately. Nothing new here. Denby instructed to assist in any way needed. Take care. Letter follows.'

The weather grew cooler as winter approached and Megan felt less lethargic, more in the mood to storm the Robard house with a battering ram. When walking on the beach and staring at the house became too frustrating, she went downtown and browsed in the bookstores looking for the latest medical texts.

This proved to be equally frustrating. As the nineteenth century drew to a close, rapid medical and scientific strides were being made, and she felt that she had been left behind. Two doctors in Vienna had published a book called *Studies in Hysteria*, suggesting that the body's ills could be caused by the mind; but she was unable to find a copy.

Her first letter from Randolph arrived and she quickly scanned the contents to see if the Chiricahua Kid had been caught. He had not, nor had A-chi-tie, fortunately. But then Randolph went on: 'A farmer and his wife and two sons were butchered near Manzanita Flats only days after you left. I do feel that the man you call A-chi-tie is innocent, since you said he had a broken ankle and the farmer's daughter – who was gathering blackberries and escaped the slaughter – saw the Kid and two other Apaches running from the house. Still, Chuck tells me that everyone hereabouts blames you for the massacre, so you'd better plan to stay in Galveston until the Kid is finally caught and we straighten everything out . . . Speaking of broken bones, Quinn's leg is mending nicely.'

Megan looked up from the letter, an image of Quinn filling her mind, his dark eyes slightly mocking, as though he could see beneath the façades others presented to the world. She wondered how Quinn, with his barely tethered energy, was coping with the inactivity necessitated by his broken leg.

Her eyes misted as she continued to read. Randolph had written, 'The house seems empty without you. I keep listening for the sound of your voice, your laughter, for the faint fragrance that whispers you're near. How I long to touch your dear face, to stroke your hair, to hold your hand. You brought joy back into my life, restoring hope to a mind that I think was as crippled as my legs. Before you came I thought that Joanna's letters were sufficient to connect me to the outside world, but I know now that without human companionship and love we cannot survive. I count the minutes until your return, and I dare to allow myself to hope that someday you will care for me a little . . .'

Megan had always loathed writing letters, but she replied briefly, telling Randolph of her woeful lack of success in meeting her father. She also asked, 'Did you discuss my metamorphosis from Joanna to Megan with Quinn? Did he tell you everything? I left for Galveston in such a hurry that there was no time for me to tell you the whole story, which you surely deserve to hear, but I believe it would be better told than related in a letter.

She visited the Robard house daily, walking up the narrow path as oleander branches slapped her and the leaves from the deciduous trees piled up in sienna drifts beneath her feet.

The ritual was always the same: Pound on the back door, then the front; leave a note.

Once she thought she heard someone inside the house

225

sobbing quietly, a despairing sound that was sadder than anything she'd ever heard, and on another occasion she again heard what sounded like the frantic crying of a child. But usually it was as quiet as a tomb.

She even tried hiding in the bushes and keeping the icebox under observation in the hope that she would see her father or his wife emerge to collect the food left by the delivery boys, but she gave up her vigil when night fell.

Denby visited her regularly. Randolph had placed funds at her disposal in a local bank, and officially the Pinkerton investigation had ended, but the agent said he just wanted to keep in touch to be sure she was all right.

One afternoon when she confessed yet another failure in flushing out her father, Denby surprised her by saying, 'I can understand your frustration. If I were you, I'd be tempted to break in. Not that I'm advocating breaking the law, mind you, but those old window shutters wouldn't keep a determined visitor out . . . if she had a little help.'

'I wouldn't want to frighten anyone,' Megan replied thoughtfully, 'but I really do feel someone should enter that house. What if my father or his wife is ill? What if one of them is dead? How do we know what's happening in there when no one has seen either of them for months?'

'I'd suggest a visit about midday,' Denby said, 'with the sun high in the sky. I have a feeling you're going to encounter some ghosts. You let me know when, and I'll be here with a crowbar.'

Megan smiled at him. For such an inoffensive and mild-mannered man, he certainly didn't lack courage or imagination. 'Thank you. I know you're risking your job, and I deeply appreciate your concern and help. Let me think about it.'

She decided to forgo her customary futile visit to the house that day, as a friendly used-book dealer had found a copy of a fairly recent medical journal for her.

Ignoring the disarray of the cottage, since Denby was her only visitor and he'd come and gone, she settled down to read of a promising new cough medicine introduced by a German pharmaceutical house named Bayer. They called the cough medicine heroin.

Just before noon someone knocked on her front door and she opened it.

Quinn stood outside, leaning nonchalantly on the porch rail. 'Stand aside and let me in, woman. Can't you see I've got a bad leg?'

He walked past her, affecting an exaggerated limp, and sat down on her couch amid a heap of newspapers and books. Stretching out his leg in front of him he asked, 'Did it ever occur to you that all the men in your life seem to end up with busted lower limbs? There's Randolph in his wheelchair and me barely out of splints, and I understand your Apache pal broke his ankle. Somebody probably should search for little dolls with smashed legs.' Glancing at the untidy room he added, 'Looks as if you need a wife.'

'A-chi-tie is a Navajo, not an Apache. What are you doing here?' Megan asked.

'Is that any kind of a greeting for a man who travelled hundreds of miles – in great pain – to see you?'

'I don't recall inviting you. Does Randolph know you're here?'

'How do you suppose I knew where you were living? Of course your husband knows. He's worried about you, all alone in a strange land.' He flashed her an evil grin. 'Of course, sending me to look after you is somewhat akin to sending a wolf to watch the sheep . . .'

Megan gathered up a pile of magazines from an armchair and sat down. 'Don't you ever work for a living?'

'Sure. But at the moment it isn't necessary. I had a streak of luck in Silver City, and now I'm part owner of a copper mine.'

'Gambling isn't working for a living.'

'Oh, no? Have you ever played poker for three days straight?'

She ignored the question and changed the subject. 'You can tell Randolph I'm quite all right. Actually, I'm enjoying

227

being by myself. Do you know this is the first time I've ever lived alone, except for the few weeks after my grandfather died and before I went to Cornwall to see Joanna. I truly love the freedom of it. I can do anything I want at any hour of the day or night.'

'Don't count on your freedom continuing. The army has cornered the Chiricahua Kid in the old Cochise stronghold. Right now they can't get in. The only entrance is barely wide enough for one man to pass through, and the Kid can pick them off as they approach it. But neither can he get out. The army's camped at the entrance waiting for him to give himself up.'

They were silent for a moment, but the space between them seemed to resonate the unasked questions. At length Megan said, 'Did you tell Randolph all of the circumstances surrounding Jo's death?'

'No.'

'Why not?'

'He didn't ask. He's so besotted with you that he didn't want to talk about anything or anyone but you. He wanted to know why you came to New Mexico with me. I told him you were falsely accused of a crime and wanted to start a new life.'

'You didn't tell him that my so-called crime led to Joanna's death?'

'He didn't ask for details of her death. Often it's best to tell people only what they want to hear.'

'Gambling that your sins of omission won't return to haunt you, I presume? As soon as I see Randolph again, I intend to tell him everything.'

'That's up to you.' He regarded her with studied nonchalance for a second. 'Tell me, how does it feel to have a man love you chastely . . . to be the object of a pure and spiritual passion?'

'It's a burden,' Megan answered without thinking and then, exasperated with herself, added, 'I didn't mean that. Besides, how do you know our marriage is . . . celibate?'

His dark eyes regarded her shrewdly. 'I could say that

you just told me, but in fact it was Chuck who passed on that bit of information.'

'Chuck? How could he possibly know?'

'Who do you think helps Randolph into bed at night and up in the morning? Chuck has always been more than just a foreman. In fact he never slept in the bunkhouse until you arrived.'

'So that's why he resented me so much. I was a usurper – in his eyes a useless one, since I never helped with Randolph. It didn't occur to me to offer and he didn't ask.'

She stood up and paced a small circle, running her hand distractedly through her hair. 'I should have thought of that. I helped my grandfather with enough crippled colliers. But you know, after the initial shock of meeting Randolph, I just didn't see the bath chair. He seems so . . . at ease in it.'

Quinn leaned forward. 'Doesn't that strike you as odd? I was like a wounded bear after I broke my leg. If I thought I'd be paralysed for the rest of my life I'd probably put a bullet in my head. But Randolph . . . oh, he makes an effort to curse the chair once in a while, but did you ever get the feeling he doesn't really mean it? That he's putting on a show for the benefit of whoever is listening?'

'No,' Megan said shortly. 'He's soft-spoken, a gentleman, and gentlemen don't fly into rages or create scenes.'

Quinn raised one black eyebrow. 'Nor do ladies. What does that make us, Megan, you and me?'

Once again she chose to ignore his question. 'You can't stay here, you know. It would be quite improper.'

'I've taken a room at a hotel in town. Randolph tells me that your father has become a total recluse and won't see you.'

'That's true.' Megan stopped pacing. 'But I've decided to get into the house anyway. Tomorrow, probably.' She told him briefly of Denby's offer to help her break in. Quinn listened without comment.

She went to the window and looked out at the amber water of the Gulf, lazily lapping at the shore. It seemed almost too calm today, as if resting prior to some upheaval.

Behind her Quinn said, 'You got any food in the house?'

'Bread and cheese and some leftover shepherd's pie.'

'I never ate a shepherd before, but I'm starving . . .'

Halfway through his meal Quinn looked up at her with a twinkle in his eyes. 'You're not much of a housekeeper and you've had ink on your nose ever since I arrived . . . but you sure can cook.'

Megan absently rubbed her nose with her napkin. 'I was making some notes, although I don't know why I bother. Did Randolph tell you I applied to three medical schools and was turned down by all of them?'

'That's one of the reasons I came to see you. Randolph told me that your father doesn't practice medicine anymore and that he once had a reputation as a seagoing drunk. I figured that was why you wanted to be reunited with him. You can't be a doctor yourself, but with either a senile old man like your grandfather or a drunk like your father, you can practice medicine under someone else's license.'

Megan flung her napkin down. 'Don't sit in judgement of me! I'm a better doctor than many men who went through medical school. Just because I'm a woman –'

'Whoa! Sorry, but that old excuse doesn't hold water any longer. Randolph said you were turned down because you're too old.'

'Randolph tells you too damn much.'

'Why, Miss Thomas, please, mind your language!'

She rose and started gathering up the dishes. Quinn intercepted her between the table and the kitchen and firmly removed the pie dish from her hands. 'I didn't mean to make you mad. But you've got to face reality. Besides, I have a plan that should make both you and Randolph happy.'

'If you're going to suggest I take up nursing, I'll break your other leg,' she warned.

'I was going to suggest that we persuade Doc Sedgewick to set up shop in Manzanita Flats. The town is growing so fast there'll be plenty of patients. You can work with him.

Nobody's going to complain if you take over for Sedge when he's on a binge.' He paused, giving her a penetrating stare. 'It was you who operated on Becky at the Jade Palace, wasn't it?'

She turned her back and rested her hands on the sink. 'You're mad. Sedge belongs exactly where he is – in a painted wagon hawking nerve tonic and snake oil to gullible people who aren't ill in the first place and so can't be harmed by it.'

He took her arm and jerked her around to face him. 'That's not fair. Sure, he drinks once in a while, but he was a good surgeon once and he still keeps up with all the latest medical news. That wagon is full of journals from all over. And if you must know why he travelled about the territory, it was because he was searching for his wife and son.'

'What happened to them?'

'She was a Chiricahua maiden, very beautiful. After he was kicked out of the army he was bitter. He didn't want to practice medicine, but didn't know how to do anything else. He carried a triple stigma: he'd caused unnecessary suffering to some soldiers while he was drunk; he was responsible for the death of some others when he was absent without leave; and he was a squaw man. The settlers weren't about to forgive or forget his sins. Sedge and Migina were run out of town and I guess he went on a long binge. Finally she returned to some of her own people who'd managed to avoid being shipped off to the reservation with Geronimo. They were hiding out in the Sierra Madre when their *rancheria* was raided by Mexican troops who killed all the men and made slaves of the women and children. Only Sedge didn't know that then. He bought the medicine wagon and began a long search for his wife and son.'

'Did he ever find them?'

'No. But I . . . I tracked Migina and the boy to San Carlos. It was true that she was given as a slave to an officer's family, but the boy, Sedge's son, had light hair and fair skin and the Mexicans figured he was a captive, a

231

settler's son. The Chiricahua often took settlers' children and adopted them into the tribe. The boy was given to an American lawman returning to Arizona. We haven't been able to trace either the lawman or the boy.'

'And Sedge's Indian wife? What of her?'

'She died in San Carlos a few months after she was separated from the boy.'

'How terribly sad,' Megan said.

'Sedge only recently learned she was dead. That's why I think now is the time to get him to give up the medicine wagon and settle down. Enough time has passed, too, so that Sedge's past history has faded from most people's memories.'

'You don't think he'll want to continue the search for his son?'

'He wants to believe the lawman adopted the boy and is raising him as his own. Sedge said he doesn't want to disrupt the boy's life; he must be twelve or thirteen years old by now.'

Megan was silent for a moment, thinking about the sad-faced Sedge and feeling a little guilty that she had condemned him without inquiring about the reason for his behaviour. 'Perhaps . . . when I return to the ranch, Dr Sedgewick and I could talk about his starting up a new practice.'

Quinn clasped her hand. 'Good.'

His hand was warm and she couldn't prevent a slight tremor from making itself felt beneath his touch. Aware of it, he stared at her for a second or two, then said raggedly, 'Oh, hell, why do we pretend . . .'

Their lips met swiftly, sweetly, and everything spun out of focus. She was in his arms, where she'd wanted to be for so long, and Randolph was so far away it was as if he'd existed only in a dream.

Quinn's mouth was on hers, his hands were travelling over her body, and she was all pliant flesh and burning need. When he swept her up into his arms and carried her into the bedroom she didn't resist.

232

His fingers opened the buttons of her blouse with practised ease, freeing her breasts for his warm mouth and tongue, and somewhere deep in her throat she moaned with pleasure and anticipation.

A little warning voice at the back of her mind was stilled – a moment more of bliss, she told it, and then I will stop him . . .

But something strange was happening to her body. She writhed under his caress and she was panting with need. Inside her, a coiled spring of desire tightened unbearably. Then, somehow, she was naked and he was stripping off his own clothes, and when their bare flesh fused, it was like no other sensation she'd ever known.

For several minutes he merely held her close to him, his hand cupping her breast. She felt his male hardness and lay very still, waiting for him to move, but he kept his body under control while only his mouth touched hers, gently exploring, a leisurely journey that caused stars to explode behind her eyelids.

'I love you, Megan,' he murmured against her parted lips. 'I want you . . . not just now, for this moment, but for always. It's important to me that you know that.' His hand slid down to her thigh and rested there.

She couldn't speak, dared not speak, for fear all her shocking thoughts might spill from her in the same way that this moist warmth now radiated from the core of passion she felt, just a few tantalising inches away from his hand. Unable to lie still another moment, she twisted her body so that his fingers slipped closer to her scalding need, but still he held back.

'Love me, Megan, please love me.' His lips moved from her mouth to her throat, then to her breast, and he whispered, 'You're so beautiful, your skin is softer than silk.'

'Quinn . . .' Even his name tasted sweet on her lips, but vestiges of her shyness and inexperience lingered and she could not bring herself to tell him that she wanted him to make love to her. Was he waiting for her permission? Why

233

couldn't she tell him she loved him? For she did; she knew that beyond any shadow of doubt. Every nerve in her body yearned for him.

Unable to say what was in her heart, she cast aside her inhibitions and reached out to touch him, her trembling fingers finding his virility, awed by the pulsing life force she felt, astonished that she who had studied anatomy had no conception of what the human body was really like, or how well men and women had been created in order to complement one another. Or how the mind and, yes, the spirit, too, seemed to soar to a mystical union as flesh pressed against flesh, warm breath mingled, and desire blended, so that his need was as palpable as her own. She no longer felt shy or modest, but caressed him lovingly, as though it were the most natural action in the world, and surely, feeling as she did, it was.

He caught his breath then, and she felt him grow even harder in her hands. As if with a will of their own, her thighs parted and she guided him towards her.

She gasped as he entered her, first with pain and then with the sheer pleasure of joining. He was gentle, tentative at first, but after a moment his ardour swept them both away. They rode some ancient chariot together, whirling faster and faster towards the edge of the earth, not stopping even when they plunged over the edge.

They lay entwined for a long time, not speaking, too stunned by the intensity of their feelings to express them in words. Then Megan said breathlessly, 'Your leg seems much better.'

'True. But you still have ink on your nose.'

She laughed and he kissed her and pushed back a damp strand of her hair. She was so filled with wonder that when the full realisation of what they had done struck her it was like a physical blow.

Sitting up abruptly, she said, 'Oh, God. I've committed adultery.'

Instantly his arms were around her. 'You were never married to Randolph. Not in the real sense of the word.

234

Megan, look . . .' He pointed to the streaks of her blood on the sheet.

'It doesn't matter. I have broken my marriage vows. I promised to be faithful. I hate myself. I wish I'd never been born. How could I do this to Randolph?'

His hands gripped her shoulders and he shook her. 'You're a woman; you can't deny your destiny. You were made for a real union with a man. Megan, I love you; you know I do. Why can't you admit that you care for me? You told me you did once; those feelings must still be there.'

'We don't have the right to love each other,' she whispered. 'We gave up the right when I married him. Please, just go. I need to be alone.'

For a second he hesitated, then gently kissed her cheek and rose from the bed.

She pulled the sheet around her and lay curled up, not moving, for a long time after she heard the cottage door close behind him.

The afternoon shadows lengthened and a cool breeze came in through the open window. She felt bereft, deserted, and wished he had not allowed her to send him away. Yet the memory of passion kept coming back to haunt her, and some devil deep within her relished the images of making love with the only man she had ever loved, or would ever love, and this feeling clashed unbearably with her sense of guilt.

The waters of the Gulf, so still earlier, had begun to churn and break against the shore in increasing force as the tide turned. How could she ever face her husband again? Her shame was so great that it immobilised her. She simply could not get out of the bed.

A sullen dusk fell and her stomach growled with hunger, but she ignored it. The wind rose and rain blew in through the open window. She felt both hot and cold, her flesh clammy yet pulsing with life. The memory of the lovemaking both enraptured and repulsed her and she felt torn in two.

Loud pounding on her door made her leap out of bed.

She grabbed her dressing gown and pulled it on as she ran to answer the insistent knock.

Quinn was outside, rain dripping from the brim of his hat. 'Get dressed. We're going out.'

'Out? In this storm? Where on earth . . . ?'

'To visit your father. I've seen him, told him about you and he wants to see you. Come on – hurry! He's waiting for us.'

'But how did you get in?'

'I climbed through a bedroom window. He's deaf, Megan. He simply doesn't hear unless you're right next to him. But I got him to listen to me.'

28

New York City seemed gentler at night, although the stars and sky were lost in the halo of light from street lamps and windows. Joanna and Magnus walked together, away from their building, past the shops, and along a street of brownstone houses.

A late warm spell had brought many families out to sit on their stoops to talk with their neighbours, and children still played on the sidewalks. Voices were less strident, and occasionally music drifted from an open window. Someone played a piano with surprising brilliance, a mother sang a lullaby in a soft Irish brogue, somewhere in an attic over their heads a tenor sang an aria in Italian, tugging at Joanna's heartstrings. She looked up at Magnus as he walked beside her, and the sight of his broad shoulders and craggy features in profile was comforting, as was the warmth of his hand as he held hers. She wanted him always to be there, at her side, and knowing this could not be was unbearable. Why, oh, why, did she fall in love with unattainable men?

They walked in silence for a while, happy just to be together, knowing that when they spoke their words must of necessity deal with reality.

'Joanna,' Magnus began. 'I must explain . . .'

'Please don't take up boxing again. I'm so afraid for you.'

'I have to fight tonight; it's all arranged. I wanted to talk to you about Delta.'

'She told me about the baby. I'm . . . happy for both of you. Will you invite me to the wedding?' Her voice sounded strange, as though it belonged to someone else.

He stopped under a street lamp and placed his hands on her shoulders, looking down at her. 'I'm going to be honest with you, Joanna, because you don't deserve any less. There was a time when Delta and I . . . we –'

'You don't owe me any explanations, Magnus, really.'

'No, I want you to know. The baby she's carrying could be mine. After we got off the boat and you were still on Ellis Island, I was lonely. I missed you . . . Oh, sweet Jesus, listen to me make excuses for myself. One night I had a few drinks, and the next thing I knew Delta was in bed with me . . . But, knowing her, that officer aboard the ship could be the father, too. Still, she's my responsibility now and I won't shirk it. I have to marry her.'

Joanna lowered her head so he wouldn't see the tears that stung her eyes.

Clumsily he put out his hand to touch her hair and she laid her cheek against his palm and kept it there as he went on quietly, 'You and I both knew that there was never any hope for us. Maybe that's why we feel as we do. It's human to want what we can't have, isn't it?'

She nodded, numb with despair.

'After tonight we won't speak of this again. But, Joanna, I must be sure you're all right. I wouldn't be able to rest if I thought you were all alone in this big strange country.

237

I wish you'd write to your cousin in New Mexico again, but if you won't then I'll just have to keep an eye on you until you're settled. I can't believe working as a parlour maid will make you happy, but perhaps you'll meet someone . . .'

For answer she turned her head and pressed her lips briefly to his palm. He withdrew his hand, curling his fingers over his palm as if to keep the imprint of her lips there. For an instant he looked down at his fist, then wordlessly pulled her into his arms and held her.

Oblivious of the fact that they stood in a pool of yellow lamplight and passersby turned, smiling, to observe what they undoubtedly perceived to be a pair of young lovers, Joanna clung to Magnus as if she were drowning.

He whispered against her hair, 'We must go back now. I'm due in the ring in thirty minutes.'

She raised her tearstained face. 'Is there nothing I can say that would persuade you not to fight tonight?'

He smiled sadly. 'I need the purse to pay for a marriage licence . . . and soon for a child. Don't worry. Digging ditches these past weeks has been good training.'

Delta was asleep when he returned to the room after the boxing match that night, but Joanna, hearing his muffled groan as he lay down, longed to go to him. The following morning she had to hide her dismay when she saw the ugly cut over his eye and the purplish bruises on his jaw. He moved stiffly, as though he hurt in other places, too. She was astonished to hear he had won the fight, and shuddered to think of the other man's injuries.

Magnus, despite his cuts and bruises, accompanied Joanna to the home of the Abercrombys later that morning, and they stood for a moment observing a handsome town house on a most elegant street on the Upper East Side. The neighbourhood was such a contrast to the one in which they lived that all at once she was acutely aware of her worn and old-fashioned clothes and nervous about her chances of being hired. 'It looks very nice,' she said uncertainly.

'Not much like Traherne Hall, but better by far than where we just came from,' Magnus said.

In the daylight his bruises were livid, and blood had seeped through the plaster across the corner of his eye. There were also bruises on his knuckles.

'I think perhaps we should find the back door,' Joanna suggested. 'At home the servants never enter the front door.'

They walked around the block to an alley. Magnus gave her hand an encouraging squeeze. 'Good luck. I'll wait here for you.'

She was shown into a large kitchen filled with chattering servants who glanced at her briefly and then went on with their tasks. A formidable-looking woman who was probably the cook informed Joanna that Mrs Abercromby personally interviewed all the help.

After waiting for half an hour Joanna was taken to a study on the parlour floor where a regal-looking woman with honey-coloured hair sat behind a Queen Anne desk. She looked up, her eyes taking in every detail of Joanna's appearance.

Joanna felt a self-conscious flush creep up over her face and shrank inside the clothes Justin Bodrath had given her, which now seemed even more out of date and moth-eaten.

'Normally, I would never hire a maid who has no references,' Mrs Abercromby said, 'but I understand yours are en route from England and our last girl has vouched for you. We are in the midst of making arrangements for our daughter Edith's wedding, and guests will begin arriving tomorrow. I'm in desperate need of a maid, so I'll give you a two-week trial. You'll take care of the guests' rooms and help the other servants when you're told to do so. The butler will instruct you, and Cook will find a uniform for you. Have you any questions?'

Joanna considered confessing that no references would be forthcoming from England, but decided against it, since either Jacob or the previous maid had invented that tale. Perhaps at the end of the two-week trial she would be kept on without references. She cleared her throat. 'Thank you, no. Except . . . when shall I start work?'

'Why, right away, of course.' Mrs Abercromby picked up her pen and bent her head to write, evidently dismissing her. Joanna backed out of the room, wishing she had been less abrupt with the maids who had served at Traherne Hall.

She slipped out to the back alley to tell Magnus she'd been hired. He took her hand and held it awkwardly. 'Good luck, then, Joanna. You know where to find us if you need anything.'

She nodded, then turned and ran back to the house.

For the next few days Joanna was at the beck and call of everyone in the Abercromby household. Apparently the newest maid was the lowliest of employees, and not knowing exactly what was expected of her, she obeyed every command.

At home in Cornwall the maids had been all but invisible. As if by magic, order was restored, clutter was removed, beds were warmed and turned back, laundry disappeared, rooms were cleaned, floors were polished, and fresh flowers appeared. Joanna assumed all of this was accomplished by the maids, although her own personal maid was the only one she ever really saw and then only when she needed to have her hair dressed or her clothes laid out.

Somehow she stumbled through her tasks, carrying piles of fresh linen to the bedrooms and making the beds, dusting and sweeping, polishing furniture and floors with beeswax, washing windows with vinegar and water, folding endless towels, and picking up discarded clothing, soiled handkerchiefs, and muddy shoes.

When Joanna had met the guests' wants, the butler gave her another list of chores to do, and after she finished those, she had to contend with the demands of Cook and the senior maids. Joanna collapsed into her bed after midnight so weary she could not even think, let alone talk to the other maid with whom she shared a tiny spartan bedroom.

On some nights, before falling into an exhausted slumber, she would remind herself of the terrible price she had paid for a moment's pleasure with Oliver Pentreath, and she would wonder why women should suffer so for breaking society's rules while men went scot-free.

Randolph Mallory had asked her to write and explain her presence in New York, but she was simply too tired to do so. Besides, remembering that arrogantly handsome man she'd met in Cornwall, and the fact that he knew of her shame, there seemed little point.

On her day off she went to visit Magnus and was told that he and Delta had been married the previous day. She assumed a justice of the peace had performed the ceremony, but neither of them went into detail. Delta still languished in bed and was not at all happy to see Joanna, who didn't stay long. Magnus walked her to the streetcar stop.

'Joanna, I know you wanted to come, but –'

'It's all right,' Joanna said wearily. 'I understand.'

A grey drizzle of cold rain had started to fall, washing the soot on the pavement into oily rivulets. The world seemed drained of all colour, all warmth, all hope.

'Do you have any prospects of employment?' Joanna asked, not wanting to talk about his marriage.

'There's not much call for a tin miner nor a fisherman in New York,' Magnus said. 'The only other trade I have is boxing. After a couple more fights I should be able to move Delta into a better place.'

Joanna's feeling of hopelessness was echoed in his voice and in the bleak expression on his face. At least, Joanna noted, he wore no new bruises.

When the streetcar arrived, Joanna climbed aboard and shrank into a corner away from the smell of wet horseflesh and rain-damp clothes.

Arriving back at the Abercromby house she was met at the door by Cook. 'A new guest has arrived. A Mr

241

Whitman. Take towels and linens up to his room and unpack his bags.'

Too dispirited to point out that her day off had not yet ended, Joanna plodded up the stairs to the guest bedrooms. On the landing outside the newly arrived Mr Whitman's room she paused, hearing a strangely familiar sound – the clacking of typewriter keys.

The door was ajar and a second later she heard a man's voice utter an expletive. She smiled, knowing the frustration one felt after striking the wrong key, and moved closer to the door, although she knew she could not enter while a guest was present.

Curious as to why a guest would bring a typewriting machine with him on a social visit, especially for a wedding, she peered around the doorjamb and found herself staring into the eyes of a bespectacled young man in the act of ripping a sheet of paper from the typewriter.

As she started to back away, he called, 'Oh, come on in. You might as well make up the bed, because I'm certainly having no luck with this dag-blasted article. Confounded infernal machines – how I hate them! Can you imagine someone having the gall to build one small enough to be carried about? My editor insisted that I write up this wedding *while I'm here*. The man's a Tartar, I can tell you. Bad enough I have to attend the wedding of that simpering fool Edith, without being put to work at the same time. Great balls of fire, you'd think being a blasted usher in the so-called wedding of the year would be punishment enough for my sins –'

He broke off, cocked his head to one side, and peered at her through his glasses. She recognised that nearsighted search for details, since Megan was also a bit myopic. 'Are you going to stand there holding all those sheets and things, or are you coming in to make my bed?' He gave her a leprechaun's grin. 'I know what we shall do: *You* write a description of Edith's wedding gown and *I'll* make the bed.'

His laughter was hearty, considering his diminutive size,

but it was cut off abruptly when Joanna responded, 'Very well.'

'What?'

'I agree to the arrangement. You make the bed and I'll write about the dress. I'm so tired of being on my feet it would be a welcome change to sit down and use the typewriter.'

Whitman's glasses slipped down his nose, and he regarded her with astonishment over the wire-rimmed lenses. 'Are you telling me you know how to use one of these infernal machines?'

'Yes, I am.'

'Holy Moses. Dare I hope you have some vague knowledge of spelling and grammar also?'

'I do. What I don't know is what Miss Edith's wedding gown looks like.'

'Then we'll sneak you into her room and you can see it. Great Caesar's ghost, what a find! A soft-spoken woman who is not only domesticated but who types! Hallelujah! Will you marry me?'

Joanna laughed. His exuberance was catching, and for the first time she felt that she was being treated as an equal.

'It's not *that* funny,' Whitman grumbled. He stood up, disclosing the fact that he was barely five feet tall, a pixie of a man with a devilish grin and a voice, laugh, and mannerisms that would not have been out of place on someone a great deal bigger and brawnier. He strode across the room purposefully. 'Come on, there's no time like the present – strike while the iron's hot and all that sort of thing.'

Placing the linen on the bed, Joanna followed.

She had caught an occasional glimpse of Edith Abercromby, a pale and petulant-looking girl with the same spun-honey hair as her mother, flitting about the house in the throes of prenuptial arrangements. Edith was marrying one of the wealthiest men in New York, a man who was many years her senior and who seemed to have

243

little to offer other than money. Joanna wondered, recalling Adele's sudden interest in Oliver after he inherited a fortune, if Edith would have married her elderly suitor had he been poor.

Whitman paused at the end of the upstairs landing, his hand on a doorknob. 'I happen to know Edith and her mother are out shopping, so we can just pop into her room. The wedding gown was delivered this morning.'

'Wouldn't it be better to ask her maid to show it to us?' Joanna whispered.

But the door was already open and he was inside the room. Joanna followed. The dress hung from the top of the dressing room door, a drift of white lace over satin, its bodice embroidered with tiny seed pearls. Whitman went to it and held up the end of the train to show her its length. 'There must be a headdress and veil somewhere, too,' he announced in a stage whisper, looking around.

Joanna stood behind the door, studying the dress to determine if the seed pearls formed a flower pattern, while Whitman went into the dressing room. He popped out under the dress a moment later holding up a veil and a pearl tiara.

At that moment an icy voice from the landing asked, 'What are you doing, Mr Whitman?' and Mrs Abercromby swept into the room.

29

Quinn sheltered Megan under his arm and leaned into the rain-slashed wind as they tramped over wet sand to the Robard house. Quinn swung his recently healed broken leg a little stiffly, but Megan still had to hurry to keep up with him.

An oil lantern cast a feeble yellow glow over the front entrance to the house. Quinn tested the door, which was unlocked. He pushed it open and they went inside.

Megan shivered as the musty gloom closed around her. The only light came from a half-open door at the end of the hall. She could feel, rather than see, dust and cobwebs. Quinn's arm remained around her shoulders and she resisted an urge to bury her face against his chest, all at once not sure that she wanted to meet her father.

'Come on. He won't bite,' Quinn whispered.

'Are you sure he's expecting us?' Megan asked for the third time.

'Yes. I told you – I've talked to him.'

'You didn't . . . bully him?'

Quinn sighed and propelled her down the dark hall.

When they reached the lighted room he called loudly, 'We're here, sir. May we come in?'

'Must you shout?' Megan asked, horrified.

'Yes,' Quinn answered. 'He's quite deaf.' He held the door for her and she walked into a book-lined study, her eyes fixed on the man seated behind a desk piled high with books and papers.

The first thing she noticed was his hair, which was still as red as hers. But when he looked up, she saw that his eyes were not true green like hers; they were more blue-green. He was handsome once, she decided, before his skin became scarred. Had he removed those lesions from his forehead and nose himself? His skin was much too fair to withstand his years aboard a ship plying the Caribbean. The lower part of his face had been protected from the ravages of the sun by a luxuriant moustache, as gloriously red as his hair. Had he secluded himself in this dreary house because of a combination of cancerous skin lesions and loss of hearing? It seemed a drastic solution.

His study was a veritable treasure trove of books and medical journals. Megan scanned the shelves enviously, then glanced at the piles of magazines and journals on his desk.

Dr Robard wiped his fist across his eyes. 'You weren't lying, Mr McQuinn. This is my little girl. I'd know her anywhere. She's got her mother's lovely features and my colouring.'

There were still echoes of the Welsh mountains in his voice, that slightly singsong accent that made even the guttural Welsh language sound like music. For an instant Megan felt a great wave of homesickness, of longing for all that she had left behind, wondering if she could regain at least a part of it through this man. She quelled the yearning by reminding herself of his reclusive life and his refusal to see her until now.

He rose and came around the desk and opened his arms. Megan held herself stiffly as he hugged her, still uncertain about this stranger.

'Your friend tells me your grandfather named you Megan.'

'Yes, after my grandmother.'

'I'm sorry, my dear, I don't hear very well. You must speak up. I'm teaching myself to read lips, but I'm not proficient at it. How we do take our senses for granted, don't we?'

Quinn said, 'I'll leave you two alone –'

'No,' Megan said quickly. 'Don't go, please.'

'I'll just wait in the hall.' He was gone before she could speak again.

Dr Robard – she could not think of him as her father – bent to remove a pile of journals from the only other chair in the room, and she felt a shock of recognition. The action reminded her so much of herself. She wondered if she'd inherited his untidiness, or was it simply that they both became too engrossed with more important matters to worry about putting things away, especially books and papers that would be read many times?

She accepted the chair he'd cleared for her and he leaned against his desk, remaining closer to her than she would have preferred. She wished he would return to his chair and keep the barrier of books and papers between them.

He smiled at her suddenly, and she was transfixed. How could that smile be anything but sincere?

'I don't understand,' she began, then raised her voice, 'why you wouldn't see me when I came alone nor even reply to my notes. What did Quinn say to persuade you to change your mind?'

He picked up an ear trumpet and held it to his ear. 'This helps a little. Can't have you going hoarse, can we? We've a lot of catching up to do. Now, to answer your questions – first, I was convinced my baby was dead and you were another of those prying journalists who had somehow found out I'd had a daughter with my first wife. I can't tell you how many different ploys they've used to get in here and see me. I didn't doubt they'd be cruel enough to pretend my dead baby was still alive.'

'Journalists?' Megan asked, but he evidently didn't hear, as he went on, 'As to what Mr McQuinn said . . . why, he told me that you have a burning desire to become a doctor and have gone to great lengths to accomplish that goal. But what really intrigued me was to learn that you actually removed a diseased appendix and the patient lived!'

'Quinn had no right to tell you that. He assumed it anyway, because he wasn't present.'

'Doesn't matter. *You* were present. You can tell me all about it later. But first I owe you some explanations.'

'None are necessary. I understand why you never returned to Wales. After Grandfather died I found some of your letters. You thought I was dead. We both have to forgive Grandfather for telling you that. He was lonely and wanted to keep me with him.'

'The old man didn't want me to take your mother away from him either. Megan, there's much you need to know before you decide to accept me as your father.'

'I am curious about why journalists try to see you.'

He leaned closer, straining to hear. 'You haven't been

247

in Texas very long, have you? You see, everyone in Galveston believes I am a murderer.'

Megan felt another shock of recognition. So he, too, had been accused of killing someone. 'A patient died?'

'No. My wife disappeared. At least that's what outsiders believed. Rumours flew that I dissolved her body with acid or took it out to sea and weighted it down and sank it, or buried it under the oleanders. There were even vague hints in the newspapers about human experiments and unnatural practices, including devil worship.'

He paused to catch his breath, and Megan sat stiffly in her chair, glad that Quinn was waiting in the hall. What if she'd taken Denby's advice and broken into the house alone?

Denby! Of course! Now his continuing interest in her became clear. He must have known all about the rumours surrounding the Robards, and yet he hadn't passed the stories along to her. Was he hoping she would uncover the truth about the mysterious doctor? Was the disappearance of her father's second wife an unsolved case for the Pinkertons?

Her father went on, 'My wife's family raised a hue and cry, soon after she disappeared, of course. But they fell silent when they learned the truth. So that left everyone else wondering. Looking back, I see the mistakes I made, but I'm not sure I could have acted differently. I was beside myself with worry for Agnes, my wife. She was my first concern. I thought I was doing the right thing at the time. I believed that if I took her far from here she would recover from the tragedy. Everything here, especially me, seemed to be adding to her grief. More than that, *causing* her malady.'

'Oh,' Megan said, relieved. 'Your wife was still alive?'

'What's that? Yes, it's nearly nine. Oh, forgive me, are you hungry? Thirsty? It's been so long since I had a visitor I've forgotten my manners.'

Megan hadn't eaten, but she was too curious about the missing Agnes to think of food. She shook her head. 'No, please, go on. What happened next? I assume you took your wife to a nursing home somewhere? What was the source of her grief?'

He placed his forefinger against his mouth, almost as if he wanted to silence himself, but she asked the same question, louder, more insistently, forcing him to reply.

'We lost a baby. Stillborn. It was more than I could bear. I was a madman. I'd already lost one little girl, you see . . . you. Or thought I had. Agnes went into premature labour, and I delivered the child myself. There was a terrible storm that night, and I was like a man possessed, ranting and raving. I went out and started walking on the beach. The flood tide was almost up to my waist when somehow – God knows where she found the strength – Agnes dragged herself from the bed and came after me.'

'I came to my senses then, picked her up, and carried her back to the house. But when I dried her off and put her to bed I realised that there was something terribly wrong. I didn't know if losing the baby or my own demented behaviour was the cause.

'After that I did one stupid thing after another. I started to drink again. My patients left me en masse. I refused to allow Agnes's family to visit us, and, most stupid of all, I buried our stillborn daughter in the garden and erected a tiny shrine over her grave. When I was drinking, I apparently sat up all night burning candles beside the grave . . . not that I recall any of that. The next thing I knew, the police were here, digging up the pathetic remains, demanding to speak to Agnes. I asked them to wait until morning, told them I'd given her something to help her sleep, which was true, and I allowed them to look into the bedroom to see that she was indeed there. That night I managed to get her out of the house. I took her to Houston.'

He looked at Megan, his eyes pleading with her, begging her to understand. She wondered why he had waited so long to talk to somebody about this. Surely this wasn't the way to greet a long-lost daughter. Wasn't he interested in her, in her life?

'You said her family believed you'd murdered her. When you were accused, why didn't you take them to see her?'

His lips compressed into a tight line. 'Agnes became hysterical when anyone but me entered her room. I had to spirit her back here, keep everyone away from her. Eventually I did, of course, have to allow her father to see her, to prove she was still alive. He called off the law, sent the reporters packing. They all left me alone after that. But the rumours persisted.'

He laid the ear trumpet down on top of a pile of papers on his desk. 'I had to tell you all this right away, Megan, so that you'd know what had happened. I couldn't simply march you upstairs and introduce you to Agnes. You see . . . she never did return to me, not really.'

30

Whitman stood in Edith Abercromby's dressing room doorway holding her wedding veil in one hand and the pearl tiara in the other, his expression that of a mischievous elf.

Mrs Abercromby had not yet seen Joanna, who was hidden by the open door.

'I asked, Mr Whitman, what you are doing here?' Mrs Abercromby repeated, her voice dripping frost.

'Oh, merciful heaven! Caught in the act,' Whitman said. 'It's like this, you see, Mrs Abercromby. I was just going to try on the veil and headdress. I swear by all the saints I wouldn't have touched the dress itself. No, ma'am, no indeed. That would have been going too far, even for me. Although I must admit I was tempted. Yes, indeed.'

'What on earth are you talking about?' Mrs Abercromby asked faintly.

'I'm throwing myself on your mercy, ma'am, confessing that I'm a transvestite – that is, I enjoy wearing women's clothes. In private, of course, and only the finest quality material and the most tasteful designs. I'm rather partial to silks and velvets; they cause a certain type of friction against the skin . . .' He gave a dreamy sigh.

Mrs Abercromby looked ready to faint.

'Not many transvestites ever get to wear a wedding dress, and . . . well, ma'am, you can imagine how difficult it would be for me to acquire one. I can always say I'm buying the odd skirt or blouse or pair of bloomers for a wife or sister, but no one would let me buy a wedding gown. So there it is . . . a harmless sin, but a sin nevertheless, and I do beg your forgiveness and assure you that you arrived before the dastardly deed took place, so have no fears on that score.'

Mrs Abercromby's nostrils had clenched, as though the room were filled with an abominable odour. 'Bartholomew Whitman, you will leave this house immediately. I never wanted to invite you in the first place. I should have known you were up to something when you arrived without warning days before the wedding. Why, your own family won't have anything to do with you because you're such a disgrace to them. I'll never know why my son wanted you to come.'

'Possibly because we've been friends since school?' Whitman suggested pleasantly.

'You've gone too far this time. You will never be welcomed into this house again, and I –' She broke off, catching sight of Joanna's reflection in the dresser mirror.

Mrs Abercromby slammed the door shut and glared at Joanna. 'And you, I presume, are a voyeur? Here to witness this disgusting spectacle?'

'I . . . I . . . we –' Joanna stammered, taken aback.

251

Surely Whitman was joking and Mrs Abercromby realised this?

'You're dismissed,' Mrs Abercromby said coldly. 'Go. Leave my house at once. I should have known better than to hire you without references, and had it not been for the wedding –'

'But I haven't done anything,' Joanna protested.

'How dare you answer me back! Get out! You no longer have a position here, do you understand?'

'Hey, wait a minute –' Whitman began, but Mrs Abercromby screamed, 'Don't *you* say another word. If you're not both out of my house within ten minutes, I'll call the police.'

Joanna crept from the room, feeling more humiliated than she could bear.

Five minutes later she and Whitman stood on the street, their belongings hastily thrown into suitcases, as the butler shut the Abercrombys' front door with a final thud.

'Mr Whitman,' Joanna said indignantly, 'why, pray tell, didn't you explain about the article you're writing?'

He cocked his head to one side, looking up at her like a woebegone gnome. 'Ah, yes, the article. Well, you see, the Abercrombys have been keeping the design of little Edie's dress a secret until after the wedding. There's a lot of interest about it in certain circles, and my editor is among the curious. Great balls of fire, though, I certainly didn't mean to have you sacked over it. But never fear, Whitman's here and it's your lucky day, Miss . . . What's your name, by the way?'

'Smith, Joanna Smith, and I'd hardly say it's my lucky day. I've no job and nowhere to go, and Mrs Abercromby didn't even pay me.'

'The devil you say! Smith, is it? Sounds like an alias to me. I'll call you Joanna and you can call me Bart. Now, a lady who can use one of those confounded typewriting machines certainly should aspire to greater heights than making beds. I'll take you to my editor and ask him to find a job for you.'

'Why on earth did you tell Mrs Abercromby that ridiculous story about wanting to wear a wedding dress yourself?'

He winked. 'It was better than admitting I intended to sell a description of the dress to a newspaper days before the wedding. I'll just be ostracised for the transvestite story . . . but for telling the secrets of high society? That, dear lady, is a crime punishable by death.'

'I take it you are – *were* a member of high society yourself?'

'My father disowned me years ago. Haven't seen the old bastard – oops, excuse me – the old curmudgeon for over a year.' Bart grinned and added cheerfully, 'He never did like me. I was supposed to be tall, dark, and handsome, you see. I'm not sure what went wrong, but I strongly suspect that a little bowlegged, nearsighted, silver-tongued iceman had something to do with it.'

Joanna shook her head disbelievingly. 'How can I give credence to anything you say? You really are outrageous.'

'Well, we can't stand on the street all night. Let's walk to the corner and hail a cab, and I'll take you to a hotel.'

'I don't have any money – at least, not enough for a hotel.'

'It's on me, love. This is the least I can do after getting you the sack. Tomorrow we'll meet old Dragonbreath.'

'Dragon . . . ?'

'My editor.'

E. B. Duggenbrand, a man of considerable girth with a mop of yellowish-white hair and a penetrating pale-eyed stare, leaned back in his chair, balancing his hands on his paunch. 'You're crazy, Whitman. There's no place on *my* newspaper for a woman.'

Bart perched on the edge of the editor's desk. 'Sure there is. Joanna can use a typewriter, she can spell, her grammar is perfect. Hell's bells, E.B., I'm not asking you to send her out as a reporter. She can do rewrites, proofread, run copy, make coffee, pay bills, do the filing –'

'No. It's out of the question. Take her out and find her a sewing machine someplace. She can't work here.'

Joanna fixed her gaze on her feet, pressed primly together in front of her chair, feeling like an idiot child while the two men spoke over her head as if she were not even present. She also felt a seed of anger beginning to sprout. If a woman had neither father nor husband to support her, surely her skills and capabilities should determine her choice of employment, and she could certainly write more articles like the one Bart was now waving under Dugganbrand's nose.

'Wait till you see this story, E.B.! Great God of all Creation, it's perfect. If you won't hire her, then you can kiss the Abercromby wedding details good-bye. It's Jo's piece. She wrote it, and she will damn well sell it to another paper.'

It was true that Joanna had typed the article, and the description of Edith's wedding gown was hers, but Bart had supplied the guest list, which included the cream of New York society and several titled English visitors, one of whom was a member of the royal family. He had also divulged the menu for the wedding feast and the plans for the honeymoon. The Abercrombys would surely seeth with rage if all that information was disclosed before the day of the wedding.

Joanna looked up to see Duggenbrand scowling at her, but when he spoke it was to address Bart. 'Aw, come on, Whitman, you don't mean that. It's your damn article and you know it. Gimme the piece and I'll give you a bonus. You can share it with her.'

Rising to her feet, Joanna was about to forget she was a lady and tell this obnoxious man that she would rather starve than work for him, when Bart jumped down from the desk and grabbed her arm.

'Come on, Jo, let's go talk to the *Herald*.'

They wended their way through the maze of desks, some of which were occupied by grinning reporters who had overheard the heated exchange. Although she kept her eyes fixed on the door, longing to escape from the leers and stares, she was fascinated to see that that modern marvel, the telephone, was very much in evidence in the city room. What a boon it must be to be able to call in a story as it happened! She felt a deep sense of disappointment that she was to be barred from this exciting world of journalism.

Halfway across the room Duggenbrand bellowed after them, 'Oh, hell, come on back, you two. We'll put a desk for her in the storeroom and see what she can do. A two-week trial in return for the Abercromby article. That's the best I can do, and at that the boss is going to have my hide.'

Joanna managed to remain calm, fighting an urge to clap her hands and toss her bonnet in the air. She tried to quell her excitement by warning herself that she'd failed miserably the last time she was given a two-week trial. In any event, she decided, this was just a ploy to get the article. No matter how well she did her work, she would surely be dismissed in two weeks . . . but, oh, how she looked forward to those two weeks!

To celebrate her first week on the paper Bart took her to a restaurant that was popular with journalists and writers. He ordered steaks and champagne and raised his glass in a toast: 'To the first woman to breach the male bastion of the *Chronicle*!'

'My position is still too tenuous for toasts,' Joanna protested. 'I'm sure Dragonbreath will send me packing next week. And I may be the first woman at the *Chronicle*, but there are lots of women working on other papers.'

'Great balls of fire, we'll have no pessimism and no self-denigration in the ranks! Now, I've a couple of bits of advice for you. Take your first week's salary and buy yourself something decent to wear. No offence, Jo, but those clothes look as if they came out of the ark.'

Joanna glanced down at the faded bombazine gown that had belonged to Justin Bodrath's mother and for once felt no embarrassment. After a week in the rough-and-tumble company of men, she was beginning to be inured to blunt observations. 'I can't afford new clothes. I need to rent a room. I can't go on borrowing from you for the hotel.'

'I've been meaning to talk to you about that . . .' He tilted his head back in order to peer through his glasses, which had slipped down his nose. 'See, I have this aunt who spends more time in Europe than here, and she has a nice apartment that stays empty most of the time. She'll be gone for most of the winter. She sort of likes me because I make her laugh. Her apartment's yours for the next four months, if you want it.'

Magnus came into the apartment slowly, his cloth cap in his hand, his brilliant blue eyes darting about as though he didn't want to see what he was seeing. 'It's very grand, Joanna.'

Joanna still held the door open. 'Delta didn't come with you?'

'No, she wasn't feeling well. I have a bout tonight, so we thought I'd just stop in for a few minutes to explain. She was glad to get your note, though, and said thanks for the baby bunting.'

Joanna gestured for him to sit down, and he perched awkwardly on the soft leather sofa in Bart's aunt's living room.

'I know the baby isn't due for months, but, well, I wanted to buy something out of my first week's salary. Oh, Magnus, I have the most wonderful position!'

He was looking at her strangely, but as she told him in swift excited exclamations about meeting Bart and going to work for the *Chronicle*, she didn't notice that he was not responding.

'. . . and so Bart suggested that, since his aunt is away a great deal, I should stay here. It's lovely, isn't it? I had no idea a flat could be so spacious, and she has exquisite taste in furnishings. That's a Chippendale dining table and —' She broke off, realising he was staring at her new gown.

Bart had insisted on going shopping with her and had selected the burgundy wool dress she was wearing. It was cut in classically simple lines and, as he roguishly pointed out, displayed her excellent figure to best advantage. 'Oh . . . yes, this is new. Do you like it?'

'It's very nice.' He glanced at the china clock on the mantel as if wondering how soon he could safely escape.

She was puzzled by his aloofness. She'd looked forward to telling him of her good fortune and had expected him to be as excited as she was. Instead, he regarded her unsmilingly, twisting his cap in his hand and watching the clock. 'Oh, Magnus, how rude of me – let me take your cap.'

He stood up so abruptly that a cushion slid from the sofa. 'No! I can't stay. I told you, I'm on my way to a bout.' Bending, he picked up the cushion and replaced it.

Joanna felt a stab of disappointment. She'd been so looking forward to seeing him. But perhaps he felt awkward because Delta had not accompanied him and he didn't want to be alone with a single woman. She said, a little breathlessly, 'Oh, I do wish you'd stay for dinner. Bart will be here soon and you can meet him –'

'No!' The word shot from his lips like a bullet. 'I don't want to meet him. Good night, Joanna.'

31

Dr Robard lit an oil lamp. 'I need to replace the gas mantles in the hall and landing. I must try to remember to do that. But I keep plenty of light on in Agnes's room.'

As they stepped out of the study into the hall a tall

shadow detached itself from the deeper darkness. In the faint light Megan saw that it was Quinn. He lightly touched her arm. 'Everything all right?' he asked.

Dr Robard raised the lantern to peer at him. 'I'm taking Megan upstairs to meet my wife,' he told Quinn. 'Agnes doesn't receive visitors, so I must ask you to remain here. Don't worry if you hear a commotion. Agnes may get upset, but she's quite harmless and I do want my daughter to meet her.'

'Megan?' Quinn's tone was doubtful.

'It's all right. You wait here.'

She followed her father up a flight of creaking stairs. Outside the wind howled mournfully under the eaves and the rain beat a tattoo against a window on the landing. Megan realised that her heart was thumping erratically.

The landing was as dark as the hall below, and she followed the yellow pool of light cast by the lantern. Her father opened the first door at the top of the stairs, then turned to motion for her to remain on the landing.

As he went into the room, leaving the door open behind him, Megan heard a child's voice cry out, 'Daddy! Can I have a drink of water, Daddy? Please, please, can I? Can I?'

Puzzled, since Dr Robard had not mentioned the presence of a child, Megan inched closer to peer into the room, which was illuminated by a gaslight suspended from the ceiling.

The first thing she saw was a window seat, where several china dolls sat on attractively arranged pink ruffled cushions. Lace window curtains were tied back with pink velvet bows. Megan's gaze moved from the wallpaper, with its pale rosebuds and delicate tracery of leaves, to a shelf on which stood a doll house, several music boxes, and some rag clowns.

In the centre of the room stood a four-poster bed with a pink canopy edged with a white eyelet flounce. In the middle of a frothy pile of pillows lay a woman whose grey hair lay over her shoulders in long thin braids tied with pink satin ribbons. She wore a fluffy pink bed jacket and held an elaborately dressed doll in her arms. There was no child in the room.

'Darling, I want you to be very good –' Dr Robard began. At the same instant the woman in the bed caught sight of Megan in the doorway. A piercing scream filled the room. Dropping her doll, she clutched one of the pillows, tried to hide behind it, then hurled it at Megan.

Footsteps thundered up the stairs and Quinn appeared at Megan's side, his arm protectively around her.

Dr Robard gave Quinn a reproving glance over his shoulder and moved quickly to hold the woman as she thrashed wildly around the bed, sobbing uncontrollably.

'Shall I leave?' Megan asked.

'No. She'll quiet down in a minute. There, there, dearest child, I'm with you; you're safe. But I do want you to meet this young lady. I must insist.'

Agnes's penetrating screams became even more hysterical. Megan said to Quinn, 'Step back, out of sight.' He obeyed reluctantly, standing within arm's reach to one side of the doorway where Megan remained in full sight.

It was obviously difficult for Dr Robard to restrain his wife, and for a few minutes they wrestled on the bed, Agnes alternately screaming and lashing out at him with clawlike hands. Whenever she managed to break free of her husband's grasp she lunged towards Megan.

Watching, Megan wondered if a competent neurologist had examined Agnes and if so, what his conclusion had been. Disorders of the brain were so terribly difficult to treat. From a clinical point of view, Megan found the woman's condition intriguing; apparently a lesion had formed on Agnes's brain shortly after her husband's violent reaction to the birth of their stillborn baby. But of course the neurologists would deny any connection between the two occurrences.

It was obvious why the doctor had kept everyone, including her own family, away from Agnes. She had somehow turned into a grotesque, ageing little girl. She sounded like a child, threw childish tantrums, and clearly exercised no adult control over her own actions.

Eventually, after what seemed an eternity, Agnes exhausted herself and lay limp in her husband's arms, gasping for breath and occasionally giving another long shuddering sob. Her husband said, 'I've brought Megan to see you, dear. She won't harm you.'

'Go 'way! I hate you. Don't want you here,' Agnes mumbled.

'Come in now, Megan,' Robard called.

Ignoring Quinn's muttered protest, Megan stepped into the room, gesturing with her hand for him to remain out of sight.

Agnes promptly buried her face in her husband's shoulder and clung to him in pathetic desperation. She was very thin, almost emaciated, and Megan saw that a food tray remained untouched on the bedside table.

Over his wife's head Robard gave Megan a helpless look, but he spoke calmly, repeating several times that Megan was related to him and that she was a doctor who perhaps could help her.

'I not sick,' Agnes cried. 'I *not*.'

'Darling, you must be. You didn't eat your supper again tonight.'

'Not hungwy.'

'Megan came a very long distance to visit us, Agnes. She came all the way from Llanrys in north Wales. Perhaps tomorrow you'd like to get dressed and come downstairs so –'

Immediately the hysterical thrashing and screaming began again.

Megan turned and left the room. She felt Quinn's hand find hers in the darkness, and they went downstairs and back into the lighted study.

'What in God's name happened to her?' Quinn asked.

Megan let out her breath slowly. 'I'm not sure. Neurologists insist that behaviour like that is caused by a brain lesion.'

'Could she be acting the part of a child? She was almost a parody of a little girl, as though she knew exactly what she was doing and saying.'

'Yes,' Megan said thoughtfully, 'I got that impression, too. But why would someone – Hush, here comes the doctor.'

'The doctor? Isn't he your father? I thought that red hair was pretty convincing.'

'Yes, he's my father; I'm just not ready to call him that yet,' Megan whispered as Robard came into the study.

He collapsed into his chair behind the desk and buried his face in his hands for a second. When he raised his head again, he looked suddenly very much older. He gave Megan a tired, hopeless look. 'So you see the problem. She's been like this ever since we lost our baby. I didn't dare tell her that you are my daughter. I'm not sure what would happen if I did.'

'Have you sought other medical opinions?' Megan asked. He looked puzzled and she repeated the question, slowly and distinctly.

'Oh, yes. Two doctors insisted she needed surgery, three advised me to give up and place her in a home for the mentally unbalanced, and one suggested using fright treatment.'

'Dear heaven, are they still trying to *frighten* irrational behaviour out of patients? I thought they'd given up on that type of treatment.' She turned to Quinn and explained, 'In the old asylums they would drag unfortunate mental patients out of bed in the middle of the night and throw them into an icy pond . . . or fire a cannon near them without warning. Doctors would dress up in weird costumes and jump out unexpectedly.'

'That was supposed to cure them?' Quinn asked. 'I should think it would scare them still further out of their wits. What about the surgery?'

Dr Robard said, 'I would rather my wife stayed permanently in her present condition than subject her to the knife. I've seen too many disastrous results of brain surgery. In fact, I am adamantly opposed to all of the so-called medical cures being used for mental illness. One Austrian neurologist actually claims that the injection of an extract of tubercle bacillus into a mentally disturbed patient might induce a curative fever.'

'Dear God in heaven!' Megan exclaimed.

He turned to her. 'I'd like to spend some time with you, as soon as possible. I've been reading about a new treatment a doctor in Vienna has been using with patients like Agnes, but I haven't been able to find out very much about it. Perhaps you could help with my research. Apparently this doctor is considered a crank or worse in most medical circles.'

'Vienna? Not Dr Freud?' Megan asked.

'You've heard of him?' Robard looked astonished.

'Yes. He and Dr Breuer wrote a book called *Studies in Hysteria*. I haven't read it yet.'

A bell clanged noisily, echoing down from the upper reaches of the house, followed by a thumping on the ceiling that made the entire room vibrate. Dr Robard rose instantly. 'Agnes is upset. I'd better go to her. If you wouldn't mind showing yourselves out . . . and please, please come back soon. I keep the tradesmen's door locked, but I'll leave the front door unbolted for you.'

The rain had abated slightly, but the wind was still strong and Quinn held on to her as they raced back to her rented cottage as fast as the elements and the wet sand underfoot would allow. Quinn's recently healed broken leg didn't slow him down, and it was clear that he had exaggerated his earlier limp, probably in a play for sympathy and an attempt to distract her from his unannounced arrival.

At the cottage door Megan looked up at him, unsure what to do or say, wondering how much things had changed between them since that afternoon.

Quinn didn't give her a chance to speak. He pushed open the door and pulled her inside. 'We're both drenched to the skin, tired, not sure where we stand with each other, what we're going to do next . . . not to mention the situation with your father and his wife. If you think I'm going to leave you alone tonight, you're loco, lady.'

Megan felt relieved, for once, to have a decision taken out of her hands. She nodded and led the way into the kitchen. 'Let's light the stove and get warm. Are you hungry?'

'Starved.' He helped her off with her coat, his hand lingering for a second against her neck. She couldn't suppress a shiver and, to cover it, said quickly, 'It's very chilly, isn't it?'

'We can't help our feelings, you know, Megan,' he said, ignoring her question.

'No . . . but we can help what we do about them,' Megan said shortly. 'You start the fire and I'll find you something dry to wear.'

An hour later Quinn finished the last of his bacon and eggs and looked up to find Megan grinning at him.

'Have you any idea how ridiculous you look in my dressing gown?'

He glanced down at her burgundy velvet robe, which despite its fullness, didn't meet across his chest. 'I could take it off and we could curl up in bed to keep warm.'

Her grin vanished. 'Quinn, stop and think before you say something you'll regret. Even a casual joking remark could destroy this rather fragile truce we've constructed between us.'

'Is that what it is? Look, I did some thinking while you were discovering your long-lost father. I think we should head back to New Mexico right away and settle things with Randolph.'

'No, we can't!'

'Megan, I love you. I want to be with you. Are we going to spend the rest of our lives paying for the mistakes we made?'

'If by doing so we can avoid hurting a man as fine as Randolph, yes.'

'Did it ever occur to you that you could hurt him more by masquerading as a loving wife?'

263

Megan jumped to her feet. 'I'm going to bed. You can sleep on the couch.'

He caught her arm as she reached the door and spun her around to face him. 'Oh, no, you don't. We'll settle this now. You can't have it both ways – a gentleman husband at home and me hanging around waiting for a kind word. I don't want little pieces of you. I want all of you, and I don't intend to share you. Either you agree to come back with me and talk to Randolph or we say good-bye now, tonight, and go our separate ways.'

Megan stared at him. 'Is that an ultimatum?'

'Yes. Patience isn't one of my virtues. I want you, but I won't wait around for you to make up your mind. Either you love me or you don't.'

'I . . . I can't go back. I'm in trouble with the army in New Mexico because I released the Indian –'

'The hell with the army. Randolph was a fool to send you away. I wouldn't have. Megan, come back with me and I'll deal with the army. You don't have to go back to Randolph; you can stay in a hotel in Silver City. We'll go and see Randolph together, tell him the whole story.'

Megan closed her eyes for a moment. 'No, no, I can't.'

Wordlessly Quinn went to the makeshift clothesline they had strung across a corner of the kitchen, where his wet clothing hung. He peeled off her velvet robe and tossed it on a chair, then dressed in his own still-damp clothes and walked out of the cottage.

She stood staring at the closed front door for several minutes after he'd gone, feeling more bereft even than she had that afternoon. There was a finality in this parting that she had not felt earlier, perhaps because she had sent him away the other time and was sure she could bring him back . . . She flung herself at the front door and yanked it open, calling, 'Quinn!' into the stormy darkness.

The only reply was the moaning of the wind and the restless churning of the sea.

*   *   *

264

Denby gave Megan an ingratiating smile and tugged at his collar. 'Are we ready for the confrontation with your father?'

Megan didn't invite him in. He stood at her cottage door on a chilly grey morning that matched her mood. 'Why didn't you tell me the whole story about Dr Robard and his wife?'

His smile slipped. 'Uh . . . er . . .'

'It doesn't matter now. I've already seen my father. I shan't be needing your services again, Mr Denby. Please don't bother to call in the future.'

'You talked to him? What about her . . . his wife?'

'Good day, Mr Denby.' Megan closed the door firmly.

She waited for an hour, to be sure he was not still nearby, then slipped out the back way. A little while later she pushed open the unlocked front door of her father's house and called, 'It's Megan. May I come in?'

Remembering her father's hearing loss, she went directly to his study.

He was seated at his desk, engrossed in a medical paper. With that sixth sense she'd noticed before in those whose hearing was impaired, he glanced up and saw her.

'Sit down and look at this,' he said, as though she had always been with him. He thumped the paper with his fist, his eyes alight with excitement. 'Free association. That's what this Viennese doctor advocates, and apparently he's having incredible success with it. Free association . . . *talking* about the problem. By God, it's revolutionary, yet so simple it's unbelievable.'

Megan slipped off her coat and sat down opposite her father, who pushed the medical paper across the desk to her. She swiftly scanned the article written by Dr Sigmund Freud. When she looked up, her wonder exceeded his. 'His theory is that mental disorders are not always caused by physical symptoms,' she said, 'that the mind itself can become ill! My God . . .'

'We must get hold of everything this Dr Freud has written. Do you realise the possible consequences of his theories? Megan, he may have spawned a whole new school of medical science!'

'Yes . . .' Megan said slowly, 'and is it possible that women might be equally as adept as men at talking about problems of the mind? Perhaps, since we're more intuitive, we'd be even better.'

'You must bring all of your belongings over here and we'll prepare a room for you. There's much work to be done and I shall need you at all hours of the day and night.'

Megan leaned back in her chair, wondering if her father was interested in her only as a medical and research assistant. He was so completely absorbed with caring for his wife. Still, her own interest in the new science that Freud called psychoanalysis was intense enough that she would stay and not question her father's motives for inviting her to help him with his studies.

By the time Randolph's telegram arrived some three weeks later, Megan was so intrigued with what she and her father were discovering that she read her husband's message with dismay: 'Chiricahua Kid caught. Please come home immediately. All my love, Randolph.'

32

Joanna awoke each morning with a feeling of eagerness and, despite the cramped and windowless storeroom in which she worked, was always first to arrive at the *Chronicle*.

By the end of her second week, many of the newspaper's reporters were coming to her for rewrites or advice about their articles.

'You have a knack for using simple language, but you still manage to draw vivid pictures,' Bart told her. 'And you grab the reader's attention in the first paragraph. The mark of a real journalist, love.'

The society page had carried the article about the forth-coming wedding of Edith Abercromby under Bart Whitman's byline, but everyone in the city room had recognised the beautifully written piece as Joanna's work.

Bart was elated. 'Great balls of fire, Jo!' he had roared on the day the piece appeared. 'With my nose for sniffing out news and your elegant writing style, what a combination we are! Buy yourself a new bonnet, love, old Dragonbreath will keep you on for sure. The description of little Edie's dress is making today's edition disappear faster than snowballs in hell.'

But E. B. Duggenbrand had not addressed Joanna directly after that first day, not even to respond to her 'Good morning' when she passed his desk. He acted as if she did not exist. Joanna had grave doubts that she would be kept on, and she dreaded the approach of Friday of the second week.

She had become so caught up in the dissemination of news that she hadn't had time to miss Magnus or to brood about his marriage to Delta and his approaching fatherhood. When she did become aware of this apparent oversight, it occurred to her that perhaps she had stumbled upon the reason why men seemed less absorbed with the women in their lives than women seemed with their men. If one spent most of one's time in the pursuit of an interesting profession, one simply didn't have time for lovelorn longings. To Joanna this was an incredible discovery and she decided that even if old Dragonbreath fired her on Friday, her sojourn at the *Chronicle* would have been worthwhile.

Friday morning she donned her stylish wool dress and matching coat, put on a brave face, and marched into the city room with her head held high. Instead of going directly to the storeroom, she walked up to Duggenbrand's desk and, when he didn't look up, said, 'Good morning, Mr Duggenbrand. I believe my two-week trial period ends today. May I know your decision about my future with the *Chronicle*?'

At that instant the entire city room fell silent, as though all of the men were holding their breath.

Duggenbrand appeared taken aback by her directness and shifted his weight in his chair as he shuffled papers on his desk. 'You can stay on,' he mumbled.

A cheer went up, reverberating about the room, and suddenly reporters and copyboys surrounded Joanna, patting her on the shoulder and shaking her hand. Joanna was touched that they cared, a little embarrassed by all the attention, and elated that she'd been given a permanent position.

Bart hung around on the edge of the group of well-wishers, wearing a smug I-told-you-so expression. Duggenbrand glowered at the group. 'Doesn't anybody have any work to do?' Then to Joanna he said, 'You sit down. I want to talk to you. Whitman, you get over here, too. This concerns you.'

She pulled up a chair and sat down near the editor's desk as Bart made his way through the departing crowd.

The editor addressed his remarks to Joanna. 'The owner of the paper was impressed with the Abercromby wedding article. None of us realised how many readers are interested in the lives of the upper crust. Oh, we've always published wedding news on the society pages, but your piece was different. It was a glimpse behind the scenes – more than that, an advance glimpse . . . and none of the other papers had it. The big man liked that. The way the edition sold out told us that more women read our paper than we realised. Anyway, the owner wants you to write a regular weekly column about high society. All the scandal and inside stuff you can dig up.'

Joanna digested this silently, as Duggenbrand turned to Bart and said, 'Now, here's where you come into the picture. You're the one with the society connections, but you're probably *persona non grata* everyplace after the Abercromby piece, so nobody's going to tell you anything. We're going to keep the identity of our society columnist a secret – we'll come up with a pen name for you, Joanna – and Whitman, you are going to introduce her to the people most likely to pass along the gossip. Joanna, we'll give you an advance against your salary to buy some appropriate clothes, and we'll concoct a past for you. What do you think about that?' He was beaming now, like a magnanimous Buddha bestowing largess on an unworthy worshipper.

'I'm not sure I like the idea of becoming a professional gossip,' Joanna answered thoughtfully.

'She's just joking, E.B.,' Bart said quickly, grabbing her hand to yank her away. 'She's ecstatic about staying on.'

Duggenbrand called after her, 'Course you'll still run copy, help out the reporters, do the filing, and make the coffee. A weekly column won't take that long to write.'

Joanna walked along the shabby hallway, stepped aside to make way for two small boys racing by, and when she reached the last door, knocked tentatively. The sounds and smells of the tenement seemed more oppressive than ever, after the weeks she had spent in Bart's aunt's comfortable apartment.

She was very much aware of her fashionable suit, topped with a dramatic fur-trimmed cape, as a woman wrapped in a threadbare wool shawl walked by, her shoulders drooping under the weight of the packages she carried. Joanna's decision to come to see Magnus and Delta had been made on the spur of the moment, but even if she'd planned it, she couldn't have dressed down because she no longer owned any of the clothes she had brought with her to America. Bart had gathered them up one evening and made off with them. 'Holy Moses, Jo, we can't let anyone even suspect that Princess Natalie owns any of these relics.'

It had been Dragonbreath's idea to bestow the title upon

her. 'If we tell everyone you're a princess,' he had said, 'more doors will open.'

After a moment the door opened a few inches and she looked into Magnus's brilliant blue eyes, which showed more dismay than joy at the sight of her. Still, she was relieved to see there were no fresh bruises on his face.

He opened the door with obvious reluctance, murmuring, 'If you had let me know you were coming, I'd have tidied up a bit.'

The room needed more than a little tidying. Clothes, magazines, dirty dishes, were everywhere. There was no sign of Delta. Joanna looked at Magnus questioningly.

'Delta's feeling better. She . . . she went to visit one of the neighbours.'

'Perhaps I'd better not stay, then. I just wanted to know how you both were. I hoped I'd hear from you.'

For a second his eyes blazed with an emotion she couldn't define. 'Why? For God's sake why do you have to come around here to torment me? The only way I can bear to be away from you is if I don't see you.'

'Oh, Magnus,' Joanna breathed. 'Can't you understand my life would be too bleak if I thought I'd never see you again? Just for a moment, to know you're well and happy.'

'Happy?' There was so much bitterness in the word that Joanna felt as if a knife had twisted in her heart. 'You mean in the way you're happy, living in your fancy flat with your Bartholomew Whitman?'

Bewildered, she said, 'But I don't live with Bart. I told you, that's his aunt's apartment. He has his own place across town. Actually, I shall be moving to an apartment of my own shortly. That was another thing I wanted to tell you . . . my new address.'

She paused, then added gently, 'So that was why you seemed so distant that night. You thought I was living with Bart.'

He turned away, scooping up a bundle of feminine underwear as he did so. 'We're leaving here. Tomorrow.'

'Oh? Where are you going?'

270

After dropping the clothing into a drawer, he slammed it shut. 'Someplace where we won't have fingers pointed at us.'

She caught his arm, forcing him to look at her. 'There was gossip because you lived here with Delta before you were married? Is that what you mean?'

'We aren't married.'

'What? But you told me you were.'

'I thought it best you think we were. The truth is, I couldn't find anyone to marry us. They all said it was against the law, because I'm white and she's coloured.'

Joanna didn't know what to say. Underlying all other reactions was relief that Magnus was still free. But his next words dispelled any lingering hopes she nurtured.

'I met a man who wants to be my manager. We're moving in with him. Look, Joanna, there's no point in my telling you where. It's better if we don't keep in touch. You've made a place for yourself in this country and so have I, and we're just as far apart now as we were in England. Now you'd better go. I've got to get ready for a fight tonight.'

She hesitated. The idea of two men punching each other to a bloody pulp for the pleasure of a sadistic audience appalled her. Still, she couldn't walk out now; if she did she might never see Magnus again. Drawing a deep breath, she said, 'I'd like to come and watch. I've never seen a prizefight.'

For a moment she thought he might refuse to take her, but then his mouth twisted into a bitter smile. 'Why not? It's time you saw how I make my living . . . how I live and with what kind of people.'

Mauve spirals of smoke rose in the air above the boxing ring like malevolent genies, and a babble of harsh voices and raucous laughter assaulted Joanna's ears.

She was surprised to see so many women present – shabby women in worn shawls, flashy women with paint on their faces, even some fur-draped society women

271

accompanied by pale gentlemen in evening dress. The hall smelled of sweat and tobacco, whisky and beer. Joanna sank as low as she could in her seat on the front row, wishing she were a million miles away.

Magnus was fighting the second bout. She had kept her eyes closed throughout the first, mercifully short, fight. But the memory of the sickening sound of bone meeting flesh, the grunts and groans of the fighters and the manic yelling of the crowd, lingered in her mind. They had screamed for blood, like ancient Romans in an arena, and Joanna felt physically ill.

A great roar went up as the two new opponents entered the ring and she forced herself to open her eyes. She was vaguely aware of the referee in the centre of the ring, of the big brute in the other corner, of raised fists around her as the crowd saluted their favourite contestant, but her eyes were fixed on Magnus.

A slow shiver rippled up her spine. She felt her palms grow clammy and her heart begin to pound. Magnus stood in his corner like some remote god, magnificent, lonely. His seconds pulled his robe from his powerful shoulders, and Joanna felt her breath stop somewhere between her heart and her throat at the sight of his powerful pectoral muscles and bulging biceps.

She had read several articles on what the Americans called the sport of fisticuffs and knew that many fight organisers were now observing the rules drawn up in England by Sir John Sholto Douglas, Marquess of Queensberry, which required that the fighters wear gloves and refrain from wrestling each other or hitting an opponent who was on one knee. The most important innovation was that of the three-minute round with a one-minute interval between rounds. But this was a bareknuckle prizefight, in which a round would end only when a knockdown occurred.

In the instant before the bout started Magnus's eyes found hers through the smoky haze and he inclined his head slightly in her direction, as if proclaiming himself her champion. Joanna felt a vague urge to remove her scarf and toss it to him, as a lady of some bygone era might have offered her talisman to her chosen knight.

But when Magnus's fist crashed into the jaw of his opponent, grim reality replaced fantasy. Joanna's own fist flew to her mouth and she pressed her knuckles against her teeth, hoping to stem the bile that rose in her throat.

Watching through half-closed eyes, Joanna was both repulsed and fascinated by the spectacle of the two Goliaths duelling with their bare hands. The other fighter managed to land several blows to Magnus's body and face, and a cut opened above Magnus's left eye. But he remained on his feet, moving as lightly as a ballet dancer, despite his size.

She heard the man beside her say he was sorry he'd bet on the underdog, and from other comments around her, Joanna realised that Magnus's opponent was favoured to be the next bare-knuckle champion. Magnus was not expected to win.

She cringed as yet another blow struck the side of Magnus's head. According to the newspapers, some fights lasted for fifty or sixty rounds before one fighter prevailed over the other. How could she stand to watch such brutality for so long?

Unsteadily she rose to her feet to leave, but at the same moment Magnus began to fight back, pounding his opponent, driving him against the ropes.

The spectators leaped to their feet, shouting, cheering. Magnus's fist slammed into his opponent's jaw, and the favourite hit the floor, then rolled over and lay still. The referee began to count and, when he reached ten, seized Magnus's fist and raised it over his head.

Around her there was bedlam. She was vaguely aware that she was being swept along with the crowd surging towards the ring, and she felt panic replace her relief that the fight was over. She would surely fall and be trampled to death in that mad crush. The noise receded, the spectators blurred into an indistinguishable mass. Surprised, she thought, I'm going to faint!

A second later Magnus jumped over the ropes and landed beside her. He swept her up into his arms as the smoky blackness closed around her and squeezed away consciousness.

When Joanna opened her eyes she was lying on a hard table, a folded towel under her head. She looked up to see Magnus hovering over her. Somewhere, distantly, the roar of the crowd continued, or perhaps it was merely an echo inside her head. They were alone in a small dressing room, just as once they had been alone in a cave in the cliffs of Cornwall.

'Oh, God, Joanna, what was I thinking of, bringing you here? When I thought you were going down under the boots of that mob I wanted to kill every last one of them.'

'Magnus,' Joanna whispered. 'Hold me in your arms. Please.'

Thickly muscled arms went around her, wrapped her close to his chest. She could smell sweat and blood, but because it was his, it neither frightened nor disgusted her.

Raising her hand, she stroked his damp, tousled hair back from his forehead. 'Oh, my love, you were magnificent.'

For an eternal moment he didn't speak or move, but simply stared into her eyes, and all the longing of her own soul was reflected back at her in his gaze. Then his big powerful hands loosened the ties of her cape and laid it aside. He unfastened the buttons of her gown, his callused fingertips stroking the soft skin of her throat.

The roughness of his skin, the friction of his touch, brought an immediate response and she felt herself tremble, every nerve suddenly alive.

When he bent his head and pressed his mouth to the hollow of her neck, her hands clasped his head to her and a shuddering sigh slipped away from her.

He was breathing rapidly, his big powerful frame taut, muscles rigid as if braced, or perhaps tethered. She kissed his forehead and then his lips and murmured his name. Then she was no longer in control; he was sweeping her away, pulling her gown from her shoulders, running his fingers through her hair until it tumbled free.

Picking her up as if she were a doll, he held her in his arms, kissing her eyes, her mouth, her breasts. Then he pulled the towel from the table and spread it on the floor. Carefully he laid her down, pressed his lips once more to her breasts. She watched as he removed the rest of her clothes, then his own boxing tights.

His naked body, still glistening from the fight, thrilled her as nothing ever had before, and she stared at him, lost in admiration, her heart pounding with excited need.

Now he, too, was swept away with a passion that burst free from the boundaries he had imposed on himself. Somewhere, far back in the intuitive part of her mind she sensed that the excitement of tonight's victory was still with him, and her own presence was perhaps such a contrast to her surroundings that he was no longer able to control his desire for her.

She didn't care what had brought about the release of passion; she had waited too long to express her own. She opened her arms, parted her thighs eagerly, and he came to her, his manhood surging against her eager flesh as a force as old as time enveloped them.

There was no holding back. Every part of their bodies fused, with the urgency born of long need. Joanna felt stronger, as if his strength poured into her body through their joining. She raised her hips to meet his thrusts, pushed her breasts against his hands, wrapped her legs around his body in wanton abandon.

Except for a sharp intake of breath at the exquisite sensation of new pleasure, they were silent, too engrossed in the expression of physical love to speak.

She felt as though everything they did was new, while at the same time they were so in tune it seemed they had been together for a very long time, their demands and responses flowing easily.

When someone knocked on the dressing room door and called that the hall was to be locked up for the night, it was Joanna who suggested they go to her apartment.

Magnus nodded. Neither of them mentioned Delta.

33

'I wish you would reconsider,' Megan's father said, placing her bags in the train compartment. 'It's not too late to come home with me. I need you, Megan. Agnes is just beginning to accept you, and with my deafness, it's difficult for me to talk to her in the way Freud suggests.'

There was no point in repeating that she had a husband to whom she must return, so Megan replied, 'You'll manage and we'll keep in touch. Don't forget to send me anything new you find on the subject of psychoanalysis. I'll talk to Dr Sedgewick in New Mexico and see what he can dig up.'

'You never told me anything about the young man who came with you that first day,' Dr Robard said unexpectedly. 'Mr McQuinn with the physique of a lumberjack and the eyes of a road agent.'

Another passenger had entered the compartment. Megan said, 'He was my husband's best friend.'

'Was?'

'Is.'

'Ah,' her father said.

Megan forced herself to smile. 'Don't try any of Freud's tricks on me, Father.'

The word hung in the air between them and each was equally surprised by its impact. It was the first time she had called him Father, although she had spent every waking minute with him during the past weeks. It sounded right, she thought.

Tears welled up in her father's eyes and trickled slowly down his cheeks. Wordlessly he put his arms around her and held her. 'I shall miss you dreadfully, my dear. Please come back soon.'

She nodded, too overcome with emotion to speak.

As the train rattled over the tracks towards New Mexico, she pondered the fact that life always had something new to offer, perhaps as compensation for something lost. The thought didn't help ease her longing for a dark-eyed rogue named Quinn and she told herself despairingly that the two of them really should have attempted to synchronise their feelings for each other. When he wants me, I shy away . . . and now that I want him, he's gone for good. Perhaps it was just as well.

At the train station in Deming, Chuck collected her baggage and started across the platform.

'Goodness, there's one of those new horseless carriages I've been hearing about,' Megan said. She squinted in the bright sunlight. 'Surely I'm seeing a mirage! Can that be *Randolph* in it?'

'Yep. I tried to talk him out of it – sure don't want to have to learn to drive the durned thing myself – but he had to have one. Had it shipped out from the East.'

'At least it got him out of the house,' Megan said, quickening her pace.

Randolph's handsome face was wreathed in a broad smile as she hugged him, kissed his cheek, then stepped back to scrutinise the vehicle.

'Welcome home,' Randolph said. 'What do you think of our motorig? It's gasoline-powered and will go twenty miles an hour. Look closely at the cowl – you'll see my initials on it.'

Megan dutifully examined the handsome black-lacquered wooden hood, found the gold initials, which seemed to her somewhat diminished by the bicycle wheels with which the vehicle was fitted.

Seeing the direction of her glance Randolph added, 'The wheels are a small problem. The eastern wagon-wheel base is narrower than ours, so they set the motorig wheels the same and they don't fit into western wagon wheel ruts. This makes the ride a bit bumpy, but you're looking at the transportation of the future, Megan. Come on, Chuck, crank her up. I can't wait for Megan to have her first ride. I brought a scarf for you to tie over your hat, Megan.'

Chuck helped her into the seat. She saw she would have to sit between Randolph and Chuck, who would operate a tiller in order to steer. 'They're called motorigs?'

'Motorig is my personal favourite. Also proposed have been motor fly, automotive, autometon, autobaine, and several others. This one was made especially for me by a distant relative of my father; it's a Winton.'

'It's dreadfully noisy, and it smells terrible,' Megan commented laughingly a few minutes later as they lurched off down the dirt road. Randolph was right about the wheel base. The wheels on the one side rode in the wagon-wheel ruts and, on the other side, on higher ground, which meant she either had to cling to Randolph or slide into Chuck. 'But it brought you out into the world, so I shall get used to it.'

There was so much news to exchange that Megan and Randolph talked all the way to the ranch, through dinner, and on into the late evening, sometimes simultaneously.

'You're no Joanna when it comes to writing letters,' Randolph commented.

'Yours were beautiful, thank you. Tell me about the Chiricahua Kid.'

'He turned out to be Mexican, not Apache at all. The men in his gang were all Mexican or American. They dressed as Apaches when they went on their raids, then simply donned suits and moved freely about the towns. That's how they escaped the army for so long. If a patrol

278

hadn't chased them into the Cochise stronghold, they might have gone on killing and robbing for years.'

'I saw several unfamiliar cowboys as we came in. I take it they replaced the ones we lost?'

Randolph nodded. 'We're still shorthanded, though. Tell me more about your father. You did invite him to visit us?'

'He's even more of a recluse than you are. I doubt he'll come.' She told him briefly about Agnes and about the neurologist in distant Vienna who believed the mind could become as ill as the body. 'But I suppose Quinn told you all about Agnes?'

'I haven't seen him. He dropped me a note saying you were well and then went on to New Orleans. Said he had a sudden longing to take a paddle wheeler up the Mississippi.'

Just before midnight Randolph said, 'You haven't told me about your trip to New York. Did your father ask you to go? I kept waiting for a letter of explanation, but –'

'New York? I don't understand.'

'You did go there, several weeks ago?'

'No. I never left Galveston.'

Randolph looked perplexed. 'But your telegram . . . You sent me a wire from New York asking if you could come back to the ranch.'

Megan shook her head. 'The only time I was in New York was when our ship docked. I never sent you any such message.'

'Come with me,' Randolph said. He wheeled his chair through the living room archway, along the hall, and into his study. After opening the top drawer of his desk, he pulled out a Western Union envelope and handed it to her. 'I'm not sure why I kept it. I certainly wouldn't have forgotten to ask you about it.'

Megan read the message and then looked up at him. 'Randolph, it's signed "Joanna."'

'I know. I thought perhaps you'd become so accustomed to the name that you used it out of force of habit.'

'Who could possibly have sent this? No one but you and Quinn and I knew about Joanna,' Megan said.

But someone had sent that telegram and a strange possibility tugged at Megan's mind. Was it possible? Could it have been sent by Joanna herself? When Megan left Cornwall, Joanna's body had not washed up with the tide. What if she had *not* died?

'Megan?' Randolph asked. 'What is it? You don't believe in ghosts, do you?'

'I never told you all the circumstances of Joanna's death,' she said slowly. 'I think perhaps I should.' She related briefly the events leading up to her leaving with Quinn, finishing, 'But Joanna's body had not been found when we left.'

'Do you think there's a possibility she's still alive? Surely we would have heard from her,' Randolph said.

Megan looked at the telegram in her hand. 'Perhaps we have.'

She sat down weakly, the implications of the telegram rushing through her mind with the force of a hurricane. 'No, no she can't be alive,' she said after a moment. 'It would be too much to hope for . . . and even if she *is* alive, how on earth would she have ended up in New York?'

'There's a return address,' Randolph said. 'I sent a wire . . . lord, she must have thought it strange that I told her she couldn't come here. Still, we can send another wire. We'll have Chuck drive us into Manzanita Flats in the morning; there's a Western Union office there now.'

Megan was astonished at the changes that had taken place in Manzanita Flats during her absence. What had once been a straggly row of wooden buildings along a dusty boardwalk was now a thriving community. She saw a bank, several stores and – was it possible? – a theatre.

At the end of Main Street the green canopy of the Jade Palace protruded almost defiantly beyond those of its more sedate business neighbours, and Lallie's ornate green-lacquered carriage, harnessed to a sleek pair of horses, waited in front under the watchful eye of her burly Oriental driver, Mr Chang.

'How could all these buildings have gone up so fast?' Megan said, looking around wide-eyed. 'Why, this will be a town before long.'

'If they don't run out of water first,' Chuck grumbled. 'Territory ain't got enough to support this kind of growth.' He parked the car at the Western Union office and went inside to send the wire.

Randolph observed the number of people on the street despite the early hour and shook his head in amazement. 'My mother never would have believed this.'

'That saloon across the street looks quite posh,' Megan commented. 'As nice as anything I saw in Silver City or even Galveston. And, Randolph, look – there's a café. Oh, let's have lunch there.'

Tight lines formed on his face. 'Have you forgotten? I can't walk.'

She was about to suggest that Chuck carry him to the café, but the look on his face made her change her mind. 'If only we could get your wheelchair into the rig . . . Randolph, have you ever tried to get about on crutches?'

His head snapped back as if she'd slapped him. 'Would you display me as a cripple for everyone to see?'

'I'm sorry, I didn't mean to upset you. But, Randolph, you had an accident and I don't see that it's anything to be ashamed of that you can't walk.'

He stared straight ahead, apparently not listening. She sighed, wondering if Dr Freud had any magic formula for getting a person to talk. Sometimes she suspected that Randolph's feelings about his paralysis were more of a burden to him than the actual handicap.

Megan leaned forward suddenly. A familiar figure, staggering slightly, had launched himself out of the front doors of the Jade Palace. 'It's Dr Sedgewick . . . Oh, I must speak to him.'

'The man is drunk –' Randolph protested, but she was already out of the Winton.

Dr Sedgewick had crossed the street to the cafe, and the effort had apparently exhausted him. He clung to a hitching post and looked around in bewilderment, as though uncertain where he had been going. He blinked as Megan appeared at his side. 'Why, it's pretty Mrs Mallory . . . Heard tell you were in Galveston.' Although his speech was slurred, he seemed to be reasonably coherent. He glanced shamefacedly back at the Jade Palace. 'I was just checking on our patient, Becky . . .'

'Yes, of course,' Megan responded, knowing full well that Becky's incision would have healed by now. 'I would like very much to talk with you. Will you come out to the ranch and visit me?'

'Your husband wouldn't like that, ma'am.'

'He won't mind if you're sober when you call.'

Sedgewick gave a maudlin sigh. 'Sometimes a man has to drink to drown his sorrows. I guess you didn't know that my wagon burned to ashes last week.'

'Oh, I'm so sorry,' she said at once. 'Did you lose all your books and medicines?'

'Everything.' He hiccuped, then covered his mouth with his hand.

Out of the corner of her eye she saw Chuck emerge from the Western Union office and start cranking the car.

'I must go, Dr Sedgewick . . . Please come soon. I have a lot to tell you.'

When she told Randolph of the invitation, he frowned. 'I wish you hadn't done that. I loathe drunks; they're so unpredictable. You never know when they're going to turn ugly.'

'Perhaps he won't come,' Megan answered. 'But I hope he does. I need to talk to someone with interests similar to my own. Please don't deny me that.'

To Megan's surprise, Dr Sedgewick called on her the following afternoon. He had shaved and dressed neatly, but his hands shook as he accepted a cup of coffee from her.

Randolph murmured something about having business to discuss with Chuck; then he left them alone.

She was eager to tell Sedge all she had learned about Dr Freud and the fledgling science of psychoanalysis, especially the strange case of Agnes Robard's regression to childhood, and to ask if he could obtain any journals on the subject, but before she could begin, Sedgewick asked abruptly, 'Did Quinn talk to you about helping me set up a practice here in Manzanita Flats?'

'Yes, he did, and I think it's a wonderful idea for you to hang your shingle in Manzanita Flats,' she answered. 'The town must need a doctor desperately.'

'That's for sure. 'Specially after the Saturday night shoot-ups. In these parts, more men die of gunshot wounds than of any disease.'

She nodded sympathetically. 'Lead poisoning can certainly be quick and deadly. My grandfather treated many a wounded poacher at home in Wales. Once we even had to remove a bullet from the lord of the manor himself . . . I believe it was the only way they could have brought him down, as he was a great powerful giant of a man. That was the first and only case of acromegaly I ever encountered. When we first met Lord Evan Athmore the affliction hadn't even been identified –' She broke off, realising he had no idea what she was talking about. How long ago that episode seemed now and how far away the rugged hills of north Wales.

Dr Sedgewick leaned forward. 'What do you think? Would your husband let you come and help me out? I don't think I could handle a practice alone.'

'I couldn't possibly mention such a proposal to Randolph. I'm sorry, Dr Sedgewick.'

'Call me Sedge, and I'm going to call you Megan, because I'm going to talk to you like a father . . . well, maybe like a brother, since I'm not that old. Now, listen to me, Megan. Quinn told me all about your grandfather and how you practically took over his practice towards the end. I know you tried to get into medical school. I know how much you want to be a doctor . . . Hell, don't you think I know what it means to want it so bad that you'll do anything, anything at all, to have the right to help the sick and the hurt? Christ almighty, would any of us go through what we have to go through to call ourselves doctors if we weren't born with some demon in our gut that drives us?' Megan was silent, considering the truth of what he said. Already she missed her father who, despite his deafness, spent every waking hour seeking answers to the same questions that constantly hammered away at her own mind.

'I've got me a backer who's willing to put up the money for me to open an office, buy equipment, and replace my library,' Sedge continued. 'A party who wants to remain anonymous.'

A quick vision of Sedge staggering out of the Jade Palace the previous morning flashed through her mind. Since he had recently lost his medicine wagon, had he moved into the Jade Palace, perhaps paying his way by treating Lallie's girls? Knowing that Lallie, too, had a silent partner, Megan wondered if he was the same one who had offered to back Sedge.

'If you'd just come in and help me set up shop,' Sedge went on. 'Maybe give me a few hours a week of your time. I figure if there's a woman with me maybe I can get some female patients to come in. Too many of 'em die in childbirth, Megan. Oh, the midwives do fine with straight-forward deliveries and uncomplicated pregnancies, but –'

Megan raised a hand to stop him. 'All right! I'll talk to Randolph. Let's see what he says.'

To Megan's surprise, Randolph voiced no objections to her helping Sedge whenever she wished. His only stipulation was that she not travel to Manzanita Flats alone, in view of the recent escape from prison of the renegade the territory still called the Chiricahua Kid.

'I'll find Chuck right away so we can go and tell Sedge,' Megan said. They had just finished breakfast.

'Chuck has already left. He rode into town to try to hire some more hands. He says nowadays there's usually a

284

drifter who's lost his stake in a poker game, or a drover who's fallen in love with one of Lallie's girls and wants to prove to her he can settle down and hold a steady job.'

While Chuck was gone, the scruffiest and most unkempt cowpoke Megan had ever seen rode up to the ranch looking for work, and Randolph hired him.

Later, when Chuck returned, Megan overhead his comments about the new hand. 'Christ, if he takes care of the herd the way he takes care of himself we'll be in trouble. He's practically in rags. Did you see his boots and that worn-out saddle?'

'Clothes do not always maketh the man,' Randolph commented. 'Young Wyatt certainly seems down on his luck, and, yes, I did notice the worn-out saddle, but I also saw that his horse was well groomed and well fed and had recently been shod. And Wyatt took care of his animal before he even took a drink of water for himself. Give him a chance, Chuck. I'm sure he'll work out fine. Incidentally, one of the men you hired has the look of a gunslinger.'

'Braddock,' Chuck said. 'I wouldn't be surprised. But did you see the one they call Tex? He's a former Texas Ranger. I reckon one will balance out the other.'

'I suppose beggars can't be choosers. We need them all.'

That evening Megan was passing the bunkhouse on her way to the smokehouse to bring in a ham when she heard music and laughter and what sounded like someone dancing on the wooden floor to the accompaniment of hand-clapping and thigh-slapping.

Curious, she approached the window and, concealed by the lavender twilight, peered inside.

The ranch hands were sprawled on their bunks or seated in a semicircle around the newest and youngest cowpoke. Wyatt squeezed a concertina, producing a raucous, cheerful melody, to which his worn-out boots stamped an enthusiastic jig.

Megan smiled, feeling her spirits lift. Wyatt's shock of blond hair stood up in spikes around his earnest, pink-cheeked face. A patched and faded shirt hung loosely on his skinny frame and a threadbare kerchief was knotted around his scrawny neck.

She watched, entranced, until she noticed one of the other new hands who sat with his back to the wall rolling a cigarette. His fingers sprinkled tobacco into a paper, but his eyes unblinkingly regarded her through the window glass. Embarrassed at being caught, she immediately withdrew. What a frightening stare the man had. He must be the man called Braddock, who Randolph and Chuck suspected was a former gunslinger.

Lallie's flamboyant carriage drew close to Megan seconds after she left the doctor's office. The green-lacquered door opened and Megan climbed inside. She smiled at Lallie, who kept well back in the shadows, away from prying eyes, although the carriage certainly called attention to its owner.

'You really don't have to resort to this,' Megan said. 'If you're uncomfortable visiting me at the ranch, you could come to the office.'

'There's enough gossip about you for working with Doc,' Lallie said, 'without being seen with me.'

'I'm glad to see you under any circumstances, Lallie. I haven't made many friends of my own sex, and I do long to talk to another woman sometimes.'

'This ain't a social visit, Megan. It's like this, see. One of the Jade Palace's clients needs you. Well, his wife does. She's had female troubles for months now; that's why her husband came to my girls. Well, last night he breaks down and tells me this fancy doctor in Silver City wants to operate on his wife. He's going to take out something called ovaries.'

Megan felt a chill. It had become a fairly common practice to remove one or both of a woman's ovaries on the flimsiest pretext in the belief that it would cure a woman's 'female problems.' Many women died on the operating table, but that did not deter the surgeons. 'Try to get your friend to bring his wife to see Dr Sedgewick.'

'He won't do that. Folks know Doc's a drunk who hawked snake oil before he set up shop in Manzanita Flats.' Lallie paused, then her eyes lit up. 'I've got an idea! A Mr and Mrs Simmonds of Silver City are giving a big soiree for Joshua Pennington – he's my client with the sick wife – and he's running for governor. I could ask him to get the Simmondses to send you an invitation so you could talk to Mrs Pennington then. You could slip away from the festivities and have a private chat. Wouldn't be like going to another doctor at all.'

'Randolph wouldn't accept. He refuses all social invitations.'

'He goes riding in that new horseless carriage of his.'

'But he never gets out of it. I'm sorry, Lallie.'

Lallie glanced at her out of the corner of her eye. 'How about letting Quinn take you to the Simmondses"? Oh, don't look at me like that! I know all about you and Quinn.'

'There's nothing to know,' Megan protested, although her heart gave a familiar lurch. She and Randolph had heard that Quinn was back in Silver City, but he hadn't called on them.

'I know about Quinn tricking you into coming here and . . . Well, tell you the truth Megan, he drank a bit too much whisky at the Palace one night, and he told me if Randolph wasn't his friend, and crippled like he is, that he –'

'Lallie,' Megan interrupted, 'please don't go on with this. Surely you realise that people say things they don't really mean when they drink too much.'

'Quinn loves you, Megan. You must know that.'

'I know nothing of the sort. Besides, I'm married to Randolph.'

Lallie gave her a crafty glance. 'Quinn says Randolph loves you, too. Enough that he would have let you go away to medical school. If he loves you that much, wouldn't he let you go to a dinner party with Quinn so you could talk to a sick woman?'

287

'I'm not a doctor, Lallie, and even if I were, I couldn't treat someone who hasn't asked to be treated.'

'I already talked to Quinn. He said he'd explain the situation to Randolph tonight. I daresay when you get home they'll both tell you to go.'

That wasn't likely, in view of the fact that Quinn kept his distance. 'I'll see what transpires. Oh, I must go. There's Chuck across the street glaring at me. Randolph insists that Chuck bring me in to town and take me home, although I'm sure I could handle the motorig myself.'

Lallie's wide-eyed admiration at this claim was brief. 'Ain't you forgetting? The Chiricahua Kid busted out of jail and he's prowling the territory somewhere.'

'I doubt that. He's probably back in Mexico by now. Goodbye, Lallie. Take care.'

All the way back to the ranch with the taciturn Chuck, Megan alternately told herself there was no chance that Quinn would be there, then hoped against hope that he would be. Her heart leapt as she saw his magnificent black stallion hitched to the post in front of the house. Not many men in the territory owned a horse like that; from all accounts Quinn was doing very nicely financially nowadays.

She entered the cool dimness of the house, peeling off her gloves as she crossed the entry hall. Through the archway she could see a pair of long legs stretched out in front of the living room hearth.

Instinctively her hand went to her hair, windblown from the ride, then dropped again to her side. Why primp for a man who was merely doing a favour for the local madam?

Quinn rose as she entered the room, his dark-eyed glance moving over her almost imperceptibly. 'Good evening, Megan.'

She went directly to Randolph and bent to kiss his cheek. He caught her hand in his and raised her palm to his lips. 'Hello, my love. Just when I thought I couldn't stand being here without you another minute, here you are.'

'But you had Quinn for company,' she pointed out. 'Good evening, Quinn, how are you?'

288

'Tolerable, ma'am, thank you. I hear you're helping out my old compadre Sedge. Sounds like an ideal arrangement for both of you.'

Megan sat down near Randolph, whose eyes searched her face anxiously. 'Quinn has been invited to attend a ball given by the Simmondses of Silver City for Joshua Pennington, who's running for governor. Quinn wants us to go, too.'

Us to go, Megan thought. 'Why, that would be lovely, Randolph. We could have one of the hands take the wheelchair in the buckboard.' She avoided meeting Quinn's gaze, afraid he might sense the churning of her emotions.

'You know I never go to social affairs,' Randolph said quietly. 'But if you'd like to go, I won't object.'

She gave him a quick glance, but a mask had descended over his face and she couldn't tell if his acquiescence was sincere.

'I should like that. I hear the Penningtons are charming.' She excused herself and went to her room to change into a new and rather severely tailored gown of forest green.

Minutes after she returned to the living room, Consuela announced that dinner was ready, and for the next hour Megan forced herself to eat and sip wine and listen to Quinn's amusing tales of his travels. His trip by paddle wheeler up the Mississippi had evidently been very profitable: During a poker game he had acquired part interest in a Louisiana plantation.

Occasionally Quinn turned his attention to her, flattering her and flirting. 'How charming you look this evening, Mrs Mallory. Your gown is a perfect foil to set off your hair and eyes, yet unobtrusively so, so that we see the woman first.'

His glance lingered a fraction of a second too long on the curve of her bodice and Randolph frowned, but Quinn went on, 'I noticed that the ladies in New Orleans tend to overdress. Their gowns overpower them so that at first glance one is aware of only the dress, not the woman. You'd love New Orleans, by the way. It's probably the most exotic city in all of America. It was old at the beginning of the century, when Andrew Jackson led his triumphant ragtag brigade beneath the wrought-iron balconies of the French Quarters –'

Breaking off, he affected an exaggerated expression of woe. 'Oh, do pardon me. It was bad manners to refer to Jackson's triumph, since it was over your countrymen.'

'My countrymen are Welsh, have you forgotten?' Megan responded shortly. *Have you forgotten making love? Have you forgotten your declaration of love?*

'In any event, Jackson fought that final battle of the War of 1812 *after* the peace treaty had already been signed,' Randolph put in. 'So it was an exercise in futility.'

'Ah, yes,' Quinn agreed, his eyes fixed on Megan. 'Some events do turn out that way, don't they?'

Megan stared at him, trying to pick up the undercurrents in his comments. Surely he, too, felt the turmoil of being forced to pretend that nothing had changed between them, when in fact everything had. But his expression gave nothing away.

He raised his glass in a toast. 'To the loveliest lady to grace our wild frontier. I hope you realise you're the envy of every man in the territory, Randolph.'

The two men sipped their wine, but Randolph regarded Quinn strangely. From time to time Megan felt her husband's eyes on her in a questioning way. She grew increasingly angry with Quinn.

Perhaps Quinn caught the gleam in her eye, since he smoothly changed the subject to the coming election and the possibility of statehood for New Mexico. Not knowing much about American politics Megan felt left out, but after a few minutes Quinn turned to her again and said, 'Forgive me. Politics is far too boring a subject for a beautiful woman to concern herself with.'

Don't flatter me, Megan thought. Don't flirt with me as if I were merely a casual acquaintance. We were much more to each other than that. As the evening wore on, she became increasingly irritated and regretted having agreed to accompany Quinn to the home of one of Silver City's most prominent citizens for the ball to honour Joshua Pennington.

When Randolph suggested they go into the living room for brandy, Megan abruptly said she was tired and would like to retire. 'I'm sure Quinn has lots of stories to tell you, dear, and my presence will no doubt put a damper on the details.'

Megan lay in bed, hearing their muffled voices and laughter, feeling angry without quite knowing why.

Sleep came reluctantly, and she had just begun to dream that she was home again in Wales, flinging herself breathlessly upon a windswept hillside with the valley unfolded beneath her, misty green and beautiful – when she felt hands on her body, lips pressed urgently to hers.

At first she thought she was still dreaming. She was lying on the edge of her bed, one arm dangling over the side.

An exploring hand had slid inside her nightgown and was fondling her breast, while the stranger's mouth seemed bent on devouring her lips.

As she struggled towards consciousness she thought for one delirious instant that Quinn had come to her, but then reality prevailed. His kiss was different, his touch less frantic.

Her hand touched something cold and unyielding in the darkness beside the bed. Her fingers traced the curve of a wheel. She pushed the hand away from her body, jerked her face away from the devouring mouth. Randolph! It was Randolph, his wheelchair pressed to the side of her bed.

He spoke then and she knew this was no dream. 'You're my wife and I have rights. Did you think you could deny them to me forever? I've loved you purely and chastely all these months, but I'm a man, not a priest. All evening I watched him flirting with you and you blushing like a schoolgirl, and I was filled with rage . . . and, yes, with jealousy and lust. I want you, Megan. I want you now. This marriage is finally going to be consummated.'

34

Magnus visited Joanna regularly at her apartment. They made love, dined together, spent quiet hours sitting close together holding hands, touching, glad just to be safe, warm, well fed, and in each other's company.

The second time Magnus spent the night with her, Joanna's conscience drove her to ask, 'Magnus, I can't help but wonder about you and Delta . . .'

'We go our separate ways. I hardly ever see her, except when she wants money.'

'Do you make love to her?'

'No. The only time I did was after we got off Ellis Island. I told you about it. I was drunk. I've never got drunk since. I love you, Joanna. Now, then, always. I never cared for Delta and never led her to believe I did.' He reminded her gently, 'She isn't my wife, you know.'

'But she's expecting a child. I feel guilty, keeping you here with me when she's alone.'

'Alone? Delta? Do you really think pregnancy has changed her?' He gave a short, bitter laugh. 'She still goes out every night to meet men. Sometimes she doesn't come home at all.'

'Yet you continue to take care of her.'

'Delta lives only for the moment. Now that she's feeling well again she doesn't think the time will come when none of her male friends will stand by her. So I have to stay until then.'

Joanna sighed and nestled closer to him. She loved the way his powerful body seemed to enclose hers, his strong arms wrapping her in a love so passionate that she knew instinctively few lovers were blessed with such perfect sensual compatibility. They were creatures of the flesh – primitive, urgent, inexorable. When he held her and her breasts were crushed against his hard muscles, her legs wrapped around him, she felt fragile and yet strong, too, since his strength was hers to command.

The nights they made love were made of black velvet, studded with diamonds, disconnected from the mundane details of their daily lives. When they were together, nothing else existed for them.

They never discussed her column in the *Chronicle* or the people she met, nor did they talk about his steadily increasing record of wins in the ring. Neither of them mentioned Delta again. They were an island of two adrift upon an ocean of passionate, desperate love.

When Magnus left her, Joanna had no idea where he went. She did not allow herself to wonder about the other woman in his life or to think about tomorrow. In her mind she and Magnus were married, although no minister had performed a service, and Delta was simply a shadowy back-street liaison to be tolerated.

As Joanna's circle of society acquaintances grew and she was invited to parties almost every night, she and Magnus were forced to meet at odd times of day. Magnus was content to see her on her terms, and if Delta or his training schedule made any demands on his time, he never mentioned it to Joanna. Her only nagging fear concerned the fact that Delta would soon give birth to her child. Then what would happen? she wondered. Even though Magnus was not sure the baby was his, fatherhood, real or imagined, might change him, might it not?

Bart Whitman knew immediately that Joanna was seeing someone secretly. Late one evening as he walked her home after a musical evening he asked abruptly, 'All right, princess, cough up his name. I can't stand not knowing who he is.'

Joanna knew Bart well enough by now to realise he

wouldn't be put off by demurral. 'A man I knew in England. No one whose name you'd recognise.'

'Is he married?'

'Why do you ask that?'

'Holy Jerusalem, Joanna, I don't know of any other reason for you to keep him hidden.'

She stopped walking as the impact of this statement struck her. There had been occasions when Magnus might have accompanied her, to the opera, to the ballet, to the theatre – perhaps not to a dinner party, since he preferred simple food and would have been overwhelmed by a multiple-course meal. She told herself she hadn't invited him because he would have been uncomfortable. Would he ever truly be at ease in her world?

But now she wondered if in reality it was she who balked at presenting him to the society in which she moved. Recalling with a shudder the one and only night she had watched him fight, she had to ask herself, too, if she could ever become a part of his world. This had always been Magnus's contention – that neither could live in the other's world.

'What is it, love?' Bart asked solicitously. 'Some revelation you weren't prepared to face?'

'Perhaps. Bart, come up and have a cup of tea with me and let me tell you about the man I love.'

How wonderful it was to have a friend like Bart, she thought as she put the kettle on and he examined the telephone she'd recently had installed.

'Doesn't it startle you out of your wits when it rings?' he called to her through the kitchen door. 'Bad enough to have the pesky things in the city room, but at home, too?'

'It doesn't ring too often.' She carried the tea tray into the living room. 'The first time I thought it was the front door. Dragonbreath called me about the column and *that* was an ordeal – you've heard how he bellows over the line?'

'He's the main reason I've resisted getting one of the dag-blasted contraptions.' Bart eyed the cup of tea she handed him hopefully. 'A dash of brandy would make it drinkable.'

'You know you never stop with a dash, and it's so late.'

He sighed and settled down on her sofa. 'All right. Tell me about Mr Wonderful.'

'He's a prizefighter.'

Bart blinked.

Although Joanna confided a great deal in Bart, she decided not to tell him how she and Magnus had met, instead allowing him to think they had met aboard the ship.

When she'd finished, Bart shook his head, as though trying to digest everything she'd said. 'You're the last woman on earth I'd expect to take up with a fighter. Beauty and the beast, I guess.'

'Not at all! Magnus is sweet and gentle and –'

'And beats men to a pulp with his fists for a living.'

'Boxing isn't quite so brutal nowadays. He wears gloves most of the time now, and the Queensberry rules are observed. Magnus says it's becoming a legitimate sport.'

'Not quite, love. It's still banned in all but a couple of states. Magnus? I don't know any boxers by that name.'

'He calls himself Max Morgan in the ring.'

Bart whistled. '*Max Morgan!* He's the next contender.'

'Contender?'

'For the heavyweight title, love. Hasn't he told you?'

'We . . . don't talk about boxing much. I'm a little sickened by it.'

Bart raised an eyebrow but didn't comment on her aversion. After a moment he frowned. 'There's going to be plenty of interest in him as the championship fight draws closer. Great balls of fire, Jo, it will cause quite a stir if the press finds out about you *and* his mulatto mistress. Hell, I'd be tempted to break the story myself.'

Joanna winced. 'I hadn't thought about that. I should have, of course, being in the business of ferreting out such information myself. I should explain that Magnus would have married Delta, but he couldn't find a justice of the peace who would perform the ceremony.'

'I'm surprised she got into the country in the first place and even more surprised she came by way of England. When I was there it appeared to be a completely homogeneous society. Could she pass for white?'

'Her skin is like milky coffee and she's absolutely beautiful, with long straight hair and huge amber eyes . . . but no, she doesn't look white.'

The telephone rang, its clarion call causing both of them to jump. Joanna picked up the earphone and listened for a moment, then said, 'Yes, I understand. Thank you for letting me know. Good night.'

She looked at Bart. 'Delta gave birth to a baby girl this evening.'

Two weeks later Bart insisted on cooking dinner for Joanna at his apartment after they left the *Chronicle* offices.

'You've seen Delta and the baby.'

It wasn't a question, but Joanna nodded. 'A beautiful little replica of Delta, with a slightly lighter skin.'

'And the mighty Max Morgan?'

'Magnus, you mean. Yes, he was there. They're living with his manager in a neighbourhood called Hell's Kitchen.'

She suppressed a shudder, recalling her mercifully brief visit. Bart mustn't suspect how it had torn her heart in two to see the exquisite baby nestled in Delta's arms and the way Magnus hovered protectively over the two of them.

'Listen, Jo, I'm going to have to give you this straight. Delta had an affair with Magnus's manager during the latter part of her pregnancy, and before that, she slept with several other men. Apparently she's been sleeping with everyone but your friend Magnus.'

Joanna didn't comment. She wasn't surprised by this information, but felt uneasy to learn that Bart had investigated Magnus and Delta so thoroughly.

Bart had brought home a pair of lobsters, and Joanna

looked away as he dropped them into a pot of boiling water. 'Great Caesar's ghost, Jo, but you are the most tenderhearted little thing I ever did encounter. I suppose I'm going to have to make a ham sandwich for you instead?'

'Why did you want to see me tonight, Bart? You're obviously in the throes of some inner battle with yourself.'

'You know me too well, love.' He handed her a glass of wine. 'Fact of the matter is . . . I had a few drinks with a reporter from the *Herald* and he spilled all the dirt about Magnus and Delta. Furthermore, he knows that Magnus has been slipping off to see some society lady, and he expects to find out exactly who this woman is before long.'

Joanna drained her wineglass in a single gulp. 'If he finds out about me, will it hurt Magnus in any way?'

Bart's eyebrows went up in amazement. 'Hell, no. It will turn him into a romantic figure. You're the one who'll be in trouble. It will be the end of Princess Natalie and her weekly column.'

'Do you think Dragonbreath would keep me on in some other capacity?'

'Jo, love, will you please open those lovely eyes of yours and see the world as it really is? Consider the situation of Delta and her baby. Interracial affairs, especially those that produce offspring, are tolerated not at all. It smacks too much of the old master-slave scandal. If it gets out that Magnus is involved with you *and* Delta, you'll be – forgive the choice of words – tarred with the same brush. You'll be seen as part of a *ménage à trois*. I doubt any paper will hire you.'

Joanna reached for the wine decanter and poured herself another glass. 'I find it hard to believe our private lives would interest anyone to that extent.'

'Like it or not, love, you and your fighter have become celebrities, each in your own way.'

She sighed. 'Isn't it peculiar how we worry about all the wrong things? When I got up this morning I was petrified at the prospect of going to a party tomorrow night because the Abercrombys are going to be there.'

'So?'

'Mrs Abercromby or Edith will surely recognise Princess Natalie as their former parlour maid.'

Bart laughed shortly. 'Hardly, love. Have you looked at yourself lately? You bear absolutely no resemblance to that wide-eyed, skinny little immigrant girl who was terrified of her own shadow. The gaunt hollows have filled in, and you've acquired a certain sophistication. Your clothes, your hair, and your demeanour and bearing say "quality," "class." Besides, people like the Abercrombys don't really see their servants. They're only aware of silent, subservient shadow-figures creating order around them.'

Joanna knew this to be true. She surely would not have recognised any of the staff of Traherne Hall had she met them anywhere else, especially without their uniforms.

'I'm sure you're right,' she said. 'Besides, even if I'm recognised it won't really matter, since you feel my days as Princess Natalie are coming to an end because of my love for Magnus.'

Joanna moved restlessly around Bart's living room, glass in hand, too tense to sit down. There was a stack of newspapers and magazines on the coffee table, and she paused, looking down at the sports page of a rival paper.

Her throat constricted as she looked at a picture of a brawny young man surrounded by several other men. She did not even read the caption as one face stared at her from the page.

Bart glanced over her shoulder at the picture. 'Ah, that's the English heavyweight boxer Jeremiah Hollis. If your Magnus wins his next fight, he'll defend his title in an international bout with Hollis. I should think . . . Jo? What's wrong? You look as if you just read your own obituary.'

With a shaking finger Joanna pointed to the older man who stood just behind the young boxer's shoulder. 'That man . . . it's Paxton, Justin Bodrath's butler . . .

Oh, dear God, I have the most awful premonition of disaster.'

'Paxton? Bodrath? Who are they?'

'Ghosts,' Joanna answered, 'from the past – Magnus's and mine.'

35

A full moon had risen. Its pale silver light flooded Megan's bedroom, illuminating Randolph's tortured expression as he strained to drag himself from his wheelchair to the bed.

Megan had rolled away from him, fully awake now, and she watched him for a moment, still disbelieving. Was it Randolph who had kissed and caressed her, or had it been a dream?

He managed to grab the bedpost and pull himself away from the chair, which began to roll backwards. A second later he crashed to the floor and lay in a crumpled heap.

She jumped up and lit the lamp. When she reached his side he looked up at her helplessly, his eyes filled with tears. 'Oh, God, what have I done? Megan, forgive me, please. I had too much to drink and –'

'It's all right.' She slipped her arm under his shoulders and pulled him up into a sitting position. Crouching beside him, she reached for his wheelchair.

'Go to the bunkhouse and get Chuck,' Randolph said through clenched teeth. 'I'm too heavy for you.'

'We don't need Chuck,' Megan answered firmly. 'Get hold of the edge of the bed and haul yourself up. I'll lift your legs.'

'Please – just get Chuck.'

'I won't go for him, Randolph, so unless you want to spend the night on the cold floor, you'd better do as I say.'

Beads of sweat formed on his brow as he grasped the iron bedsprings and tried to pull himself up. When he fell again and struck his head on the adobe tile floor, she almost relented and went for help, but forced herself to harden her heart. 'You can do it. Come on . . . try,' she urged.

After several failed attempts, he raised his torso into position over the bed and she quickly grabbed his legs and swung them up with him.

He lay on the bed, panting, as she sat down beside him. For a moment his triumph in moving without the aid of his foreman was enough to temporarily block from his mind the reason he was in her room.

But then he clapped his hand to his head, covering his eyes. 'I don't know what to say to explain my behaviour. I don't know how to ask your forgiveness. I don't know what came over me.'

Megan cleared her throat. 'Randolph, please don't feel shame with me. I had no idea that you were able to . . . that you felt –'

'What other men feel for a woman?' he finished bitterly. 'Oh, yes. In my mind, my imagination, I've made love to you many times. Tonight I think too much brandy distorted my thinking to the point where I actually believed I could put my yearnings into practice, which is impossible, of course.'

'Why is it impossible?'

He turned his head away from her. 'Don't mock me. You know I'm paralysed from the waist down.'

'Randolph, I want to see your legs.'

'What?'

'Will you allow me to remove your trousers and look at your legs?'

'I don't understand . . .'

'I'd like to examine the scars from your accident.'

'There aren't any.'

300

Taken aback, Megan stared at him, her mind racing. 'You move the upper part of your body easily. You reach for books, bend over to retrieve something you've dropped. You just twisted around in several directions in order to get onto the bed. This indicates that your spinal cord is intact, so I'm curious to know what happened to your legs.'

His head rolled slowly towards her and he regarded her reproachfully. 'They were crushed.'

'The bones broken? The ligaments and cartilage mangled? The flesh torn? All without leaving scars?'

'You're not a doctor, Megan, so don't play the part with me. I knew it was a mistake for you to help out that drunken snake oil hawker.'

'Who took care of you after the accident? Which doctors?' Megan persisted.

'I saw several doctors. Why are you delving into this now? Can't you accept the fact that I'm no saint? I got drunk and came in here and forced myself on you and I'm sorry. Now will you fetch Chuck? As far as I'm concerned, tonight's regrettable incident is over. I've apologised and I swear it will never happen again. We'll put a lock on your door if you like.'

'That isn't necessary. Randolph, please, we must talk.'

He gritted his teeth and pulled himself into a sitting position. 'Would you mind bringing my wheelchair closer to the bed?'

For answer she pushed the chair even farther away. 'Would you like to walk again?'

'Now you're being cruel. Megan, I've apologised to you, what more can I say?'

'You can answer my question. Would you like to walk again?'

'Do you think I *like* being helpless?'

'I think,' Megan said slowly, 'that you like the life you lead now. You live in a quiet world of books and art; you never have to leave the sanctuary of this house or socialise with other people. Most of all, you don't have to associate

301

with rough-and-tumble ranchers and cowboys. You can avoid doing all the things you hated to do before your accident.'

'I can't believe you're saying these things to me.'

'Randolph, I've been thinking about it a great deal since I came back from Galveston. I intended to tell you about a doctor in Vienna and his theories about the influence of the human mind on the body. I hoped you'd read some papers I brought back with me.'

Gripping his thighs with his hands, he picked up his legs and swung them over the side of the bed. Before she could stop him, he pitched forward on the floor, his knees cracking against the adobe tile. Then, grunting, panting, he began to drag himself forward on his elbows, inching painfully towards the wheelchair.

Megan could feel the tears pouring down her cheeks. 'Randolph, I have something else to say and if I don't say it now I probably never will.'

He rested for a moment, looking up at her with soul-deep pain in his eyes. 'If you're going to tell me you're in love with Quinn, don't bother. If I hadn't been blinded by my own feelings for you, I'd have recognised it long ago.'

She swallowed hard. 'I was going to ask if it's possible that you've been punishing yourself by staying in that wheelchair . . . because you lived and your parents died.'

The instant the words were out of her mouth she regretted saying them. If she had taken a knife and plunged it into his heart he could not have looked more shattered.

After she had summoned Chuck to help Randolph back to bed, ignoring the foreman's muttered diatribe about good-for-nothing women who caused more trouble than they were worth, Megan sat down to write to her father.

'. . . and I wish I'd never heard of Freud! I can't describe the look on my husband's face when I suggested he was suffering from an extreme case of guilt, doing penance, as it were, because he believed he was the cause of his mother's running away, which led to the death of both parents. She ran away. Therefore Randolph would never run, or walk, again.

'I thought I'd reasoned it all out, that he blamed himself because he was the one who introduced Quinn to his mother, and then she became infatuated with him. Then, too, Randolph had never liked the life of a rancher. His father taunted him because he loved books and music and art, and by not walking, of course, Randolph was free to spend all his time in these pursuits. Oh, how neatly I arranged all the facts in my own mind and came up with perfect answers! But we humans are really too complex for one of us completely to understand another.

'Father, it's almost dawn and I've been up all night and I'm probably not making much sense, but I wanted to tell you all that happened tonight and ask what you think about it. Do you feel, as I do now, that Freud has the right idea – that indeed there is an unconscious mind – but that his method of dealing with deeply buried problems doesn't work? Or is it that we just don't know enough about his so-called talking cure to make it work? God knows, enough doctors recognise medical disorders without coming up with an effective treatment. To digress for a moment, a case in point: I've just learned that a local doctor wants to remove the ovaries of the wife of an important politician here . . .'

Megan laid down her pen, her hand cramping, and the thought crept into her mind that tonight had irrevocably changed everything between herself and Randolph, and between Quinn and the two of them. The ball for Joshua Pennington and his wife was only days away. What a pity everything had gone awry just now. She might have been able to persuade Mrs Pennington not to allow her physician to remove her female organs.

She stretched out on her bed, muscles twitching with fatigue, too weary to contemplate what might happen next. Her sheets were crumpled and the faint scent of the bay rum Randolph used to tame his hair clung to her pillow. The masculine smell disturbed her in a way she was unable to define, or perhaps, she thought, she didn't want to define it. Quinn didn't use bay rum and usually smelled of wild chaparral, but Randolph's mere presence in her bed, despite the circumstances, made her feel disloyal to Quinn. 'Ah, Dr Freud,' she murmured just before she fell asleep, 'what would you make of that?'

Consuela awakened her with a breakfast tray a short time later. 'Senor Mallory said to bring you *desayuno*.'

Megan groaned. 'Thank you – *gracias*, Consuela.' Another hour's sleep would have been more welcome. It was, she was sure, Randolph's way of saying he wanted to see her.

Half an hour later she walked into the living room. Randolph's wheelchair was positioned near the window and he was engrossed in reading a letter. A number of other letters, all written on the same fine parchment paper in delicate copperplate handwriting, were scattered around him, on his lap, the table, the floor.

When Megan approached, he said, without looking up at her, 'I'm rereading Joanna's letters.'

Feeling tired and irritable, Megan snapped, 'And no doubt wishing you'd never heard of either of us.'

'Not at all. In different ways you both enriched my life.' He raised his eyes to meet hers. 'I want so much to believe the woman who wrote these letters is still alive. Her words express an appreciation for truth and beauty, a love for all that is noble in life, that is strong enough to overcome personal loss or disappointment. How I wish I could meet her.'

He carefully folded the letter he was holding and slipped it back into its envelope. 'The wire I sent to New York to the address Joanna gave in her telegram wasn't delivered. Western Union advised me that the party in question had moved and left no forwarding address.'

Megan didn't comment. How could she tell Randolph that even if Joanna was alive and in this country, there was little likelihood that she would come to New Mexico, since she believed that Quinn – who knew she had aborted Oliver's child – was actually Randolph.

'Chuck has to go to Silver City,' Randolph said

304

unexpectedly. 'I thought perhaps you'd like to accompany him and have a gown made for the Pennington ball.'

Blinking, she wondered if she'd heard correctly. 'You mean . . . you still want me to go to the ball with Quinn?'

'I want you to be happy,' Randolph replied quietly.

Chuck's voice, raised in anger, shattered the early-morning peace. 'Look at you! You're a disgrace to the Mallory ranch. You're not going into town looking like that. Hell, the worst saddle tramp I ever saw dressed better'n you.'

Megan hesitated, halfway between the house and the barn, hidden from view by a row of cottonwoods.

She heard the hesitant drawl of the young cowboy, Wyatt. 'I done washed my shirt and pants, Chuck. They're clean, honest. An' I polished my boots, too. I gotta go to town, Chuck; it's real important.'

'Mr Mallory gave you an advance on your wages. What the hell did you do with the money? You were supposed to get yourself some new duds.'

There was no response.

Megan wheeled around and walked between the trees towards them. Wyatt was astride his horse, hanging his head before the foreman's wrath. Chuck had grabbed the reins to halt him.

How very young Wyatt looked in the clear morning sunlight, and how woebegone. He managed a grin as she approached, and touched the brim of his battered Stetson. ''Morning, ma'am. Mighty fine day, ain't it?'

'Good morning, Wyatt. Chuck, I couldn't help overhearing your conversation. I do think that if it's Wyatt's day off he should be allowed to go into town. Furthermore, his wages are his to do with as he pleases.'

Chuck's glare turned to pure venom. 'I run this ranch, Mrs Mallory. Maybe you're forgetting?' He jerked his head at Wyatt. 'Go on, git. We'll talk about this later. Right now I need to settle a few things with Mr Mallory's bride.'

They watched Wyatt ride off and, moments later, heard his happy tenor voice singing a cowboy ballad.

'You know what you just did?' Chuck demanded. 'You just undermined my authority.'

'I'm sorry, but you were wrong,' Megan answered. 'Wyatt is a hard worker. I saw him in the corral with the horses last night long after everyone else had quit for the day.'

'We'll see what Mr Mallory has to say about this,' Chuck said grimly and turned on his heel to head for the house.

He was supposed to drive her into Manzanita Flats. Megan watched his lanky figure disappear into the house. If she followed, there would be a confrontation over the incident with Randolph. Perhaps by the time she returned from town, things would have cooled down. She went instead to the bunkhouse to see if any of the other hands had the day off.

The only man present was the cold-eyed Braddock, sitting with his back to the wall rolling a cigarette. Megan gave him a tentative smile. 'Would you mind taking me into Manzanita Flats in the buckboard? My husband doesn't like me to go alone or I wouldn't bother you.'

'No bother, ma'am.' Braddock uncoiled himself from his chair and rose, his movements vaguely serpentine. Stifling a shiver, Megan led the way outside, a prickly feeling causing the hair on the back of her neck to rise.

She had heard all the stories about the Lincoln County wars that had raged through the territory years ago, and even now there were clashes between gunfighters and lawmen. All of the other ranch hands seemed nervous around Braddock, which indicated that he had been one of those dangerous quick-draw artists. But considering the alternative of facing chastisement for interfering between Chuck and Wyatt, she decided having Braddock accompany her to town was the lesser of the two evils. Surely she would be safe with him, since no one would dare to attack him.

The journey to Manzanita Flats was accomplished in

silence. Megan's attempts at conversation were met with monosyllabic responses, and after a time she gave up. Braddock had erected an impenetrable barrier around himself that no one was going to breach. She felt sorry for him, sensing that there was a very lonely man behind that icy façade.

In town she noticed that no one looked him directly in the face, and when he accompanied her to the general store they were served first and none of the other customers objected.

The only time he spoke to her was to remark laconically, 'You could have had young Wyatt bring you in. He was coming anyhow.'

'I believe he had other plans.'

'He just came out of the Western Union office,' Braddock said. 'Reckon that's all he come for, since he's hitting the trail out of town.'

All the way home Megan silently wondered which of the two men was more of an enigma.

36

In the candlelit café Bartholomew Whitman lowered his voice and said, 'Your old friend Paxton is apparently an extremely wealthy man with an interest in the sport of boxing. He's Hollis's owner.'

Joanna gasped. '*Owner*? How can he own another human being?'

'He doesn't actually own him. He puts up the money for training and . . . well, never mind about that. Tell me why you're frightened out of your wits by him.'

'He came here to destroy Magnus.'

'Destroy? In what way?'

'I'm not sure. But I am quite sure that his interest in boxing has to do with Magnus. Bart, please don't ask me to go into detail. It's an old grudge, a quest for vengeance.'

Bart regarded her with a faintly amused grin. 'What a flair for the dramatic you have, love. Great balls of fire, you should write it up. I can see the headlines now, "Fight to the Death, Blood Feud to Be Settled in Arena. 'Vengeance is mine,' sayeth the fighter."'

'Don't mock me, Bart. I'm serious about this.'

Immediately contrite, Bart patted her hand. 'Look, love, be reasonable. First of all, Magnus hasn't won the title yet, and there won't be an international challenge until there's a new American champion, so Paxton couldn't possibly have brought his fighter to New York with the intention of destroying Magnus, as you put it, since they don't know who Hollis will fight yet. Second, if Magnus and Hollis do fight, it's possible Magnus will win, and even if he doesn't, the worst that will happen is that he'll take a few lumps.'

'Do you think Magnus will win?'

'Well, he's quite a bit older than Hollis, but then, he's more experienced in the ring, too.'

Joanna snapped open her pendant watch, a gift from Magnus after his last win. 'I must go, Bart. Magnus promised to come over later.'

Bart caught her wrist as she was about to stand up. 'Jo, this Paxton character doesn't have a grudge against you, too, does he?'

'Why do you ask that?'

'No particular reason. I guess maybe my intuition is working overtime, too.'

Joanna didn't reply, but she felt that Paxton might very well seize any opportunity to punish her for having attempted to aid Magnus – not to mention any other real or imagined transgressions against his beloved master.

An hour later when Magnus let himself in to her

apartment she was seated on the sofa holding a battered tin box. Bending over to kiss her, he tapped the box with his finger. 'What's this? The family jewels?'

He sat down beside her and wrapped his muscular arm about her shoulders, drawing her close and pressing his face against her hair. 'You always smell like fresh flowers. I've missed you so. I can't stay long, I'm afraid, lass. Delta wants me to watch the baby.'

'She's going out? So soon?'

Shrugging, he tapped the metal box again. 'Are you going to tell me about this?'

'Harry Bodrath's death certificate is in here, and several letters that puzzle me.'

'You brought this box from Bodrath House? Why?'

'Because what happened to Harry Bodrath is going to haunt you for the rest of your life and there's still so much I don't understand.'

Magnus stood up so suddenly that Joanna was startled. He strode into the middle of the room, then spun around and faced her.

'Let it rest, damn it. I don't want to hear Harry's name mentioned again. It's over. Done with. We're in a new country, starting a new life. The Bodraths can't touch us here. You're Princess Natalie and I'm Max Morgan. What have the Bodraths to do with us now?'

'Paxton is here, in New York.'

Magnus looked blank for a moment.

'Justin Bodrath's butler,' Joanna added. 'Paxton must have inherited a tidy sum, because he brought the English contender here. He owns Jeremiah Hollis. Didn't you see his picture in the paper?'

Magnus looked away. 'I don't read the papers.'

'You don't? Not even the sports news?'

'Damn it, Joanna, I can't read.'

'But . . . you sent me a note once, when I was at Bodrath House.'

'Delta wrote it for me.'

Joanna was unsure what to say, feeling his embarrassment

309

ment and her own jolting realisation of how great the differences between them really were. They came together to satisfy the most primitive of human needs, the comfort of physical bonding, warmth, food . . . yet they shared nothing else. But she loved him and he loved her, so what did it matter that she couldn't bear to watch him box and he could never read anything she'd written for the *Chronicle*?

'I was hoping,' she said, 'that you would give me your opinion of the letters in this box. You see, I believe someone was blackmailing Justin Bodrath.'

'I've told you, I don't want to talk about the Bodraths.'

'Magnus, we can't avoid it. Paxton is here in New York with a boxer you might very well have to fight.'

A dull flush suffused his craggy features. 'Let it rest, Joanna. You don't want to know any more than you do now about the Bodraths.'

'But I do!' She rose to her feet and went to him, her eyes searching his face. 'What do you mean? More than I know now . . . ? There *is* something more, isn't there? Something you're not telling me. Magnus, I read those letters again for the first time since I left Cornwall. When I read them originally some significant portions had no real meaning for me. But since I've been here, working on the paper, I've learned some things about the world I didn't know before and frankly would have preferred never to know.'

He didn't meet her eye, but she caught his hands and held him near her. 'There's a mention of Justin's brother's "perversion." I didn't know before what that meant, but I do now. It means that one of the Bodraths – I expect it was Harry – preferred men to women.'

Magnus groaned.

More sure of herself now, Joanna plunged on. 'Ironically it was because you took up boxing again that I'd heard about the Marquess of Queensberry. Then I read an old newspaper story about the Marquess publicly accusing Oscar Wilde of homosexual practices. Wilde filed a libel suit, but then he was arrested, convicted on a morals charge, and sent to jail. As I read about that case, the meaning of those blackmail letters to Justin Bodrath became clear.'

Magnus looked resigned now. 'Sit down, Joanna. I can see I'm not going to get you to leave this alone until I tell you everything that happened.

'I went to work in the Bodrath tin mine when I was ten,' Magnus began. 'Even then I was big for my age and stronger than most boys. A friend of mine went to a fair where a prize was offered to anyone who could stay on his feet for five minutes with a professional fighter. My friend knocked him out and got his job. When I was sixteen I started going to fairs myself and did some bare-knuckle fighting.

'Joss, Delta's brother, also worked in the tin mine. He was big, handsome, much darker skinned than Delta. He was a better fighter than me. In fact, Joss was the only man who ever knocked me out.

'We used to go to boxing matches on our day off, mostly to watch and learn at first. Then, later, some of the fighters would hire us as sparring partners. We began going to fairs and knocking out the professional prizefighters. Often the fair was so far away we'd spend all our time off travelling just to get to a fight, and we would have to box after being up all night.

'Well, the trouble started one summer when young Harry Bodrath came home from university. Boxing was catching on with students then, too. He brought this professor with him – I don't even remember his name anymore. He was from London, never been to Cornwall before and wanted to see a tin mine, so Harry brought him down into the pit, and it would have to be the shift Joss and I were on.

'The professor stopped to watch us work. It was Joss who caught his eye. Joss looked like one of those statues you see in museums. You've seen Delta. Imagine a young man with features as perfect as hers and a body that was all solid muscle. There was something else about Joss . . . a happy kind of innocence. Even when he punched the hell out of somebody, there was no malice in it. To Joss it was all just a game, all in fun.'

Magnus paused, his bright blue eyes gazing off into some distant point in his memory as he recalled his friend. After a moment he continued, 'The professor just stopped dead in his tracks to stare and I heard him say, "My God, he's magnificent." But young Harry Bodrath wanted to get back up to the surface as fast as he could. He was whining about it being dark and clammy and how he wished he hadn't come down the shaft, but the professor just stood there, staring at Joss.

'Then he started asking Joss questions. Was he African? Where did he come from? How long had he been in England? Had he ever played any sports? Did he lift weights?

'That's where Joss made his mistake. He said that he and I were boxers. So then the professor turned to Harry and said, "Aha! I seem to unerringly find the gladiators, don't I?" Then he punched Harry on the arm and said to Joss, "My young friend Mr Bodrath rather fancies himself a boxer also."

'Well, the next thing we knew, the professor and Harry were popping up everywhere Joss and I went. They found out where we practised our punches and our footwork, and they would come there, too. I was a bit slow to realise what was going on at first. I knew Harry didn't like Joss, because he was always making nasty remarks about him, but I didn't recognise that he was acting like a jealous woman.'

Magnus broke off, staring into space.

'A triangle?' Joanna asked. 'Joss was coming between the professor and Harry?'

He nodded. 'Fortunately the summer came to an end, and Harry and the professor went back to university. Well, during that winter Harry really got into training, although we didn't find that out until later. By then I'd saved enough

312

money to leave the mine and go prizefighting all over the country. I wanted Joss to go with me, but he didn't want to leave his sister and he was a bit timid about meeting new people. So he stayed in the mine.

'I forgot about Harry and the professor. The following summer I went back to Cornwall, bought a little boat, and planned to spend the season fishing. I stopped in to see Joss and Delta. Joss was in a stew because Harry and his professor were back and the professor kept asking Joss to meet him alone. Joss didn't know what to make of this – he was just about as innocent in things like this as you, lass.

'Then Harry challenged Joss to a boxing match.

'Joss didn't want to fight him. They were mismatched, and Joss was afraid he'd lose his job if he knocked out the favourite son of the owner of the mine.

'I asked Harry to call off the fight, but he was a hothead and he said Joss had insulted him. Now, Joss was as sweet-tempered a man as I ever knew and never said an unkind word about anybody. He'd spent most of his life on a plantation in Martinique kowtowing to a white boss, and I knew he'd never insulted Harry. When Harry wouldn't listen to reason, I went to his brother Justin. Soon after that, Harry called off the fight.

'But a few days later the professor cornered Joss and tried to do some things that Joss wasn't going to put up with – so he picked the man up and flung him across the room.'

'Good gracious!' Joanna exclaimed.

'The professor told Joss he could either face assault charges or fight Harry. Joss was talking about letting Harry win, but I was afraid that just winning wouldn't be enough for Harry and the professor. What if he brought assault charges afterwards? I didn't like the smell of the whole situation, and I told Joss the best thing would be for him to disappear for a while.

'Now, I knew my way through the caves at Dutchman's Point by this time, because I liked to sail into the cove and just be by myself. So I persuaded Joss to go up there and Delta and I would take food up to him. Joss didn't want to give up his job, but we convinced him it was for the best.

'Harry and the professor were furious. Especially the professor. It made my skin crawl to see the look on his face and . . . well, let me tell you, there's something sickening about a man who gets pleasure out of seeing other people suffer, and I believe the professor really loved to see pain. He wanted to watch Harry and Joss beat each other. I think he hoped one of them would kill the other.'

Magnus fell silent for a moment and Joanna thought, but didn't say, that that was exactly what had happened – only it wasn't Joss who beat Harry; it was Magnus.

'The professor went to see Delta. I happened to be in her cottage that night. He said the arrangements for the fight were all made. She was to tell her brother he'd better be at the appointed place or a warrant would be issued for his arrest. The fight was to be held in secret. It was to be outdoors with just a scratch line in the dirt. Only four of us would be present – the professor would be Harry's second, and I'd stand up for Joss.

'I never would've told Joss; I'd have left him safe up in the caves. But Delta was afraid of the professor . . . He was . . .'

'Sinister?' Joanna suggested.

'More than that. There was such a coldness about him.'

'So Delta told Joss that the fight had been arranged?'

'Yes. I didn't find out about it until just before the match was to begin. I managed to get to Dutchman's Point before Joss left and . . . well, I had to use a sneak punch on him or I probably couldn't have brought him down. I only hit him hard enough to gain time to tie him up. Then left him in the cave and went to the place where the fight was going to be, to tell them Joss wouldn't be coming.

'I thought the professor was going to burst a blood vessel. He told Harry to fight me instead of Joss. To give Harry his due, he didn't want to fight me because I didn't have a second. But then the professor pulled a pistol from under his coat and said we were to fight until one of us was unconscious. He threatened to shoot me if either of us refused.'

'What a sadistic brute!' Joanna said. 'He must have been a madman. So you and Harry fought?'

Magnus nodded. 'Harry was very good. Quick on his feet and able to dodge most blows. He hit me a few times. But then I landed a punch to his head and down he went, out cold. I've known other fighters like that; in this country they call it a glass skull – can't stand a blow to the head. The professor was kicking him, telling him to get up, calling him a coward. I grabbed the pistol and threw it away, shoved the professor into a bramble patch, then picked Harry up and carried him home.

'I swear to God that when I handed him over to Justin and his butler, Harry was only unconscious, not dead.'

Magnus sighed deeply. 'They came for me the next morning. Delta and Joss visited me in jail right away and Joss said he'd back me up at my trial and tell the whole story beginning to end.

'But the next day his body was found floating in the sea among the rocks. We knew he hadn't fallen – he'd been up on Dutchman's Point for weeks and the cliff's far more treacherous there.

'Delta was terrified. I told her to stay away from me, not to come to the jail. There was nothing she could do anyway, since she hadn't seen the fight. So the only witness at my trial was the professor, and he testified that I'd beaten Harry to death. Justin Bodrath and the butler said Harry had died only minutes after I took him home. I never got a chance to tell my side of it. The barrister defending me said it would be better for me not to speak, as I would condemn myself with my own words. He said nobody would believe an educated man like the professor would behave in such a way. It was a working-class man against an aristocrat, you see. The Bodraths and the professor and Paxton . . . my word against theirs.

Furthermore, I'd fought in the ring for a living, while Harry was just an amateur. The barrister said he could save me from the gallows if I stayed off the witness stand. He was as good as his word. I went to Dartmoor instead. But prison was a living death for me. I can't describe what it was like. I thought I'd go mad. I knew I had to escape or die in the attempt.'

Joanna wrapped her arms around Magnus and held him close.

After a long silence she asked, 'I suppose you never found out who tried to blackmail Justin?'

Magnus picked up Justin Bodrath's metal box and lifted the lid. He stared at the contents. 'I didn't know anybody had until you told me.'

Glancing at the clock on her mantelpiece he dropped the box and jumped to his feet. 'Great God, but I'd better run. Delta said she'd leave the baby alone if I wasn't back by nine.'

He kissed Joanna on the lips and searched her face with a worried gaze for a moment. 'I'll be back as soon as I can. I don't like to leave you with so much on your mind, but –'

'Of course, you must go at once and take care of the baby.'

She didn't trust herself to say anything else. After he left she glanced at the telephone, wishing Bart had one so that she could call him. Instead, she went to her dressing table and took down her hair.

A parcel tied with a ribbon sat on the dressing table, and Joanna realised she had forgotten to give it to Magnus. It contained a christening gown for the baby, whom Delta had named Sari.

Delta was the last woman on earth who should have been entrusted with an infant, Joanna thought, and immediately told herself that what she felt was envy. How she would have loved to bear a child for Magnus! One that he knew for certain was his.

She put the thought out of her mind and began to worry

about all that Magnus had told her and about Paxton and his burly young boxer.

After drifting off to sleep later that night, she plunged into a nightmare. Paxton, clad in his butler's garb, was systematically pounding Magnus's face to an unrecognisable mass, while in the background the ghost of Justin Bodrath danced with manic frenzy.

Awakening abruptly, Joanna found herself gasping for breath. In that moment, she knew what she had to do.

37

Randolph suggested that Consuela travel to Silver City with Megan to help her prepare for the ball.

Megan asked, 'As a chaperone, you mean? After all, I'll be spending the night with the Penningtons' hosts, and so will Quinn.'

'That remark was unworthy of you, Megan. I just thought you'd want Consuela to help you with your gown and your hair. You don't always give your appearance the care it deserves. You're a very beautiful woman, but you seem to believe that scrubbing yourself clean is all the toilette necessary.' Randolph picked up his book and began to read.

'I shan't need Consuela,' Megan said. 'She'll be more useful to you here.'

'As you wish.'

He refused to argue with her or, during the following days, to discuss anything more serious than the weather. In fact, now that she was no longer pretending to be

Joanna, she and Randolph had very little to talk about. She no longer feigned interest in his books and poetry, and he no longer inquired about the medical journals she brought home from Dr Sedgewick's office. They coexisted in an uneasy vacuum, often giving each other startled glances when they chanced to meet around the house. They consumed their meals rapidly, with little conversation. Then they went their separate ways. She would have to do something about the situation, she mused, the moment she came back from the Pennington ball.

Then, a few days before the ball, Wyatt, the scruffy young ranch hand, rode out one morning to round up strays and didn't return.

Everyone had grown to like Wyatt, despite his careless appearance, threadbare clothes, and the apparent squandering of his pay on his forays into town. If Wyatt spent all he earned on the ladies of the Jade Palace or at the poker tables of the local saloons, then his engaging personality and willingness to work twice as hard as anyone else, earned him the respect and affection of all.

Even the cold-eyed Braddock, who always wore a gun and whose hand never strayed far from his hip, seemed to brighten when Wyatt squeezed a tune from his concertina and sang and danced. Only Chuck maintained his distance, refusing to be captivated.

A search party went out to look for Wyatt the morning after he disappeared, but they had no success. Tension at the ranch mounted, and Randolph ordered half of the hands to keep looking for the missing cowboy. Chuck muttered that no doubt Wyatt had wandered into a saloon someplace and was sleeping off a drunk.

Then in the middle of the third night after his disappearance, Tex went out to answer the call of nature and found Wyatt sleeping peacefully on the bunkhouse porch, both arms neatly wrapped with leaves and bark. His horse was tethered to a nearby post.

Consuela awakened Megan and gestured that she was wanted in the bunkhouse. Chuck explained what had happened. 'Seems Wyatt tangled with a cougar. Got hisself clawed and bit pretty bad – arms, hands. Lucky for him, your pal A-chi-tie happened along. Wyatt looks okay, but the boys figured you'd best bandage him up. Me, I'd say let the redskin's medicine poison him; it'll teach him a lesson.'

Megan immediately went to tend to Wyatt's injuries. She carefully peeled back the leaves and bark and scraped a small area free of an herbal ointment that had been applied to the wounds.

He opened one eye and winked at her. 'Your redskin pal made up that paste with white pine, wild plum and cherry, and a root or two – boiled it all up and pounded it into a mash. He said the flesh wouldn't rot – reckon he meant gangrene wouldn't set in. Didn't have the heart to stop him. 'Sides, his decoction sure took the sting out.'

'You'd better wash it off,' Chuck said curtly. 'Tex, fetch some water.'

'No, I'm going to leave it alone,' Megan said, replacing the bark and leaves. 'Animal bites are the worst kind of wounds. Infection sets in almost immediately. But Wyatt's wounds are clean and already healing. If I didn't know they had been inflicted only a couple of days ago, I would have thought the cougar attack occurred weeks ago. It's amazing.'

Wyatt closed his eyes, perfectly relaxed. Just before he dropped off to sleep he murmured, 'The redskin hangs around that cave up near the top of the ridge overlooking the river. If any of you cowpokes was in need of a poultice, I daresay he'd oblige. He asked me if I worked for the squaw with the copper hair before he fixed me up. Reckon he meant Miz Mallory.'

The following day while all of the hands were working, Megan visited Wyatt in the bunkhouse. He looked at her sheepishly 'Chuck told me to take the day off. I done told him I could do my chores –'

'Mr Mallory gave instructions that you weren't to do any

319

heavy work for several days,' Megan said. 'But if you're up to a short ride, perhaps you could take me to A-chi-tie. I assume you speak the Navajo language?'

'Sure do, ma'am, and I'd be mighty glad to take you. Can't stand lying around here nohow.'

They rode up to the cave near the top of the hill, stopping well short of the opening, and Wyatt cupped his hands around his mouth to give a long low call that sounded a little like that of an owl. Moments later A-chi-tie appeared on the ridge over their heads. He observed them for a second, then swiftly descended the almost sheer cliff with the surefooted ease of a mountain goat.

Watching the Indian's approach, Megan said to Wyatt, 'Ask him if he will teach me his herb medicine.'

A-chi-tie greeted her in sign language, then spoke to Wyatt, who grinned and responded in Navajo. Turning to Megan, he said, 'He says he never got a chance to thank you for saving him from the soldiers. He says anything you want to know, he'll be glad to teach you.'

'First, I'd like some samples of the roots and herbs he put on your wounds, so I can take them back to the ranch for identification. Then I'd like to see how he mixes them.' She smiled at A-chi-tie. 'Oh, yes, and please tell him that I should also like to thank him for saving me from the bear.'

She learned that day that A-chi-tie's maternal grand-father was a Chippewa medicine man who had taught his grandson his healing methods. She was amazed to find that in addition to treating wounds, he could make medicines to treat diseases of the nervous system, the circulatory system, the respiratory system, and the digestive system. He could treat burns, haemorrhages, and diseases of the eye and ear. It was clear that she would have to spend many hours with A-chi-tie to acquire even a fraction of his knowledge.

When she reluctantly told Wyatt they should return to the ranch, she added, 'On the way home, would you teach me a few words in Navajo? I'm going to visit A-chi-tie as often as I can, and you may not always be able to come with me.'

The strained atmosphere between Megan and Randolph had intensified as the date of the ball for Joshua Pennington approached, and she was relieved when at last she was in the Winton bouncing down the dirt road towards Silver City.

Chuck drove in tight-lipped silence, but Megan had the feeling that he would gladly have driven her straight to the gates of hell and out of Randolph's life forever.

Their hosts for the ball in honour of the Penningtons, the Simmondses, were a charming older couple who lived in a rambling mansion on the edge of town. Some of their guests were invited for the weekend, but most would come only for the Saturday evening reception and ball.

Mrs Simmonds proved to be a short, plump woman with a dazzling smile and a tendency to drift away in the middle of a sentence. Since a dozen or more guests were already in residence and over a hundred more were expected for the ball, Megan thought Mrs Simmonds's vagueness was understandable.

'So glad you could come, Mrs Mallory. Your husband made a generous contribution to Joshua's campaign, as, of course, did Mr McQuinn. Now, let me see . . . I think we put you in the Wallace room. I'll have a maid take you up and then you can . . .'

She fluttered her hands and moved on, disappearing into a group of guests who were apparently admiring a new objet d'art in the entry hall. Megan had been about to ask whether Quinn had arrived.

'The Wallace room,' a deep voice whispered in her ear, 'is at the end of the landing on the second floor. It's the best room in the house, although if Lew Wallace ever really slept in it I'd be very surprised. You can't believe how many New Mexico homes that man is supposed to have slept in.'

Turning, Megan looked into a pair of twinkling eyes that

321

lit up a somewhat stern, bewhiskered countenance. She recognised Joshua Pennington from his photographs even before he introduced himself.

'I heard Mrs Simmonds address you as Mrs Mallory.' He glanced over his shoulder and then, conspiratorially, back at her. 'Our . . . uh . . . mutual friend could not speak highly enough of your medical skills. I want you to know that I would be most appreciative of any help you could give my wife. She's resting presently, but I'll see that you two are alone later on.'

Raising his voice to a normal pitch, he went on, 'I daresay I should have slept in the Wallace room myself. It might have brought me luck in the election, but I wanted to be at the back of the house where it would be quiet for Mrs Pennington.'

Noticing Megan's blank expression, he added, 'Forgive me, I forgot for a moment that you're new here. I take it you didn't know that Lew Wallace was the governor of New Mexico in addition to being a famous author? I understand *Ben Hur* was very popular in your country.'

Before she could respond, a male guest approached, slapped Pennington on the back, and said, 'Trust you to find the prettiest woman here, you sly old dog.'

For the next several minutes Megan was presented to various other guests until at length she was rescued by Mrs Simmonds, who appeared with a uniformed maid in tow to show her to her room.

'Most of the ladies are going to rest this afternoon,' the maid volunteered shyly as she finished unpacking Megan's bag, 'so they'll be fresh for tonight.'

'Yes, thank you. That sounds like a good idea.'

Megan was too wide awake and excited to take a nap. She removed her gown and stays and prowled around the room in her shift. A framed photograph of a handsome man with a luxurious black moustache and long beard stood on a dresser. It was autographed by Governor Lew Wallace.

Megan had not heard of *Ben Hur*, but then, she didn't

322

read novels. Probably Joanna would have known of it and been thrilled to sleep in the same bed that the author had used. So often Megan's thoughts turned to memories of her friend, and lately, since Randolph had become convinced that Jo was not only still alive but actually in America, Megan found herself wishing by some miracle it could be true.

Randolph had grown distant and withdrawn since the disastrous night when he came to her room and she foolishly tried to get him to talk about his paralysis. Still, there was an air of expectancy about him, as if he were waiting for something important to happen. For Joanna to be resurrected from the dead.

Recalling that just before Chuck delivered her to the Simmondses' home they had picked up the mail and there was an as yet unread letter from her father tucked into her handbag, Megan retrieved it and sat on the bed to read it.

'My dear Megan,' her father had written. 'I'm sorry your experiments with Freud's free association methods didn't work on your husband any more than mine helped restore Agnes's sanity. I was thinking about it last night, wondering what we're doing wrong. Suddenly it came to me in a blinding flash.

'Megan, do you remember Freud's thesis that most of our repressed, unconscious conflicts are sexual in origin?'

Megan caught her breath. Randolph had confessed that he had the same sexual longings as other men. That was why he had come into her room that night, his guard down because he'd been drinking with Quinn. Why hadn't she pursued that avenue instead of concentrating on the accident and the death of his parents? Randolph had shown her the way and she had ignored it!

The possibility so excited her that she almost jumped up and ran downstairs in order to rush home to Randolph – until she remembered that Chuck would not return for her until Sunday morning.

Pacing back and forth, Megan came to another, more sobering realisation. She hadn't wanted to discuss

323

Randolph's sexual conflicts with him. It was one thing to be the object of a pure, chaste, spiritual love and quite another to be the object of the physical desire of a man she didn't love. Especially when this man was in fact her husband and, as such, had certain rights.

She paused to stare at herself in the dressing table mirror and whispered, 'What a terrible fraud you are.'

There was a tentative tap on her door. Hastily flinging on her dressing gown she opened the door to find a pale, thin young woman standing there. She would have been pretty had she not been so obviously debilitated. She seemed to droop in every aspect of her person.

'Please forgive the intrusion. I'm Cecilia Pennington. My husband insisted that I come to see you.'

'Come in, please.' Megan glanced up and down the landing before closing the door.

Mrs Pennington's gaze did not connect with hers. 'Joshua suggested this would be a good time for us to talk, while the other ladies are resting. I'm not sure why he thinks you can help me.'

The woman accepted the chair Megan offered. She folded her arms across her scrawny bosom, clamped her feet and knees together, and seemed to shrink away from Megan, who sat on a dresser stool. 'I studied medicine with my grandfather,' Megan said firmly. 'And I have a special interest in women's health problems. I'm not a doctor – I must tell you that right away.'

Cecilia Pennington was flushing scarlet. 'I'm so embarrassed that someone told you about my . . . ailment. Was it Mrs Simmonds?'

'No, no! I have no idea what ails you. All I know is that a doctor has recommended that you have your ovaries removed and I want to plead with you not to allow this.'

'They say it's the only way I can be cured. As I am now I . . .' Her voice had sunk to a whisper.

'If you could give me a little hint as to your problem? I don't want to pry, but the surgery the doctors suggest is terribly serious.

Mrs Pennington wrung her hands, nervously kneading the material of her gown as she did so. 'I can't be a wife to my husband.'

So the doctors would turn you into even less of a woman and send him permanently to the Jade Palace for his sexual satisfaction, Megan thought grimly. Aloud she asked, 'Would you confide in me more specifically what the problem is?'

The woman hung her head miserably. 'You're not a doctor, you said so yourself. You're not even a friend; you're a complete stranger to me. I don't even know how my husband knows you.'

'I met him for the first time this afternoon. The woman who asked me to talk with you is a good friend, please believe me. Will you tell me what prompted you to consult the doctors? Were you in pain?'

'Yes.'

'In your abdomen?'

'My . . . female parts.'

'Constantly? Occasionally? Are there other symptoms?'

'When . . . when my husband wanted to . . . it was impossible, the pain was so intense. I had palpitations and nausea also. Oh, I'm so mortified that Joshua told someone else such intimate details.'

'He didn't tell me anything, nor did the friend who suggested I talk with you – except that you're considering the surgery. Mr Pennington loves you,' Megan said. 'And a man who loves a woman also wants her . . .' Her voice trailed away as her own words echoed mockingly in her head. A small voice whispered, *You're a fine one to talk*.

Cecilia Pennington's voice sank to a barely discernible whisper. 'I would submit to his base needs if I were able to do so. My condition prevents it. I'm not to be blamed for my illness, am I?'

Megan jumped to her feet. 'No, by God, you're not! And neither is Randolph!'

'Please don't . . . It upsets me to hear a woman blaspheme. Bad enough that men do it. Who is Randolph?'

'He's my husband. I'm sorry, I didn't mean to be blasphemous.' Megan walked around the room, thoughts flying into her mind so rapidly she was scarcely able to assimilate the revelations they brought. Oh, if only her father were here!

When she turned to Cecilia Pennington she knew she wore an expression that brooked no nonsense. 'I'm going to examine you to be sure there is no physical abnormality. In all probability your male physicians have never even looked at your private parts. I expect they asked you to describe your symptoms or even point to a doll to indicate the part of your anatomy that bothers you. But an examination is necessary because certain conditions could cause painful intercourse. Once we eliminate those possibilities, we can treat you – make you well.'

Mrs Pennington was on her feet now, backing away, her eyes wide with fright.

More gently, Megan asked, 'Do you love your husband?'

She nodded, biting her lip.

'Then let's find out why you refuse him.'

'But . . . what if you don't find anything physically wrong with me?'

'I have a feeling that's exactly what will happen. Then, Mrs Pennington, we're going to talk, and – eventually – we'll find out what happened to you that makes you believe you can't be a wife to your husband.'

And perhaps, Megan reflected silently, at the same time I'll learn how to reach that part of Randolph's mind that tells him his legs are useless.

Dressed in a shot-silk gown of jade green that flashed violet rainbows as she moved, her auburn hair piled in gleaming curls on top of her head and fastened with tortoiseshell combs, Megan entered the ballroom on Quinn's arm. Every head turned in their direction as their names were announced.

'Mrs Randolph Mallory and Mr John McQuinn.'

Out of the corner of her mouth Megan whispered, 'So your name really is Ramblin' Jack.'

Quinn winked at her. He looked particularly dashing tonight in his evening clothes, and Megan was glad that she'd taken the time to style her hair. Randolph's remark about her carelessness with her appearance still stung, but she had taken some pains to impress Quinn.

He had sent a maid to her room with his card, which read, 'John W. McQuinn, owner, Black Horse Copper Mine.' Scrawled on the back of the card in his handwriting were the words, 'I'll be up at eight to escort you to the reception.'

There had been no opportunity to talk, and she assumed he preferred it this way. As they walked into the crowded room, almost everyone they passed greeted him. Megan felt a stab of envy of his wide circle of friends and acquaintances, which bespoke a far more gregarious way of life than Randolph pursued.

Passing a handsome marble fireplace flanked by full-length mirrors, Megan caught a glimpse of their reflection. As Quinn paused to introduce her to several friends, she looked with almost clinical interest at the mirror images of a tall black-haired man with flashing dark eyes and a rogue's grin and his vivacious companion. The gown made her eyes sparkle and in taming her hair she had enhanced her oval features. Tonight her face was more animated than usual, her smile quicker, her dimples deeper. She was aware of the admiring glances cast her way, and for once this attention pleased her, since Quinn obviously noticed the way other men's eyes lingered on her.

Her dance card was quickly filled except for the first and last waltz, which good manners demanded she save for her escort. When the music began and Quinn led her out onto the highly polished parquet floor, she realised that they had not exchanged more than two words of a personal nature.

She had once watched him dance with the English sisters aboard the ship that brought them to America. Now as he placed a firm hand around her waist and whirled her in graceful turns, she recalled how she had longed to dance with him then. Like most athletic men he was light on his feet, despite his size, and it was just as wonderful waltzing with him as she had imagined it would be. Lurking at the back of her mind also was relief at not having to measure her steps or slow her pace so that a wheelchair could keep up with her, and this brought such a feeling of guilt that she told herself she was merely enjoying the music and party atmosphere after the solitude of the ranch.

Looking down at her, Quinn said, 'You look positively enchanting tonight, Mrs Mallory.'

'So do you, Ramblin' Jack.'

He turned her faster and faster, the other dancers and the lights blurring as he whisked her around the floor at a heart-pounding pace, slowing only long enough to ask, 'Were you able to speak privately with Mrs Pennington?'

Megan could barely manage a nod in response to his question, yet he wasn't the least bit breathless. She thought enviously that he was not encumbered by stays that pinched or heels on his shoes that threw him off balance.

When the dance ended, he led her to a sofa. 'Would you like some punch? You need to keep up your strength, since you blithely promised every single dance.'

Seeing a familiar gleam in his eye, she realised he had deliberately tried to tire her with his fast waltz.

Suddenly solicitous, he added, 'I'll explain to your next partner that you're fatigued, if you like.'

'Don't you dare! I'm going to dance all evening.'

She noted with some satisfaction that as her partners came to claim their dances with her, Quinn wore the look of a male whose territorial rights were being threatened. The instant the strains of the last waltz filled the hall, Quinn swept her into his arms and they glided out onto the floor. He danced less aggressively this time, pausing and reversing the turns so that she could catch her breath.

'You're quite the belle of the ball,' he remarked.

'Perhaps partly due to the stir you caused by attending with a man other than your husband.'

She looked up at him in astonishment. 'Surely everyone knows that Randolph is confined to a wheelchair?'

'That wouldn't have prevented him from coming if he'd wanted to. He could have chosen to sit on the sidelines and listen to the music or join in some of the fairly lively political discussions that are going on. Joshua Pennington's wife has been ill, too, but she puts on a brave face and sits quietly with the older ladies while her husband circulates and dances with, I noticed, only the prettiest women.'

Joshua had danced with Megan twice, and each time she had looked at Cecilia over his shoulder, convinced now that the woman's frail health was mostly in her mind. Megan's examination had found nothing to indicate a physical problem. She wondered why a robust, vigorous man like Joshua had chosen to marry a shrinking violet like Cecilia, who seemed to fade deeper into the background as the evening wore on. Little wonder Joshua had sought his pleasures at the Jade Palace.

'Are you going to see Cecilia again?' Quinn asked as the dance ended. He slipped her arm through his in a proprietary manner as they left the floor.

'I hope so. I asked her to come and visit me, either at Sedge's office or at the ranch, and I offered to go to see her. But she was somewhat evasive.'

'Did you at least talk her out of having the surgery? Lallie felt that alone would be a triumph for you.'

Megan gave him a frosty glance, annoyed that he'd reminded her he was also a friend of the madam of the Jade Palace. 'It's quite improper for me to discuss Mrs Pennington with you.'

'I thought she was the only reason we were here.'

Some of the guests were now departing, and Megan started towards the staircase, saying over her shoulder, 'I'm going to retire. Thank you for being my escort tonight. Good night.'

She didn't look back as she went quickly up to her room.

Feeling curiously let down, she closed her door and leaned back against it. The music still rang in her ears and every nerve in her body pulsed with energy. Sleep would not come easily tonight.

A moment later there was a light tap on her door. Opening it, she looked into Quinn's quizzical gaze.

38

Joanna alighted from the cab in front of the canopied entrance to the hotel where Paxton was staying, thanked the doorman for his help, and walked into the lobby.

She felt surprisingly calm as she asked the desk clerk to inform Mr Paxton that she wished to see him. She gave her real name. There were two armchairs sheltered by potted palms and she sat down in one of them. Less than ten minutes later Paxton appeared.

He looked, she decided, less like a servant and more like the soldier he once was. Carrying himself rigidly erect he strode across the lobby with the gait of a much younger man. His impassive features showed no surprise at the sight of her.

'Miss Traherne,' he murmured through barely moving lips.

'Won't you sit down, Mr Paxton?'

Taking the chair next to her, he fixed her with an unblinking stare. 'What is it you want from me?'

'To ask you to leave us alone.'

'Us?'

'Magnus and me. Don't pretend he isn't the reason for your sudden interest in boxing and your presence in America.'

'I didn't have the slightest idea you and Magnus were here until this moment.'

Joanna leaned against the unyielding back of her chair, unprepared to deal with this response. Paxton continued to regard her with a disdainful stare. 'Nor am I particularly interested in the news that you are here. Now, is there something you want from me? If so, please state your business, as I have better things to do than sit here chatting with my late employer's amanuensis.'

She drew a deep breath. 'You must know that I have in my possession the Bodrath journal and Justin's blackmail letters. I could, if I chose, divulge the whole sordid story of the Bodraths.'

One iron-grey eyebrow twitched slightly. 'And what purpose would that serve? Do you think anyone here would be interested? Assuming such letters exist, even if you were to return to Cornwall with them, how could you prove they were not written long after the death of the last of the Bodraths?'

The interview was not going at all as Joanna had planned. She gripped the arms of her chair in rising desperation. 'I will not use the documents I have if you will give me your word that you will not harm Magnus or allow your boxer, Hollis, to fight him.'

Paxton gave a short, mirthless laugh. 'I don't know what kind of back-alley bouts your convict friend engages in nowadays, but I can assure you that Mr Hollis is not here to waste his time with bare-knuckle brawlers. We will issue an international challenge to whoever wins the championship fight next week. From what I hear, that is likely to be Max Morgan.'

Joanna stared at him incredulously. Paxton betrayed no sign whatsoever that he was aware of the identity of Max Morgan. Surely no man on earth could pretend so well? Paxton had not lied. He hadn't known they were here.

He went on, 'Let me suggest that you also consider the teachings of the Bible. Are we not advised to let him who is without sin cast the first stone? A particularly appropriate

331

suggestion since it concerned the harsh punishment meted out to a fallen woman. You came here to attempt to blackmail me yourself, but you have a skeleton tucked away in your own cupboard, do you not?'

With a shock, Joanna realised he was right. She had been so blinded by her love for Magnus and her fear for his life that she had acted contemptibly. 'I came only to beg you not to hurt Magnus. I'm sorry . . . I shouldn't have threatened you.'

Confused, she rose unsteadily to her feet. 'I suppose you'll find out sooner or later . . . Magnus uses the ring name Max Morgan.'

Paxton digested this news in silence, although his expression registered surprise and, Joanna thought, dismay. After a moment, as though anxious to drop a bombshell of his own, he said, 'Before you take your leave, Miss Traherne, you might be interested to hear my personal belief, although I can't say for certain, regarding the identity of the person who made the feeble attempt to blackmail Mr Justin.'

Joanna turned to face him, uneasily aware that if Paxton wished to reveal such information it was bound to be hurtful.

He gave her a malevolent look. 'The letters were written by an old fool besotted by her, of course. She could hardly have composed them herself, although I understand she could read and write. But her orchid fancier – who, incidentally, made one last foolhardy and fatal attempt to sail through the suicide gap and so is no longer among us – probably wrote the letters for her.'

Delta, Joanna thought, pure horror racing along her veins in icy rivulets. 'Oh, dear God in heaven!'

Paxton watched Joanna walk across the hotel lobby, thinking that despite the fashionable clothes and smartly styled brown hair, those gentle hazel eyes still wore the look of a startled fawn. She was the last person on earth he had expected to find amid the hurly-burly of a city like New

York. He could hardly believe she had taken up with a pugilist.

He went back up to his hotel room, thinking how ironic it was that Jeremiah might face Magnus in the ring. If Joanna Traherne hadn't popped up so unexpectedly today, Paxton would have been more surprised at this turn of events than anyone else.

Entering his room, Paxton went immediately to Jeremiah's adjoining room.

The young boxer lay on the bed, his mouth slack, his eyes closed. One powerful arm was thrown over his head and the morning sunlight gold-dusted the hair on his chest. He was nude.

For a moment Paxton merely stood observing him, marvelling again at the perfection of his physique, the symmetry of bone and muscle and sinew, the flawless skin that was fair and tender looking, yet had the tensile strength of the toughest sailcloth.

How very different Jeremiah was from the Bodrath brothers. In the beginning, Paxton had been so repulsed by the muscular young man with his crude speech and barracks manners that he had coached, cajoled, threatened, and bullied him into becoming a little more refined, at least in private. Yet in some ways Jeremiah reminded him of Colonel Bodrath, whom Paxton had served as a batman long ago, and whom he had hero-worshipped.

Jeremiah opened his eyes and gave a lazy smile. 'What did she want?'

Crossing the room, Paxton sat on the edge of the bed. 'To beg us not to hurt Magnus, who is here in America with her and apparently is still boxing.'

'You didn't know they were here?'

'Had no idea.' Paxton reached out and ran his hand slowly over Jeremiah's right bicep, then down his arm.

The young boxer's deep-set eyes, his worst feature as far as Paxton was concerned, flickered questioningly. 'You told me a long time ago that you wanted me to kill him

333

for you. In the beginning, when we started the training, I thought it was the only reason you got into boxing. But you haven't mentioned him lately, not since –'

'No, I haven't. Jerry, when you first walked into Bodrath House I had just lost someone I cared for very deeply. It was his need for revenge that drove me then. We all make vows that later seem . . . excessive. I felt I'd lost everything I cared about. Justin was the last of the men I served, the one I loved the best. It didn't seem fair that he was dead and his brother's murderer was still alive. Especially since, indirectly, Harry's death had destroyed all of the Bodraths. But that was then and, as you know, much has changed in my life since. For one thing, I now have you.'

Jeremiah rolled over onto his stomach. 'My neck's a bit stiff.' Paxton obligingly massaged his neck and shoulders and Jeremiah grunted with pleasure. 'It must have been tricky for you when the old man was alive. Unless he was –'

'No,' Paxton said quickly. 'The colonel was a womaniser, and so was his eldest son, Neville.'

'What about Harry? Did you and he . . . ?'

'Absolutely not. Harry was far too indiscreet.'

'You should've found out where Magnus is and I'd have done him in for you anyway. It's the least I could do to repay you.'

'But you see, I know now that Magnus didn't kill Harry.'

Jeremiah's head swivelled around abruptly. 'Go on! Who did, then?'

'I believe it was his professor. I think he found Harry an encumbrance in the pursuit of his other affairs. Harry was always a spoiled, clinging individual. I suspect that the professor had been feeding him small doses of arsenic for some time. It's a wonder Harry was in any condition to fight at all that night. At Magnus's trial we testified that Harry died immediately after Magnus brought him to Bodrath Hall, but in actual fact it was dawn the next day before he expired, and the professor was with him all night

334

– with plenty of opportunity to give him a fatal dose of poison. But of course we didn't know that then.'

'How the hell did you find out?'

'Shortly before we left England the professor was arrested and charged with the murder of another undergraduate. Apparently he had tired of the young man, but was afraid their relationship might be revealed, with resulting criminal action from the boy's family. He'd been giving the student small doses of arsenic, and the boy had been ill for some time. When he died, his doctor was suspicious and insisted upon an autopsy. The arsenic poisoning was discovered, and when I read a description of the symptoms, I realised that they were exactly the same as the ones Harry experienced that night – which, incidentally could also have resulted from a beating. Now, I have no proof that it was the professor who killed Harry, and I'm certainly not going to go to the police about it. It wouldn't bring Harry back, and besides, it's my sworn duty to protect the Bodrath name.'

Jeremiah snorted, 'Not to mention the fact that you'd just as soon not have too many questions asked about you and Justin.'

'Watch your tongue, Jerry. I created you and I can destroy you, and don't you forget it.'

Jeremiah chuckled unpleasantly. 'If I don't destroy you first, you old sod.'

Several days passed, and Magnus didn't come to see Joanna. She knew he was in training for the championship fight, and since Delta had made it clear Joanna was not welcome to visit them, she had no alternative but to wait.

If she hadn't been worried about Paxton's presence in New York she would have welcomed the quiet evenings alone, which were a rare treat nowadays. She had time to read and play her new phonograph, to write for her own pleasure rather than for the newspaper. She had even written letters to Randolph, which she tucked away in a drawer instead of mailing, since his tersely worded telegram had made it clear he no longer wished to correspond with her. The only possible reason for this had to be that he had learned of her disgrace and she had attempted to tell her side of it in her letters but none seemed adequate.

She had not been able to acquire a taste for the society gatherings to which, as Princess Natalie, she was invited. She was able to tolerate them only by reminding herself that it was her job to report on high society at play.

The day before the fight Bart was in a particularly belligerent mood and insisted on taking Joanna out to lunch. The moment they were seated in a corner alcove he exclaimed, 'Great Caesar's ghost, Jo, but you're too fine a woman to throw yourself away on a man who keeps you in the shadows like some backstreet tart. When are you going to wake up? I know of at least three fine upstanding men who would ask you to marry them in a minute if you'd give them half a chance.'

Joanna smiled. 'Three? Do tell me who they are!'

Bart looked sheepish. 'Well, me for one.'

'Oh, Bart, you're too dear a friend for me to inflict marriage upon you.'

'What about your boxer? When is he going to pop the question?'

She pleated and unpleated her napkin on her lap. 'You know that's impossible.'

'Why is it impossible? Because he's already married? You know he isn't.'

'Delta –' she began.

Bart gave an indelicate snort. 'What's to stop him making an honest woman of you and setting *her* up in a love nest somewhere? Wouldn't that work just as well as the present arrangement? He's using her as an excuse, that's all.'

'If you brought me here to lecture me, I'm leaving.' She started to rise, but he leaned across the table and caught her hand.

'Sit down, Jo. I brought you here to tell you that the

reporter for the *Herald* plans to reveal Max Morgan's love life and the identity of the ladies in question. The story will run tomorrow morning, to take advantage of the fact that the championship bout is tomorrow night.'

She took a sip of water. 'Well . . . we've been expecting it. There's very little we can do about it, is there? Why don't you write up the story yourself so at least the *Chronicle* will carry it, too. No sense in both of us infuriating old Dragonbreath.' She gave him a ghost of a smile.

Bart clapped a hand to his forehead in frustration. 'Woman, you're hopeless. What am I going to do with you? Have you no instinct for self-preservation?'

'My life is in Magnus's hands. It has been from the moment I met him. I love him, and as long as I can be with him, nothing else matters.'

Bart let out his breath in a long, exasperated sigh. 'All right. My first plan was to persuade you to marry me tonight and take you out of New York in the morning. I have even been reconciled with my family, so I can take you to the ancestral home.'

'Oh, Bart, how very sweet you are.' She paused. 'If that was your first plan, did you have others?'

'One other, love. Let's put it into action. Let's go see Magnus and Delta and tell them what the *Herald* plans to print tomorrow. If she cares anything about him and he cares anything about you, *he'll* marry you today. Tomorrow the *Chronicle* can carry the story that you're secretly married. This will counteract the dirt the *Herald* publishes and maybe save your hide.'

She stared at him in amazement.

Bart glared back at her. 'Don't look at me as if I'm suggesting you hand over your firstborn son to Herod! Nobody's getting sacrificed here, except maybe me.'

'I would never force a man to marry me.'

'Magnus doesn't love you, Jo. If he did, he wouldn't treat you like this. If a man truly loves a woman, he makes her his wife.'

'It isn't that easy with Magnus and me. He feels obliged

337

to Delta and her child, and besides, he and I live in different worlds.'

'Jehoshaphat!' Bart exclaimed under his breath. 'Will you listen to what you just said? It's you, Jo, isn't it, who wants the mad passionate affair without the humdrum daily routine of marriage? Great God, what's the world coming to?'

Joanna had refused all social invitations for the night of the championship fight, but as she sat in her apartment she regretted the decision to wait alone for the outcome. The minutes ticked by slowly, leaving far too much time for agonising.

Glancing at the clock she saw there was still an hour until the match began. She walked over to the telephone, wondering whom to call. Who could provide company without asking questions? Bart had left her immediately after lunch the previous day claiming he had a story to cover, and she hadn't heard from him since. Joanna had stayed home, unwilling to face Dragonbreath when the rival papers hit the streets.

The story about Max Morgan and the *Chronicle*'s society columnist had appeared that morning in not one but three newspapers. The boxer's secret romance with 'Princess Natalie' was revealed, along with the fact that the princess was actually an English immigrant named Joanna Smith, recently arrived via Ellis Island. Delta was described as Magnus's coloured commonlaw wife, with whom he had a child.

Except for a quick early-morning trip to the corner to buy newspapers, Joanna had not ventured out of her apartment all day. There was no point in even going to see Dragonbreath and suffering through a screaming diatribe, which would culminate in her being fired. She decided to forgo any salary she had coming to her in order to be spared that ordeal.

She was reaching for the phone when her doorbell rang. Bart, she thought, oh, bless you. But when she opened the door Magnus stood on her threshold, holding the shawl-wrapped baby.

'Joanna . . . she's gone. Delta left, and this time I don't think she's coming back. I didn't want to leave the baby with my manager's housekeeper because I think she drinks.'

Taking the sleeping baby from him, Joanna raised her face for his kiss. 'Surely you should be leaving –'

'If you'd just watch the baby for tonight –'

'Yes, of course. Pull out the bottom drawer of my dresser. We'll put a pillow in it and Sari can sleep in there.'

'I brought a bottle and a teat. If she gets hungry you can just add a drop of warm water to some milk.'

'Cow's milk? But –'

'She's used to it. Delta wouldn't feed her because it tied her down too much.'

'I suppose you heard about today's news stories?'

'Yes.' He looked indescribably tired, she decided, certainly not in peak condition to box tonight. Damn Delta, why couldn't she at least have stood by him until after the fight?

They settled the baby into the makeshift crib and then faced each other, knowing there was no time to talk.

'Good luck tonight,' Joanna said. 'I love you.'

'Joanna, no matter what happens tonight, after it's over I'll come back here and we'll talk about the future. We can't go on like this.'

She nodded and he held her close, his arms painfully tight, as he kissed her hair, her eyelids, and finally her lips.

As he turned towards the door Joanna raised her hand to stop him, a terrible premonition causing her heart to thud. 'Magnus . . . don't go. Please don't fight tonight. I fear something horrible is going to happen.'

He looked back at her, his eyes soft with love in his battered face, and he smiled. 'Don't worry. I'll be back before you know it, and I'll have the title. I'm going to win it for you, Joanna.'

39

Megan stood aside to allow Quinn to enter her bedroom, knowing she would be lost if he so much as touched her. Her heart had begun a familiar slow, thudding response to his presence.

To hide her turmoil, she walked away from him, towards her dressing table. 'If you think I'm going to tell you about Mrs Pennington's problems so you can regale the ladies of the Jade Palace with the lurid details –'

He caught up with her in two long strides, grabbed her arms, and spun her around to face him. 'You know damn well what I want to talk about. About how you keep saying no with your words and yes with your eyes. That last evening I spent at the ranch you nearly drove Randolph crazy with jealousy because you kept fluttering your eyes in my direction.'

'I did not, you conceited, overbearing –'

'Oh, don't start that rigmarole again. You think I don't know why you danced yourself silly tonight, tossing those fiery curls and giving everything in britches a dimpled smile? You're just not cut out to be a flirt, Megan. It doesn't come naturally to you. You prefer more direct methods of achieving your goals.'

'And you believe *you* are one of my goals?' Despite her attempt at incredulity, she couldn't meet his eyes.

'I believe that neither of us will be happy until we're together. Maybe we can't be together all the time, but we need to know that we can always come back to each other.

Look, Megan, when I left you in Galveston I swore to myself I wouldn't see you again. But here I am.'

'But nothing's changed since then,' she said miserably.

Placing his hands on her cheeks, he tilted her face upward. The mocking glint in his gaze was gone, replaced by a look of yearning. His voice was very low. 'Just for now, for this moment, be honest with me. If you weren't married to Randolph, would you marry me? A straight yes or no, Megan, that's all I ask.'

His mouth was a fraction of an inch from hers, she could feel the warm eddy of his breath against her lips, and his eyes seemed to look into her soul. A long, shuddering sigh slipped away from her. She wanted to say, Yes, yes, of course I would. I love you. I hate being away from you, I think about you constantly, wonder what you're doing, whom you're with. Instead she asked, 'Is that a hypothetical question?'

To her surprise he laughed. 'One of the things I love about you is the way that logical, analytical streak pops out when I least expect it. You look like a guileless beauty with nothing more complex on your mind than what to wear for your next ball; then you floor me with a question like that. No, my love, that was not a hypothetical question. It was a declaration of my honourable intentions. I want you to be my wife.'

'In that case,' Megan said slowly, 'if I were not already married to Randolph, yes, yes, I would marry you. But –'

'Do you love me?' he persisted.

'Yes, I love you. Oh, Quinn, Randolph knows about us.'

That silenced him for a moment. At length he said, 'Randolph is just as unhappy with the present situation as we are. But he's too much of a gentleman to tell you.'

'He discussed our marriage with you?' Megan was outraged.

'No,' Quinn answered quickly, 'he didn't. But I know him well enough to sense his misery. He's like a lot of men who don't always know what – or who – will make them

341

happy. He was dazzled by you – by your beauty, your animation, your intelligence – but he couldn't foresee that you're not the type of woman he could happily live with. He needed a quiet woman, a homebody who would be content to share his solitude. Even before he lost the use of his legs he couldn't abide parties and crowds. He would have died before he'd have attended the ball tonight. It would make him happy to sit reading for hours with his woman beside him doing exactly the same thing. You've got too much energy and ambition for that. You prowl around his house like a caged tigress; I'll bet it wears him out just to watch you.'

'Quinn, knowing this about Randolph, why in the name of heaven did you take me to him?'

'If I answer that question truthfully, you're going to hate me.'

'Didn't you suggest that for this moment we be completely honest with each other?'

'All right. I'm not proud of what I believed then – and I want you to know I no longer think that way – but in view of your circumstances when I met you, I thought you would gladly *become* the kind of woman Randolph needed. I assumed you'd see the situation as a bargain, in other words. Wealth and security for you . . . Megan, I didn't know you then, or love you as I do now.'

'"Oh, what a tangled web we weave,"' Megan quoted softly.

'"When first we practice to deceive,"' he finished for her. 'I'm going to suggest to Randolph a quiet annulment of your marriage. I think he'll be relieved. He confessed to me that lately he finds himself behaving in ways he doesn't like, and he doesn't understand why. I've seen a change in him, too. Frankly, Megan, you don't bring out the best in him.'

'I've touched some nerves with him, made him think about things he didn't want brought out into the open.'

'But that isn't your function as a wife. Lord, no wonder he's uncomfortable with you. You've been treating him like your patient, not your husband.'

342

'Quinn, I suspect there's no physical reason why he can't walk.'

'Hypochondria?'

'No, nothing like that. Something much more complex.' She slipped out of his embrace and went to the desk, opened a drawer, and found a sheet of paper. Lew Wallace's photograph watched her from the far side of the blotter.

She dipped a pen in the inkwell and swiftly sketched a diagram of an iceberg with only the tip showing above the surface of the sea, and the vast bulk below. 'According to a neurologist named Sigmund Freud in Vienna, this' – she indicated the tip of the iceberg – 'is our conscious mind. All the rest, below the surface, is our unconscious. Freud attempted to reach into his patients' unconscious, first with hypnosis and later with what he calls free association, to resolve conflicts they are not even aware they have, conflicts that can actually cause physical symptoms.'

She felt Quinn's arms slip around her, and his lips moved the hair on the nape of her neck, finding the flesh beneath so that he might kiss her. 'If you feel so strongly about Randolph's paralysis, then put yourself in a position where you can really help him. Become a doctor.'

Exasperated, she exclaimed, 'You know that's impossible. I can't get into medical school.'

His hands moved insistently around to the front of her body, rose to briefly caress her breasts, then slid to her shoulders.

Gently, he turned her to face him. 'Because the venerable gentlemen who run our medical schools say you're too old. I know. Megan, I do admire your innate honesty, but sometimes when you run up against a brick wall all you can do is batter your way through it.'

'What do you mean?'

'I mean that you know and I know you'd make a damn fine doctor. But you need to get into medical school to prove that to the dunderheads who are keeping you out.

343

So . . . tell them what they want to hear. If you're too old at twenty-five, then be eighteen.'

Her mouth fell open. 'Lie about my age?'

'Why not?'

'But I already applied to several schools. They know my correct age.'

'What about your correct name, did you give that?'

'Well, no . . . On my marriage certificate I'm Joanna Mallory, *née* Traherne, so that's the name I used on my applications.'

'So now you'll apply as Megan Thomas-Robard . . . or, better yet, as Megan McQuinn.'

She was silent, savouring the sound of it. Her eyes closed as for a blissful instant everything seemed possible. Then, rather than let go of the dream and face reality, she slipped her arms around his neck and turned her face upward for his kiss.

He was immediately aroused. Picking her up, he carried her to the bed. She opened her eyes and smiled at him. 'I love you, Ramblin' Jack.'

'And I love you, Megan Thomas-Robard, soon-to-be McQuinn.'

'It's shameless of me, I know,' she said softly, 'but I feel we're married already. I feel bonded to you in a way no minister reciting words could ever accomplish.'

'Nevertheless, you hussy, I won't be happy until you make an honest man of me. I want that minister to recite the words.'

He kissed the hollow at the base of her throat, traced a path with his warm mouth to her face and gently nibbled her lower lip. 'Tell me you love me.'

'I do love you, Quinn. Even when you're being impossible. I love you even when I try to hate you . . . I suppose that's how I know that my feelings won't go away.'

He sighed with pleasure. 'Knowing that, I can surmount any obstacle, even your stubbornness, my sweet.' He looked at her and as their eyes met it seemed their hearts touched, too. 'Megan, I love you so much.'

His fingers were busy with her hairpins and when her hair streamed onto the pillow he bent to kiss the soft strands, then turned his attention to the buttons of her basque.

Megan felt an intoxicating languor creep over her and, paradoxically, a rising urgency, a need to be even closer to him. She began to unbutton his shirt, then pressed her lips to the firm flesh beneath, inhaling his masculine scent, savouring the anticipation of lovemaking.

Minutes later, naked limbs entwined, they were lost in a magic joining of flesh that transcended everything but their sensory awareness of each other.

Just before dawn he murmured, 'I'd better get out of here before the maid comes. Go home with Chuck and wait for me. I have to leave for Santa Fe this morning on business. I'll be gone for about a week. As soon as I get back I'll come to the ranch.' He kissed her mouth, a long slow meeting of lips that was exciting yet comforting, like a promise for the future.

'Quinn, wait . . . I can't let you leave believing that I'll agree to all you suggested last night. Oh, I think we should ask Randolph if he'll agree to an annulment, but I won't lie to get into medical school. Besides, when I'm your wife, I don't think I'll want to leave you.'

He looked down at her. 'You're saying you'd give up your dream for me? Megan, for pity's sake, don't you see that your dreams are the essence of you. Without them you wouldn't be the woman I love, and if I let you sacrifice them for me, then I'm not the right man for you. Each of us should bring out the best in the other.'

A slow smile broke across his face. 'Besides, you're forgetting my name – Ramblin' Jack. How do you suppose I got it? I'll move back east with you when you go to medical school. Who knows, maybe I'll even let my family welcome home the black sheep. They'll love you, although they'll probably try to convince you that I'm not good enough for you. There's even a family business waiting for the only son and heir to take over. Maybe when I'm a respectable married man I might consider settling down.'

Megan laughed. 'I very much doubt that.'

Suddenly serious, he said, 'I'll be there with you, I promise, while you go to medical school. I'll be waiting for you when you come home with ink on your nose.'

'Quinn, my darling,' Megan murmured, 'I love you, but I just don't know . . .'

Megan didn't see the Penningtons before leaving, but she left a note with Mrs Simmonds, repeating her offer to see Cecilia Pennington any time or anywhere and again begging her not to undergo surgery.

On the one hand, Megan wondered if Cecilia might benefit from Dr Freud's talking cure, and on the other she couldn't help remembering that when A-chi-tie explained the Indian use of plants and barks and herbs to treat various diseases, one of the disorders he had mentioned was 'female trouble.' Megan had been surprised to realise that men who were considered savages showed more compassion for their women's medical problems than their white counterparts did.

She fervently hoped that Cecilia Pennington would get in touch with her again after she returned to the ranch.

Chuck drove her back from Silver City in disapproving silence, but for once Megan didn't care. She felt light-hearted, filled with the joy of being in love, certain that only good things could happen.

Halfway back to the ranch they had to drive across a shallow neck of the river. Chuck slowed the car down as the wheels rolled over the gravelly riverbed.

As they reached the opposite bank two horsemen emerged from a copse of cottonwoods, blocking the trail in front of them. Chuck braked so suddenly that plumes of water sprayed all around the car, splashing Megan's face.

When she wiped the water from her eyes she saw that both riders faced them with drawn guns. Her heart leapt into her throat.

One man spoke in rapid Spanish.

346

Chuck said, 'He said you're to get out of the car.'

'Just me?'

'That's what he said.'

The two men watched silently. Although the outlaw who had spoken was obviously Mexican, the other man looked like an American. In the split second she wondered about this, Megan noted the slack jawed expression on the American's face and the faintly Mongoloid features that suggested mental retardation. He was also a very large man, much taller and heavier than the slim Mexican. Both wore dirty ponchos, and the Mexican rode without a saddle. Instead there was a blanket on the back of his horse, Indian style.

'Get out, senora,' the Mexican said softly in English, 'or we come get you.'

As she stepped out of the car Megan recalled with icy dread that the Chiricahua Kid was Mexican.

40

Just before midnight Joanna wrapped Delta's sleeping baby in a blanket and went in search of the doorman of her apartment building.

Her nerves were frayed to the breaking point. Surely by now the championship fight was over? Why hadn't Magnus returned?

The doorman looked up in surprise as she hurried across the lobby towards him. 'Have you heard the result of the Max Morgan fight?'

His mouth dropped open. 'Why . . . sure. Morgan won by a knockout in the nineteenth round.'

Joanna closed her eyes briefly in a silent prayer of gratitude. She thanked the doorman and went back up to her apartment. No doubt Magnus, his manager, and his seconds were out somewhere celebrating his victory. Exhausted, she put the baby back into the makeshift crib and then collapsed into her own bed.

She awakened to the sound of insistent knocking on her door and sat up with a start. Dawn was creeping in through a gap in the draperies and Sari was stirring, making soft cooing sounds.

Certain that Magnus had at last arrived, she didn't bother to reach for a robe, but scrambled out of bed and ran to open the door.

Bart stood outside, his expression grave. There was none of the usual jocularity in his tone as he said, 'I guess . . . you haven't heard yet?'

'That Magnus won last night? Oh, yes, I have. Isn't it wonderful?'

For answer he stepped into the room and closed the door carefully behind him.

'Bart, please! Give me a chance to dress.'

He grabbed her arm and led her towards the nearest chair.

'What on earth are you doing?'

'Sit down, Jo. I've got some bad news.'

As she looked into his eyes, she felt her mouth go dry.

He crouched in front of her, holding her hands tightly. 'You can kick the messenger, if you like . . .'

'Something's happened to Magnus,' Joanna whispered.

He nodded. 'I'm sorry . . . Christ, I can't tell you how sorry I am. It was so senseless.'

'No, you're mistaken,' Joanna cried, clutching at straws. 'He won the fight.'

'Yes, he won the fight. He was the new champ for a little while.'

Joanna tried to stand up. 'Where is he? I must go to him.'

Bart forced her back into the chair. 'He's dead, Jo.'

For a moment there was a silence so intense that it seemed every creature on earth had been stilled.

'Jo?' Bart shook her slightly.

'No,' she said firmly. 'You're wrong.'

'I'm not wrong, Jo. We've got to get you packed and out of here before the reporters arrive – and they will descend on you like vultures now.'

The baby cried suddenly, an impatient wail of hunger.

Bart looked at her questioningly. 'Delta's baby? Where is she?'

'I don't know. She left Magnus yesterday. Bart, why are you doing this? Why are you frightening me like this?'

'Magnus was set upon by a gang of thugs on the street last night – I guess he was on his way to you. They were waiting for him when he left the arena. They beat him . . . He was dead before his manager could get help.'

'Paxton!' Joanna said in a strangled whisper.

'No. Paxton and Hollis are in New Orleans for an exhibition bout. I checked.'

'Then who? Why?'

'Who, we don't know. Why, was pretty obvious – the stories about Delta and the baby. A witness said the men were drunk and yelling racial epithets.'

'I must see to the baby,' Joanna said. 'Let go of my hands, please.'

Bart reluctantly released her. He followed as she went to Sari, picked her up, and rocked her back and forth.

Calmly Joanna said, 'If you'll pack a bag for me, I'll feed and change the baby. Then we can leave.'

During the days that followed Joanna found that caring for an infant was too time-consuming to allow her to grieve. Indeed, she did not truly accept that Magnus was dead and constantly expected him to appear at the door of Bart's apartment.

Bart refused to bring home any newspapers or to tell her what was happening in the aftermath of the tragedy. She and Sari remained in his apartment as the days slipped away. Bart had tried to find Delta, but she, too, had dropped out of sight.

He did bring a message from the *Chronicle*. 'Dragon-breath put out the word that if anyone knew your where-abouts they were to tell you that if you'll give him an exclusive story – all the details – of your affair with Max Morgan, he might consider rehiring you. Not as a columnist, but in some capacity.' Bart scowled. 'Copy girl, probably.'

'He can go to hell,' Joanna responded.

One evening when Bart returned from the *Chronicle* offices, Joanna was walking around the living room, softly singing a lullaby, the baby in her arms. She raised her finger to her lips and mouthed the words, 'She's almost asleep.'

Bart nodded and went into the kitchen. By the time Joanna had put the baby down he had pork chops sizzling in a pan and was peeling potatoes. 'I brought a cabbage, too. Do you like cabbage?'

'I should be cooking dinner for you,' Joanna said. 'I'm not much use now that I'm no longer Princess Natalie, am I?'

'I like to cook,' Bart answered. 'But hate to type. If you'll type up my article for me, we'll call it even.'

'Gladly. What would I have done without you?' Joanna said. 'I don't know where I could have turned. Especially with the responsibility of taking care of Sari.'

'A responsibility you didn't really have to assume, you know. Oh, don't misunderstand me. Sari is as cute as she can be, and she's welcome to stay with us, but, Jo, I'm worried that you're getting too attached to her. Delta is around somewhere, don't forget, and from what you've told me about her, I suspect she'll pop up again when it suits her.'

Joanna bit her lip. 'Yes, I know that. I suppose I've just been living from day to day. Magnus wasn't even sure that Sari was his child, but . . . well, she's all I have left to remind me of him.'

Bart pushed his glasses back up his nose and scrutinised a peeled potato with more concentration than it warranted.

'Maybe that's all the more reason you should take the baby to somebody else. You'll get over Magnus faster if you aren't reminded of him.'

'Bart! I'll never get over him. I loved him with all my heart, against all logic and reason. We had nothing in common, yet he lit up my life, cared for me, and protected me. When I was with him I felt beautiful, desired. As though that wasn't enough of a gift, I always felt safe when I was with him.'

He turned to face her, his customary leprechaun's grin missing, his myopic gaze searching her face as though desperate to find something there. 'You don't feel safe here, with me?'

'Oh, Bart, forgive me,' Joanna said. 'I didn't mean to imply . . .' She went to him and put her arms around his neck. Standing, he was several inches shorter than she was, and she brushed his forehead lightly with her lips. 'Of course I feel safe with you.'

The baby awakened and began to fuss.

'Damn,' Bart said.

'I'll get her back to sleep before the vegetables are done,' Joanna answered.

'The hell with the vegetables,' Bart growled. 'This is the first time I've had you within arm's reach.'

Not taking him seriously, Joanna laughed and went to take care of the baby.

A week later Joanna was folding diapers when Bart arrived unexpectedly in the middle of the morning.

'We're leaving,' he announced abruptly.

'Leaving? The apartment?'

'The city. We're getting out of New York. How fast can you pack? There's a train in two hours.'

Bewildered, Joanna stood up. 'But what about your job?'

'I quit the *Chronicle*.'

'But why? And where will you go?'

'*We* are going to Chicago. I've got a job on a paper

351

there.' He opened a closet and pulled a suitcase down from the shelf.

'Bart, wait! I can't go traipsing across the country at the drop of a hat, not with a baby. Besides, Sari and I have imposed upon your hospitality long enough. It's time I pulled myself together and decided what to do next.'

A second suitcase tumbled from the shelf. 'You're coming with me. You have no alternative.'

'There are always alternatives. I'll get another job, pay someone to take care of Sari.'

'I haven't got time to argue with you, Jo! You're the main reason we've got to go, so get your things together.'

'What do you mean, I'm the reason?'

He rooted around on the floor of the closet and found a carpet bag. 'Here, this will do for Sari's stuff.'

Straightening up, he looked at her. 'A week ago a man came to the *Chronicle* office asking about you. We've had plenty of inquiries since the big fight, of course, but there was something different about this man. He wasn't a reporter . . . Anyway, he was back again today and this time he was trying to find out where I lived. It's only a matter of time before he tracks us down, and you know what will happen then. Every newshound in the city is going to be panting at your door for a story about you and Max Morgan – not to mention the tricky situation in regard to Sari.'

'But why do you think this particular man will find us? No one else has.'

'Because,' Bart answered grimly, 'today I found out who he is – or rather, what he is, and just how much he already knows about you. Is your real name Joanna Traherne?'

She nodded, a dry lump in her throat. 'How could he possibly have learned that? I haven't used that name since I left home.'

'Snooping is his business. He's a Pinkerton detective, and he's going to find you, Jo, unless we leave right now and take care to cover our tracks.'

352

'But I can't take the baby out of the city. Sooner or later Delta will come looking for her.'

'She's more likely to find the baby if we take her to a foundling home and tell them who she is.'

'Bart! I'd never take Sari to an orphanage. What a horrible suggestion. What about Magnus's manager? Could we let him know where to find us in Chicago?'

Bart picked up one of the suitcases and walked towards his bedroom. 'Sure, we could do that. We'll write to him after we get to Chicago.'

41

Chuck sat immobilised in the driver's seat of the Winton, staring at the gun in the hand of the Chiricahua Kid. Megan stood rooted to the spot as the American slid from his mount and approached her. He grinned at her. 'She's for me, huh? You promised, Kid. You said the next one was for me. You said that, you did say that.'

Flat brown eyes, as cold as stone, regarded Megan for an instant. '*Si*, Lonnie, *amigo*, I say that. Sure did.'

The big American quickened his pace. One more second and a grimy hand would reach for her. Megan bent down and scooped up a handful of river rocks and hurled them at him. The stones caught him full in the face and he yelped. At the same instant Chuck reached under his seat and a gun appeared in his hand.

There were three explosions in rapid succession and blood flew in every direction. Chuck slumped over the driving wheel.

It had happened so quickly that Megan could only stand

and stare. Only when Lonnie grabbed her and started to paw her breasts did she react. Kicking, screaming, she felt herself being lifted into the air and swung around in a manic dance of triumph as Lonnie howled with laughter.

Another shot, fired into the air, calmed him. He looked up at the Kid in bewilderment, Megan still clasped in his arms.

Megan saw then that Chuck had managed to fire one shot, which had struck the Kid in his left shoulder. Despite his wound, he remained astride his horse, smoking gun in his hand. 'Put her down, Lonnie. Now. Come here and help me.'

Lonnie hesitated, and the Kid fired again, this time the bullet struck the dirt near Lonnie's feet and Megan cried out in fright as she was flung in a heap on the ground.

Without looking up at them, she began to inch backwards, into the water. She was a strong swimmer. If she could just get out into midriver, perhaps . . .

She felt a gun barrel touch her cheek and looked up into the pitiless eyes of the Kid. Behind him Lonnie was dragging Chuck's body from the Winton.

'You know how to make go?' the Kid asked, jerking his head in the direction of the car.

They wanted the vehicle, she realised, but they didn't know how to drive it . . . and if she said she couldn't drive, Lonnie would rape her, and the Kid would undoubtedly shoot her . . .

'Yes,' she said. 'I know how to drive it.'

They didn't bother to clean Chuck's blood from the seat. She managed to brush away most of the shards of glass from the shattered windshield before Lonnie shoved her behind the wheel.

She had ridden as a passenger enough times to be vaguely aware of what to do, but her hands were shaking and her voice was little more than a whisper as she instructed Lonnie to turn the crank to start the engine.

The Kid climbed in without help, but she could hear his laboured breathing over the sputtering of the engine as she tried to coax it to life.

Please, please, she prayed silently, let it start. Lonnie jerked the crank around again, his face beet red, and swore when the engine failed to ignite.

Fortunately the engine was still warm and it started with less cranking than Chuck normally gave it. Megan gave a sigh of relief when it roared to life after four or five attempts. But as they lurched forward it occurred to her that it surely wouldn't take long for the Kid to realise that driving was a very simple procedure. With a bullet in his shoulder, he would be unable to handle the car himself, but even slow-witted Lonnie could take over from her. And when they no longer needed her . . .

Oh, if only Quinn were not on his way to Santa Fe! She comforted herself with the thought that when she and Chuck didn't arrive home, Randolph would send men to search for them.

Randolph waited tensely as the two cowboys shuffled into the house. Young Wyatt, frayed and shabby as ever, but always eager to please, gave him an uncharacteristically sad look. At his side the grizzled Texan who had once been a Ranger, according to Chuck, pulled his hat from his head and surveyed Randolph gravely.

'They were bushwhacked, we're pretty sure by the Chiricahua Kid. I'm sorry, sir, but it looks like they took your wife with them in the horseless carriage.'

Randolph felt fear for Megan flood over him in an icy wave. What the Kid and his men had done to women captives had horrified the entire territory. For Megan to be in the hands of those sadistic monsters was unthinkable. He made a small strangled sound and smashed his fist into the armrest of his wheelchair. 'How do you know it was the Kid and his men?'

Tex answered, 'We found Chuck's body by the river, some brush tossed over it. Two bullets in him and . . .

355

well, sorry, sir, but he had the mark of the Chiricahua Kid on him.'

Randolph turned away swiftly so they wouldn't see the tears that sprang to his eyes. Chuck had been like a father to him even before the death of his real father, and since the tragedy, he had been more than a father – custodian of the ranch, sole caretaker of a helpless invalid, friend, mentor.

Wyatt added, 'They left two worn-out horses – stolen, prob'ly – and took the Winton. There were two men, one of 'em big and heavy. Wheel tracks went south. We rode after 'em for a while, but it was getting dark and Tex figured we'd best come back and get help.'

'What about Chuck? You didn't leave him for the coyotes?'

'No, sir, we went back for him. He's here. We laid him out in the bunkhouse,' Tex said. 'I'll send one of the boys into town for the mortician in the morning.'

Randolph's hands gripped his wheelchair until the knuckles whitened. Quinn, he knew, was on his way to Santa Fe to meet some prospective buyers about selling his copper mine. Without either Quinn or Chuck to rely on, Randolph felt helpless, adrift. For a long minute paralysis, of mind as well as body, immobilised him.

Then Tex cleared his throat and said, 'We'll hit the trail as soon as it's light.'

'The tracks went south, you said.'

'Heading for the border, I reckon.'

'Across a lot of open country,' Randolph said. 'The Winton had already come from Silver City. It will run out of gasoline before they reach Mexico.'

Tex looked at him blankly.

'Wake up one of the other hands and tell him to saddle up and ride to the marshal's office. Get Braddock up, too, and send him to me. Then harness the trap to the two fastest horses we own.'

'Now?' Tex asked.

'Yes. I'll be leaving in ten minutes to go after my wife.'

'You . . . *you're* going? But –'

Wyatt cleared his throat. 'Mr Mallory, sir, I'd be proud to go with you. I ain't tired.'

'Thanks for the offer, Wyatt, but I believe I need Braddock for this particular mission. Don't stand there, Tex. Move. We're wasting time.'

The engine sputtered and died halfway across a dry lake bed. Megan had been aware of the changes in the moonlit countryside – the appearance of an occasional tall saguaro cactus, a monolithic boulder formation, the sparse growth of chaparral.

From the occasional comments that passed between the Chiricahua Kid and Lonnie, Megan inferred that they hoped to cross the border into Mexico. She also noticed that the Kid was beginning to feel the effects of loss of blood.

'Wha – what's wrong?' he asked, his speech slurred. 'Why . . . you stop?'

'The motorig needs fuel,' she answered. 'I told you we'd have to stop in a town, but you –'

'Shut up.' He poked Lonnie's shoulder and said something in Spanish, and Megan saw that he was becoming weaker and more confused. She would have to try to escape while it was still dark.

Lonnie apparently understood some Spanish, for he lifted his companion out of the Winton and laid him carefully on the ground, then covered him with a blanket.

'I . . . need to get out, too, to stretch my limbs,' Megan said.

In the moonlight Lonnie's expression was blank, giving his Mongoloid features a sinister inscrutability. When neither man objected, she cautiously climbed out of the driving seat, rubbing her stiff shoulders with her hands.

She took a tentative step and then another, walking close to the Winton but avoiding the two men.

They couldn't have run out of gasoline in a more exposed area. There were no covering trees or cacti, just the salt flats of an ancient lake bed. The moonlight was bright enough so that they could certainly shoot her if she attempted to dash across the flat ground. But if searchers were looking for her, the exposed position might work to her advantage.

Lonnie appeared at her side so suddenly that she jumped. He gave her a slack jawed grin and with one finger touched her cheek, then traced a path down her throat to her breast. She tried to draw back, but the Winton was in the way. When she moved sideways, Lonnie's brawny arm shot out to stop her.

His face moved closer, blocking out the moonlight. She smelled his sour breath, then heard the sound of tearing silk as his hands sought entry to her bodice. She opened her mouth to scream, but his lips and tongue cut off the sound.

He pushed her down on the ground beside the Winton and the gravelly sand cut into her back. His hands savagely closed around her breasts, but the pain she felt was nothing compared to the disgusting sensation of his tongue exploring her mouth. Once when she was a little girl she had been picking watercress along the edge of the river and her hand had closed around a giant slug. She recalled the horrid feel of the creature now.

Lonnie forced her legs apart with his knee, and one great hand dropped to her skirts. She struggled more desperately, still impaled upon that sluglike tongue, held down by those enormous hands. A whimpering sound, like the whining of a puppy, came from Lonnie's throat, overpowering her own feeble choking and gagging sounds.

She felt her senses slipping away as his hand tore at her underwear. His erection prodded her thigh, fearfully insistent, but at the same instant she felt another hardness against her hip. His gun! He still wore his gun belt with a holstered pistol.

Forcing herself to sag limply, as though yielding, she heard his small cry of excitement and triumph as he prepared to force himself into her.

The moment the pressure on her arm eased, she slid her fingers up the leather holster and found the grip of the pistol.

In the following split second she realised that merely pointing the gun at him would not stop him. Jamming the pistol against his thigh, she squeezed the trigger.

The gun went off with a roar that reverberated through the stillness of the night. Lonnie lurched upward, then rolled off her, clutching his hip.

For a few seconds he rolled about on the ground, gasping and moaning. Then, incredibly, he started to crawl towards her again.

Megan scrambled to her feet, fear driving her. At the far side of the moonlit lake bed a shadowed cluster of giant boulders beckoned, offering sanctuary. Surely she could evade two wounded men in those rocks until help came. She started to run.

She had taken only a few steps when a hand closed around her ankle, pulling her down.

She crashed to the ground, the pistol slipping from her fingers. The jolting shock to her body dazed her for a moment; then she turned her head and looked into the flat stare of the Chiricahua Kid.

'Let me have her,' Lonnie screamed. 'Let me kill her, Kid. She hurt me. Look, I'm bleeding.'

Megan twisted onto her side, one ankle still held in the Kid's relentless grip. Her mind raced, seeking a way to stay alive. 'I can help him,' she cried. 'I can help both of you. I'll remove the bullets. I'm a doctor.'

The Kid snorted. 'You no doctor. Woman can't be doctor.'

'Under the seat of the motorig – there's a black bag,' Megan said desperately. 'Have Lonnie get it out. I'll show you forceps and probes and scalpels and bandages and . . . Look!'

She pointed to the dark stain on the ground under him. 'You're bleeding to death. You'll get weaker as the night wears on if you don't let me help you. I can save your life.'

Lonnie was on his knees, moaning, his hands pressed to his thigh. 'Let me kill her, Kid. We don't need her now. The carriage thing won't go. Come on, Kid, let me have her.'

The Kid hesitated. 'Look and see if there's a bag.'

'I can't . . . I'm hurt bad, Kid.'

'Get over there, *amigo*, and find the bag.'

Lonnie crawled towards the Winton.

The cold night air of the desert crept through Megan's torn clothing and chilled her flesh, but her hands were clammy.

Minutes later Lonnie dropped her grandfather's medical bag on the ground beside her. The Kid handed Lonnie his gun and said something in Spanish. Lonnie grinned and nodded.

Megan opened the bag with shaking fingers, certain that the Kid had just told Lonnie that no matter what her medical skills proved to be, he would soon be allowed to do whatever he wished to her.

42

Joanna knew the moment she set foot in the home of Bart's parents that she had made a mistake. The house itself, although beautifully situated on the shores of Lake Michigan, was over-poweringly furnished with huge dark mahogany pieces and cluttered with statuary and bric-a-brac. Heavy velvet brocade draperies remained permanently closed on the windows, and all the hardwood floors had been stained almost black, creating a deeper gloom.

Bart's mother, an elegantly thin woman with a perpetual

aura of peevishness clinging to her like a second skin, took one look at the baby and said faintly, 'But she's . . . coloured.'

'Well, just a little bit,' Bart responded, hastily stepping between his mother and Joanna, who held Sari in tired arms. 'Look, Mater, as I explained in my letter, the baby is just a temporary arrangement. She isn't Jo's child. Come on, now, give us a smile and say it's all right. Great balls of fire, you've got plenty of help in the house. One little baby isn't going to upset the apple cart.'

Mrs Whitman's lips compressed into a thin line. 'I don't understand how a baby can be classified as a temporary arrangement, nor do I understand how she can be just a little bit coloured. Is this infant a Negro or not? If she isn't Joanna's, then whose baby is she?'

Joanna, who was exhausted from the long journey, depressed by the gloomy house and Mrs Whitman's disapproving stare, and anxious to heat a bottle for the baby before she began to fuss, said as politely as she could, 'Mrs Whitman, I realise this is a dreadful imposition and we certainly don't want to put you out. Perhaps we should go to a hotel.'

As if she hadn't spoken, Mrs Whitman said to Bart, 'You always were so gullible when it came to women, Bartholomew. I know you're self-conscious about your short stature and your poor eyesight, but that's no reason to take up with –'

To Bart's credit, he didn't let his mother finish. 'Great God, I knew I shouldn't have come back here. Holy Moses, Mater, how can you be so friendly and forgiving in a letter and then keep us standing in the hall after we've travelled over eight hundred miles to see you? Are we welcome or not?'

A maid in a black dress and a starched white apron and cap hovered at Mrs Whitman's elbow. She turned to her and said curtly, 'You can put Miss Traherne and the baby in the old nursery. Bartholomew, your room is ready and waiting for you.'

The nursery had clearly been unused since Bart's infancy. Joanna was dismayed to find mildew spots on the walls and a coating of dust on the crib. The sheets were damp and musty, and a faint fungal odour permeated the room. A single bed, separated from the baby furniture by a screen, had evidently been used by a nanny.

'I didn't know there'd be a baby coming, mum,' the maid said. 'I'll clean the place up right away.'

'Just heat her bottle and bring me some clean sheets for the bed,' Joanna said wearily. 'We'll clean in the morning.'

Bart's father, a prosperous investments broker, was as thin and peevish as his wife. They reminded Joanna of a pair of rapiers, sharp and cold and lethal.

When she entered the dining room at eight that evening after a struggle to get Sari to sleep in a strange bed, the elder Whitman was already halfway through his soup.

Mrs Whitman looked pointedly at the glass-domed gilt clock on the mantel. Bart jumped to his feet to pull out a chair for Joanna.

'I'm sorry I'm a little late. I stayed upstairs until the baby was asleep,' Joanna said. She remained on her feet, waiting to be presented to Mr Whitman.

'The baby,' Mr Whitman repeated. 'Yes. We'd better get that little mess cleared up immediately.'

'Little *mess*?' Joanna felt several blood vessels expand.

'You must realise that we entertain a great deal,' Mrs Whitman put in. 'We have many influential friends. It would be impossible to keep such a secret.'

'Look, Miss Traherne, since our son brought you here, we assume he has honourable intentions towards you,' Mr Whitman went on. 'He tells us that the infant was deserted by her mother, who was a friend of yours. Be that as it may, people are going to talk about Bart bringing home an unmarried woman with a coloured baby. Oh, boy, are they going to talk.'

'Pater . . .' Bart pleaded.

'It needs to be said, son. The baby has to go.'

'What do you suggest I do with her?' Joanna inquired. 'Drown her like an unwanted kitten?'

She had the satisfaction of seeing Mrs Whitman's thin lips open to an outraged O, while Mr Whitman's entire face seemed to clench.

'Jo, Mater has a plan,' Bart said quickly. 'We'll put out the story that Sari is the baby of your maid, who got sick on the way from New York and who will be here in a couple of days. Then we will hire a coloured maid for you. That way, you can keep an eye on the baby without embarrassing the folks.'

'We'll have the wedding as soon as is decently feasible, of course,' Mr Whitman said.

Joanna gasped. 'The *wedding*?'

'Jo, they assumed . . . since we came home together . . .' She had never seen Bart at a loss for words, but felt less sympathy for him than anger at his allowing this situation to develop. Looking directly at his mother, Joanna said, 'Your son and I are friends and former colleagues. Nothing more. We have no intention of getting married.'

'If you don't intend to marry my son,' Mr Whitman said, 'what are you doing here?'

'I really don't know,' Joanna said. 'But rest assured the baby and I will be gone as soon as I can pack.' She ran from the room.

Bart caught up with her halfway up the stairs. 'Jo – wait. I'm sorry about this. My fault. I should have known that leopards would change their spots before the Whitmans would relax their conventional views. I thought we could stay at least long enough for me to get another job.'

She paused, one hand on the banister, and looked down at him. 'I thought you already had another job, on the *Tribune*.'

'Well, I haven't actually applied there yet, but I'm sure . . . Listen, don't go. Just let Mater and Pater think we're getting married, and go along with the coloured maid idea until we get on our feet and can afford to move out.'

'I can't do that, Bart. It would be dishonest. I see now that I allowed my grief over Magnus to paralyse me. I took shelter behind your kindness and concern when I should have been finding a way to take care of the baby and myself.'

'But where can you go? What can you do? This isn't New York, Jo. No paper here will take on a female reporter without references. And you can hardly tell them you were Princess Natalie.'

She continued on her way up the stairs. 'Then I'll find some other way to support myself.'

'I'll go with you, then.'

'No, Bart. Not this time. Stay here with your parents.'

'But I can't just turn you loose in a strange city,' Bart said miserably.

'If you could borrow a carriage and take me to a hotel, I'd appreciate it.'

She went into the nursery and looked down at Sari sleeping in Bart's old crib. The tiny girl had become dear to her; she felt a wave of fiercely protective love wash over her. She whispered, 'We'll find a way, little one,' and bent to kiss the baby's petalsoft cheek.

The manager of Chicago's largest hotel looked with amazement at the young woman who insisted upon seeing him in his private office.

She was fashionably dressed, quietly confident, not pretty but possessed of classic features that would wear well. 'Are you a guest here, may I ask?'

'No, I'm not. I've been staying at a . . . much more modest establishment. I came to you because I believe your hotel could use my services.'

'Indeed?'

'You have a number of businessmen staying here, do you not? They are in town for various reasons, while their offices and clerks are in some other place. Wouldn't it be convenient for them if they had their offices and clerks along with them?'

'What exactly are you getting at, Miss Traherne?'

'I'm proposing that you install an office in the hotel. An amanuensis with a typewriter who would be available to write business letters, type orders, and perform other secretarial tasks for your guests. There would thus be no interruption in their work. They wouldn't have to wait until they returned home to carry on with their business.'

'You want the job yourself? Do you own a typewriter?'

'A friend does. He'll lend it to me until I've earned enough to buy one for myself. All I'd need is a room with a desk and a couple of chairs. You and I could work out an agreement whereby a percentage of the money I earn would go to the hotel, in addition to a rent payment, of course. I've brought a sample of my work for you to see.'

Joanna handed him several neatly typed letters. He read them carefully. She had made sure there were no typing errors and no spelling or grammatical mistakes.

She smiled as he stroked his upper lip thoughtfully. Joanna had learned that the hotel business was highly competitive, and she suspected that the extra service she offered could give this establishment an advantage over its rivals.

'We could try it for a while,' the manager said. 'See how it works out.'

'Good. I can start right away. I've already had a sign painted to hang on the door.'

'You were pretty certain I'd agree, weren't you?'

'I knew the manager of one of Chicago's hotels would. I just wasn't sure it would be the first one I approached.'

As she replaced her sample letters, she added matter-of-factly, 'By the way, I care for a baby. She's very good, hardly ever cries. She sleeps in a large basket, which I'll put in a corner of my office. She won't bother anyone, I assure you.'

She smiled, shook his hand, bade him good day, and disappeared before he could recover from his shock.

*　　*　　*

'It's the latest Remington,' Joanna said. 'Isn't it beautiful? Bart, I'm so grateful to you for letting me use your type-writer all these weeks while I saved money for this one.'

He rocked Sari in his arms and surveyed his neatly boxed typewriter gloomily. 'I suppose this means I won't get my articles typed anymore?'

'Of course I'll type an occasional article for you when you have a deadline to meet – but, Bart, you really should conquer your fear of that machine. Tell me, how do you like your new job?'

'A magazine is different from a newspaper. The writers sit around drinking coffee and smoking for most of the month. Then, the last few days before we have to get out an issue, all the office doors close and people begin pounding out stories. I guess I found it easier to cope with the daily deadlines of a paper.'

The baby gurgled happily as Bart held her up in the air. 'Are you still living with your parents?'

'Yes, but I'll be moving out the minute I get my first month's pay.'

'Bart, forgive me, but I have a report to type. You can put Sari on the rug.'

Bart looked at her wistfully. 'We're not friends anymore, are we? Not the way we used to be before that disastrous stay with Mater and Pater.'

'We're friends, Bart. But you must go now. I have get to get back to work.'

An hour later she finished the report, fed the baby, and put her down for her nap. She felt pleased with herself. Everything was going so well. She had so many clients she was considering hiring someone to assist her, and she had even managed to put a little money in the bank.

Realising that she had half an hour or so before her next appointment, she picked up an accumulation of news-papers and magazines and sat down to catch up on the news. At night after she closed the office and took care of the baby she usually preferred to relax with a novel or a book of poetry, ignoring newspapers and magazines, perhaps because she blamed the news stories for causing Magnus's death. But enough time had passed now that she was curious about what was going on in the world.

She flipped through one of the newspapers and was about to discard the sports page when she noticed a small item near the bottom of the last column. The headline read, 'Morgan's condition unchanged.'

Joanna gasped as she read the rest of the item: 'No improvement has been reported in the condition of boxing champion Max Morgan, who was beaten by unknown assailants after winning the championship bout in New York two months ago.'

43

Megan closed her medical bag and leaned against the Winton. Lonnie was asleep, his snoring blending with the nocturnal sounds of the desert – the scurrying of rabbits in the chaparral, the soft swoosh of an owl's wings overhead, the howling of coyotes on a distant ridge.

Lonnie wasn't badly hurt. The bullet had passed right through the fleshy part of his immense thigh. Chuck had done more damage with his shot. A bullet had lodged in the Chiricahua Kid's shoulder, shattering part of the bone. It had taken all of Megan's skill to remove it, and she feared that septicaemia might set in, given the length of time the bullet had remained in place and the poor light in which she was forced to work.

She had offered the Kid a little laudanum, but he refused it. Probably afraid he'd fall asleep, she decided. Instead of the laudanum he had taken a swig of whisky, clenched his jaw, and made no sound while she probed for the bullet. Afterward he slept for half an hour while Lonnie kept watch. Now, awake but exhausted, he lay on his side, his gun pointed at her.

'Why don't you put that gun down and rest?' she suggested, calm now. 'I'm not about to shoot you after going to all that trouble to cure you of lead poisoning.'

He fingered the bandage she'd made from her petticoat, then the rawhide strap cut from his saddlebags, which served to immobilise his right arm. 'You shot my compadre, senora.'

Megan glanced at the sleeping Lonnie. 'He would have raped me.'

'*Sí*. Now he will rape you *and* kill you, first chance.'

Just before Lonnie fell asleep he had inquired fretfully as to how they could get across the border in a rig without fuel. The Kid had replied that sooner or later riders would come this way. It wasn't necessary for him to elaborate. Megan knew what would happen to any unwary travellers.

Her own usefulness was over. She was still alive only because she had tended to their wounds; any gratitude they felt would be fleeting. She dared not recall the horror stories of the atrocities the two outlaws had committed.

The Kid suddenly pressed his ear to the ground and kicked at the sleeping Lonnie. 'Riders coming. Night riders no good. Maybe a posse. Tie her up. If there's too many of them, we bargain with her.'

Megan leapt to her feet to run, but Lonnie's long arm shot out and tripped her. She fell to the ground, and he twisted her arms viciously behind her back and tied her wrists with rope. Then, following the Kid's instructions, he fastened the rope to the door handle of the Winton so that she was forced to stand beside it. He pushed a vile-tasting kerchief into her mouth and tied another tightly around it.

The two men crawled behind the Winton, and she heard muttered instructions from the Kid and the sound of rifles being loaded.

Spread before her, the dry lake bed was silver in the moonlight. She stared across its barren surface, feeling naked, exposed, a lamb tethered to await the jaws of the wolf. She strained to hear the sound that had alerted the Kid, but in this predawn hour even the nocturnal animals were quiet and the silence of the desert was complete.

Then, in the distance, she heard, faintly, the thud of hooves and . . . She cocked her head to one side. Did she also hear wooden wheels grinding over the salt flats?

What would the approaching travellers see? A motorig with a woman standing beside it. They would have to be fairly close before they saw the gag in her mouth. They would assume the vehicle had broken down and her husband had gone to collect wood for a campfire. Since no one had ever heard of a bandit who rode in a horseless carriage, they would not expect to be waylaid by gunmen.

Megan tugged at her bonds, feeling the skin on her wrists bleed. She made futile mumbling sounds inside her gag.

The hoofbeats grew louder. Moving shadows materialised on the far side of the lake bed. She could make out a single horseman, followed by a pair of horses pulling a trap. Oh, they were doomed! They would be cut down before they ever realised the Chiricahua Kid lay in wait. The wounded outlaw probably believed Providence had given him this means of escape across the border.

But suddenly the rider wheeled off to the left, heading for a cluster of boulders, while the trap continued directly towards them. She heard the Kid mutter something in Spanish behind the car, followed by Lonnie's plaintive query, 'You see 'em, Kid? How many? Can I have the women, huh? Don't shoot the women, Kid.'

What could the driver of the trap be thinking about? Why hadn't he followed his outrider when he detoured away from the lake bed? But the horses pulling the trap were driven at a breakneck pace, and then, in the instant before the driver turned them to avoid running into the Winton, Megan saw the face of the man who held the reins.

Randolph! She could scarcely believe her eyes. The moonlight blanched his golden hair so that it appeared white, and that certain set of his head and squaring of his shoulders as he shook the reins, urging the horses forward, was unmistakably his. How many times she'd noticed that the upper part of his body seemed unusually strong, as if to compensate for his useless legs.

He was riding to his death and there was nothing she could do to stop him. She tugged harder at her bonds and heard her silent cry of warning ring inside her head. She raised her foot to pound with her heel against the side of the car in a futile attempt to warn him away.

Then Lonnie reared up over the cowl and the roar of his rifle shattered the night. There was the scream of a falling horse, a blurred flurry of dust and a flying shadow that must have been Randolph, and the trap went over.

For a moment there was silence, broken only by the creaking of one wheel of the trap as it continued to turn in diminishing revolutions. Then Lonnie cried, 'I got him, Kid. You see that? I got him.'

'Shut up and keep down,' the Kid croaked. 'What happened to the other one?'

Megan slumped against the car in shock. Oh, Randolph, what a brave, gallant, foolhardy gesture! To come after the most dangerous men in the territory, hampered by paralysed legs, riding in a trap that kept his hands occupied and therefore unable to use a gun! He'd come to her rescue with that same quiet courage she had witnessed when the ranch was attacked, the same stoicism he exhibited in his day-to-day living.

Two shots rang out in rapid succession. She heard them thud into the wooden cowl of the Winton.

Lonnie screamed. The other horseman must have managed to get around behind them while Randolph drew the outlaws' fire.

Then all was confusion. More shots, hooves pounding closer. Megan crouched as low and as close to the car as her bonds would allow. She squeezed her eyes shut, partly

370

to pray for deliverance, partly out of sheer unbridled terror.

For several minutes she felt as if she had fallen into a void. Sounds and movement registered vaguely, without form or meaning. She could think only of Randolph, wishing she had been kinder to him, wishing she could go back and undo the havoc she had wrought in his formerly ordered life.

Then hands touched the rope binding her and a voice said, 'You're all right now, ma'am. You're safe.' She recognised the toneless voice of Braddock, the ranch's most sinister hand.

The moment he freed her, she raced towards the fallen trap. Both horses were now back on their feet. Searching the shadows frantically, she saw the crumpled figure of a man lying face down beside a clump of mesquite. He was very still.

44

The train hurtled towards New York, and as the wheels ground over the steel tracks Joanna's thoughts tossed her back and forth between anguish at the thought that Magnus must believe she had abandoned him, worry about the extent of his injuries, and anger at Bart's perfidy.

Immediately after reading the item about Magnus on the sports page of the newspaper, she had gathered up the baby and gone to the offices of the magazine where Bart worked. Their confrontation had been brief but illuminating.

'Why did you lie to me?' she had demanded.

Bart, seated behind a cluttered desk, an overflowing wastepaper basket at his feet and a blank sheet of paper in his typewriter, looked up at her in surprise. 'Jo, what –'

'You told me Magnus was dead.'

All the life seemed to drain from him. His gnome's body shrank still lower in his chair as his face crumpled into woebegone lines. 'Jo, you've got to believe this, because I swear it's the gospel truth. The doctor said he wouldn't last through the night. His head had been beaten to a pulp, and they didn't think he'd regain consciousness.'

'You kept me from going to him –'

'He wouldn't have known you were there, but the press would. They'd have put you through the wringers of hell.'

'You had no right to decide that. Bart, I will never forgive you for this. We stayed in your New York apartment for weeks. In all that time you never once hinted that Magnus was still alive.'

'I thought it was best.'

'For whom? Certainly not for Magnus or me.'

'Don't go back to him, Jo. Please, I'm begging you. He'll bring you nothing but trouble. He's no good for you.'

She had stormed away then, too disgusted with him to spend another moment in his presence.

Now as she stared out of the train window, the long journey to New York stretched interminably before her, as flat and empty as the endless vistas of the Midwest.

Sari awakened and cooed at her. Tiny fingers curled trustingly around hers. Joanna looked down at the baby in her arms, a warm glow of love flowing through her, able in that one moment to put aside both bitterness and anguish.

E. B. Duggenbrand gave Joanna a contemptuous glance and said, 'Last I heard, he was in the charity ward. Seems all his money, including the purse from the big fight, vanished along with his mulatto mistress and his manager. Isn't it a bit late for you to come down with a case of conscience about him now? And if you've come to sell me the story of your romance, you're too late for that too. Max Morgan is no longer news, and neither is Princess Natalie.'

Having braved the stares and whispers of the reporters in the city room of the *Chronicle*, Joanna thought that entering the charity hospital would be less of an ordeal, despite her anxiety about Magnus, but the moment she set foot in the dismal barrackslike building her spirits sank to their lowest ebb. Despair seemed to permeate the drab wards, and hope had clearly long departed from the hearts and souls of the pathetic patients.

A matron, girded into her starched apron like a suit of armour, glanced at Joanna with disinterest. 'Max Morgan, the boxer? Ward six, seventh bed on the left.' Joanna had to find her own way.

Avoiding looking at the scarred walls, the filthy floor, and the emaciated men, she walked to the seventh bed. A very old man slept in it. She continued along the length of the ward searching for Magnus.

Some of the patients lay two to a narrow bed, others thrashed feebly amid grey and threadbare blankets. One man, she saw to her horror, had expired. She fled back to the armoured matron, whose deep sigh conveyed clearly how irritated she was at the interruption. 'Oh, yes. I forgot. Morgan is with the mental patients now, waiting to go to the asylum.'

Joanna felt her blood turn to ice.

This time the matron accompanied her to a ground-floor room with a heavily locked and barred door. She summoned a burly male orderly to take Joanna inside.

It was, Joanna decided, like stepping through the gates of hell. She knew she would never forget the old man systematically banging his head against the wall, or the youth who sat screaming in a corner, plucking at his tattered clothes as though they were alive with insects. Others muttered, mumbled, sobbed, clutched themselves, jerked their bodies convulsively, lay curled on the floor in the fetal position, or simply stared glassy-eyed at the padded walls. One man was pulling clumps of hair from his head, another was pummelling his companion, who appeared oblivious of the blows.

Had they been like this when they arrived? Surely not, or they would have gone directly to the asylum. There were no more than a dozen men here, yet surely Bedlam itself contained no wider range of madness.

'He's over there, by the window,' the orderly said, shoving a wild-eyed old man out of the way.

The light from the barred window behind Magnus momentarily blinded Joanna, whose eyes had grown accustomed to the gloom of the wards, and he appeared as a silhouette, sitting peacefully on a straight-backed wooden chair. His arms were at his sides and his feet were placed exactly in front of the chair legs. He was so still, Joanna thought, that he might have been cast in stone. Then she saw that his wrists and ankles were manacled to the chair.

Outraged, she turned to the orderly, but before she could speak he warned, 'Don't get too close to him. He's been known to break free of his shackles and strike out at anybody in reach.'

Ignoring him, Joanna hurried to Magnus's side. As she approached, his brilliant blue eyes met hers without a glimmer of recognition. His nose had been broken again, and a myriad of cuts and bruises had not yet healed.

'Magnus, my darling,' Joanna murmured, placing her hand gently on his shoulder.

His eyes seemed to focus on her face and his lips moved, but he made no sound. She bent and kissed his bruised lips. 'It's me. Joanna. I've come to take you away from here.'

A slow smile lit up his face and for an instant Joanna thought that he recognised her. She thanked God that he was all right and assumed that it was this dreadful place that had caused him to act deranged.

But then she realised that the glazed look in his eyes remained and still he didn't speak. His smile was like that of a baby who experienced pleasure from his mother's touch without comprehending all that it implied.

'Oh, dear God,' Joanna said aloud. 'He doesn't know me.'

'He don't know *nobody*,' the orderly said. 'I seen a lot of fighters get punch-drunk, some worse'n others. Some of 'em just get a bit befuddled and don't think too clear or talk too straight. More'n likely old Max here had taken too many blows to the head before he ever got beat by that gang of thugs. They finished him off, you might say. His brain don't work no more.'

Joanna distractedly stroked Magnus's cheek, smoothed his shaggy hair back from his brow. He continued to smile even as he stared vacantly at her. Not one word passed from his lips.

One of the other patients approached silently and, before either the orderly or Joanna could intervene, spat on Magnus. He still didn't react.

Feeling tears well up in her eyes, Joanna wiped the spittle from his face with her handkerchief and said to the orderly, 'Please take me to whomever I must see to get him released.'

'You're wasting your time. Max here's already been committed to the asylum.'

'He's leaving with me,' Joanna answered, 'no matter what I have to do to get him out of here.'

She sat on a hard chair in a drafty office until the chief of staff could spare the time to talk to her. After a two-hour wait she was informed he had left the premises and she would have to return the following morning.

Reluctantly she made her way out of the building, hating to leave Magnus behind but anxious to return to her hotel, where she had left Sari in the care of one of the permanent residents who had been recommended by the manager.

The moment she set foot on the street she was accosted by a tall, portly man who appeared to have been waiting for her. 'I'd like to have a word with you, miss.'

She felt a flicker of fear. This was not a choice

neighbourhood, and as the dinner hour approached, there were few other people about.

'You are Miss Joanna Traherne, are you not? You've led me on a merry chase, I can tell you. Probably never would have found you if you hadn't gone to the *Chronicle* today. Please don't be frightened. I'm with the Pinkerton Detective Agency.'

She recalled Bart telling her that a detective had been looking for her. 'Surely you aren't going to dredge up a scandal involving myself and Mag – Max Morgan now?'

'No, ma'am. My assignment was only to find you and let you know that Mr Randolph Mallory would very much like to have you visit him in New Mexico. I'm instructed to place at your disposal whatever funds you need.'

Delta smoothed the delicate silk nightgown over her slim hips and moved one shoulder so that the narrow strap slipped, revealing one softly rounded breast. Her body was almost as perfect as it had been before the birth of the baby – only a few silvery lines on her abdomen hinted that she was a mother.

She certainly didn't feel like a mother. The infant belonged to Magnus. There had never been any doubt in Delta's mind about that, because he was the only man with whom she had not practised birth control. But Magnus had rejected her for another woman. Therefore Delta owed nothing either to him or to his child. Besides, a baby required a great deal of time and work and at present Delta needed to concentrate on the unexpected development in her life. Perhaps some time in the future when Sari was older . . .

Delta touched the glass stopper of a perfume bottle to her hair and to her throat, then lightly pressed it to the cleavage between her breasts. Slowly she raised the nightgown and perfumed her inner thighs. Smiling, unhurried, she used the crystal stopper with sensual pleasure, pausing to inhale the delicate sandalwood fragrance, fully aware of the effect she was having on the man watching her.

Turning from her dressing table, she took a bottle of champagne from the ice bucket and smiled at the man lying on the bed.

He was no longer young, but she found his fierce hawk-like features compelling and there was no doubt that he was as virile as he had ever been. More than that, he reeked of old money, rank, power.

'I'm still surprised that you found me,' she said as she filled a glass with the sparkling champagne.

'Your sulky maid in Cornwall, Lizzie, told me you'd gone to America. She was happy to relate all she knew, including the fact that Magnus had accompanied you. I came to New York, city of immigrants, and searched for you. Of course I was unsuccessful for months, but I persisted, wild for you, needing you as no man ever needed a woman before. Then suddenly the newspapers were filled with stories of the prizefighter Max Morgan and his beautiful mulatto mistress.'

The viscount accepted the glass she offered him and raised it in a toast. 'To you, my beautiful one. To our reunion. To the rest of our lives together.'

Delta sat on the edge of the bed, her gaze still inviting, but speculative. 'But what about your wife?'

His fingers closed around her wrist, gripping it painfully. 'Listen to me carefully, Delta. I have given up my wife and my home – my entire way of life – for you. That's how thoroughly you have enslaved me. I couldn't exist without you. How very clever of you to leave me, because I didn't know how much I needed you until you were gone. When you left, I was shattered. I stormed about like a madman, unable to think of anything but how to get you back. I knew then that I had to have you, to keep you with me always, no matter what.'

She shivered, partly with excitement at learning the true power of her hold over him, and partly with intuitive fear that this could not be easily discarded.

He went on, 'My wife and family believe I am dead. A victim of a storm tide and a reckless attempt to sail through

377

the suicide gap. My boat was found wrecked on the rocks, articles of my clothing floating in the cove.'

'But if you gave up everything' – Delta's fingers played lightly along the taut muscles of his abdomen – 'then how can we possibly go to the Lahamas to live?'

'You may rest your mercenary little mind in that regard. Before I planned my untimely death I transferred certain assets abroad in such a way that they cannot be traced. You will be able to live in luxury, my sweet' – he paused, his penetrating stare momentarily unnerving her – 'as long as you are faithful to me.'

To mask the twinge of fear she felt, she leaned closer, blew the foam from his champagne so that the bubbles sprayed his chest; then she bent to lap them up. He caught her long hair in his fist and held her to him.

She smiled then, feeling the intensity of his need, thrilled by the power she wielded over him. 'Yes, my darling, we shall go to the Bahamas and make love in the sun.' She reached down to caress his erect member, murmuring, 'I'm ready to leave with you. There's nothing to keep me here.'

As she spoke her mouth moved slowly in the direction of her fondling hand and although he sighed with pleasure he added harshly, 'Give me your word that you'll be faithful. Don't give it lightly, because if I find you with another man, I shall kill you.'

Teasing him with her lips, her silky hair falling about his thighs and causing him to throb with desire, she murmured, 'But, darling, of course I'll be faithful. Just so long as you keep me in luxury. I never want to be poor again.'

'The baby you had,' he continued hoarsely. 'I don't want children, especially not one you had with another man. You swear you've given her up for good?'

'Yes, yes. Hush, now, while I make love to you. Haven't you waited long enough?'

Her tongue flicked playfully, while her hands stroked him. She would keep him on the brink, the very edge of climax, until he agreed to her own conditions for their future. He had stated his terms; now he would agree to hers. The Viscount was going to provide for her future, her entire future, before she tired of him and moved on to another man. This time she had him exactly where she wanted him and he would pay, handsomely, in advance of their living together. What fools men were, how easily deceived, such slaves to the dark gods of their loins.

He was built magnificently. Not even Magnus had a more impressive organ and heaven knew Magnus was as perfectly formed as a Greek god. Delta could feel the Viscount's passion building, and she carefully slowed him down by plunging her fingertips into the cold champagne and gently touching his chest and thighs and the tip of his manhood.

She paused in order to peel off her nightgown, and he caught his breath as he looked up at her body. She was proud of the fact that childbirth had changed her so little. For a moment she swayed from side to side in the cobra dance that she had learned long ago in Martinique from a most accomplished lover. As she moved, she touched herself, calling his attention to the delights she had in store for him.

He groaned and called her name and it was a primitive cry of need that transcended reason. She lowered herself onto him and began to move in langorous circles.

'Before we sail for the Bahamas, my darling,' she whispered huskily, as her body quivered over his, 'I shall need a large sum of money.'

He gasped, his hands clutching her breasts as she rode him. 'Yes, yes, all right. I want you to buy clothes. Ah, sweet, sweet . . .'

'Jewellery, too. Lots of jewels.'

He nodded, too much a captive of his senses to speak, his body rising to meet hers, his eyes half closed in ecstasy. She lost herself in the frenzy of her own climax then, pinching him to prevent his.

She collapsed on him, tremors rippling through her body. 'I shall need cash in the bank also.'

'Yes . . . don't . . . pull away –'

'My dear . . . we've barely begun.'

45

Megan gently turned Randolph over and cradled his head in her arms. His eyes were closed, and he was bleeding profusely from a cut on his forehead.

Quickly she ran her fingers over his scalp, neck, shoulders, seeking bullet wounds. She laid him down and felt his chest and arms, peered at his clothing for signs of blood. She felt a faint heartbeat, but she was terrified that he was seriously hurt, that he might not regain consciousness.

One of his trouser legs had ripped open on a clump of cholla, exposing most of his lower thigh, knee, and calf. Even in the pale light of the moon she saw the cruel scars on his atrophied leg, mute evidence of the irreparable damage that had been done in the accident that killed his parents. He had told her that his legs were crushed, and he had not lied. And when she asked to see the scars he said there were none simply because he couldn't bear to show her how badly he'd been hurt.

It was more than she could stand. She bent to press her lips to the withered flesh, tears scalding her face.

'Megan . . .' Randolph's voice whispered. 'Don't . . . please. I'm all right. I haven't been shot. I think I hit my head on a rock when we went over.'

She raised her head to look at him, unable to believe

that he had been spared – or that she had been given a second chance to right so many wrongs.

'Randolph, oh, thank God!'

For an instant she pressed her cheek to his chest and hugged him. Then she straightened up and tore a strip from what was left of her petticoat. 'Lie still. I must bandage your head.'

A shadow fell across the ground beside her and a voice over her head said, 'I'll set the trap upright. The Chiricahua Kid and his sidekick won't be doing no more looting or murdering.'

Megan looked up at Braddock. 'Thank you for saving my life.'

He shrugged. 'Your husband took all the risks. I just shot straight.'

Megan insisted that Randolph stay in bed for a few days, although he protested that the cut on his head – which she sutured with such care that he suggested with a grin he would be deprived of a fine conversational scar – did not warrant such coddling.

'I'm going to wait on you hand and foot,' Megan responded. 'I shall cook all your meals – I'm actually not a bad cook – and from now on I will bathe you and help you and do all the things Chuck used to do for you.'

She paused. 'I'm sorry about Chuck. He and I didn't get along very well, but I know what he meant to you. He died a hero's death, trying to save me.'

Randolph held out his hand to her, and she slipped her fingers into his, agonisingly aware that any day now Quinn would return from Santa Fe and they would have to tell Randolph they loved each other and wanted to be married.

She said breathlessly, 'Have I truly expressed to you how much I admire you – what a hero you are?'

Randolph smiled. 'Yes, many times.'

'To come riding gallantly to my rescue like that, with only one man. Why didn't you bring more of the hands? Better still, the army or a posse of lawmen?'

'Tex saw the tracks of only two men near Chuck's body. I thought we'd be more likely to get close if we appeared to be harmless travellers. In the past the Kid easily dodged both army patrols and large posses. Besides, I suspect that Braddock was once a more dangerous desperado even than the Chiricahua Kid. He certainly proved to be more than a match for him, didn't he?'

'Why did Braddock immediately pack up and leave the ranch?' she asked. 'He seemed almost angered by our gratitude.'

Randolph considered for a moment. 'He probably came to work for us because he wanted to retire from his former profession; that's not easy for a gunfighter. But when the word got out that he had killed the Kid, Braddock knew he would become a target not only for lawmen interested in his past but also for every young gunman wanting to make a name for himself by drawing against the man who killed the Chiricahua Kid.'

'Still, knowing that, he rode out with you.' Megan sighed. 'I do hope he finds peace somewhere.'

Randolph smiled. 'I daresay the bonus I paid him will help. By the way, I've made Tex foreman.'

'Good choice. I hope he doesn't pick on poor Wyatt the way Chuck used to. I saw Wyatt a little while ago, looking more bedraggled than ever, but whistling as he rode out. He's such a happy soul, I always feel uplifted when I see him. What do you suppose he does with all his money? He certainly doesn't spend it on himself. His shirt was so faded I couldn't tell what colour it was supposed to be and he'd cut his own hair again.'

'I'll let you in on a little secret,' Randolph said. 'When Chuck came to me complaining that you'd interfered with his order to Wyatt to buy himself some decent clothes or not go into town, I sent for Wyatt and we had a private little chat. I finally got him to tell me why he's so miserly. Wyatt sends every penny of his pay to a girl in Wyoming. As soon as she has enough to buy herself a wedding gown and a train ticket to New Mexico, they plan to get married.'

'Oh, how very touching and romantic!' Megan exclaimed. 'Why don't we buy Wyatt some clothes?'

'No, we can't do that. It would hurt his pride. He'd consider it charity.'

Megan thought about the problem for a moment. 'What about Chuck's clothes? Consuela is an excellent seamstress. We could ask her to cut down some of his shirts to fit Wyatt.'

'Good idea. Why don't you ask her?'

'I must run to the kitchen. I have a pie in the oven.'

'You'll be making Consuela feel unwanted, but I must admit I'm enjoying your cooking.'

Megan had just put the pie out to cool when Consuela came to tell her that a carriage was approaching the house.

Slipping off her apron, Megan went to the front door just in time to see Lallie's green lacquered carriage arrive. Resplendent in emerald satin with a dyed-to-match feather boa, Lallie swept up the driveway and hugged Megan.

'We heard what happened . . . Thank God you're safe. I reckon I shouldn'ta come, but I had to see for myself you were all right.'

'Come in,' Megan said. 'Let me make you a cup of tea.'

'But your husband –'

'He won't mind. Besides, he's in bed.'

They went into the kitchen and Megan put the kettle on while Lallie peppered her with questions about her ordeal. She wasn't satisfied until she'd heard every detail.

'What about Quinn? How come he left you at the Simmonds place after the ball for the Penningtons?' Lallie asked, sipping her tea.

'He had to go to Santa Fe to sell his copper mine. He'll be back shortly.'

Lallie gave her a shrewd glance, but made no further comment. After a moment she said, 'I feel so sorry for Josh Pennington.'

Puzzled, Megan said, 'Why? Did he lose the election?'

'No, honey. He lost his wife. I guess she hadn't told

383

anybody she'd already made the arrangements to have that operation the day after the ball.'

'She had her ovaries removed?' Megan asked, aghast.

Lallie nodded. 'I heard tell she died on the operating table.'

'Damn,' Megan said. 'Damn, damn, *damn*.'

The following morning Megan went into Manzanita Flats and made her way to Dr Sedgewick's office. She had not spent any time with him since before the ball and hoped he had not neglected the practice they had steadily been building. At first the townspeople had been reluctant to trust Sedge, knowing his history, and many patients, particularly the women, made a point of visiting his surgery only when Megan was present. But new settlers were flooding the territory and, knowing nothing of his tarnished past, they accepted Dr Sedgewick unquestioningly.

Two miners lounged on the boardwalk beneath the doctor's shingle and as she approached, one of them said, 'If you're looking for the doc, he ain't here, ma'am.'

'I expect he's out visiting a patient, then,' Megan said, fumbling in her pocket for her key to the office. 'Would you step aside, please? I must go inside.'

'Wouldn't go in there, if I was you,' one of the men said. 'Doc went on a rampage and smashed everything before he left.'

'What?' Megan had already turned the key in the lock and pushed open the door. The furniture, equipment, all of their bottles and jars of medicine and lotion – everything lay broken and splintered on the floor, swathed with unrolled bandages.

An overpowering smell of ether rose from the debris, and two sedated mice lay on their backs, feet straight up in the air. A bag of plaster of Paris had burst, covering the devastation with a white film of dust.

Megan stared for a moment speechlessly, then whispered, more to herself than to anyone else, 'But why, why?'

'A drunk don't need no reason why,' one of the miners volunteered. 'Once they fall off the wagon, ain't no telling what they'll do. Hell, they don't even know what they're doing themselves most of the time, and sure as hell don't remember afterwards. Old Doc just up and smashed all his stuff and rode out of town yelling something about getting hisself another wagon on account of he wanted to go travelling again.'

Not wanting to return to the ranch to tell Randolph what Sedge had done, Megan locked the office and walked slowly down the street. Someone in town had invested a great deal of money in setting up the office and surgery for Sedge. She wondered who. Damn the man for his irresponsibility. She felt personally betrayed.

As she reached the gaudy façade of the Jade Palace, Mr Chang emerged and, on impulse, she said, 'Good morning. Is Miss Lallie up and about yet?'

Bowing, he turned and gestured to the ornate doors behind him.

Megan hesitated, then decided that it was a little late for her to start worrying about what people would think. She went inside.

'Why, Miz Mallory, it sure is nice to see you,' a soft female voice said.

'Good morning, Becky, how well you look!' Megan felt some of her anger at Sedge dissipate at the sight of the young woman who had nearly died of appendicitis. Becky was now the picture of health, her step sprightly and her eyes bright, despite the early hour.

Although Megan felt revulsion at the services performed by the women of the Jade Palace, she had found that most of them were either somewhat dull-witted or had been convinced by their life experiences that prostitution was their only recourse, and her revulsion was tinged with pity. She wondered if one day Dr Freud or one of his students would study the problem of women who chose such a degrading way of life. To Becky she said, 'I'm looking for Lallie.'

'She's having breakfast,' Becky answered, pointing towards the dining room. 'Go right on in. You're always welcome here, Miz Mallory.'

Megan found Lallie eating an enormous plateful of eggs and fried potatoes. She was clad in an ostrich-trimmed peignoir, traces of last night's face paint marring her complexion, and she blinked in surprise as Megan made her way to her table.

'Honey, you'll have tongues wagging again if anybody saw you come in here. Still, too late now – might as well sit down and eat.'

Megan took a chair. 'No, thank you, I've had breakfast. But I'd like a cup of coffee. Lallie, you know everything that goes on and I'm sure you're aware that Dr Sedgewick has left town after wrecking his surgery. I was wondering if you knew who his financial backer was. I'm hoping to find a way to make restitution.'

Lallie delicately wiped her lips with a napkin and answered offhandedly, 'Forget it, honey. The Jade Palace is making me rich. I don't need the money.'

'*You* put up the money?' Megan swallowed a sip of coffee along with her surprise.

'Sure. Sedge and me kept it quiet on account of we figured the good folks of Manzanita Flats wouldn't patronise a doc who was financed by the likes of me.' Lallie gave her a calculating glance. 'But if you really want to – what did you call it? – make resti . . . resti –'

'Restitution,' Megan finished for her.

'Yeah . . . that means paying me back, right? If you want to do that, then you can take over Sedge's practice. This town sure needs a doctor.'

'I'd love to, Lallie, but it's impossible.' Megan rose to her feet. 'I must get back to the ranch. Thank you for the coffee.'

Megan had driven the trap into town herself, and on the way back she passed several buckboards and carriages on what was formerly merely a trail marked by wagon-wheel ruts. More and more settlers were moving in every day,

386

and now that the Chiricahua Kid no longer menaced the territory it wasn't necessary for her to be accompanied by one of the hands when she travelled about.

Randolph had dispatched Tex to retrieve the Winton, which Tex insisted would be pulled by his horse since he wasn't about to attempt to drive the durned thing. Megan would have loved to drive it herself, but didn't suggest it. It was one thing to be forced to drive that night in peril of her life, but no doubt a woman driver would be as unacceptable as a woman doctor. How tiresome it was to be so shackled by convention.

When she arrived back at the ranch, Randolph listened sympathetically as she told him of Sedge's fall from grace. 'I wondered how long he'd last. I think there must be some sort of inborn flaw in the men who let alcohol rule their lives. I'm sorry, Megan. This means you've lost your last link to the world of medicine, doesn't it?'

'Well, there's still my father in Galveston, but he isn't practising conventional medicine any longer. He's deeply involved with Dr Freud's treatment of mental disorders.'

Randolph decided that he'd had enough of lying in bed and the following morning asked Megan to help him dress and get into his wheelchair. He actually needed very little assistance, and Megan adopted a matter-of-fact attitude that soon eased any embarrassment he felt.

As the days passed, Megan began to count the minutes until Quinn returned. As she awoke each morning her first thought was to wonder whether he was close. She felt a thrill of happiness at the prospect of being reunited with him, now that they had both made promises and plans for the future.

Toward the end of the week Consuela came to her one morning to tell her, in a mixture of Spanish and English with many gestures, that one of the ranch hands was ill.

Megan hurried out to the bunkhouse.

Tex met her at the door. 'Consuela shouldn't have bothered you, ma'am. I reckon she's like everybody else around her. She's so fond of young Wyatt that she spoils him. Ma'am, he ain't sick. He's just got the granddaddy of all hangovers.'

'Oh,' Megan said. 'You're sure?'

'Yep, he's just hungover from a night on the town, ma'am.'

'I find it hard to believe Wyatt got so drunk. He never goes into town other than to go to the Western Union office to send money to his fiancée.'

'Well, ma'am, that's the whole problem . . . That's why he went on a big drunk in the first place. See, he got a letter from his girl . . . She ain't coming. She up and married somebody else back home in Wyoming.'

'Oh, no!' Megan said, deeply saddened. How very cruel people could be. A sudden image of Quinn riding back from Santa Fe to tell Randolph of their love for each other leapt into her mind. Wouldn't that be just as cruel – perhaps even more so? She had to get back to the main house in case Quinn arrived, keep watch for him and tell him . . . what? The lines of tension returned to her brow. Oh, please, she prayed, let there be a way for Quinn and me to be together without hurting Randolph.

Tex was watching her, his expression concerned. 'Don't worry about young Wyatt, ma'am. He'll get over it. We all do.'

She wasn't sure if he meant lost love or the hangover. 'Well, since I'm here, I might as well take a look at him. At least let him know we care about him.'

'He just don't want to work today, Miz Mallory, but I think it would be the best thing he could do.'

The young cowboy's groans became louder as she approached, and he thrashed about the bed dramatically. His distress seemed almost as comical as his jigs and concertina recitals.

'Where do you hurt, Wyatt?' she asked.

'Terrible pains in my head, ma'am.' He clapped one hand to his forehead. 'And in my eyes, too.'

'Nausea? Vomiting?'

'Oh, yes, ma'am. Something fierce.'

'Lie on your back,' she instructed, already convinced

Tex was right and the young hand was malingering, but prepared to check to see if she had come upon another case of appendicitis.

Wyatt didn't wince as she probed his abdomen, but continued to roll his head back and forth.

'I think you'll be all right if you sleep a little longer, Wyatt,' Megan said, ignoring Tex's scowl. 'Then drink several cups of black coffee.'

She patted his hand before she left and murmured, 'I'm so sorry to hear your girl jilted you, but a nice young man like you will soon find someone else.'

Wyatt gave several more piteous moans as she walked away.

Megan prowled restlessly about the house the rest of the morning, changed her gown three times to try to determine which was the most fetching, pinched her cheeks to bring colour to her face. If Quinn didn't come soon, she thought, she would be a quivering mass of nerves.

They had just finished lunch and Consuela was clearing away the dishes when she paused, glancing out of the window. 'Carriage coming,' she said.

Megan's heart leapt, but a moment later she realised Quinn would have come riding up; he wouldn't be in a carriage. 'I wonder who it could be?' She rose and went to the window herself.

For a split second she peered nearsightedly at the woman being helped down by the driver. She was dressed in a smart linen travel suit, wearing a hat with a jaunty feather and a wisp of veil. Only when she walked towards the house, carrying herself with easy grace, did Megan realise who their visitor was. She blinked, wondering if she could be dreaming, then pinched herself. No, she was definitely awake.

Then she was running for the door, crying over her shoulder to Randolph, 'It's Joanna! Joanna is here. She's alive; she's here!'

46

For several minutes Joanna hugged Megan, wept with her, marvelled that they had been reunited at last, expressed astonishment that they should meet again so far from home.

She held her friend at arm's length and looked at her. Megan had changed in appearance not at all, she decided. Her glorious auburn hair was as usual slightly untidy, her lovely face vivacious, her green eyes lit with tiny gold lamps that could flash with angry fire or express a wide range of other emotions so vividly.

Megan wore a forest-green gown with a row of tiny buttons down the bodice, but she had missed one of them, throwing all the rest out of sequence. Still, despite her careless appearance, she was so beautiful that Joanna wondered if perhaps the mismatched buttons and tousled hair simply made her appear more approachable, thus adding to her charm.

Her face tear-streaked, Megan said, 'We thought you were dead . . . Jo, what *happened* to you?'

Joanna, who had as yet seen little beyond the totally unexpected vision of her friend, suddenly became aware of the man who sat in a bath chair under a Spanish-style archway on the far side of the tiled entry hall. Her reply to Megan's questions – she had been about to say that it was a long story – faded from her mind before it was uttered.

The afternoon sunlight, slanting in through a narrow window in the thick adobe wall, gilded a head of golden hair framing the most handsome features Joanna had ever seen. Apollo on Olympus could not have captivated her more, in spite of the fact that the man in the bath chair wore a bandage around his forehead. He was regarding her with a warm smile, quietly waiting for her to finish greeting Megan.

As his eyes met hers, Joanna felt as though every question she had ever asked about her life was being answered. Her gaze dropped briefly to his hands, folded on top of the blanket covering his lap. Beautiful hands, with long tapered fingers. She could imagine those hands holding a pen, writing long letters to her; she could picture those sensitive eyes glancing up, seeking exactly the right word, the right phrase to convey what was in his heart. She knew before he spoke, before she even wondered about those blanket-wrapped legs and the use of the bath chair, that this was Randolph; this was the man she had always been destined to meet.

Beside her Megan was explaining, in almost the same words Joanna had been going to use for her own recital of what had happened in Cornwall, 'Jo, it's a long story and we'll tell you everything later, but briefly, the man who came to Adele's wedding was Randolph's friend, John McQuinn. This is Randolph Mallory, your distant cousin, with whom you corresponded.'

'Yes,' Joanna said softly, 'I know. I believe I would have known you wherever we met, under whatever circumstances.' She crossed the room to him and they reached out simultaneously to clasp hands.

Randolph said, 'I've waited for this moment for so long, Joanna, that even now that I see you standing here, I'm not quite sure you're real.'

At that moment Consuela came into the hall and said to Megan, '*Excusar*, Señora Mallory, I make ready room for the *señorita, sí?*'

For a second, listening to Megan indicate which room was to be prepared for her, Joanna did not realise the implications of Megan's presence here, her instructions to

391

the maid, or the fact that she had been addressed as Señora Mallory.

Then the full realisation struck her like a physical blow. In that split second she was back at Traherne Hall on the day her beautiful half sister had married Oliver Pentreath. Joanna fought to maintain her composure as Randolph said, 'Consuela will take you to your room, Joanna. After you've had a chance to rest, we can talk.'

Megan had recognised Joanna's look of dismay and guessed the reason for it instantly. When Consuela showed her to her room, Megan followed, carefully closing the door behind her.

'Jo . . . I am going to ask Randolph for an annulment of the marriage the moment Quinn returns. We're in love, Quinn and I, and . . . oh, please don't look at me like that. I truly believed you were dead.'

'That doesn't explain why you married Randolph if you love the man you call Quinn.'

The chill in Joanna's voice momentarily took Megan aback. Never, in the entire time they had been friends, had she ever heard Joanna use such a tone to anyone, not even the humblest servant in her parents' home. It was simply not in her nature to chastise anyone.

'No, it doesn't,' Megan responded, feeling guiltier than ever. 'But perhaps when I tell you that your parents were about to have me charged with murdering you as a result of an illegal operation, you'll understand the desperate situation in which I found myself.'

'Oh, my God, Meg! How dreadful for you! I had no idea.' Joanna removed her hat pins and placed her hat on the dressing table, her movements graceful and unhurried. 'Perhaps you and I should have a long talk before we rejoin Randolph. I have a couple of rather startling revelations of my own to make.'

Two hours later, when Consuela knocked on the door to announce that Randolph would like them to join him for tea, Megan had told Joanna almost all that had happened to her since the day of Adele and Oliver's wedding.

Joanna had listened quietly, mentioning only her father's death and the fact that the Traherne housekeeper had performed the abortion.

They had been sitting side by side on the bed and now Megan rose and, glancing at the clock on the mantel, said, 'Randolph will think we're terribly inconsiderate. We'd better go to him.'

Randolph sat in the atrium next to the tiled fountain, and Joanna exclaimed in delight over the bright-coloured vines and clay pots trailing flowers and remarked at how cool the sound of the running water was and how different the way of life seemed here in the West compared to the teeming cities of the East.

'You speak the same way you write,' Randolph said, 'with such wonder and awe and curiosity about everything you encounter.' He paused. 'In some indefinable way, you even look the way you write. Shy, yet eager, vulnerable yet resourceful.'

The comment was so intensely personal that Megan felt like an intruder. Randolph and Joanna appeared to be unaware that they were looking at each other like intimate friends who were all alone. When Randolph finished speaking, Joanna glanced at Megan. She knew her friend was wondering why Randolph hadn't known immediately that she was an impostor. They were, after all, so completely different from each other.

Megan pulled a chair over to the shady side of the atrium to protect her fair complexion from the sun, a habit acquired after seeing the ravages the sun had caused to her father's skin. Joanna sat on the edge of the fountain and raised her face to the bright sky like a flower seeking the life-giving warmth and light. Why, she belongs here in a way I never would, Megan thought. She even has the right colouring, a complexion tawny enough to resist the sun's burning rays.

'I was so surprised when the detective you hired tracked

me down,' Joanna said. 'Especially after that rather cold telegram you sent to me earlier.'

'I'm sorry,' Randolph replied. 'I thought your telegram was from Megan. Has she told you –'

'Yes. There's something I must tell you both right away. I can't remain here with you.'

They both interrupted with protests and at length Joanna raised her hand. 'Please! Let me explain. I must go back to a boarding house in Manzanita Flats. There are two people there who are depending on me.'

Megan and Randolph waited expectantly.

Joanna looked from one to the other. 'I have a baby to care for . . . two babies, really. Let me explain . . .'

Magnus cradled the baby in his arms and rocked her gently back and forth. He had been afraid of hurting her at first, but Joanna had assured him that if he was very careful with Sari she wouldn't break.

To his surprise, handling the baby seemed to come naturally to him, as if he'd done it before. Perhaps he had. He couldn't remember. There was a great deal he couldn't remember.

Joanna seemed to be someone he'd known once, but he couldn't be sure. Before she came there was a terrible place filled with men who hit and kicked him, spat and cursed at him, and when he defended himself, they chained him to a bed or a chair. Joanna was so kind to him that his one fear was that she would leave him. But she said she wouldn't. He thought she truly meant that.

He liked this place where she'd brought him. It was quiet, peaceful, and nice and warm. There weren't many people about. The man with golden hair who couldn't walk, the very pretty lady who smiled a lot, another dark-haired woman who spoke a foreign language, and the men who worked outside with the horses and cows. He couldn't remember their names. He liked the animals – horses and cows and goats and chickens. A man named Tex was in charge, and he let Magnus feed the goats and chickens.

He liked the trees and flowers, too, and the way the birds sang in the morning. He often took the baby down by the river. She seemed to like to hear the sound of water running over the pebbles, just as he did.

'Can we stay here, Joanna?' he asked on the second day after they came to the ranch. 'Sari likes it here, I think.'

Joanna had given him that same strange look she gave him sometimes. Vague memories had stirred, but like the half-remembered images from a dream, they refused to take shape. She had leaned close and kissed his cheek. She smelled so sweet. 'Perhaps we'll stay, Magnus. We'll see.'

He did remember travelling on the train with Joanna and Sari. It was a very long journey. They stopped off a couple of times. Joanna had been very sad then; she wasn't so unhappy anymore. But on the train he had often looked up to see her watching him with tears in her eyes.

The man in the wheelchair was called Randolph. He had kind eyes and a soft voice, and he was very patient, like Joanna. He didn't interrupt or finish off what Magnus was trying to say, or prod and poke him when he couldn't get out the words fast enough, as the men back in that terrible dark place had done. But best of all were the times when they let him take care of the baby. Little Sari didn't talk at all and he didn't have to rack his brain to think of something to say to her. It was so hard to find the words he wanted. He had terrible headaches sometimes.

The other lady – Joanna called her Meg – tried to talk to him. But she asked too many questions and seemed disappointed when Magnus couldn't answer them. Then she felt all over his head with her hands, gently, and held a light in front of his eyes.

Magnus felt comfortable here, as though he'd come home.

The wire Lallie sent to Quinn arrived in Santa Fe late one afternoon. By the following morning he had sold the copper mine for less than it was worth in order to conclude his business quickly. He then rode day and night in the

395

hope he could catch up with Sedge before he did anything foolish.

Lallie's wire had told him that Sedge had heard his son was dying, a victim of his adoptive father's violence. In a rage of grief, Sedge had apparently destroyed everything he owned, then ridden out of town swearing to kill the man. He was bound for a small town in Arizona called, expressively, Dustdevil. Lallie had concluded by saying she had told no one else of Sedge's intention, as she hoped Quinn could 'fix things.'

As he headed south, Quinn cursed the intrusion into his own life, his own plans, and swore this would be the last time he attempted to rescue Sedge, or anyone else, if it meant he had to stay away from Megan.

The town of Dustdevil was exactly what he expected it to be. A huddle of sun-bleached wooden buildings in the middle of a windswept plain, roasting in the desert heat a couple of miles north of the Mexican border. In the distance the purple-hazed mountains kept rearing cumulus clouds at bay.

A few saguaros, rising starkly from the baked sand, seemed to be the only other living things left on earth, the crunch of his horse's hooves in the gravelly sand the only sound. Even when he reached the edge of town there was no sign of life. Was Dustdevil a ghost town? He looked around for any indication that there had been mining activity here, or any other reason for the town's existence. It had probably been a stage stop, he decided, perhaps no longer needed after the coming of the railroad, which had bypassed the town. Despite the weather-beaten buildings, it didn't look like a ghost town. But where were its inhabitants?

His horse balked, startled, as a giant tumbleweed blew across the street. Somewhere a shutter banged in the arid wind. Quinn spoke soothingly to his horse, urging him forward.

Halfway down the main street stood a jailhouse with a single barred window. Bullet holes pockmarked the adobe walls. He could see an abandoned Butterfield stage station at the far end of the street. There was a saloon, a livery stable. Everything appeared to be in order, in reasonably good repair, except that the town was deserted. There did not appear to be a single living creature in the entire town, not even a stray dog.

Dismounting, he peered into the front windows of a couple of stores, then moved on to several houses. From what he could see, everything inside indicated that the occupants had been there recently. One table was still set for a meal. A plant thrived on a window ledge. In one house dominoes were set up; the game had been abandoned just before one player lost.

As he remounted and rode on, an eerie, prickling sensation accompanied him, a sense of impending doom that seemed to shimmer like the haze over the bleak landscape.

He reached the far side of town. Ahead lay boot hill. Among the weathered headstones and rotting wooden crosses Quinn noticed a disproportionate number of new graves, several of them still open. Four pine coffins lay on the ground. shovels flung down beside them.

Quinn looked out across the plain, watching a spiral of yellow dust whirl mindlessly through seared clumps of cholla. The tumbleweeds rolled like an advancing army towards him, then abruptly, as the wind changed, retreated. No doubt somewhere on the hazy horizon beyond the scorched plain there would be another tiny town, built around a plaza, its inhabitants speaking Spanish.

Border towns, Quinn knew, were havens for the lawless – men escaping to or from both countries. The bounty hunters and lawmen who pursued them were often more brutal than the thieves, rustlers, and murderers they chased. Still it was unlikely that Mexican *bandidos* or raiding Indians could have killed every living creature in Dustdevil without leaving, in addition to those coffins and open graves, other evidence they'd been there. There were no smashed windows, broken boardwalks, dead horses, stray livestock – no debris of any kind. Just a few bullet holes in the jailhouse wall, holes that had been put there long ago, no doubt by a disgruntled cowpoke who'd cooled his heels in a cell after hurrahing the town. What could have caused every man, woman and child simply to vanish, leaving their possessions behind?

He was about to turn back when he noticed a second plume of dust that had been hidden from his view by a cluster of occatillo. Not a dust devil this time, but the dust thrown up by a horse's hooves. Someone was riding hell-for-leather towards the town.

Quinn's hand slid towards the handle of his gun, holstered to his belt, and he eyed the rifle strapped to his saddle. Riding alone in the Southwest necessitated such protection.

The approaching horseman was close enough to recognise now. He relaxed. It was Sedge. He didn't seem surprised to see Quinn.

'What the hell happened here –' Quinn began.

Sedge didn't slow down. He yelled as he thundered past, 'Follow me.'

Back along the deserted street, reining to a halt in front of the saloon, Sedge jumped to the ground, grabbed his saddlebags, and ran inside. Quinn followed.

The moment they were inside Quinn heard the low murmur of human suffering, so weak and faint it had not carried beyond the walls to the street. He blinked in the dim light creeping in through the shuttered windows. The smell of alcohol was overpowering, as though someone had emptied bottles of liquor all over the place.

Sedge made his way to a storeroom at the rear of the saloon. Inside Quinn could make out the shapes of several people lying on pallets. Sedge had dropped down beside a boy, who tossed fitfully. 'I'm back, Nat, I'm here. Can you drink some water?'

He looked over his shoulder at Quinn. 'Thank God you came. I didn't want to leave them, but I had to have help. Nobody would come. I did manage to get some formaldehyde; we can disinfect properly now. I threw whisky all over this room, hell of a waste. We'll use the formaldehyde in one of the houses, carry the patients over there. If we disinfect thoroughly and then isolate the sick, maybe we can get some of the townsfolk to come back. Some of 'em are camped in the foothills.'

'This is your son?' Quinn asked, looking down at the ravaged body of the boy.

Sedge nodded. 'The US marshal who adopted him called him Nathaniel.' He wrung out a cloth in a bowl of water and gently mopped the boy's brow. 'Seems that a couple of months ago the marshal brought a fugitive back from Mexico and the man was sick. By the time they reached Dustdevil the prisoner was dead and the marshal was in the early stages of smallpox.' Sedge looked up at him. 'You were vaccinated, weren't you?'

'A fine time to ask,' Quinn said. 'But, yes, I was, when I joined the army. Can you save the boy?'

Something akin to a sob came from Sedge's throat. 'Oh, Christ, Quinn, this is my fault. I should have vaccinated him when he was an infant, but right after he was born I was court-martialled, and then there was the trouble in town . . . then Migina took the boy and left.'

He pressed a cup of water to the boy's lips. 'There's no treatment for smallpox; prevention is the only hope. The best I can do is make him and the others comfortable and hope the disease will run its course. We'll have to get some vaccine for everybody who came into contact with these people and the dead and . . . there's too much for me to do by myself. The dead have to be buried. Everybody dropped everything and ran the minute I told them it was smallpox.'

'How did you find out about this?'

'The marshal who adopted my son, it seems he talked to Migina in San Carlos before he took the boy, and she told him Nat was my son. He could have found me any time, but I guess he'd grown too attached to the boy to give him up. When he realised he was dying and had infected the boy, he sent a man to tell me. The message I got was garbled; I was told that the marshal had killed the boy, which was true in a way. The marshal probably knew what he had and didn't want to panic the town or the messenger. I thought . . . well, I don't know what I thought. I didn't think of illness. A beating, maybe, or neglect. Blamed myself, him. I flew into a rage, started drinking. You know me; when I drink I smash things.'

One of the huddled shapes on another pallet called weakly for water and Quinn picked up a pitcher.

Sedge said sharply, 'He's got his own cup. Keep the lip of the pitcher away from it. Scrub your hands after you touch any of 'em or you're liable to pass the disease to somebody else. Smallpox is a plague. It terrifies people. You can see what it did to this town. Even people who've been vaccinated fear it. Do you think Megan's been vaccinated? Would she come to help? There's a Western Union office here, and you know Morse code.'

'I'll send a wire. I'm sure her grandfather made sure she was vaccinated. She can take the train to the end of the line and I'll meet her there.'

Quinn wrapped his arms around Megan and their lips met in a hungry, urgent kiss.

'Your wire was so mysterious,' she said as she stepped back from him. 'Is Sedge ill?'

He took her grandfather's battered medical bag from her hand. 'There's been an outbreak of smallpox. Sedge was trying to care for the victims alone. One of his patients is his son.' He explained briefly what had happened.

'I should have realised something was wrong when I saw what he'd done to his surgery. But shortly after I discovered it we had a tremendous surprise . . . Joanna arrived.'

He whistled. 'Joanna Traherne?'

'Alive and well. I'll tell you about her on the way. Do you have a horse for me?'

400

'A wagon. We have to take food back with us, and gallons of formaldehyde. Nobody will go near the town.'

She clutched his arm in sudden fright. 'You *have* been vaccinated?'

Quinn nodded. 'We've wired Tucson to send vaccine. With luck we'll stop this epidemic before it spreads any farther.'

He helped her into the wagon. 'Tell me about Joanna. What happened to her? What was Randolph's reaction to her?'

Megan paused for a moment before answering. 'I know what you're thinking . . . and I was just remembering what I saw a few minutes before your wire arrived. Joanna had pushed Randolph's wheelchair to a grassy bank sprinkled with wildflowers, not far from the house. I can see her now, sitting with her skirt spread around her, her arms clasped about her knees . . .'

The images were still vivid in Megan's mind. Over their heads the sunlight dappled the leaves, and a breeze blew wisps of Joanna's hair about her face. There was a madonna-like serenity about her that suggested she'd found what she'd been seeking.

She went on, 'Joanna was gazing up at Randolph and he was completely engrossed in what she was saying. They'd talked nonstop for several days and, I suspect, nights.'

'Sounds promising. But where has she been all this time?'

'I'll explain in a moment, but first I must tell you about Magnus and Sari.'

Quinn listened without comment, and by the time they reached Dustdevil he was no longer as hopeful as Megan that Joanna's arrival might help Randolph accept Megan's departure. To Quinn it sounded as though Magnus was Joanna's first concern.

After they entered the plague town they had no time for anything but work. Megan rolled up her sleeves and plunged into the formidable task of nursing desperately ill people with a cheerfulness and energy that amazed and inspired the two men.

Megan insisted that Sedge and Quinn wear handkerchiefs over their mouths and noses, as she did, even though they had been vaccinated. She told them, 'We must be careful about breathing particles of the infectious agent of the disease. I read that even immune people can carry it to others.'

They lost two of the stricken people, but the others, including Sedge's son, clung to life.

Watching Megan deal with the horrors of the disease, noting how she was able to calm a frightened child and ease the suffering of a man racked by fever, his skin a mass of haemorrhagic eruptions, Quinn felt both admiration and a certain dismay. This was what she'd been born to do, to heal the sick. He wasn't sure that until now he'd recognised that she really did have a calling.

He'd envisaged that when they were married she might be content to do occasional volunteer work at a hospital or even work part-time with some accommodating doctor. He had not expected – did any prospective husband? – that he would be the part-time element in her life. Even though he had urged her to try to get into medical school, by devious means if necessary, Quinn hadn't truly envisioned how her medical ambitions might affect their life together. Now he brooded about their chances for a successful marriage. He wondered if he was capable of sharing her. During those desperate days in the parched little border town she barely had time to nod and smile in his direction.

After they had scrubbed and disinfected everything, burned the clothes and possessions of the dead, moved the sick to clean beds in the largest of the private houses, Quinn finished the work at boot hill. He was digging the last grave when Sedge's shadow fell across the ground beside him.

'We've got to round up everybody who was in town and

had contact with any of the sick people, Quinn. They've got to be vaccinated. Will you ride to the camp in the hills and start there?'

Quinn looked up, squinting in the relentless sunlight. 'You want me to bring them in at gunpoint?'

'If necessary, yes. But I'm hoping you'll use your gift of the gab instead, not to mention your personal charm. I know you're possessed of both. You must be, to persuade a woman like Megan to marry you. Yes – she told me. Congratulations.'

Quinn vaulted out of the hole in the ground. 'Pick up the other end,' he instructed, gesturing towards the coffin.

'You know any words from the Scriptures?' Sedge asked, as they completed the burial.

Glancing back at the other three graves he had filled in, Quinn straightened up and took off his hat. He said softly, 'Yea, though I walk through the valley of the shadow of death, I will fear no evil: for thou art with me; thy rod and thy staff they comfort me . . .'

They walked back to town in silence. As they reached their makeshift hospital Quinn said, 'I'll saddle up right away and ride over to the encampment.'

Sedge laid his hand on Quinn's arm. 'You're not sure anymore, are you . . . about Megan? Your doubt was written all over your face when I congratulated you, and you made no comment.'

Quinn sighed. 'You know me too well. I'll be honest with you, Sedge; it's me I'm not sure about. I don't know if I can live with her dedication, her total absorption in healing. I think maybe there are times when she believes she can be my wife, and other times when she has doubts, too. It's been like that from the beginning with us, up and down, on and off. We never seemed to be able to synchronise our feelings for each other. Hell, maybe we should have recognised that as a warning sign.'

'Listen to me, Quinn. I've known you a long time.

You're a different man when you're with Megan. She brings out a side of you I hadn't seen before and I suspect no one else had either, including you. I think with Megan you'll finally be able to shake off that Ramblin' Jack handle and settle down . . . Now, don't get mad at me. You're successful at everything you do, I know that, maybe too successful, but that isn't the point. You rush in to accept a challenge. Then when you've conquered it, you lose interest. What I'm getting at is this: You're the most adaptable man I know. If anybody can figure out a way to be married to a lady doctor, it's you. Think about it.'

Quinn was buckling his saddle strap, but something caused him to glance up. Megan was standing at the open second-storey window of the house, watching them, her expression troubled. He cursed under his breath, wondering how much of their conversation she'd overheard.

He called up to her, 'I'm going to ride out to the camp, bring back the people who need to be vaccinated.'

She nodded, then turned her head in Sedge's direction. 'Nat is awake and says he's hungry. Sedge, I think he's past the crisis.'

47

They said good-bye to Sedge and Nat when the last of Dustdevil's evacuees returned. There was already talk of renaming the town in honour of its rebirth.

Megan hugged Sedge. 'Are you sure you don't want me to stay and help you start your new practice?'

'We'll manage. I've got Nat, and several of the local

ladies have offered to help. You and Quinn got important matters of your own to take care of.'

Sedge took Quinn's hand, then pulled him into a rough embrace. 'You take care of her, hear? Or you'll answer to me.'

Nat smiled shyly as Megan hugged him. His dark Apache eyes made a striking contrast to his fair skin and sandy hair. The boy had been lucky; most of the smallpox lesions had been on his body and there would only be a couple of pockmarks on his face, most of them hidden under his thatch of hair. 'Thank you for taking care of me,' he said.

'You were a very good patient. Remember what I told you: Get plenty of sleep and eat your vegetables.'

Nat grimaced and Sedge laughed.

Quinn said, 'You're a hero, here, Sedge. You saved this town and people are grateful. This is a whole new life for you and there's no need for you to bring along any baggage from the past, is there?'

Sedge slapped his shoulder. 'I've got a good reason to make it work for me here, Quinn, so don't worry. My shingle is out and my diploma's on the wall. My son, I promise you, is going to be proud of me.'

'I'm going to be a doctor when I grow up,' Nat said earnestly.

'You'll learn a lot from your father,' Megan said. 'He's a very good doctor. I learned all I know from my grandfather, who was also a physician.'

Quinn turned to Megan. 'Let's head for the ranch. I feel an urgent need to talk to Randolph and straighten out the mess I made.'

'*We* made,' Megan said. 'Let's hope by now he and Joanna . . .'

The spring evening at the higher elevation of New Mexico had turned cool and Consuela had lit a fire in the living room, but after dinner Quinn suggested to Megan that they go for a walk. That afternoon Quinn and Randolph had closeted themselves in the study and talked for a couple of hours. Megan was anxious to hear what had transpired.

They left Randolph and Joanna in front of a blazing mesquite log. The baby and Magnus were both in bed. Magnus now slept almost as much as Sari.

Quinn slipped his arm around Megan's shoulders as they walked, and she liked the way she fitted so comfortably into his side. She continually had to suppress an urge to press herself close to him, to touch him and to hold on to him, as though if she were to let go he might vanish.

'You and Randolph talked so long this afternoon that I'm almost afraid to ask what passed between the two of you.'

'I told him the truth – that I love you and you love me. He agreed to a quiet annulment.' Quinn stopped and embraced her, holding her close. 'Will you marry me the minute you're free?'

She nodded happily and offered her lips for his kiss, marvelling at the swift rush of passion that passed between them.

'If it weren't so cold out here,' he murmured against her mouth, 'I'd make love to you right here under the stars.'

For a few moments she nestled in his arms, tempted to respond that they would generate too much heat to be aware of the night chill, but she knew they ought to take this opportunity to discuss what could not be said in front of the others.

'Quinn, what do you think about the situation with Joanna and Magnus? I understand that he saved her life back in Cornwall, but I wonder if there's more she isn't telling us. I'd almost believe she loved him, but the idea of Joanna falling in love with a prizefighter, so rough and uneducated . . .'

'It's almost as strange as the lady doctor falling in love with a gambler named Ramblin' Jack, you mean?'

She laughed, because it was inconceivable to her that she and Quinn could not be considered equals, partners, in every sense of the word, despite their vastly different histories. But after a moment she realised that Quinn wasn't laughing with her. In the moonlight his face was set in serious, concerned lines.

'You're not really a gambler, Quinn. You were a soldier, a rancher, a mine owner, a businessman.'

'Jack of all trades, master of none?'

'I think you just haven't found the type of work you can be happy with yet.'

'Maybe it's time I told you exactly where I'm going, Megan, albeit along a winding path. You see, like a lot of young men, I was in competition with a highly successful father. I wanted no part of his empire – he owns several companies, including a large printing company. I knew I could never work with him, because we clashed constantly, so the minute I got out of college, I headed west. But everything I've done in the twelve years since has helped me understand why I wanted no part of my father's business. The people who work for him work under miserable conditions for hellish long hours –' He broke off.

'I didn't mean to get started on this,' he said after a moment. 'I guess what I wanted to say was that experience has shaped me into a man, ready to take on my father. The company is called McQuinn and Son – he added "and son" the day I was born. So I figure one day I'll go back with my own plans for some reforms.'

'When? Soon?'

'Well, I'm figuring on an extended honeymoon first . . .' Quinn kissed her cool cheek, then took her hand and tucked it inside his pocket to keep her warm as they walked on.

Feeling happy, in tune with him, Megan said, 'You know, there was a time when becoming a doctor was all I could think about. Now my mind is full of plans for being with you, becoming your wife, living with you, doing wonderful things together . . . like having children. A cocky self-confident little boy and – who knows? – maybe a little girl who will grow up in a world that doesn't object to women in the medical profession.'

'Have I told you lately how much I love you? How much I want you to be my wife?'

'No,' Megan murmured. 'Tell me again.'

'Marry me, be my wife.'

'I'd love to.'

They walked in silence for a while, contemplating a future that was filled with promise.

After a while Quinn said, 'Judging by the long looks Joanna and Randolph have been exchanging, I'd say they're soul mates. But where will Magnus and the baby fit into the grand design?'

'I don't know,' Megan said. 'Joanna has changed so much from the timid, self-effacing schoolgirl I knew that I hardly know what to expect from her anymore. She's done so many things – worked as an amanuensis, a parlour maid, a journalist, even had a clerical business of her own. She crossed the Atlantic in steerage, hobnobbed with the richest people in New York. I suspect, too, that she had a passionate love affair. She wears that look of a woman who has been much desired.'

'Magnus,' Quinn said sagely.

'I wonder what he was like before . . .' Megan mused. 'But, getting back to Randolph, you're right about how attracted she seems to be to him and he to her. They speak the same language, I suppose.'

'You're shivering. Your blood probably thinned out in the desert heat,' Quinn said. 'Come on, let's go back. Tomorrow morning we'll go to Silver City and find a lawyer, and tomorrow night, my love, we'll share a hotel room and I'll make love to you until the sun comes up.'

'Why not tonight?' Megan murmured.

'Not even Ramblin' Jack is going to make love to another man's wife in his own home,' Quinn said. 'Unless, of course, I happen to walk in my sleep . . .'

When they returned to the house Randolph was sitting

alone before the dying embers of the fire. When they stopped to say good night, he looked up at them and smiled. 'I envy you,' he said, and there was no need for him to say more.

Happily tired, Megan went to her room.

Joanna was sitting in the middle of her bed, giving the baby her bottle. 'I hope you don't mind, Meg, but I wanted to talk to you again in private.'

'Of course not. Did Randolph tell you we're getting an annulment?'

'Yes, he told me.'

Megan kicked off her shoes and sat down beside her friend, picking up the baby's tiny hand to kiss her fingers. 'What will you do if her mother reappears to claim her? Won't it be an awful wrench for you?'

'I'll cross that bridge if I come to it,' Joanna replied. 'But from what I know of Delta, I doubt her way of life would accommodate a baby, and she certainly wouldn't want to take care of Magnus in his present condition.' Her voice broke as she spoke his name, and Megan squeezed her shoulder sympathetically.

'Oh, Meg,' Joanna sighed. 'It's so very sad. Is there any hope for him? Could his mind be restored? You told me about your father and his wife and the possibility that the new science of psychoanalysis might help her. What if someone like Dr Freud could talk to Magnus?'

'It's not possible, Jo. Don't get your hopes up. He'll never be any better than he is now. You see, there was no injury to Agnes's brain. But Magnus was struck in the head repeatedly. His skull was probably fractured, and the resulting pressure destroyed part of the brain. That's why he doesn't remember you, or anything that happened before the beating.'

'They told me at the hospital that it wasn't just that one beating, that his present state was the result of a cumulation of blows to the head in the boxing ring.'

'That's probably true. Each blow could have destroyed some of the brain cells.'

'I always hated that brutal sport.' Joanna shivered. 'Meg, there's something I want to say before you and Quinn rush off and get married. Randolph told me about your attempts to get into medical school and why you were turned down.'

Megan laughed shortly. 'Quinn suggested I try again and lie about my age. But the board would surely see through such a ruse the moment I went for my interview. Besides, I made a vow never to lie about anything again . . . ever. I just have to face the fact that medical school doors won't open for me. Fortunately I have Quinn now. Jo, I never thought I could love someone like this, so completely that I don't need anything other than to be with him.'

'Perhaps you don't need anything else now, at this time in your life,' Joanna said. 'But I've known you for a long time, and I find it hard to believe the time won't come when all your old longings for a medical career will return. You're a born healer, Meg. I think you're making a big mistake not to give medical school another try.'

Megan sighed. 'You're quite right, of course. You always did know me better than I know myself. I don't suppose I'll ever be able to give up my dream of becoming a doctor. Do *you* think I should lie about my age?'

'No, I think you should be completely truthful. Tell the medical school board that you studied all your life with your grandfather. Get letters of recommendation from your father and Dr Sedgewick and anyone else you can think of. Write a couple of papers perhaps – on that new operation you mentioned that you and Dr Sedgewick performed on the dance hall girl, Becky. What did you call it?'

'An appendectomy,' Megan answered.

'You had a good education in England. Give the board every detail about your life, your education, your lifelong apprenticeship with your grandfather, your experience since he died, the patients you've treated or helped treat. If you can convince them that your training puts you far ahead of most applicants, perhaps your age won't matter. It's worth a try. Don't give up yet.'

'Complete honesty . . .' Megan said slowly. 'Yes, I like the idea of being perfectly open and frank. But do you really think I could have a medical career *and* a husband and family? Will I have to give up Quinn? I don't know if I can.'

'Didn't you say that Quinn is prepared to go East with you? It isn't as if you wouldn't have an understanding husband.'

'Do you think he really meant it? Few men would agree to such an arrangement. He'll have to wait several years for me to finish my training before we can start a family.'

'Quinn isn't most men. He's unique.' Joanna smiled. 'He'd have to be, to captivate you. Heaven knows no other member of the male sex was ever able to.'

Megan grinned. 'When I went to Cornwall for Adele's wedding, I couldn't really comprehend your obsession with Oliver; he seemed so boring. But now I understand you loved him, and I know now that without love, our lives have little meaning. And love enhances everything else in our lives. Do you know what Sigmund Freud says about love?'

Joanna shook her head.

'He says that human beings need two things in order to be happy: love and work. He was probably referring to men, but I do feel it applies to women, too.'

'I *know* it does,' Joanna said firmly.

'While we're on the subject, Jo, I'm not going to pry, but I think there may have been a time you loved Magnus even more than Oliver. There's something about the way you look at him, touch him . . .'

'Some day I'll tell you the whole story, Meg. When it's not quite so painful for me.'

'Tell me, are you falling in love with Randolph now? Oh, I do hope you are; you'd be wonderful together.'

The baby had finished the bottle and Joanna lifted her up onto her shoulder and patted her back. Sari was more interested in falling asleep than in bringing up swallowed air.

'It's true that I love being with Randolph, talking to him . . . just watching him. He's incredibly handsome, isn't he? But I could hardly expect him to take on Magnus and the baby, too. Besides, I'm no longer sure I want to be only a wife, even if Randolph does propose to me.'

'What? But . . . Jo, that's all you wanted with Oliver.'

'That was a different time and place, and I was a different person. Since then I've been out in the world. I've travelled, earned my own living. I was a journalist and I ran my own business and, frankly, I enjoyed it.'

'You'd rather work than live in this lovely house with Randolph? But the two of you have so much in common; you could be so content together.'

'Yes, I daresay we could, for a while. But I think perhaps I'm a little more experienced in the ways of men and women together than you are, Meg. This blind, heady thrill of discovery doesn't last. Oh, I think perhaps something less exciting but more comforting takes its place. However, I feel I may need to follow other paths.'

'You don't like it here in New Mexico? You seem so taken with the countryside, the space and openness.'

'I love it here,' Joanna said firmly. 'And Magnus is happy here, too. Randolph has invited us to stay as long as we wish, but I can't impose on him too long. I've been thinking about the way Manzanita Flats is growing. It's going to need a newspaper soon. The local people won't be content to wait for papers to arrive from other towns. Then there's the question of statehood for New Mexico, getting the vote for women, and so many other causes a good paper could endorse.'

'You're not saying you want to start a newspaper?'

'I am indeed. If I can raise some capital. And if I

approach local businesses and politicians, that shouldn't be too difficult.'

Megan flopped back on the pillow. 'I can't believe I'm hearing this from you of all people. I'm at a loss for words!'

Joanna had grown accustomed to waking to the sound of Sari's cooing, but upon opening her eyes the following morning she realised that the infant was still sound asleep in her basket beside the bed.

It was still quite dark and very cool in the bedroom, so she got up to close the window shutters. Her habit of sleeping with an open window had been acquired in childhood and she always felt claustrophobic in a tightly closed room.

As she reached the window she realised what had awakened her. Voices outside, agitated, urgent, then the sound of hoofbeats as someone rode off. Then, moments later, she heard the roar of the Winton's engine starting up.

Something urgent to do with ranch business had necessitated all this predawn activity, she supposed. She got back into bed to savour a few minutes of contemplating what the day might bring.

Today Megan and Quinn would be leaving for Silver City to begin the process of annuling her marriage. Joanna could see why her friend was so swept away by the dashing Quinn. He was masculine and forceful, and his conversation could be both outrageous and ribald. He was, Joanna decided, exactly the kind of man schoolgirls dreamed of meeting but rarely did. Which was fortunate, since most girls would be unable to cope with such a man. Joanna admitted that he would wear her out with his sheer energy.

In quiet moments like these Joanna often reflected on her love affair with Magnus, knowing now that it had persisted only because the time they had spent together was always brief. Stolen hours, treasured moments that were always filled with the imminence of parting. Sadly she realised that eventually their affair would have burned itself out due to its sheer intensity.

She sensed that this wouldn't happen to Megan and Quinn. Megan had needed a man like him to penetrate that scientific shell her grandfather had helped her build around herself and find the woman within. Still, she felt that surely Megan could have both Quinn and the fulfilment of her dream.

Joanna dozed, and began to dream that she and Megan were back in Cornwall, standing on the cliffs at Dutchman's Point, watching the sea churn into the coves below. They joined hands and flew out over the indigo ocean, laughing as gulls wheeled around them and clouds parted to allow them to pass.

She awoke to the baby's hungry wail and someone knocking on her door.

Disorientated, still in the grip of the dream, she stumbled out of bed and picked up the baby, calling, 'Come in.'

The moment Megan entered the room Joanna knew something was terribly wrong. She seemed dazed, drained of all life. Her shoulders slumped and her eyes stared unseeingly in front of her.

'Meg! What is it? What's wrong?'

'*Primum non nocere*,' Megan said in a dull voice, moving trancelike towards her.

'What?'

Megan's eyes found hers, then filled with tears. 'It's the first rule of all physicians, since the beginning of time.'

'What does it mean?'

'First . . . do no harm.'

'You believe you've harmed someone?'

'I have killed a man with my neglect.'

'You can't be serious. Who?'

'There was a young cowboy named Wyatt. We were all so fond of him . . . He complained of pain in his head. The foreman thought he'd had too much to drink the night before and was malingering. I looked at Wyatt, but didn't

414

examine him properly or question him as to how long he'd had headaches. I should have insisted he go into Silver City to see a doctor, but I didn't.'

'He died?'

Megan nodded. 'Quinn and Tex tried to get him to a doctor last night, but Wyatt died on the way.'

Joanna put the baby back into her bed and wrapped her arms around Megan. 'Don't blame yourself. If you hadn't been here, no doubt Tex would have been even harder on him. In any case, I doubt the poor young man would have seen a doctor.'

'*Primum non nocere*,' Megan said again, and buried her face in Joanna's shoulder.

48

'Look,' Quinn said, 'there's nothing to be done here. We're going to Silver City as we planned and find a lawyer to handle the annulment.'

Megan knew she should feel happy that soon she and Quinn would be married, but she found herself unable to overcome her distress over the death of the young cowboy, Wyatt.

Over and over in her mind she relived that morning she had been summoned to the bunkhouse to look at him, rewriting the scene in her mind, doing the things she should have done, asking the proper questions, desperately trying to make it come out right. But none of it changed the grim reality that the young ranch hand was irrevocably dead.

Quinn was patient but firm. He ushered her through the

days that followed, in the same way that once he had probably herded reluctant steers on the long cattle drives north in the days before the railroad.

Getting the annulment proved to be a simple procedure, although it necessitated Randolph's appearance before a judge to corroborate Megan's testimony that the marriage had never been consummated. He travelled to Silver City with Tex, and after the brief hearing Quinn helped carry the wheelchair down the courthouse steps.

There was an awkward pause as the three of them surveyed one another, their new status legal but not yet comfortable.

'Perhaps you'd like to be married at the ranch,' Randolph said hesitantly.

Recalling her marriage ceremony with Randolph, Megan felt a tightening in her throat.

Quinn moved swiftly into the breach. 'Thanks, but we've got an appointment with a justice of the peace this evening.'

'Joanna will be disappointed,' Randolph said, although his relief at the refusal was obvious.

'We'd really prefer to get married quietly,' Megan added, 'in view of . . . well, you know.'

Randolph offered his hand to Quinn. 'Take good care of her. She deserves it.'

'We'll come and visit you after we get back from our honeymoon. Let you know what our plans are,' Quinn said. 'Maybe by then you and Joanna . . . ?'

Randolph smiled. 'She isn't ready yet. I won't make the same mistake with Joanna as I did with Megan. For now it's enough that she seems inclined to stay.'

Impulsively Megan kissed Randolph's lips. 'Perhaps we needed to be married for a little while, you and I, in order to prepare ourselves for Jo and Quinn.'

'That's one way of looking at it,' Randolph replied, his eyes brighter than usual. 'Another would be to consider that we haven't lost a spouse, but gained a friend.'

The following morning Megan awakened within the comforting circle of her husband's arms, her senses still tingling from a night of lovemaking that had driven away every guilty thought, every qualm, perhaps even reason itself.

She wanted nothing more from life than to be joined with this man, connected in every way possible, minds in tune as flesh fused into one being, whole and perfect. This mystical bonding was all the more precious because both Megan and Quinn knew that separation could not destroy it, nor could their different goals.

We're committed to each other totally now, Megan thought, forever. Together we have abilities, strengths, opportunities, that are limitless. How miraculous a true marriage is . . . It allows us to be separate yet joined.

Quinn stirred and kissed her forehead, asking with love-sated huskiness, 'Is this Mrs John McQuinn I'm holding, or am I still dreaming?'

But as she came fully awake, the rosy haze of contentment began to fade as the face of the young cowboy, twisted with pain, flashed into her mind again. She sighed and buried her face against Quinn's chest. He pushed her away and jumped out of bed. 'Come on, get up. We've a lot of miles to cover.'

'What? I thought we were going to stay here in Silver City for a while.'

'So you can mope about what you can't change? No, my love. We're heading for my favourite city – New Orleans. We'll take a paddle wheeler up the Mississippi to St Louis, and along the way I'll show you some fine old southern towns. Your mind is going to be filled with so many dazzling images that there won't be room for gloomy ones . . . But first we'll stop off in Galveston and see your father.'

He was already tossing clothes into a bag. Megan scrambled up on her knees on the bed. 'Quinn, we can't –'

'Oh, no? You just watch us.'

*   *   *

Dr Robard wept unashamedly when he saw them. Although Quinn had been prepared to break into the house through a window, they were surprised when the front door was opened by a uniformed maid who conducted them to a sunny drawing room with the windows wide open to catch the sea breeze.

Even as her father embraced her, Megan's gaze was fixed on the woman seated at the open window, serenely watching their reunion. Surely that couldn't be Agnes?

But it was. Little girl ribbons and bows gone, her silver hair neatly dressed in a bun, a smart blue shantung gown showing off a figure much more rounded than Megan remembered.

'Dearest, allow me to present Megan and Quinn. They've interrupted their honeymoon to come and visit. Isn't that kind of them?'

Agnes smiled as Megan bent to kiss her cheek, but there was no recognition in the smile. She clearly did not remember her previous visit.

'How lovely to meet you at last,' Agnes said. 'Your father has told me so much about you that I feel I know you already.'

Megan found it difficult to contain her curiosity about the woman's transformation as a tea tray was ordered and an hour or so passed while they chatted about everything but what was foremost on her mind.

Her father positioned himself beside a strange-looking contraption on a table, picked up a horn-shaped object and held it to his ear. Beaming at them he said, 'Now . . . no need for you to bellow in order for me to hear you.'

'What is that?' Megan asked.

'It's my hearing helper,' Dr Robard replied. 'I tried an ear trumpet, but it didn't really help. Then I read the principles of the operation of the telephone. It works by means of a transmitter that converts sound energy into

418

electrical energy and a receiver that converts the electrical energy back into sound energy.'

He explained about the amplification of sound and how his machine could be used presently only as a stationary hearing aid. Megan listened, fascinated, but clearly Agnes had heard all of this before and wanted to hear from Megan all of the details of her wedding.

At length Agnes said, 'Well, it's time for my afternoon nap and you two must surely need to rest after your long journey. Darling, pull the bell cord, will you? We must have a room made up for our dear daughter and son-in-law.'

When Agnes departed to her room, Quinn said, 'I guess you two have a lot to talk about. I'll take a walk along the beach.'

He paused at the drawing room door. 'Megan, tell your father about Wyatt, won't you?'

Dr Robard looked at her questioningly when they were alone, but Megan said, 'First I want to hear how you brought about the miracle with Agnes.'

'I'm still not entirely sure,' her father said slowly. 'At the time I was afraid I might be doing irreparable damage. I decided to stop catering to her fantasy of endless childhood. Oh, I didn't do it overnight. But gradually I got rid of all the dolls and toys and little-girl clothes. I'd say, "You're fourteen now, Agnes, too big to play with dolls." Then a week or so later I'd pretend it was her sixteenth birthday. She threw tantrums at first, but I ignored them. I suppose the big change came about when I acquired my hearing helper. At last we were able to really talk. I dressed up one day in my old Sunday-best suit and came calling. When she called me Daddy I quickly said, "But I'm not your daddy, Agnes. I'm your fiancé, Davydd Robard, and we're going to be married, remember?"'

'What was her reaction to that?' Megan asked.

'Puzzlement. But I plunged on, talking about her father and mother. Now, all of this didn't happen immediately, but after a while she began to speak, albeit reluctantly, about her real childhood, and I learned something I had never suspected. She was, as I believe I told you on your last visit, an only child. But there was another birth – a son born when she was four years old, who lived only a matter of days.'

Megan caught her breath. 'Oh, dear Lord!'

'It's even worse than you imagine. Apparently Agnes's father was so distraught – and how can I condemn him, since I, too, behaved irrationally when my child was stillborn? – that he rejected his daughter completely. Couldn't bear to have her near him. For months the poor little girl couldn't understand what she had done to cause her father's coldness. Eventually she came to believe it was *her* fault her little brother died.'

'How ghastly!' Megan said. 'So that early rejection by her father was locked into her unconscious, and when she lost her own baby some thread between unconscious and conscious was broken?'

Her father nodded. 'She couldn't face another rejection, or the feeling that she was responsible for a child's death, and so she quite literally *became* the lost child.'

Megan thought about this for a moment. It seemed at once too simple and yet too complex an explanation of Agnes's behaviour. Later, she decided, she would examine all the facts again.

'Now tell me why your husband is so concerned about someone named Wyatt,' her father said.

Megan felt her eyes fill with tears and she was back in the bunkhouse that morning, blithely assuming that Wyatt was suffering from a monumental hangover. Hesitantly she told her father what had taken place.

'But, my dear, don't you see that all any of us can do is guess? Sometimes we guess correctly, but more often we don't. Why do you suppose we say we *practise* medicine?'

'But I should have suspected a brain injury that required surgery.'

'It could also just as easily have been meningitis,

encephalitis, a tumour, or an epidural abscess that would have been fatal no matter what anyone did.' Dr Robard played with his hearing helper for a moment, then looked up and added, 'Or it could have been a migraine headache or' – he paused and gave her a piercing glance from beneath a tangle of bushy eyebrows – 'nothing more serious than a hangover.'

For three months Quinn and Megan travelled. They listened to the new and exciting music of New Orleans, ate exotic food and danced until dawn, slept a few hours and then made love in the heat-hazed afternoons. They boarded a riverboat and steamed triumphantly up the Mississippi, calliope wailing, paddle wheel churning the muddy waters. Along the way gracious old cities awaited their exploration, with charming antebellum mansions, intriguing museums, and lovely gardens that had been spared during the war between the states. Megan marvelled at the great variety of landscapes that blended one into the other in this vast country, the different cultures and styles of architecture, terrain that ranged from arid desert to lush tropical forest, with everything in between. Surely every country on earth was represented here in America, Megan thought.

Despite her wonder, when she least expected it there would come the inevitable plunge into desolation. She simply could not forget Wyatt. The unkempt young cowboy squeezing his concertina and dancing a jig, always cheerful and good-natured, taking all the gibes and insults the other hands made about his tattered clothes. She remembered him whistling as he rode into town on his battered saddle in his worn-out boots time and again, to send his pay to his fiancée in Wyoming.

Quinn would hold her and try to comfort her, but she was inconsolable. At last he took her into his arms one night and said gently, 'Megan, you can't go on punishing yourself like this. There are no quiet moments for you anymore. Unless we're engaged in some frantic activity, you sink into grief.'

'I'm sorry, Quinn,' Megan said miserably. 'I love you so much and I know I should be happy, but –'

'There's only one cure for what ails you,' Quinn said shortly. 'Come on, let's start packing.'

'Where are we going?'

'North. To do what we should have done right after young Wyatt died. We're going to meet my family, and then you, love, are going to start applying to medical schools again.'

Joanna met them at the railway station in Deming months later, when they returned from their travels. She had driven Randolph's Winton, and Megan was green with envy.

'You're still at the ranch?' Megan asked.

'No, but I try to visit Randolph every weekend even though I've been rather busy. I rented a house in Manzanita Flats, and I'm putting out a weekly newspaper. I don't have a printing press yet, but I've ordered one. In the meantime I'm using a machine that duplicates a master copy. It's quite amazing; it works by –'

Laughingly Megan held up her hand. 'I don't need to know, honestly! I'm still trying to understand typewriters and telephones and a hearing helper my father built. What about you and Randolph?'

'He's the most considerate, thoughtful, sensitive man I've ever known. We've spent hours discussing our favourite books –'

Joanna jerked the tiller in order to avoid a jackrabbit bounding across their path, and the resulting bump over the rutted road caused Quinn's hat to fly off. By the time they'd stopped to retrieve it, Joanna was bursting with her other news.

'Remember I told you about the Bodrath journal I was hired to write? Well, it's really a fascinating story, and I pored over old letters and documents until I could hardly see, so I know their history . . . plus a few dark secrets that Magnus filled in before he was injured . . . Well, anyway, I hated to waste all that work. Besides, I was intrigued by what was missing from my research – information about the Bodrath women. What were their lives like? After all, there had to be women, or there wouldn't have been sons. I began to invent stories about them and – guess what! I've completed the first draft of a mostly imaginary account of the women in the Bodrath family. It's highly fictionalised, of course. I call it *The Rathbone Women*, and a publisher is interested in it.'

'Congratulations,' Quinn said, holding on to his hat.

'Jo!' Megan shrieked over the roar of the engine. 'That's wonderful. You're a novelist and a journalist, you clever creature. Now, what about you and Randolph?'

Joanna let go of the tiller to squeeze Megan's hand, eliciting a yelp of alarm from Quinn. 'Why is it, pray tell,' Joanna demanded, 'that newly married women instantly turn into matchmakers? Randolph and I are very good friends.'

'Oh,' Megan said, disappointed. 'How's the baby?'

'She's the most extraordinary infant on the face of the earth. She just cut a tooth. Magnus is well, too. He's helping out on the ranch and the hands are very kind to him. Now . . . before we arrive at the ranch, I'm dying to know what it is that you came to tell us.'

Quinn took Megan's face in his hands and looked at her for a long moment. 'You're doing the right thing. It will all work out; you'll see. Come on, they're waiting for us. Magnus and Joanna and the baby have already left for the station in the buckboard. Randolph will come with us in the carriage.'

'We're not going in the Winton?'

'It isn't running. Apparently Randolph will have to send to the East for some parts.'

'Strange how it worked out – that the first train out of

Manzanita Flats will take us on the first leg of our journey east.'

Megan looked around the living room, through the arched entrance to the atrium, at the tiled fountain and clay pots of flowers. She recalled pleasant, peaceful times she'd spent there with Randolph. The attack by the Chiricahua Kid and his outlaws seemed only a bad dream now – a dream that had taken place somewhere else.

Quinn pushed a strand of her hair back behind her ear, then handed her her hat. 'Ready?'

She nodded and they went out into the bright sunshine.

The ranch seemed strangely quiet as the carriage rolled past the bunkhouse, corrals, and smokehouse. Megan realised there were virtually no ranch hands visible. She assumed they were all out on the open range.

They said little as they rolled through the lovely countryside, although Quinn frequently leaned over and kissed her cheek. Once he asked, 'Why so quiet? You're not worried –'

'No, oh, no. It's just that . . . I don't know. I expected when the time came that I was actually accepted to medical school . . . I'm being silly. I just thought perhaps a few bells would ring somewhere.'

Quinn chuckled. 'I could whoop and holler for a while if you like.'

'I know that Jo and Randolph are coming to see us off, but . . . well, didn't you think they were just a bit offhand about the whole thing? Blasé, really. As if it hadn't practically taken an act of God to make it happen.'

'You perhaps expected a big party with everyone coming from all over the territory to tell you how clever you are?'

'No, nothing like that.' She was embarrassed, and told herself surely it was enough that she was going to the finest medical school in the country and that her husband would be nearby during the harrowing years ahead. A congratulatory wire had arrived from her father, and Quinn had produced a bottle of vintage champagne at dinner one night. Still, they didn't all have to behave as though it hadn't taken a great deal of effort on her part to achieve this nearly impossible goal.

'Oh, look, they've decorated the main street of Manzanita Flats for the arrival of the train,' Megan said as they approached the outskirts of the town. 'And what a crowd! I didn't think railroad fever was still rampant. The tracks are everywhere now.'

'Um-hum,' Quinn murmured.

She peered nearsightedly at a banner strung across the street between the Jade Palace and a livery stable. 'What does it say . . . oh, my goodness!'

Emblazoned across the banner were the words 'Good luck Dr Megan. Come home to us soon.'

Suddenly they were surrounded by a cheering, jostling throng, their voices raised in a single refrain, to wish her Godspeed. She saw Becky hanging over the Palace balcony, oblivious of her dishabille, and Lallie atop her lacquered carriage shrieking and waving. Mr Chang bowed and grinned approvingly as the carriage went by.

In front of the railroad station Dr Sedgewick stood surrounded by the patients Megan had helped treat during her time in his surgery. All of the Mallory hands and most of those from the Diamond T lined the street. Tex tossed his Stetson in the air and gave a rebel yell. Braddock stood alone, his back to the wall and his gun hand ready, but he gave a rousing cheer as she went by. Even Joshua Pennington and the Simmonds had come to see her off.

Pennington whispered in her ear as he helped her down from the carriage, 'I wish my wife had listened to you. Perhaps you can prevent some other woman from subjecting herself –'

The crowd fell back to allow Randolph to wheel his chair towards her. Magnus, carrying Sari, followed him. Joanna flung her arms around Megan and cried, 'We're all so proud of you.'

Almost blinded by tears of joy, Megan looked up and saw a lone figure standing on the roof of the railroad station. Slowly he raised his hand in silent salute. A-chi-tie, too, had come to wish her well. She looked up at him and waved, hoping he understood that she would not forget what she had learned from him about Indian medicines and herbs.

Quinn slipped his arm around her shoulders as they walked to the waiting train. 'I tried to get them to ring a few bells . . .'

Laughing, borne along by love and hope, Megan looked down the track at the steel rails reflecting the sunlight, cutting a shining path to tomorrow.

BELVA PLAIN

BLESSINGS

Life was at last going well for Jennie. Her recent
engagement to Jay promised happiness beyond
dreams. Her legal work in the poorest parts of the city
was profoundly satisfying. And now she had the extra
challenge of protecting a thousand acres of wilderness
from the developers.

Just that one phone call changed everything.

Long forgotten memories awaken a hurt so deep, they
threaten the loss of the man she loves. In danger both
at home and at work, Jennie finds she must face the
hard decisions she evaded so many years before.

'The suspense is real enough. And so are the emotions'

New York Daily News

NANCY CATO

THE HEART OF THE CONTINENT

Set against the unforgiving landscape of the outback, *The Heart of the Continent* tells the story of two generations of women and a dream that came true in the Australian skies.

Newly qualified as a nurse, Alix Macfarlane turns her back on her wealthy Adelaide home and family and sets out for the wild and dangerous great red centre of the continent in the first years of the century.

She meets and marries Jim Manning, a Queensland cattleman, defying him to build a clinic for the aborigines. When he, in spite of her pleading, enlists in the First World War and is killed in Palestine, Alix is left alone, with only her baby daughter Caro and her dream. A dream that will become reality a generation later as the flying doctor service brings healing from the skies . . .

HODDER AND STOUGHTON PAPERBACKS

JANET ROSENSTOCK

CHINA NIGHTS

Katie O'Farrell had hardly travelled before. A nurse, Boston born and bred, she was revelling in the luxury ocean liner that was taking her across the Pacific to a reunion with the handsome naval officer who had captured her heart.

But in exotic, crowded, often frightening Hong Kong, disillusion and heartache awaited her. Alone, too proud to return home, she took up an offer to work as a missionary nurse deep in the interior of mainland China.

But Katie would have more than the strangeness and poverty of an alien society to contend with. China in 1937 was a land of violent turmoil as Communists and nationalists fought each other, while the invading Japanese threatened to overrun the whole country.

Adventures of the heart and undreamed-of dangers lay ahead and Katie would have to prove herself tough and resourceful if she was to survive . . .

HODDER AND STOUGHTON PAPERBACKS

JUDITH MERKLE RILEY

A VISION OF LIGHT

In 1355 the idea that a woman should write a book was shocking. Yet Margaret of Ashbury's story was amazing: twice-married but still young, plague victim, midwife, inventer, accused of witchcraft. And she had been granted the one thing that the mysterious Brother Gregory, her helper, had prayed for: a Vision of the Light, a mystic, miraculous healing touch . . .

'A lovely character and somebody one would be delighted to meet'
Rosamunde Pilcher, author of *The Shell Seekers*

HODDER AND STOUGHTON PAPERBACKS

CHRISTINA LAFFEATY

FAR FORBIDDEN PLAINS

Petronella van Zyl was seventeen, beautiful and completely naive.

Rebelling against the strict conventions of her Boer farming family, she had slipped away for a naked swim in her favourite pool when Marcus Cohen saw her. Exotic, good-looking and tender, he introduced her to the pleasures of womanhood.

That day they discovered a love for which she would face exile from home and family, for which he would abandon his faith and fight in a war not his own.

Victory for the British would bring colonisation and bitterness to the Boers. The love of Petronella and Marcus was fated to flower in the shadow of a conflict that would darken the lives of generations to come.

HODDER AND STOUGHTON PAPERBACKS

MORE FICTION TITLES AVAILABLE FROM
HODDER AND STOUGHTON PAPERBACKS

NANCY CATO

☐ 52838 3 The Heart of the Continent £4.99

CHRISTINA LAFFEATY

☐ 51582 1 Far Forbidden Plains £3.99

JUDITH MERKLE RILEY

☐ 51611 3 A Vision of Light £4.50

BELVA PLAIN

☐ 53062 0 Blessings £3.99

JANET ROSENSTOCK

☐ 53715 3 China Nights £4.50
☐ 49731 3 Worlds Apart £3.99

All these books are available at your local bookshop or news-agent, or can be ordered direct from the publisher. Just tick the titles you want and fill in the form below.

Prices and availability subject to change without notice.

HODDER AND STOUGHTON PAPERBACKS, P.O. Box 11, Falmouth, Cornwall.

Please send cheque or postal order, and allow the following for postage and packing:

U.K. – 80p for one book, and 20p for each additional book ordered up to a £2.00 maximum.

B.F.P.O. – 80p for the first book, and 20p for each additional book.

OVERSEAS INCLUDING EIRE – £1.50 for the first book, plus £1.00 for the second book, and 30p for each additional book ordered.

OR Please debit this amount from my Access/Visa Card (delete as appropriate).

Card Number ☐☐☐☐☐☐☐☐☐☐☐☐☐☐☐☐

NAME ....

ADDRESS ....

....